THE
ACHILLES
BATTLE FLEET

BOOK ONE: MEI-LING LEE

BRENDAN WILSON

ISBN: 978-0-5782-2626-2 (sc)
ISBN: 978-0-5782-2627-9 (e)

LITERATE A P E PRESS

Chicago | Las Vegas

To Mei-Ling, a warrior in body and spirit.

In 2016, I awoke one night to an alarm and an announcement, "Warning: Incoming Fire Alert. Take shelter." I was in Baghdad in a reinforced bunker. A few moments later, I heard a distant thump sound, and moment later another. Then silence. A few minutes after that came the all-clear. The next day, like many times before and after, I traveled into the Red Zone, the Wild West of Iraq, where sixteen thousand people would be killed that year. And the next.

In writing this book, I drew upon all that I knew of crisis and fear, as well as love, hope, and heroism. Yes, it is a book of fiction about a future that may never happen. But the characters are real, at least to me, especially the heroes.

— Brendan Wilson, 2019

A FOREWORD

BY GENERAL WESLEY CLARK, U.S. ARMY (RET.)

Brendan Wilson's <u>Achilles Battle Fleet</u> is a story of leadership and daring set in the far future. It is a time when Earth's nations have found ways to cooperate and work together as they push to explore space beyond the solar system. There is advanced technology, of course, to have taken mankind to the stars. Others are there, non-communicative and hostile. Human forces are armed and ready.

This is science fiction, of course—but the science is plausible, and certainly the kind of technology we will need if we are ever to explore beyond the solar system. And there is risk, posed by other civilizations, not eager to communicate, apparently willing to fight to retain their own space.

But has mankind changed? Probably not, and this makes the grist of the story. From the first stories of Homer, and throughout three millennia of conflict on Earth, it has been character, which has proved decisive in the end. Hector, Achilles, Priam, and Odysseus are figures known to all who have studied Greek literature. There is the fabled Alexander the Great, who conquered much of the world known to the Greeks, and his decisive slash at the Gordian knot. There is Hannibal, crossing the Alps, then Julius Caesar, with his conquest of Gaul, Attila the Hun, and Genghis Khan, the greatest of the warriors of the steppes. All had the character to fight, to persist, and to conquer.

Of course, there is strategy, too. All modern strategists begin with the study of Sun Tzu, the legendary Chinese strategist of the Sixth Century B.C. Then there is the study of Napoleon, and his interpreters, Jomini and Clausewitz. And finally, modern strategy, with discussions of deterrence and geostrategy, as well as various theories of counterinsurgency, flexible response, anti-access and area denial, and onwards into new domains of warfare, like space and cyber.

There are other factors, too. Organizational breakthroughs—like the Greek phalanx and the Roman legions, the German blitzkrieg tactics combining rapid armored ground maneuver with close air support. Technology is, of course, a key element in determining the outcomes—from the first iron age swords against bronze, to the short bows of the pony-mounted Mongols that defeated the Teutonic Knights, to the English longbow, cannon, airplanes, the jet engine, and of course, nuclear weapons.

Then there is logistics. If Napoleon was the first to form a mass citizen army, and forced the creation of nation-states, then in the 20th Century, war was more often about logistics—massive scale, millions of troops, fronts extending hundreds or even thousands of miles.

Brendan Wilson knows all of this. He had a great career as an Army officer. In his twenty-five years in uniform he served as an artillery officer, Ranger and Airborne qualified, prepared to fight and win at small-unit level. He practiced, participated in and observed leadership at every level, including the level of a multinational alliance. He was with me at Supreme Headquarters, Allied Powers Europe, in the late 1990s as we worked to end ethnic cleansing and re-establish peace. He worked the strategy, and he also saw it at the tactical level. He was along with me on a harrowing trip into a conflict zone that was not without challenge and risk, as we dealt with the unsettled situation in war-torn Bosnia and contended with an angry and humiliated civilian populace. After taking off his uniform he served as a defense planner and diplomat. He commanded a fire base along the DMZ in Korea, and saw service in war-torn Libya, Kosovo, and Ukraine, Bosnia, and Iraq.

Sometimes diplomacy is untried or ineffective; there is just warfare. And in the first battles, especially against enemies evenly matched technically, it is leadership that is decisive. I wager that it hasn't changed much from the days of Hector, Achilles, Odysseus, and Alexander. Good leaders take responsibility; they know their people, and they bring out their best qualities. They communicate well. They inspire their followers to take incredible risks, and to accomplish feats they would never have believed. Good leaders set the example, and sometimes this means leading from the front. Good leaders set high standards and hold themselves and others to those standards. They build confidence in the team, and at the same time instill self-confidence into those that are alongside. Good leaders have a plan; they hold themselves and others accountable. And they have the character to follow through with their plans—learning as they go, accepting the hard knocks of combat, and understanding that no plan survives first contact with the enemy.

You can see the bits and pieces of this in the lives of all the great captains of history. But sometimes it is in fragments, or distorted by time, culture, the lack of accurate records. And in fact, the history in the books often doesn't tell the full story—of the struggles of ordinary men and women, of the first skirmishes, and the first battles that shape the conflict to come. These early battles are often won at the bottom—not at the top—with the courage and skills of the men in the phalanx, of the bowmen, or the cavalry scouts, and by the wiles and tactics of persons unknown to history.

In Brendan's novel character and the art of leadership are on display. It is all here, set in the future, in a compelling story that will hold you as the leadership lessons unfold. You'll see an enterprising old "flag officer" who steps forward to assume command in a crisis, and the team he builds, including a phenomenally talented young officer, Mei-Ling Lee, who is challenged in ways she never expected but comes through with flying colors. You'll see how a diverse group is molded into a winning team. You'll enjoy the story and think about it afterwards. Perhaps you can even bring some of the lessons into the present, and into your own life.

This is challenging time for the United States of America. For almost thirty years, we had no serious challenge or rival as the world's leading power. Now there are two, working together. We have come through almost twenty years of continuous conflict against terrorists, only to find that we need to reorient our military to deal with the challenge of "peer competitors." At home, partisan politics is fierce, long-held grievances have forcefully surfaced, and the winds of change are in the air. America needs courageous, thoughtful leaders at all levels, if we are to navigate the treacherous shoals of the 2020s. Hopefully, readers will take from Brendan's novel an understanding that individuals make a difference, that character counts, and with courage and competence, history is made.

— **Wesley K. Clark**

PROLOGUE

A TIME FOR WAR

Rear Admiral Jay Chambers stood on the bridge of the Troop Ship *Honolulu*, his adjutant at his side. Chambers served as the inspector general for the Achilles flotilla, a motley grouping of starships that had recently been ordered to fall back from Achilles Nine, a contested sector near the Separation Zone. Chambers looked the part of an old warrior: past fifty, gray hair, a long scar down the left side of his face, and what was clearly an artificial left hand. Lieutenant Mei-Ling Lee, conversely, was a twenty-something Asian woman, small in stature but tough-looking. She wore her jet-black hair in a long ponytail that hung down her back.

They were on the Troop Ship *Honolulu* to conduct an after-hours, no-notice inspection. This was part of the admiral's job as inspector general. Lee knew there was some sort of command problem on the *Honolulu*, and Chambers had decided to see first-hand what it was. They were waiting for the captain to arrive on the bridge, and Lee happened to be looking out at the fleet through the forward holoport when a vast, blinding light filled the screen.

It instantly polarized to save their eyes, but Lee was left with bright blotches in her field of vision. She'd been looking right at the flagship, wondering if she'd ever be assigned there, when it went up like a supernova. Blinking past the purpling afterimages, she froze as her mind tried to register what had happened, but it was almost too enormous to grasp. All around her, people began to make sounds of excitement, verging on panic. She realized she wasn't that far from it herself as the initial shock began to wear off.

Chambers remained calm, she remembered later. She admired that about him. *A warrior at heart,* she thought. Years of conflict and training had so steadied his nerves that he was, in fact, unflappable.

He addressed her calmly: "Lieutenant Lee." She made no response. Again, calmly, "Lieutenant Lee."

She turned to him, still in a state of shock. "Yes, sir?"

"Please tell the captain that I am assuming primary command of the fleet and that you will be assuming command of this battle bridge. Until further notice, the *Honolulu* carries the flag."

She stared at him numbly, unable to reply. A thousand people, at least, had just been vaporized in the nuclear fireball that had been the former flagship, the Human Alliance Battle Cruiser *Iroquois.* People she knew, had worked with, were molecular ash or dead of explosive decompression. Fleet Admiral Robertson ... *Oh, God.*

"Please do that now," said Chambers, still retaining his unearthly calm. "I'll be in the ready room, transferring the flag." That meant reassigning command and control to the *Honolulu,* issuing orders to his staff, and a dozen other things. He hurried toward a small door leading to a room off the command deck that was normally reserved for the ship's captain.

Lee finally snapped out of it, turned to look at the screen, and saw that what was left of the former command ship was tumbling out of control, forward half completely gone, the rest streaming flames, flash-frozen liquids, and atmosphere. The surviving hull was more or less swiss-cheesed by shrapnel, with little if any possibility of survivors. Quick responders were already trying to stabilize the *Iroquois* and stifle the fires with tractor and pressor fields. *No time to worry about that now,* she admonished herself. She moved swiftly to the task she'd been given, striding to the center of the bridge and announcing, "Shipwide channel. All hands to battle stations. Captain to the bridge."

The watch officer, a young ensign, stared at her blankly, much as she had done with the admiral a moment ago. She looked hard at the young officer and saw from his tag that his name was Douglas.

She barked, "Ensign Douglas?"

He seemed to jump back to reality and turned to his console to make the announcements. A second later, she heard the three-tone attack alert, followed by the call going out on every channel: "Battle stations! Battle stations! All hands to battle stations! Captain to the bridge. This is not a drill. Repeat: this is not a drill."

She waited a moment for that task to be completed and then announced briskly to the personnel on the bridge, "Listen up, everyone. Admiral Chambers has assumed primary command of the Achilles flotilla. I am Lieutenant Lee, his adjutant. This is now the flagship and command center, and I am the battle captain. Stations, report status in standard order."

By taking strong control of the situation and ordering a well-practiced routine, her actions seemed to have a calming effect. Each station reported their status to her in the order prescribed by naval operating procedure.

The technician at one console responded, "Communications: internal, fully intact. External ..." A pause. "The command net is jammed with traffic. Nothing from Flight Ops. Admin and log nets are open and quiet."

"Assume all nets are compromised," said Lee. "Emergency supersession. Establish this vessel as primary."

Immediately, the technician broadcast, "Flash traffic, flash traffic, flash traffic. Alpha Six Log has assumed primary as Achilles Actual. Emergency supersession, all nets." Alpha Six Log was Admiral Chambers' call sign. Flash traffic was an emergency order used to clear all traffic from any communications net, to await urgent instructions due to contact with the enemy. Emergency supersession meant an immediate change of frequencies to a new, predefined set. Lee knew she was taking a chance on that one; since they clearly had been ambushed, she had to assume their current com-nets had been monitored and, therefore, compromised, and couldn't be used now. But changing frequencies after a battle had started risked losing some of the stations that missed the order to make the change.

The other stations on the bridge reported in.

"Weapons and Security: external load-out includes bow and stern lasers, fifteen short-range Sprint missiles, and limited point defense. Counter-boarding gun crews fore and aft are operational. The provost platoon is at 80 percent."

Lee suppressed a wince at the light external weaponry but wasn't surprised that the onboard weapons were minimal. That was standard for a troop transport. The provost platoon was designed to keep order on board, because troop ships normally carried jarheads, and they sometimes got out of hand. At the moment, though, the *Honolulu* was fielding only a few marines, with the balance of her living space taken up by civilian staff being withdrawn from Achilles Nine. No one had expected an ambush.

"Provost to the bridge. Have him bring one squad," Lee barked. This order was a long-established precaution in combat. The command center for a fleet would always be protected. She snapped her head around. "Ensign Douglas, we'll need to establish a flight ops function. Find a senior pilot and have him report to me."

Sixty seconds later, an older warrant officer in a flight suit with master aviator wings above his left breast pocket strode onto the bridge. Lee saw a man past fifty with Slavic features, still fit and a bit grim-looking. He saluted in a relaxed but correct manner. "Ma'am, Master Warrant Officer Nemeth reporting as ordered."

The man spoke with a slight Eastern European accent. Lee knew the Navy retained a few warrant officers, most of whom were assigned as technical specialists, master pilots, flight instructors, or test pilots, but she rarely saw them. WOs were considered officers, ranking below a lieutenant but above a master chief petty officer.

Lee returned the salute quickly and said, "Flight ops is out, as you can see." They both glanced at the viewscreen, which still showed the *Iroquois* vomiting flames and debris into space. Nemeth nodded without emotion. Lee suspected he had seen a lot in his many years of service. "You are now commander in chief, aerospace, for the flotilla," she informed the WO, before turning her head to say, "Ensign Douglas, assign Mr. Nemeth a station and coms." She turned back to Nemeth. "I need to know what we've got out there in terms of fighters, what we still have available, and what we're facing. If you need help or additional personnel, the watch officer will get those for you.

"Now, who's on operations?" Lee asked as she turned toward that station.

"I am, ma'am—Petty Officer Jones," said a young man from the terminal.

Lee ordered, "Bring up the frigates to support flight ops. Warrant Officer Nemeth will give you coordinates."

The flotilla had two frigates attached to it for security. They were slow, but the extra firepower from their big guns might be useful in the developing battle. She noted that the provost platoon had arrived and quietly taken up station at the two entrances to the bridge and realized that the captain of the *Honolulu* had yet to report. She glanced at her watch and saw that six minutes had elapsed since the call had gone out. That was far too long; something was wrong. She was about to do something about it when one of the provost guard finally announced, "Captain on the bridge."

"What the hell is going on here?" Lee heard an angry male voice growl. She turned and saw a disheveled, overweight commander, only partially dressed, stumble onto the bridge, still struggling with his tunic. He looked around wildly, trying to take in what was happening. He set his eyes on the young watch officer and said, "Douglas, what's going on? Who are these people? Why wasn't I notified?"

Ignoring Lee, the commander stormed over to the watch officer. Lee could smell the alcohol on his breath. Not just his breath; actually, he was sweating it. Clearly, he had been drinking for quite a while and was still intoxicated, in flagrant violation of fleet regulations. Douglas came to attention and began to give his report, but the commander interrupted him. "Don't give me that crap! How many times have I told you I don't want to be disturbed during third watch? Are you an idiot?"

The rest of the bridge crew looked directly at their screens with expressionless faces. They had seen this type of behavior from their captain many times before, Lee suspected.

She was about to intervene when she heard Chambers say smoothly, "Captain Evans, a word, please." Chambers had correctly addressed the ship's commanding officer as captain, though his rank was commander. Per naval tradition, the commanding officer of any vessel was always addressed as captain, regardless of actual rank.

The commander spun toward Chambers' voice, fury in his bloodshot eyes. Clearly, he wasn't used to being interrupted during a tirade. He seemed not to have seen the admiral's rank insignia or didn't care, as he brusquely demanded, "Who the hell are you, and what are you doing on my bridge?"

Chambers drew a breath, nodded slightly, and said, as calmly as ever, "I am Rear Admiral Jay Chambers, primary of this flotilla. You, sir, are relieved of command." Before the commander could object, Chambers turned to the chief petty officer in charge of the provost guard and said, "Mr. Sharkley, escort the commander to his quarters, where he is to be confined until further notice. Have the XO report to me immediately."

"Yes, sir," replied the CPO. Lee could see the man trying to stifle a grin as he moved with two of his men to comply. This crew must have really hated their former captain.

Chambers said, "Now, let's have a look at flight ops." He walked over to the console where Master Warrant Officer Nemeth was working. Lee was surprised when Chambers put his good hand on Nemeth's shoulder and said, "Good to see you here, Chief. Tell me what we have."

Nemeth tapped some keys, and his display lit up to show a tactical readout. Lee could see a representation of the *Iroquois*, still listing and tumbling, trailing a comet's tail of debris and frozen liquid and atmosphere. At least the fires were out. She saw red dots indicating enemy raiders, and a few blue dots representing the flotilla's own fighters. The frigates were already maneuvering into position.

"Sir," Nemeth began, "we have the remnants of the 514th fighter squadron fighting a containment action against about three times their number."

"Looks like they're doing well," Chambers said. "Who's in command?"

Nemeth said, "Baker, the ops officer. The squadron commander and about half of the recon element were taken out by the mine that triggered the ambush."

Chambers' face reddened; he shook his head and said firmly, "That should *not* have happened."

"No, sir," Nemeth replied solemnly, "it should not have." Deploying your vessels too near each other was a cardinal sin in the Navy, for just such a reason.

Chambers asked, "Who do we have still in pre-launch?"

"We have the remaining two flights of the 514th that weren't on patrol, the 319th recon squadron, and the 221st heavy lift squadron," Nemeth said.

"Who's in command of the 319th?" Chambers asked.

"Commander Johann Schultz, but he is ... *was* on the *Nicky P*," responded Nemeth. They could all see that the Medical Ship *Nickolay Pirogov*, which housed the central sick bay, was in pieces now. "Acting command will devolve to Lieutenant Commander Stephen Bowman."

"Can he handle this?" Chambers asked.

"He can, sir. Very solid pilot," Nemeth answered without hesitation.

"What else?"

"Ops has moved the *Alabama* and the *Guangdong* into supporting positions," Nemeth said, referring to the two frigates.

Chambers turned toward the young man on the operations console and asked, "Load-out on the frigates, Mr. Jones?"

"Each has one battery of six five-inch railguns, sir. They are at full complement and are within range," responded the young PO.

"Let's get them into the fight if they can get a clear shot," Chambers said. "These bastards are going to fight to the last, and I don't want to lose another fighter if I don't have to."

"Roger, sir," Jones responded.

Chambers nodded, turned back to Nemeth, and said, "Send Bowman and as much of the 319th as we can get out. Hold everyone else back as a reserve."

"We're not going to be able to control the fight from here, sir," Nemeth said. "We don't have the right communications gear. Bowman will have to sort it out on his own."

Chambers smiled and said, "Yes, I know. I'm counting on it."

CHAPTER 1

I AM PRIMARY

Lieutenant Commander Stephen Bowman woke instantly to the sound of a repeated three-note siren, followed by an announcement on the ship's intercom: "Three-nineteenth squadron, all pilots and crew to launch hangar immediately! Three-nineteenth squadron, all pilots and crew to launch hangar immediately! This is not a drill! Repeat: this is not a drill!"

Bowman threw his legs over the edge of the bunk as the intercom called the off-duty pilots to the ready room and was moving toward his locker when the impact alarm sounded, accompanied by flashing red lights and followed immediately by a dull thud—a sound that should never be heard on a starship. He felt the slight shudder, stumbled a bit, and quickly threw on his flight suit. Grabbing his helmet, he ran out into the passageway. He'd clap on the helmet if he felt a sudden air-pressure change, indicating a breach.

He spared a quick thought about how his life had changed in a few short months. Six months ago, he'd been pulling reserve duty on the fighter transport *Boa Vista* out of Achilles Nine, a forward outpost near what used to be called the Separation Zone during the centuries-long, uneasy peace between the Human Alliance and the Others. Bowman had taken the reserve officer course while in college in order to fund his doctoral research, as had almost all of the other professors he worked with. Unlike them, however, he enjoyed his reserve duty. He loved the oily smell of starships and the order and discipline of the Navy. But most of all, he loved being a pilot. In the twelve years since he'd started his service, he had flown in space some three thousand hours, rising in proficiency and rank, and last year, he had been promoted to lieutenant commander and assigned as the executive officer of the 319th Reconnaissance Squadron.

All reserve officers had to pull a month of duty every year. But Bowman was a single college professor and had the whole summer off, so he often spent up to three months with the Navy, which was the reason he had so many flying hours and had risen so fast in the first place. But his job as XO had been a difficult one. Pilots and college professors had no responsibility beyond their own work, and so he wasn't used to being the person responsible for maintenance, training, personnel, logistics, and anything else the squadron commander wanted him to handle or was too busy to attend to.

He also found that he had to be the bad guy in the chain of command, the one who had to take a tough line toward his former peers when they wanted to report late, miss training, or deviate from military protocol some other way. But he treated this like any other challenge and quickly became more comfortable with the leadership role. He knew that his squadron commander, and every other senior naval officer, had to go through the same painful growing process.

Bowman entered the launch bay at a run, taking in the flurry of activity among the ground crews as they loaded munitions and fuel into the sleek recon versions of the FA-300, a state-of-the-art, multirole fighter that could handle a planet's atmosphere and the vacuum of space equally well. He glanced down the length of the launch tube—a three-hundred-meter-long runway with an arching roof—and saw with dismay that the stars were careening by the exit port, which was protected by a transparent force-shield, indicating the carrier either was undergoing emergency maneuvers or was out of control. Inside the vessel, the internal inertial dampers were still working, thank God, or the crew would be squashed to jelly by now.

"Chief, how many are up?" he shouted to CPO John Raymond, his ground crew supervisor.

"Six, sir," Raymond responded hurriedly, not bothering to salute. That BS was reserved for parade grounds and ceremonies. "I've got five pilots going through emergency preflight; you'll make six. I've lost coms with flight ops, so lacking guidance, I configured up for battle, not recon."

Raymond had done exactly right, just as Bowman knew he would. Bowman had trained all the squadron to make independent decisions whenever they needed to and would never criticize a sailor for making a call when the situation required it. Had Raymond waited to be told how to configure the aircraft, they would have lost desperately needed minutes. The lack of response from flight ops confirmed that something very serious was happening.

Like all modern military aerospace craft, the FA-300 could be configured for various missions. The 319th was normally configured for reconnaissance but could pull fighter duty if required. They would have less fuel but more ammo, and the sensors would be adapted for target acquisition rather than long-range imagery. Refueling and rearming would have to happen on the fly.

Again, foresight had paid off. Bowman had insisted that the fighter role should be trained, both for individual pilots as well as squadron tactics. The pilots all complained loudly until the 319th had beaten a full-time fighter squadron in force-on-force war-games last summer, a feat that had them standing tall and had earned them the grudging respect of the fighter jocks from other squadrons.

With a skip of his heart, Bowman realized that he was the commanding officer. His boss, Commander Johann Schultz, had been seriously injured three days ago, after a mechanical failure caused a botched landing; he was confined to the sick bay on the *Nicky P.* This made Bowman the acting commander. *Oh well,* he thought, *now's as good a time as any.*

After putting on his flight helmet, he looked up in time to catch a glimpse of a searing white flash from the end of the launch tunnel:

the unmistakable sign of a nuclear detonation in space, either from a missile or from the explosion of a ship's fusion reactor. Either way, the situation was dire.

Luckily, the polarizers in the visor had cut in with the first pulse of radiation, and he hadn't gotten a direct view anyway, so his vision was fine. He leaped into the FA-300's cockpit, gratified at the green lights and friendly chirping of the various systems reporting readiness. As the canopy sealed, he felt the gentle rumble of the fighter's engines. A calm settled over his being, and he realized, with some surprise, that he was happy. Strange feeling, but there it was.

He opened the com channel and broadcast, "All stations, all stations, this is Alpha Six 319, requesting omega one report." Omega one was a rarely used request, indicating the broadcasting station was entering an unknown combat situation. His call sign, Alpha Six 319, identified him as the commander of the 319th squadron, while the call "omega one" meant that the senior person in the field would either direct his actions, if that person were senior to him, or report to him the situation and request instructions if that person were a subordinate.

Before any response could be given, his afterburners blasted to life, and he shot down the launch tunnel and out into the swirling stars.

As soon as he cleared the launching bay, his fighter stabilized and he jinked hard to port, an evasive maneuver in case the enemy was targeting the bay's opening. His heads-up display (HUD) snapped up information overlays: first navigation, then enemy threats, then friendly units. At the same time, the lower part of the heads-up display flashed his own status: relative speed, fuel, ammo, shield status, and coms. For someone not trained as a pilot, it would be an indecipherable jumble, but pilots, and fighter pilots especially, had been trained to be able to make sense of the displays. He saw that the *Boa Vista*, which he had just left, was tumbling wildly and spewing debris from the port side, its stabilizers blazing as it struggled to regain control.

Finally, his coms came to life. "Alpha Six 319, this is Bravo Three 514," a calm voice stated over his headset. The call sign identified the operations officer from the 514th fighter squadron. His response meant two things: First, that the 514th commanding officer wasn't in battle, either still on board one of the vessels in the fleet, or dead. It also meant that Bowman was senior in the field, and it would be up to him to make the difficult decisions in the next few moments.

Bowman stifled the desire to shout, "What the hell is going on?" He knew that the ops officer for 514th, a Lieutenant Baker, was a solid type who would give him what he needed.

"Sir," Baker continued in his Louisiana accent, "you have thirteen fighters in the sky, including your six. The rest are remnants of the two flights of the 514th that were already on patrol when the action started. The lead scout vessel hit a mine, taking out the entire recon element. We've had enemy O-raiders coming at us in multiple waves since then. Three vessels are damaged. We've lost flight ops, sir, as you can see."

Bowman looked across the flotilla and saw the command ship *Iroquois*, which also housed flight operations, listing and spewing flames and debris, the bridge a blazing inferno. Bowman felt his fury rise as he realized the recon squadron on duty had screwed up big time. No way should they have been in a formation tight enough for all to get taken out by a single mine.

They'd paid for their stupidity in the most terminal way possible, and they may have doomed the rest of the flotilla in the process.

He glanced at the situational display and realized Baker had done a fine job of positioning his remaining forces. He noted the two frigates moving up into a supporting position. His sensors picked up the wrecks of dozens of O-raiders, meaning Baker and his team had been harvesting them like wheat. But there were far too many left.

"Recommendations?" Bowman asked.

"We're low on ammo and fuel, sir," Baker said calmly. "I need to rotate the 514's fighters back to rearm and refuel. Looks like the HC *Centurion* has the only stable landing bay, and they're ready for us. With your permission, I'll send 'em back in twos. I recommend we fall back in a defensive perimeter; your team can take point for a while. The fleet can't jump to light speed with this many vessels damaged. The enemy must have been in stasis for months because there's no base or larger vessel in the area."

Bowman knew what that meant: The O-fighters weren't going home. They'd been sent out here as part of an ambush that got triggered by the presence of the fleet. Similar ambushes had happened before, but never on this scale. No one in the Alliance had even imagined it possible, given what they knew about the Others.

Something, some inconsistency he couldn't finger, nibbled at the back of his mind. He didn't have time to study it closely. For now, what this information meant was that the Others had no way out and would fight until they ran out of fuel and ammo—and then self-detonate in thermonuclear fury.

By this time, the rest of Alpha 319 were on his wing. Counting himself, he had six in all. It would have to be enough for now.

"Attention all stations," Bowman said into his coms. "This is Alpha Six 319. I am primary." This was a formal assumption of battle command. As far as Bowman knew, until today, it was a phrase that hadn't been uttered in over a century. "Bravo Three 514 is secondary, executing rearm and refuel under his authority."

CHAPTER 2

GAUGAMELA

Bowman took stock of his situation. Baker had fallen back to a rough perimeter around the fleet, and Bowman could see the fighters dropping off the formation, two at a time, heading for the landing bay of the Heavy Cruiser *Centurion*. Damn, Baker was good. He'd have to keep that in mind.

He had his five fighters check in with him. Two of the pilots were top-notch; the other three were good but just out of flight school, having been rushed into the fleet when the hostilities had broken out six months before. They had potential, and he knew in a few more months, they would be solid.

Today, however, they were going to have to do more than their best.

He checked the scanners and saw that the Others had fallen into a rough defensive perimeter of their own. Baker had hurt them far worse than they were prepared for. The fact that he had forced a much larger adversary into a defensive posture spoke well of his ability as a pilot and a leader. Bowman knew the enemy must be doing what he had just done—sorting out who was left and who was in command.

Their numbers, though diminished, were substantial: At least sixty O-fighters remained within the flotilla. This didn't disturb him, particularly. He knew from history that smaller numbers could defeat larger forces when properly deployed. Alexander the Great had defeated Darius when outnumbered twenty to one. The principle was simple: The enemy had put himself in a defensive position, and that made them vulnerable. Despite his smaller numbers, Bowman knew that the enemy commander would not easily let himself be outflanked. Bowman's pilots were fresh, with full ammunition magazines and fuel tanks. They could afford to draw out the Others and force a weakness in the line.

And it just so happened that his squadron had a plan for that, one they had drilled a hundred times under Bowman's demanding leadership.

"Squadron 319, this is Alpha Six," he announced into his com. "We will attack using Plan Gaugamela, Option One. That's Gaugamela One. Repeat and execute."

He waited for the chorus of "Gaugamela, Option One, aye aye!" The plan called for Flight One to go black and drift toward the center of the line, where they would mix in with the debris of the earlier battle and play dead. Meanwhile, Flights Two and Three would join him for an end-run on the right flank, kicking in their afterburners and passing a lot of radio chatter back and forth, to provide plenty of light and noise. Alliance aerospace fighters were grouped in flights of two birds, a formation that allowed mutual support and could be used as building blocks to make larger formations. Flight One was the most experienced of the three now in the formation, and they'd just been given the most difficult and dangerous job.

Hopefully, the Others weren't up on human history. The plan, Gaugamela, was named for the battle of the same name in which Alexander the Great had defeated Darius in 331 BC. Alexander had drawn out the Persians by leading his cavalry on a long end run around the flank, forcing Darius to use his chariots before he was ready, opening up the line for exploitation.

"On my mark: five, four, three, two, one, *mark*," Bowman said.

Instantly and simultaneously, both Flight One fighters went dark and began their unpowered drift toward the enemy center. They did so perfectly, each ship displaying a slight tumble and trailing fuel as if their tanks had been ruptured. The space around the flotilla was filled with similar debris, so Bowman hoped the Others wouldn't consider it a threat and wouldn't even notice that two active blips had fallen off their screens. He was encouraged; his four fighters turned and blasted the afterburners, beginning a long, arching path that would lead them into the Others' flank. As in other skirmishes, the Others had been deployed mostly on a single plane, as if reluctant to abandon the Two-D tactics that must have served them well on planetary surfaces; Gaugamela Option One would take advantage of that by hitting them from above. Each of the human fighters began transmitting prerecorded, un-encrypted messages that were designed to sound like the communications traffic of a much larger force. Bowman was counting on the natural confusion of battle for this little subterfuge to work on the Others. Their sensors would tell them only four fighters were coming, but the communications traffic would conflict with this. He was hoping their commander would overreact.

Sure enough, Bowman saw that at least half the enemy force had broken off and was repositioning to meet his flanking maneuver. Perfect. As he closed the distance and began finishing the turn, he prepared himself for the maneuver he and his fighters were about to engage in. Just as he entered weapons range, Bowman began a second count: "On my mark: three, two, one, mark!"

As one, each of his fighters began to spin violently along all three long axes, throwing off clouds of chaff, fine slices of metal designed to confuse the targeting lidar and radar of the Others' fighters. Inside the cockpits, inertial gravity dampers kept the pilots from being ripped apart by centrifugal force. Bowman focused on his own targeting systems, which had been tweaked with a program that compensated for his ship's rapid rotation. The main display showed a number of circles, each indicating an enemy fighter. The compensation had sounded complicated at first, but it really wasn't, not for a flight computer, at any rate, which routinely solved much more difficult spatial problems. All he needed to do was aim and fire at each circle, and the computer and auto-aiming mechanisms would take care of the rest.

He grasped the joystick on his weapons console and rapidly pulled the trigger in bursts of three, feeling the satisfying, *thump, thump, thump* as projectiles leapt from the 30mm railguns under the fuselage. He could see from the flashes outside the cockpit as his shots connected, turning kinetic energy into blossoms of flame as each burst took out an enemy fighter. As far as he could see, none of his own fighters had been hit so far. In fact, he wasn't sure the Others had even fired a shot, such was their confusion.

Then he saw the blasts from the nukes. His sleeper team had made their infiltration of the line, in the hole that his flanking maneuver had opened up, just as planned. Their job had been for each to drop four low-yield nuclear weapons down the middle of the formation and then skedaddle out of range before setting them off remotely.

The Others had been taken completely by surprise. Their formation showed no coherence of any kind. He had personally taken out eight on his run through the flank, and he hoped his other pilots had done the same. The eight nukes had devastated the rest of the Others' formation.

"Alpha Squadron, on me," Bowman said.

The other five fighters, all unscathed, converged on his fighter and, as a single entity, flew in a loose formation back toward the flotilla. Bowman noted that Baker was back in the sky, with his fighters rearmed and ready for combat.

"Alpha Six, this is Bravo Three," came Baker's steady drawl. "Looks like y'all had all the fun. How about some tag teamwork?"

"Bravo Three, Alpha Six. They're all yours," Bowman replied.

The two formations raced past each other as Baker took six fighters into the remnants of the Others' formation. The battle didn't last long, and it wasn't pretty. In the six months of armed conflict, mostly skirmishes, no Others craft of any kind had surrendered. Baker's team hunted many of them down individually and shot them to pieces. Bowman watched the situation overlay on his heads-up display as the last few O-fighters formed a tight defensive sphere, clearly a last-ditch defense, something it would have been wise to do earlier. At this point, it wouldn't hold for long, but it did make it harder to get at them, and Baker would probably lose some of his team mopping them up.

"Bravo Three, Alpha Six," Bowman said. "Let's let the frigates have a turn. They need some target practice too."

"Roger that," Baker replied; he sent the call for fire to the fire controller on the senior of the two frigates, the *Alabama*. "Foxtrot Sierra Six, this is Bravo Three. Fire for effect, over." Baker sent the coordinates and target description.

Clearly, the frigates had been hoping to get into the fight, because FS Six came back within seconds to announce the volley had been fired. "Bravo Three, this is Foxtrot Sierra Six, shot and rounds complete, over." This indicated that the railguns had all fired, and no more were to be expected.

Meanwhile, as Alpha Squadron approached the *Centurion*, Bowman kept an eye on the screen as the accelerator rings on the two frigates flared, and twelve projectiles, 130mm in diameter and ten times that long, screamed toward their target at a significant fraction of the speed of light. These munitions were made of steel-jacketed depleted uranium, specially designed to overcome protective shields, both physical and force based, and to detonate at a programmed set of coordinates. The enormous explosions detonated just off-center of the O-raiders' defensive sphere, but it was enough: it ripped apart the remaining ships, throwing the debris outward in what, to Bowman, resembled a supernova in miniature.

CHAPTER 3

CHANGE OF COMMAND

Eighteen hours after the last of the O-fighters had been destroyed, Stephen Bowman stood in the crowded makeshift command center, hastily set up in one of the vacant bays of the HC *Centurion*. The room was filled with squadron commanders and senior staff officers. The light was inconsistent, because of the floodlights that had been run in on cables by the techs. The air smelled of grease, smoke, and sweat.

Bowman was exhausted. After the battle with the O-fighters, he had been put in charge of the rescue and recovery efforts as well as the continued defense of the flotilla, should the Others send more fighters. It was tiring and stressful work, but he was glad to do it, especially since his team had been able to find and rescue five crew members among the wreckage, hanging onto life, breathing through emergency respirators. Once again, Lieutenant Baker had proven his worth, as meticulous and thorough as he had been audacious earlier in the engagement.

Rear Admiral Jay Chambers stood on an elevated step at the front of the room, looking calm as always, his scarred left cheek and silvery artificial hand a hallmark of his presence. He was accompanied by the fleet operations officer, Captain Jim Vance, looking pissed off as usual. Vance was a tough-looking man: tall, heavyset, balding, with a permanent scowl. Bowman knew he was holding one of the toughest jobs in the Navy right now. He had a well-deserved reputation for being less than charming.

Bowman was a bit surprised to see Admiral Chambers preparing to lead the meeting. Chambers wasn't the admiral in charge of the flotilla, as far as Bowman knew. He wasn't even a line officer. He was a logistician who had been on an inspection tour when the hostilities broke out. Because there had been no way for him to return to Earth, what with all the military vessels being used for priority defense measures, he had been swept up in the ad hoc reorganization; that's when Fleet Admiral Robertson had appointed Chambers as the inspector general of what was now called the Achilles Flotilla. The entire sector had been ordered to fall back to defensive positions, which had resulted in the formation of the flotilla.

Few of the junior line officers liked Chambers. They felt he wasn't qualified to lead them, being neither a ship driver nor a pilot. But Bowman didn't feel that way. He knew from his study of military history that logistics was a necessary art for the success of any military mission. Heck, much of his own job as squadron XO involved logistics, and he knew just how difficult that task could be. He had met Chambers a number of times and found him both a solid leader and a competent officer.

Chambers had stopped by on several assistance visits in his role as IG. The other XOs dreaded these visits, seeing them as intrusive and a nuisance, if not a form of harassment. But Bowman took the offer of assistance at face value and allowed Chambers to demonstrate the ins and outs of maintenance management, how to order and stockpile spare parts, and how to schedule work crews to get the most equitable time sharing and rest periods. Most importantly, he had shown Bowman how to fill out and submit the many dozens of reports that the fleet required of each squadron.

And Bowman had found out something else about Chambers that the others hadn't bothered to learn: Chambers hadn't always been a "logy," as logisticians were called. He had started out as an enlisted man who had joined the Navy right out of high school. For years, Chambers had worked as a *salvage tech*, which was a euphemism for a Special Operations warrior—those who filled the elite ranks of the Navy's strike team Oracle. Oracle was black ops, a top-secret covert unit composed of Navy special warfare operatives and Marine commandos. For security reasons, the members of the unit were never named while they were serving. They had a well-deserved reputation for incredible toughness and great skill.

It hadn't taken long for Chambers to become a mustang, rising from the ranks to become an officer. About twenty years ago, while serving as a special ops squadron commander, he had lost his hand while on a classified combat mission and could no longer meet the physical standards of the elite force. He was offered a retirement with full pension but refused. Instead, he had himself fitted for the artificial hand and took up his current career as a logistician. He wanted to serve, even in what was mostly a desk job. Chambers had thrown himself into his new career, learning and performing his new duties with the same dedication he had shown as a salvage tech.

Bowman only found out about Chambers' history because he had seen the deference the Marine commandos paid him one day when he was inspecting their quarters. The Marines had popped to attention in a way he had never seen them do for any naval officer, admiral or not. Bowman figured something was up, and so he sought out the unit's gunnery sergeant, a guy named Davenport, and got the story from him.

He was right: The Marines couldn't care less about Chambers' rank. They knew him by reputation; apparently, he was legend in their circles. "Beyond awesome," Davenport said. "The toughest of the tough. My old sergeant major back when I was a corporal said he'd served with him in the special warfare task force when Chambers was the CO. He said Chambers was the best warrior he ever saw— an expert at hand-to-hand, marksmanship, tactics, you name it. He didn't suffer fools or cowards gladly, and he always went in first when the going got tough. That's how he picked up that shiny hand and the pretty mug."

Bowman was impressed and said as much.

"Oh, and by the way, he can fly those pretty little birds of yours just as well as you and your boys. SpecOps commanders have to qualify as ground commanders, ship drivers, *and* aviators. Don't ever try to bluff him. He'll never brag, but he knows his stuff—and yours too."

Bowman was intrigued and asked about his personal life.

"He pretty much keeps to himself," Davenport said. "But his wife died decades ago, and he has a son in the Navy somewhere. A ship driver, I think."

Shaking off the fatigue and concentrating on the meeting, Bowman looked around the room. He noted that, despite the close quarters, there were fewer officers present than there should have been for a general briefing of field officers. He guessed there were only about thirty men and women in the room, and there should have been at least sixty. With Chambers and Vance was a young adjutant whom Bowman had seen before but had not met. She was a confident, tough-looking Asian woman of about twenty-five, her black hair gleaming past her shoulders. Bowman's heart skipped a beat; she looked gorgeous.

There was some stirring up at the front of the bay, and it was clear the meeting was about to get under way. Bowman noted a small detachment of Marines standing at parade rest off to one side. He looked again at Chambers and realized that something was different about his uniform now. When the admiral turned to speak with someone, Bowman saw with surprise and approval that Chambers was wearing his trident on his chest, the symbol of his qualification as a special warfare officer, as well as his fruit salad, a colorful array of ribbons showing his awards for combat. Among these, he quickly picked out those for the Silver Star, the Navy Cross, and, to his astonishment, the Aerospace Medal, which meant that Chambers had seen combat as an aviator.

Just as he realized that his mouth was hanging open, he heard the adjutant call the group to attention. The Marine detachment snapped their weapons up with easy precision to the order arms position. Bowman had never wanted to be a Marine, but he had to admire their discipline and precision. The group stood ramrod straight, silently waiting for what might follow.

"Attention to orders," read the adjutant, her alto voice a melody to Bowman. Damn, he needed to concentrate on what she was saying. "Alliance Fleet Command, dated 2314 Zulu, 7 December 2541. By order of the President of the Alliance of Human Peoples and the Minister of War, in accordance with Wartime Powers Act 1571, and the Global Constitution of Human Alliance, Amendment 4, 'Succession of Military Authority,' the following is promulgated:

"One: Following multiple attacks on Alliance planets, colonies, military installations, formations, and civil shipping; as of 1930 hours this date, a general state of war has been declared on an unknown enemy who has made multiple attacks on both military and civilian targets within the Human Alliance.

"Two: All military personnel not currently with their units shall report to the nearest military installation for further instructions. All reservists are hereby called to active duty and, insofar as possible, are to report in accordance with their existing activation instructions.

"Three: Deployed combatant commands are at DEFCON One and should take all appropriate measures to preserve combat capability, resist armed aggression, protect civil populations, and prepare for offensive operations where tactically feasible.

"Four: While retaining all lawful prerogatives of command, the Minister of War has delegated all necessary legal, administrative, financial, and personnel authority to combatant commanders of two-star rank or above.

"Given under my hand, this seventh day of December, AD 2541, Virgil D. Simone, President of the Alliance of Human Peoples."

You could have heard a pin drop in the bay. It was as quiet as the vacuum of space. Bowman's mind raced, trying to take in the import of what had just been said.

First, the attack on the flotilla had been only one of many that had obviously included strikes against military and civilian targets elsewhere in Alliance territory.

Second, a declaration of war had been made, a clear upgrade from the general state of hostilities that had been recognized up until now.

Third, all military forces had been activated. The Alliance actually had a fairly well-thought-out mobilization plan. The fact that the government wasn't using it meant that either the situation was dire or the part of the government that was tasked to implement that plan no longer existed, or both. That the Alliance military arm was delegating broad powers down to the two-star level reinforced the view that some substantial part of the command and control mechanism was severely impaired.

Finally, and ominously, was the name of the person who had signed the order as the president of the Alliance. The last time Bowman had checked, Virgil Simone was the minister of intercultural affairs. That he had signed as president, and not acting president, meant that the previous incumbent, the honorable William J. Clifton, and a host of other officials higher in the chain of succession were dead.

"At ease," shouted the adjutant.

Immediately, the Marines popped to the new position, eyes focused straight ahead. The officers relaxed a bit and glanced around at each other, as if looking for confirmation of what they'd just heard.

Chambers let the moment stand for a long beat and then began speaking. His voice was calm and reassuring, not overconfident, but also without the slightest bit of doubt or hesitation.

"Marines, rest," he commanded quietly. The marines immediately relaxed, lowered their weapons, and looked respectfully at the admiral.

Nice touch, thought Bowman. Not many flag officers would have remembered the Marines were still at the at-ease position, a stance less rigid than attention but still uncomfortable. The Marines would have held that position until they died, such was their discipline. By this subtle gesture, however, Chambers had shown respect for the Marines and reinforced his own authority with the group.

"Ladies and gentlemen," he began. "I first want to introduce myself to those of you who don't know me. I am Rear Admiral Jay Chambers. The first blow struck at the Achilles Flotilla today was a mine that took out our entire recon element. Thirty seconds later, an O-fighter with a nuclear payload rammed the Command Vessel *Iroquois,* destroying the command cell and killing our commanding officer, Fleet Admiral Robertson, and almost all the command staff. That explosion also took out flight ops.

"As it happened, my adjutant, Lieutenant Mei-Ling Lee, and I were aboard the TS *Honolulu* on an inspection tour. When it became clear that the command vessel was no longer capable of providing command and control, I assumed primary, and we set up a limited command operation cell on the *Honolulu*'s bridge. We have since confirmed that Fleet Admiral Robertson and all the other flag officers perished in the fighting. Formally, for the Achilles Flotilla and for the record, I am primary."

Chambers said this so calmly, and yet with such gravitas, that the room was completely silent; no one seemed able to as much as draw a breath. The ancient ritual, which Bowman himself had performed earlier, was now repeated, as it must have been many times that day in the far reaches of the galaxy. As long as there was one warrior left to say those words, there would always be a human fleet in operation.

"It is a credit to our fallen leader, Admiral Robertson, that this flotilla fought so well in very difficult circumstances after the attack commenced," continued Chambers. "Many of our team fought valiantly and made the ultimate sacrifice in the effort. The survivors have done their duty, and no more praise need be given to any living warrior."

This was the Navy's tradition, Bowman knew, to praise the valiant dead and recognize the competent and steadfast survivors. Again, Chambers was subtly grounding his officers in the traditions of the service. It had a calming effect, as was surely his intent.

"We are tired now. Many of you have not so much as taken a sip of water in over twenty hours of combat. You will need to refresh yourselves and get some rest. This is one of the reasons I held back parts of the forces assigned to us. These warriors, every bit as competent as those of us here, are now on duty, protecting our perimeter and continuing with emergency repairs.

"Before we can do that, however, we need to take stock of where we are and reorganize for the fight ahead. The president has given us our general orders, and I intend to follow those in both letter and deed."

Bowman listened in awe of Chambers as he realized the mastery and ease of the speech he was now giving. Chambers had started by identifying himself and asserting his command authority with complete confidence. Next, he recognized his fallen predecessor, further establishing himself as the legitimate successor while subtly reinforcing his own status as one who had the right to praise such an exalted leader. Next, he acknowledged those who had perished, while restraining his praise for those now in the room. The message was clear: "You've done well for now, but the real fight lies ahead. And *I* will be the judge of the living." He then made clear that he had thought ahead by keeping a reserve and now was about to transition into the more complicated task of reorganizing the forces, by seamlessly linking his own orders to those of the president. Bowman had newfound respect for the man and knew that every man and woman in the room now waited attentively for his next words.

CHAPTER 4

NEW DUTIES

Chambers looked at the group, searching the faces of those present before continuing.

"You are about to receive detailed reports on the damage from my staff, but let me just say that as of one hour ago, three of the sixteen vessels within the flotilla are damaged beyond repair, including the CV *Iroquois*. Most of the 221st heavy lift aerospace squadron was lost, with the Light Carrier *Kennedy*. The Medical Ship *Nickolay Pirogov* was also a complete loss; all hands and passengers perished in the first moments of the attack. It was obviously one of the primary targets. The launch bay of the Heavy Corvette *Mississippi River* is closed due to damage. Most of the remaining ships have suffered lesser but still significant damage. We have only limited communications capability, either for conducting operations or contacting other Alliance elements. In total, 1,652 personnel are confirmed dead and forty-three are missing."

A shockwave of silence, broken with a few gasps, spread across the assembly as the scale of the deaths sank in. Bowman realized that

Commander Schultz was dead, as he'd been on the *Nicky P* when she was destroyed.

"Our priorities are force protection, followed by the rapid ability to conduct effective offensive operations. I want all of you to internalize these priorities and inculcate them in your troops. We must take every step possible to ensure our survival and that of our civilian charges. We do this—we survive—so that we can fight and inflict maximum damage on the enemies of the Alliance. We don't do this for hatred or revenge, but because it is our duty.

"Each of you will be called upon to do whatever is necessary to achieve these objectives. Some of you will need to step up to greater responsibility. Others will have to learn entirely new skills. All of us will make sacrifices. This is what we do.

"I have reorganized the Achilles Flotilla into a battle fleet. The organization is as follows:

"Captain Vance will command base support operations, which includes overall command of the thirteen remaining vessels. He is responsible for providing life support, logistics, and communications for the battle fleet. To carry out these duties, he is promoted to commodore.

"Gunnery Sergeant Charlie Davenport will command a composite battalion of Marines and Naval security forces, configured for Special Operations. He is promoted to captain of Marines.

"Lieutenant Mei-Ling Lee will serve as the headquarters commandant and my chief of staff. She is promoted to lieutenant commander."

Bowman saw all eyes turned to the young adjutant he had noticed before. Her face was completely neutral, but he saw a hint of color come to her cheeks, and he suspected that she had been taken by surprise by this announcement.

"Lieutenant Commander Stephen Bowman will command a composite aerospace wing, including the remnants of the 319th fighter squadron, the 514th reconnaissance squadron, and 221st heavy lift squadron. He is promoted to captain.

"These four officers will be my principle commanders, and I will exercise my command through them. I task them now to organize their own commands, selecting from within the ranks for key positions. Recommendations for promotions are to be turned in to me within forty-eight hours.

"I will now turn over the briefing to Commodore Vance for detailed implementation instructions. Principal staff and commanding officers in my quarters in one hour. That is all."

Chambers turned and walked out of the room. The young adjutant called the group to attention. For a moment after he left, the room was dead quiet.

Then Commodore Vance said, "As you were; let's get to work."

CHAPTER 5

THE LONELY JOB

Fifty-five minutes later, Captain Stephen Bowman and the other three officers selected as senior commanders waited outside the admiral's suite, where two stone-faced Marines stood guard.

Bowman, now truly tired, tried to remember all that had been said in the previous briefing. He longed to get back to his squadron and then remembered he didn't *have* a squadron as such. Oh my, so much to do. He hardly knew anyone in Baker's unit, the 514th, and he couldn't think of a single name to go with the 221st heavy lift squadron. It had been a long day, and his head hurt. But he refused to let it show.

At some unseen signal, the Marines came to attention. Admiral Chambers emerged from his suite and said, "Please come in, lady and gentlemen."

He asked them to sit in reasonably comfortable chairs, and he himself pulled up a stool and sat facing them. He waited while his orderly brought out ice water and coffee. When they'd all had a sip of their chosen beverages, he began, as calmly as ever.

"I have chosen you four officers because I have confidence in your potential to serve. Although we don't yet know all the details, something calamitous has befallen both the Alliance and our military command structure. Our mission, tasks, and conditions are harsh, and that will drive all of us. I realize you are all worried about your loved ones and your nations. But put your personal feelings aside, and focus on the mission and what you four as a group can do to further our success. I expect you to work together, cooperate, and be loyal to the unit, to each other, and to me."

He paused a moment. Bowman realized he did this on purpose, both to let the words sink in and to show his control of the meeting. He would not be hurried.

"You alone are responsible for the welfare, combat readiness, and performance of your units. You will answer to me and to the Navy for that, and you will not find me an easy leader in that regard. I also understand that all of you are serving in jobs you've never had before, as am I. I do not expect the impossible. In fact, I understand that some setbacks and mistakes are a necessary part of learning and moving forward. I know that you will make them, and I insist that you learn from them. What I will not tolerate is deception or quibbling or trying to avert blame from yourself when it belongs there.

"A couple of ground rules. Your word is your bond, because I will stake the lives of our sailors and Marines, as well as the success of our mission, on your word. If I lose confidence in you, I will relieve you.

"Set the tone in your units, and hold your subordinate commanders to the same standards. You will need to develop your subordinate leaders. Keep an eye out for those who show potential. Push them hard, stress them out, and see who shines.

"You have two days to reorganize your units, select subordinate commanders, recommend promotions, and report back to me on your capabilities and limitations. This is not going to be easy, because you have a number of constraints and certain things that cannot wait.

"Commodore Vance, you have thirteen vessels that need food, water, fuel, and medical treatment. Commander Lee, my flag headquarters needs to be up and running right now, and it needs to stay that way. Captain Bowman, you currently have one squadron out on perimeter duty and, if I am not mistaken, another squadron you have never met. Captain Davenport, your Marines need to provide security around the clock, but you must also maintain a quick reaction force 24/7 and maintain training for offensive operations. No rest for the weary." He smiled slightly.

"But the first thing you are going to do is call your own staffs together, give them a fragmentation order, put someone in charge, and then get some sleep. That is an order."

He stood, and they all followed suit. "Commander Lee will be around tomorrow to set you all up with secure direct communication to the command center and with me. I must be able to reach my top leaders at any time. For now, the flag will remain on the *Centurion*. That is all."

They began to file out, and the admiral said, "Captain Bowman, Commander Lee, please stand fast."

Bowman and Lee waited while the others left the room. Bowman heard the Marines pop to attention in the hallway and then come back to the guard position.

He looked at Lee, feeling a bit sheepish, wondering if his attraction to her was obvious and if she would think him a buffoon or worse. He tried to smile, and he felt like it came out as a freakish grimace. She nodded politely and smiled just a bit, with maybe a hint of amusement. *Better than a slap in the face,* he thought.

"Please sit," the admiral said. "Captain Bowman, I need your help. I know you are a professor of history in another life, and we have lost our entire intelligence section, along with the rest of the command staff. I need your analytical skills. You will have noticed that something is wrong with what happened today." It was a statement, not a question. "What's missing?"

Bowman thought a moment. Even through his exhaustion, he knew what the admiral meant. He had sensed it before, and the feeling had become even stronger during the ops brief. "The simultaneous attack," he said. "It was too well coordinated."

"Continue," Chambers said.

"Those O-fighters. The logical explanation, based on our knowledge of the Others' capabilities, is that they were left out here in stasis long ago, with a minefield scattered as part of an ambush. That would suggest that the presence of the fleet or the detonation of the mine triggered their wakeup routine. But we have now learned that these attacks took place simultaneously, all over the Alliance. The timing is too perfect. In order for the attack to start at a specific time, the Others would have to have known the exact place and time the fleet would cross a certain point, and that isn't possible."

"Why not?"

"Because even we didn't know when we would cross that point until maybe a day or so before we did, sir. I was at the ops briefing when the route was selected only forty-eight hours ago; it was worked out on the spot. The rate of movement for the flotilla varies according to the performance of the vessels within it. We slowed for maintenance and refueling; since those variations are unpredictable, the point of the ambush couldn't have been known by anyone very far in advance."

"That is exactly right," the admiral said. "What else?"

"Something isn't right about the Others themselves," Bowman said hesitantly.

The admiral nodded grimly and said, "Yes?"

"They react to battle tactics in predictable ways."

"Is that so odd?"

"I was able to draw them out of line by using deception and tactics designed for a human foe, and they reacted exactly as expected. But they *aren't* human. We don't know how they ought to respond to stimuli, but the fact that they responded as they did is either a fantastic coincidence, or something else."

"You are closer to the answer than you know," Chambers said glumly.

"Sir?" Bowman said.

"I've seen the Others before, fought them," Chambers said simply. "The enemies you faced today were not the Others."

Bowman and Lee sat in silence, thinking about what that might mean.

"Think about it. The first attacks start about six months ago. Low-level raids hitting outposts. Initially, everyone assumes it's the Others. Yes, we fought them a century ago. Technically, there is no peace agreement in place. That's because we have no diplomatic relations with them at all. In fact, we have never communicated with them, not once. We don't even know if we *can* communicate with them."

"But sir," Lee said, "you said you fought them. You mean before the outbreak of hostilities?"

"Yes," the admiral admitted. "We have engaged in low level conflict with the Others in the Separation Zone off and on since peace was declared. They continue to try to build up bases and forces in the region, and we push them back. That's pretty much what the Oracle strike force is for."

The admiral looked at Bowman and then at Lee. "What I desperately need from you is to establish some type of intelligence capability for the fleet. I know that you will be busy with the aerospace wing, Captain. But I also know you have some good people there to help. I saw Baker on the viewscreens today. He's solid. Use him to develop the aerospace wing so you can focus on your intelligence division. I need you to spend part of your time putting together a team of analysts. Commander Lee will serve as your deputy. I think you'll find she has some experience you can use. I want you two to pick out some people with the right aptitude and skill set, bring them together, and get them working on some of these problems. I need strategic intelligence, and I need someone to develop war-game scenarios based on different views of what's going on. I know you're a master at that, *Professor* Bowman. I recognize a Gaugamela gambit when I see it."

For a second time, the admiral stood to end the meeting. The two officers stepped into the corridor, where they looked at each other without a word.

CHAPTER 6

SMART GUYS

The next weeks were a whirlwind of activity, almost a blur to Bowman as he looked back. Sleep had become a fond memory. He had indeed used Baker, relied on him heavily, in fact. Typical for his normal demeanor, Baker had no reaction when he was promoted to lieutenant commander and made the deputy for the aerospace wing. He simply set about the work and got the results Bowman expected.

Captain Bowman had reorganized the wing, now called the Achilles Expeditionary Wing, into three squadrons: two aerospace squadrons and one support squadron. The support squadron had consolidated maintenance and logistics, as well as the few remaining heavy lift craft that could be used to haul anything from fuel and spare parts to troops. He had promoted the most competent officers to command the squadrons and allowed those officers to appoint their own officers to fill the leadership gaps. The same had been done with the enlisted ground and technical crews, many of them seeing promotions and new responsibilities.

Because of the devastation of the initial ambush, many sailors had to begin the difficult transition to new skills and duties. Bowman had lost a number of bright young sailors to Commander Lee's reorganized headquarters staff. The biggest and most urgent need had been for medical personnel, the majority of whom had been killed when the *Nicky P* had broken apart. Sailors who had some of the educational prerequisites in the sciences had been pulled out to begin what amounted to an emergency apprenticeship under the few surviving doctors and nurses.

Bowman, remembering the admiral's admonition to cooperate with Lee, had suppressed the desire to argue about the loss of personnel. Despite his frustration, he had to admire Lee's confident and sure administration of the rebuilt headquarters in her role as the admiral's chief of staff. But in truth, Chambers hardly needed a chief of staff. He was quite confident in running the staff, probably a trait he learned in Special Operations, where staffs were kept to a minimum and bosses were expected to lead directly.

The most interesting and, to be honest, challenging part had been organizing the intelligence staff. Here again, Lee had proved her worth. It turned out that she had majored in strategic studies at the Naval Academy and had a master's degree in linguistics. She had assembled the initial group of applicants for her and Bowman to interview. She drew from a broad range of ages and experience from within the fleet; most of these people Bowman would have considered misfits until he learned more about them. And maybe they *were* misfits when it came to the line Navy. But for what they were looking for in the intelligence staff, he was impressed.

During his first interview, a young man in his early twenties, Seaman Apprentice Andy Danner, reported to Bowman in his ready room. Danner was slightly taller than average, very skinny, somehow looking unfit. His bearing was unmilitary, his hair unruly and just on the edge of allowable length. Bowman sighed inwardly, thinking to himself that Lee had shown poor judgment by sending him in.

But Danner had surprised him. He was clearly intelligent and spoke well, in a clear, assured voice. Despite his youth, Danner had dual degrees in engineering and ancient history from a very good school back on Earth. Bowman knew this was a rare combination; it meant Danner had a wide range of interests and both the discipline and intelligence to carry out two demanding fields of study simultaneously. His scores in training had been high, and the CPO in charge of his apprenticeship had written positive remarks about the young man in his training record. Reading between the lines, Bowman could see the chief had been delighted with the recruit, recognizing the potential he saw. Probably hated to lose him.

"Danner, why are you here?" Bowman asked shortly after beginning the interview.

"Sir, I was required to report to you by my supervisor, Master Chief Johnson," Danner said crisply, no hint of sarcasm in his voice.

"What I meant was, why have you volunteered for intelligence duties?"

Danner considered that for a moment and replied, "Captain, I was not aware that I had volunteered for anything, nor was I aware of the reason for this interview until now." Danner paused again, hesitated, and then said, "But I am happy to learn about it, sir." Then Danner smiled, and Bowman couldn't help but like the guy.

"Danner, why do you think the Others attacked us?" asked Bowman.

"I don't know that the Others *have* attacked us, sir," said Danner. "We engaged in combat, clearly with some hostile force. I don't know that they were Others per se, nor am I certain that they actually attacked us, sir."

"Are you suggesting that *we* attacked *them*?" Bowman demanded sharply.

"Not necessarily, sir. There are many scenarios that could lead to conflict. The commencement of hostilities could be the result of a perceived or actual threat. Even Alliance law allows preemptive strikes when a threat is perceived as imminent."

Bowman opened his mouth to object and then realized how silly that would be in this situation. He gathered himself and then said, "Wouldn't a preemptive strike require fair notification, as you say, under Alliance law?"

"Yes, sir," Danner said, not offering to explain.

"And?"

"I'm not sure what you mean, sir."

"I meant in this case, since no warning was given, would you agree that the attack was unprovoked?" Bowman asked, beginning to get frustrated.

"Sir, I would agree that if there were no warning given, our adversaries would be in violation of our law. However, you asked what I thought, so I have to say that I have no knowledge one way or the other about whether any such warning was given."

"Surely you aren't saying the president would lie to the Alliance about the nature of the attack."

Danner looked confused for a moment and then said, "Oh, no, sir. But President Simone's announcement to the Alliance did not say that the attacks had been unprovoked. In fact, the overall conflict had been underway for some months. I have no knowledge of how those initial attacks took place or why. Since hostilities were already underway, the attacks of December 7 would in any case be lawful, regardless of how the first attack began or who began it. Again, sir, we need more information before coming to initial conclusions, and then we need to test those conclusions before allowing ourselves to be guided based on what could be false assumptions."

"You said you didn't know if our adversaries were Others. What did you mean by that?"

"Again, sir, we have no evidence that those with whom we battled are in fact Others. The war with the Others was concluded over a hundred years ago, beyond living memory. And not to be a smart-ass, sir, but President Simone did not say the Others had attacked us, only that we had been attacked by an unknown enemy and that a general state of war existed. Surely that was not an oversight."

Bowman nodded thoughtfully. "Mr. Danner, we are forming a strategic intelligence unit for the fleet. If you were selected for this unit, what would you consider our priority tasks?"

Danner thought for a long moment, nodded, and then said, "The key task of the Alliance military arm, as ordered by President Simone and reinforced by the chain of command, is to preserve combat power and prepare for offensive operations. Whatever task the intelligence unit takes on will need to be in support of those overall aims. That said, the strategic picture has to include the true nature of the threat, overall Alliance strategic aims, and the application of the principles of war within that context."

Bowman was now intrigued. "What do you mean, overall Alliance strategic aims? Isn't that clear already?"

"It's not clear to me, sir. The preservation of forces and the ability to take offensive actions are tactical, not strategic, objectives. A strategic objective might be to retain Alliance sovereignty, or to maintain access to commercial or communications routes, or to preserve the capability to expand colonization. Our strategic aims and the enemy situation, including their war aims, should drive our strategic objectives, which will further drive our tactics."

"What is the primary threat to the Alliance?" Bowman asked.

This time Danner spoke without hesitation. "The primary threat is probably not military, as such. If our adversaries had sufficient combat power to inflict decisive victory, they wouldn't have proceeded as they have so far. Despite the so-called surprise attack, and the damage done to the command structure, most of the Alliance is still intact, as is virtually all of our substantial economic power. Our system of command and control, from government through the military arm, is flexible and redundant. Note that the national command authority continued uninterrupted despite the deaths of the president and thirty other senior officials. The military command, though interrupted, has simply decentralized and continued to operate at lower levels, something it is well-suited for."

"If it's not a military threat, then what *is* the primary threat to the Alliance?"

"Historically, the biggest threat to a major power, in this case a unilateral power, is an inappropriate response to a new situation."

"Can you give me an example?"

"Yes, sir. The clearest example is that of the United States of America during its War on Terror at the beginning of the twenty-first century. In 2001, the USA was subject to a coordinated terrorist attack carried out by twenty combatants, supported by a radical group of less than two thousand conspirators. Unable to quickly catch and punish the surviving culprits, the US attacked two other sovereign nations on the justification that those nations had assisted the attackers or were sympathetic to their cause and might help them in the future.

"The resulting conflict went on for decades," Danner continued. "It exhausted national resources, demoralized the populace, and weakened the traditions of the democratic government which, up to that time, had proven quite stable. The USA's aggression actually harmed its reputation with the rest of the world and spawned far more terrorism than it originally sought to prevent. In the end, when the real threat arose, the USA was weakened."

Bowman frowned. He was troubled by what he'd heard. Every schoolchild was taught that the weakened United States, when faced with the pandemics of the twenty-first century, had led to the collapse of the international order of sovereign states, which then led to nuclear war, followed by a century of chaos, before the Alliance was established. The Alliance was a federation of states, and now worlds, as Earth colonized the nearby habitable planets. The balance between the sovereignty of the member states and the authority of the Alliance was sometimes an uneasy one.

"So the threat is that we will overreact?" Bowman asked.

"No, sir. We need to react with all the vigor and energy we can muster. But we need to do this in a way that achieves our objectives. Wars have a way of becoming their own justification."

Bowman later asked Lee why she hadn't told Danner why he was reporting to him. She smiled and said, "Because I didn't want him overthinking it. That's his only real fault. I knew you would want him if you got to see him as he is. Also, I wanted you to see him thinking on his feet. He's the kind of guy everyone underestimates because of his appearance. But there's real substance there and a lot of potential."

"I agree," Bowman said. "Let me ask: why didn't a bright kid like that go to the academy? Or, better yet, through the officer candidate program after college? Why enlist as an apprentice seaman?"

"I don't know, but I do know that the fleet is filled with bright and motivated enlisted sailors. Let's not forget that military service is mandatory, and not everyone wants to be an officer. If I could hazard a guess about Danner, it's because he wanted to do something with his hands, something substantial. I told you, he overthinks things. He probably knows this and wanted something to ground his experience. And don't forget—he'll earn enough veterans benefits to take another advanced degree when his term is up, a goal I think you know something about. So is he in?"

"Definitely," Bowman said. "Got any more like him?"

"There's no one else like him, anywhere. I do have others I'm working on, each with their own charms," she said with a smile.

"When can I see them?"

CHAPTER 7

KUMITE

Bowman and Lee faced each other on the training mat, their faces distorted by the mouthguards and face protectors they wore. Sweat streamed down their faces, and both were panting. They'd been training steadily for over an hour. Chambers wanted all the officers in the training hall at least three hours a week. Bowman had trained under his uncle, a karate master, until he had gone off to college. While there, he had fallen away from "the path," as his uncle would have put it. But as a reserve officer, he had joined a martial arts club and kept up his training, if somewhat sporadically.

Nothing sporadic about Lee's training, he thought. She had been born into a family that took their martial arts seriously. Her father had been a grandmaster and founder of one of the major fighting styles now popular on Earth. She had trained to the instructor level as a teen and then, at the Naval Academy, had been the captain of the competition team her senior year.

Though Bowman was almost a foot taller and outweighed her by fifty pounds, he had found himself exhausted and on his back on more than one occasion when they started these sessions a month ago. Now he could hold his own and was getting into the best shape of his life.

Oh my, she was fast. At first, she had been able to strike him at will; nothing he could do to even block adequately. He soon learned, mostly from her own instruction, that she was not just fast but was actually using his own awkward timing against him. He learned that he had been hopelessly telegraphing his moves, such that she would simply meet him where she knew his defenses would be dropped or misplaced.

Furious, he had forced himself to correct his deficiencies. Slowly, ever so slowly, he was making progress. She had set him doing exercises in a set of forms, prearranged movements of stances, kicks, and punches. When he had studied the martial arts earlier, he had never liked doing forms, practicing them only reluctantly because they were required for promotion tests. She had explained to him that the forms *were* the art and said that sparring was only a manifestation of the forms. She had shown him a form called *Arche*, named after the Greek word for foundation. He was learning the subtleties of breathing, muscle control, balance, and timing. Through Arche, Bowman found that he liked the forms—that he could use them to concentrate and relax. In the last few sessions, he had actually scored a few points on her. Though he refused to let it show, he was deeply satisfied that he was using her own techniques against her.

For the past few minutes, Bowman had been intentionally leaving himself open, letting her back-kick make sharp contact with his chest protector, blows that would have broken his ribs had he not been cushioned. Just as he feigned a heavy-footed lunge, she began the twist that indicated the back-kick was beginning.

This time he was ready and sidestepped, letting the kick slide past. At the same instant, his hand shot out, smacking her forehead with an open-handed technique. Her head snapped back and her feet shot out from under her as she went down on her back. The instant she hit the mat, however, she twisted and shot her right leg out in a sweep, knocking Bowman's legs out from under him. To him, it felt like he was falling for a long time, and then, smack, he hit the mat awkwardly, his breath whooshing out of his lungs. In the next instant, she was straddling him, a reverse punch striking him in his throat protector—a killing blow, he knew, if done without protective gear.

"Break!" shouted the referee.

Bowman lay there, unable to move for lack of breath. Lee moved back to her side of the ready line and knelt, facing away from him. It was the traditional way of showing respect for a fallen competitor, by not seeing the suffering of a downed opponent.

Bowman forced himself up and stood facing Lee. She stood also, facing him, and they bowed. Bowman was not embarrassed by his defeat. He was a better fighter than most of the males who trained with them. Lee was simply better than him, much better, and that was all there was to it.

As they stepped off the mat, releasing the sparring area for the next two opponents, she said, "You are improving. You took many blows to set up that counterattack. That showed discipline and patience."

"And yet, you were ready for it; the fall was a ruse to make the sweep," he said.

"No," she said. "Your strike was a good one. I wasn't expecting that particular move. But once committed, I turned the fall to my advantage. Remember: your opponent is never more dangerous than when you've put him, or her, to a disadvantage."

"Good advice. I'll remember it." He bowed and they parted, heading for their separate locker rooms to shower.

CHAPTER 8

FORCE PROTECTION

In the month following the attack, the battle fleet made steady progress on the repairs. Chambers published an overarching short-term plan for recovering and getting the fleet back to fighting order. At first, it sounded to Bowman like just more paperwork, but he soon saw the advantage. When you can't do everything that you need to do in the time allotted, prioritization is the key to getting the most done that's possible. In the fleet, with its many different requirements, ships, and units all clamoring for something, there needed to be some flow to getting things done. The real advantage was that Chambers was also assuming responsibility for what could *not* be done. It was another lesson for Bowman: the boss needs to step up and give guidance, then live with the results.

It also meant taking risks. If the highest priority was perimeter defense, the fleet would never stop putting resources into that and would never get anything else done. So Chambers set the limits, accepted some risk, and allowed teams to begin working to better other aspects of their situation.

In a perfect world, there would always be one fighter squadron on patrol and a second on standby, ready to launch whenever needed. With the assets so low, however, there was no way to meet that requirement. Chambers asked for recommendations, and Bowman tasked Baker to come up with some options to reduce vulnerability while leaving the majority of assets free for other work. Baker had done so, and together they briefed the admiral.

"Sir," Bowman said, "Commander Baker has worked up some options on defense alternatives, as you requested."

"Let's hear it," Chambers said, clasping his hands together on the surface of the conference table.

"Sir, what we need is early warning and timely response," Baker began in his flat Southern drawl. "Too many fighters out there works against that interest. The emphasis shifts from the threat to maneuvering the squadron or squadrons. That's what happened when we got ambushed. Too much moving around and chattering on the coms, with no one really paying attention to what might be out there."

Chambers frowned and said, "Your commanding officer was in charge during that attack, and he died in the battle. Are you criticizing him?"

"Yes, sir," Baker replied without hesitation, inflection, or emotion. Here was a man who said what he thought and stood by it. Bowman knew from the communications log that Baker had twice advised his commander that the recon formations were too tight. On the second instance, Baker had received a sharp rebuke heard by the entire squadron. A minute later, the squadron commander was dead, and the war was on.

Chambers nodded and said, "Continue."

"What we can do is put out long-range drones in recon and sensor mode. Some of them would be in active mode, meaning they can be seen by anyone lying in wait. Others can be in passive mode so they can receive data but create no emissions. That way, any threat seeking to mask its presence will see the active drones and move away to hide. Since they won't see the passive drones, their movement will be detected."

Chambers, now frowning, asked, "How will the passive drones inform us of any danger if they can't emit radiation?"

"We can equip them with a directed laser-com link, set up to be line-of-sight to the active drones," Baker said. "Laser coms have a very low chance of being discovered. A threat would have to be precisely between the two drones to detect it. Since the active drone would be in constant communication with the fleet anyway, we would get our info from those."

"That's early warning. What about defense?"

"We go with two fighters on the perimeter, and two on the ready line at all times."

"What's the risk?"

"It's high, sir," Baker responded in his calm voice. "But no higher than if a larger force were placed out there, moving around and making a lot of noise. And this plan has one major advantage."

"Which is?"

"The main vessels are now armed. Commodore Vance has placed proximity artillery on all vessels. And of course, the frigates have self-protection systems and point defense. These weapons can't easily be used when the sky is filled with friendlies, but with only a few fighters protecting the fleet and good IFF systems in place, the risk of friendly fire is low."

"That sounds like a plan. When can it be in place?" Chambers asked.

Bowman spoke up. "Already in motion, sir. Commander Lee and Seaman Apprentice Danner have been working on the drones and sensors for about a week. We need to do a field test and run some scenarios with our own fighters acting as OPFOR before putting it into operation, but that can be done within days." OPFOR was the acronym for "opposing forces" when used in a training scenario. The word sounded out of place, because it was a peacetime term that no one had heard since before the war. Many things were changing, Bowman mused.

It was hard to tell by the admiral's calm features, but Bowman thought he was impressed. He approved the plan with no changes.

Over the next several days, Bowman, Baker, Lee, and Danner worked to set up the drone net, as the system came to be known. Lee had the techies mount the drones with the correct sensors and transmitters. This took longer than they had thought it would because the distances, speeds, dispersal, and timing all had to be painstakingly worked out. Another problem was that the battle fleet needed to be able to change speed and course, which meant that the drones needed to maintain their relative positions. That wasn't a problem for the active drones, because no one was trying to hide those. They could simply fire their thrusters to keep pace with the fleet. It *was* a problem, however, for the passive drones. They were supposed to be silent and undetectable, but if they set off their thrusters, they would become obvious to anyone watching.

The new intelligence section, now up to four individuals, was sitting around a makeshift worktable in the operations center with Lee, Bowman, and Baker. They had been trying to work out some solution to the passive drone problem, weighing alternatives like abandoning the passive drones if necessary, depending on how many of them they could afford to lose.

It was Danner who finally came up with the solution. He was sitting in deep thought, sort of slumped over. Bowman thought he might have fallen asleep and was about to say something when Danner spoke, as if to himself.

"Let microgravity handle it. Put the passive drones in a wide orbit around the fleet. That way, they'll look like all the other orbiting debris," he said quietly. "Within limits—as long as the fleet doesn't make radical changes in speed and direction—the passive drones will maintain their relative positions. If the fleet has to make substantial maneuvers, it's likely we'll be openly engaged with an adversary, and stealth drones will be unnecessary. At that point, the passives could be recalled or re-tasked as active drones."

And that was what they did. The active and passive drones were set out over a period of days, mixed in with other traffic, in case the fleet was somehow under observation. Baker then led several aircraft well in advance of the fleet and played OPFOR. Danner ran the combined intelligence/targeting section and set up various scanning routines to try and detect the enemy as they were trying to surprise the fleet. What happened then surprised them all.

Three days into the trial, Danner spoke with urgency from his console, where he was hunched over a scope displaying radiation levels, electromagnetic emissions, and radar/lidar sweep information. "I have a bogie in Sector Five, bearing two, five, seven, nine."

"Let me see it on my screen," Bowman demanded.

He was mildly irritated because Danner had mistakenly used the term "bogie" instead of the correct term, OPFOR. Bogie was reserved for actual unknown vessels. "What the hell? How can Baker be all the way out there? He doesn't have enough fuel to have gotten that far."

"That's not Baker, sir," Danner said.

Bowman froze for a millisecond as he realized what was happening. Then he said, "Very quietly call the admiral to the bridge. Do not sound general quarters."

Sixty seconds later, Chambers stood beside Bowman, looking at the screen. "What have you got?"

"Sir, our drones have picked up a single bogie in Sector Five. It looks like a recon vessel."

"No other vessels? No support ship?"

"None that we can see, sir."

Just then, the screen seemed to flicker, and two more bogies appeared on screen. Then two more.

"What the *hell*?" Danner demanded.

"Just so," the admiral said.

CHAPTER 9

WHAT THE HELL?

"Recall Baker's OPFOR team," Chambers ordered, "but take no action to alert the fleet. I don't want the bogies to realize we're aware of them." He turned to the assembled intel section and said, "It looks like your scheme for detecting the bad guys is working. Well done. Ask the commodore and Commander Lee to come to the bridge immediately."

Minutes later, with the command group assembled, Chambers began, "Just to bring everyone up to date, intel's new drones have picked up bogies in Sector Five. For now, I want the fleet to proceed as if nothing has changed; we don't want them to know we can see them. But there's something odd going on. Captain Bowman?"

"Sir, we first detected a single vessel with no support ship in the area. The subsequent four vessels just appeared on screen. Danner, can you display the recording?"

Danner hit a few keys, and the screen displayed a replay of what they had seen earlier. A single vessel followed by a slight flicker. At first two and then four vessels appeared. "As you can see, all of them are likely recon vessels, and there is no support ship in sight," said Danner.

"What was that flicker on screen before the bogies came up?" the admiral asked.

Everyone looked at Danner, who said, "Sir, I've been running diagnostics, and it doesn't seem to be a malfunction in our system. It looks like there's some sort of environmental distortion out there. I've checked the same event from other sources, and every time, we see that same momentary ... wrinkle."

Danner keyed the console, and various images came on screen, each showing the vessels popping into existence. Every time, they saw the distortion just prior.

"So," Chambers said, "we have a little mystery here. Captain Bowman, please assemble your entire intel team, and see if we can't get a better picture of what this means. Have your group prepare some options for us to deal with the new information. Commodore," he said, turning to Vance. "Without alerting the fleet, please review our ships' proximity defenses to make sure we can meet an attack. I want to be ready, but I *do not* want the bogies to know we can see them. We need to assume they're watching and listening."

He turned to leave and said over his shoulder, "Let's meet again in twelve hours, when Baker is back. This entire situation is Close Hold, not to be discussed with anyone unless they're part of the solution."

CHAPTER 10

THE ENIGMA

They stood in the admiral's ready room in a rough semicircle around the man himself, who was seated in his command chair with a mug of steaming coffee in his hand. In addition to Bowman, Vance, and Lee, Baker was back from his daylong flight, freshly shaven and with a change of uniform. Davenport, with his still-shiny new captain's bars on his collar, was looking alert and confident. Danner and a couple of members of his newly assembled smart-guy team stood behind a waist-high console. Bowman thought the smart-guy team really did look like techie-type nerds, one a little pudgy and another with serious acne.

Bowman was surprised to see Chief Petty Officer John Raymond standing with Danner's group, seeming strangely out of place, twenty years older than the rest and decidedly not a nerd. Bowman had barely seen the man since the battle with the Others. He would find out soon enough why Raymond was in the room. Strangely, Danner, who had seemed so awkward a few weeks ago, was beginning to look like a real sailor. He stood straighter, had filled out a bit, and even had his hair cut to regulation length.

Lee looked around the room as if counting heads before nodding to the admiral, who said, "Proceed."

Lee began, "Sir, your command team and intel section are present. The purpose of this briefing is to inform you of the assessment of the recent developments regarding the bogies detected earlier and to present possible options."

It was a formal way of opening a meeting, Bowman thought. But he knew from long experience that setting the scope of the meeting from the start would save countless wasted conversations as speakers tried to jockey around what they thought might be required. The fact that Chambers had given them twelve hours and had refrained from alerting the fleet showed both his patience and his confidence in the team, but now there was no time to waste. They needed to move forward and fast.

Lee turned her head to Bowman and said, "Captain?"

Bowman said, "Sir, in the past twelve hours, we have continued surveillance on the bogies. They have remained stationary in relative position to the fleet, approximately five hundred kilometers forward of our position along our route of movement. We have seen them rotate out every four hours. Each time, we see the same distortion as the vessels disappear, only to be replaced by others."

"What's the threat?" Chambers asked.

"To the fleet, very little," Bowman said. "The vessels are configured for recon, not battle, and they number no more than six at any one time. However, we have to assume our position and operational strength are compromised, and there is no way for us to know when a more formidable threat might appear."

"And if that happens?" the admiral asked, as he turned to Vance.

"We have reviewed and validated the onboard proximity defenses," Commodore Vance reported. "Every vessel in the fleet has projectile cannons and at least a limited ability to project protective shields when required. We could probably handle an attack of up to two squadrons, maybe thirty fighters at once. Beyond that, we would need substantial aerospace support. The risk of using proximity defenses is that the fleet's vessels can't provide mutual support. The bogies could concentrate on one vessel at a time, overwhelm the local defenses, and then move on to the next target."

Chambers turned to Davenport and said, "We're not going to let them defeat us in detail. Gunny ... I mean *Captain* Davenport, do you think the Marines could rig an RAB defense?"

"Absolutely, sir," Davenport said, straightening as he spoke and flashing an evil grin. "If the commodore could lend us some barges he doesn't need back, we can fix that up nicely."

"What the hell is an RAB defense?" Vance asked, reddening.

"Tell him, Captain," Chambers said.

"It's a small vessel, sir, configured with shields, reinforced to ram, and loaded with Marines," Davenport said. "It doesn't need to be able to jump, just maneuver locally. RAB stands for 'Ram and Board.' Any barge or even a launch will work. The smaller ship size allows the shields to provide all-around protection. The Marines suit up for the vacuum and fire from the open deck. It's basically a modified strong-point defense, a firing platform the bogies can't ignore. They *have* to go for it, and when they do, they open themselves up for flanking fire from the other vessels. And every once in a while, a disabled bogie will come close enough for the Marines to board her." At the thought, he smiled and his eyes gleamed.

Seeing this, Bowman felt sorry for the bad guys if Davenport and his men ever got in close-quarters combat with them. The Marines lived for this type of combat; it was the holy grail of Jarhead lore. He saw the look that passed between the admiral and the captain of Marines, and suspected that it was in an RAB action that Chambers had received his disabling wounds.

Clearly, Davenport would follow this man to the end of the galaxy, if needed.

Chambers nodded thoughtfully and said, "Commodore, please provide two vessels of suitable size to the Marines, along with a refit section to get them up to RAB standards."

He then turned toward Danner, who looked like he was about to burst from the need to say something. Bowman thought he looked like a kid trying to get the teacher's attention to go to the restroom.

Chambers smiled and said, "I think our new head of the analysis section has something to tell me. Please proceed, Mr. Danner."

Danner opened his mouth, then paused, took a deep breath, and started speaking in a surprisingly measured tone. "The question we've been working on is how the bogies keep popping in and out of our screens. We considered a number of possibilities, and I'd like to discuss those now." His formality might have been humorous in another setting, but at the moment, he had the attention of everyone in the room. "The first possibility is that the bogies are masking their presence either by cloaking themselves—using an obstruction of some kind—or by interfering with our sensors. We can't rule this out, but we don't think that's what they're doing."

"Why not?" the admiral asked.

"Well, sir, we looked at the images from multiple angles, using different measurements. For example, the fleet uses mass detectors for navigation to detect objects that might be in our path so we can avoid them. When we checked those, there was no indication of additional mass until the vessels came up on our screens. While it's theoretically possible to alter or obscure visual and electromagnetic signals, there is no known way to modify or mask gravitons." Danner was smoother now, as he got into the subject matter he was comfortable with.

"So they're not masking themselves," Chambers said. "What about some type of interference?"

"Again," Danner said, "we couldn't rule it out, but every check we performed showed the equipment was working properly. Any kind of interference would have caused some of the equipment to run slower or to distort other data, not just in the targeted area. We saw nothing like that."

"What about that flicker we saw just before the bogies came in?" asked Chambers.

"That one we couldn't figure out. However, Chief Raymond has some thoughts on that." Danner turned to Raymond, who nodded and stepped forward.

Bowman was about to ask why Raymond was going to speak on this topic when Vance beat him to it. "Just a second," said Vance.

"Why is the maintenance chief, however distinguished, briefing us on a space-time anomaly?"

"Would you like to tell him, *Doctor* Raymond?" the admiral asked with a knowing smile.

"Sir," Raymond said in a completely neutral voice, "I had some experience working with applications of quantum physics on space travel when I worked at the Institute for Advanced Studies before I joined the Navy."

Vance opened his mouth to speak but stopped, his jaw hanging wide for a long, surprised moment. Bowman had the same reaction of dawning realization. He looked around the room and saw the astonished faces—all but Chambers, Lee, and Danner, who apparently all knew.

"You're *that* John Raymond? Professor of theoretical physics and author of the Raymond Paradox Hypothesis?" Vance asked in an uncharacteristic rush.

"Yes, sir," Raymond said easily.

"I'm sure there's a story there," the admiral said. "For now, let's just be grateful for the Navy's bounty. Chief, please brief us on your findings."

Never had Bowman been so glad he had kept his mouth shut. How had he missed that Raymond was the famous physicist, thought to have disappeared twenty years ago? He had to focus on what Raymond was saying.

"... it's possible that what we saw on the screens was what's called a macro-wave function collapse. A little background is in order," Raymond said. "We've known for centuries that a subatomic particle moves through space as a wave, only manifesting itself as a particle when it's observed. At that point, the wave function is said to collapse. But in its wave formulation, the particle can do some pretty amazing things. It can, for example, travel through solid matter, go through more than one hole in a solid barrier at the same time, and curve around massive objects—as long as it remains unobserved. We also know that macroscopic objects, things we can see and touch, also exhibit wave properties. But because they are in fact the accumulation of billions of subatomic particles, the collective wave functions basically cancel each other out. Thus, when we throw a baseball, the quantum weirdness isn't noticeable. It's there, only too small to detect or to have any consequences in the macro world."

Raymond paused to see if his audience was keeping up. He was pleasantly surprised to see that they were, with the possible exception of Commodore Vance, who still seemed flummoxed that Raymond had turned out to be some hotshot scientist. Modern naval personnel were trained in physics throughout their education; a fundamental knowledge of it was necessary for almost every job aboard a starship.

"All of that changed about thirty years ago, when the Jupiter orbital accelerator achieved velocities high enough to simulate the energies that were present in the Big Bang. A lot of good science got done then. I was a post-doc on the theoretical side of the team looking at the limits of quantum effects on larger particles. What we found astonished everyone." Raymond was speaking quickly now as he recounted his past. Bowman saw in him a passion he had not noted before. "We saw actual macroscopic objects exhibit quantum weirdness. It was only at very high energy levels, but it was present."

"So what happened?" the admiral asked. "Why haven't we ever heard of this before? It should have shocked the galaxy, as the biggest discovery since Newton's *Principia*."

"I agree, sir," Raymond said. "We thought it was big and wanted to publish, but the government stepped in, classified the whole project, and swore us, under threat of imprisonment, to total silence."

"So what did you do?" the admiral asked.

"We moved on to other research. It was frustrating to leave it, but we didn't have any choice."

"And that's when you made your name in physics, with the Raymond Paradox Hypothesis," stated Admiral Chambers.

"Yes, sir. Though as you know, the paradox deals with another area of mathematics, not macro-wave function collapse."

"Let me guess," Chambers said. "That's when you started having trouble with the government."

"That's right, sir. I started getting calls late at night, warning me to stay clear of sensitive topics. My car was vandalized, my coms were tapped, and there was even a break-in at my office." He sighed as if remembering something troubling. "Then I found out my old colleagues from my days on the Jupiter accelerator project were dying or disappearing."

This is just incredible, thought Bowman. *What the hell's going on?*

"So that's when I decided to disappear on my own terms," Raymond concluded.

"Wait," Bowman said. "You disappeared by joining the Navy using *your own name*? How does that hide you from anyone?"

Raymond smiled and shrugged. "Well, actually, it worked pretty well. I used my confirmation name as my middle name, joined up in a field they might not expect, and have been on board one starship or another for almost the entire twenty years I've been in the Navy. Their reach apparently didn't extend this far out, or maybe they've known where I was but just didn't care enough to come and get me."

"Tell us about the wrinkle," Chambers said.

"Yes, sir," Raymond said. "But first, I hope you'll forgive me for presenting you with the biggest caveat you're ever likely to hear. No scientist would confirm the cause of an event like this based on a single observation. I could be wrong in some particulars. I'll almost certainly be wrong in others, and you'll need to factor that into your decisions."

He paused, as if waiting for this information to be acknowledged, and when no one spoke, he continued, "That said, here's my best explanation: I think what we saw *was* a macro-wave function collapse. The vessels are somehow traveling via energy wave, if you like. The wrinkle we saw was the momentary transition of space-time as the wave function collapsed and the vessel returned to normal existence. I saw this before on a much smaller scale during the Jupiter trials, before the whole thing got shut down."

"What are the implications for our fleet," Chambers asked, "given this possibility?"

"A couple of things," Raymond said. "First, both the research and the engineering required to do this—configuring entire squadrons of vessels with living pilots and placing them precisely where they want—would require an almost unimaginable effort over a period of years. We're talking a substantial portion of galactic gross domestic product committed. Second, something isn't right about the whole thing. Why would a society so advanced in one area of science and technology—macro-quantum space travel—be so relatively backward in everything else?"

"How are they backward?" the admiral asked.

"*Relatively* backward, sir," Raymond replied. "The engineering for their vessels, for example, is no more advanced than ours in terms of communications, propulsion, weapons, and shields. Those are all more or less what we have. And yet in this one particular area, they're very far advanced. It's odd and lopsided. It smacks of a child with a new toy, not an advanced civilization. Third, we ought to be able to detect and predict when this technology is being used. The wave phase of any object, micro or macro, is still in the universe. It emits radiation, it has mass, and it should be detectable."

"I thought we just heard that there was no spike in gravitons before the wrinkle appeared," Chambers noted. "How is that consistent with what you just said?"

"I think we'll find it's a question of looking in the right places. The wave is spread out over a huge area, but it will be more concentrated in some areas, and we ought to be able to set up an array of detectors that could capture the event before it happens."

Vance seemed to realize something and blurted out, "You mean they're faster than our FTL drive?"

"Yes, sir," Raymond said. "Our FTL drive can reach ten times the speed of light under ideal conditions; a vessel using macro-wave function collapse technology could move an object instantly to any location. The distance would be limited only by the amount of power available."

"What else?" Chambers asked.

"One more thing, sir. The problem we faced when working this issue back during the Jupiter trials was how to control the collapse of the macro-wave function. For a subatomic particle, the wave function collapses when a conscious entity looks for it, say with a test or instrument of some kind. It's part of the quantum weirdness. You can set up a test to check on the spin of an electron, for example. If the test isn't monitored by a conscious brain—a human—then the wave function does not collapse. If someone is sitting at the test console and watches the test in real time, the wave function *does* collapse, and the particle comes into existence. To my knowledge, no one has ever determined why this is so, though there are many theories. Somehow, some way, whoever is using this technology has figured out how to control it. I believe there must be a vulnerability in this process."

"Meaning what?" Bowman asked.

"Meaning that we might be able to interfere with the process by either collapsing their wave function at the time of our choosing or by preventing it altogether."

CHAPTER 11

VESSELS OF WAR

Chambers had made the decision to inform the fleet of the presence of the bogies; he felt it was better that everyone knew what risk they were facing. The fleet, which was already working hard at recovering from the initial December 7 attack, now went into overdrive. The Marines were especially busy, modifying two shuttles into RABs. Bowman had allocated them one of the maintenance bays, and they had been in there day and night, the sound of welding, cutting, and hammering a constant refrain. They didn't want any help other than Chief Raymond, who for some reason had their confidence, though he was pure Navy.

After the third day of this, an exhausted, unshaven, but smiling Captain Davenport came to see Bowman. "Sir, the Marine detachment reports that the RAB vessels are ready for your inspection." He pronounced the acronym RAB as a single word: *Rab.*

Bowman was somewhat surprised that the Marines were deferring to him. Davenport didn't report to him but rather directly to the admiral. "Captain Davenport, I'm not clear why you're asking for my clearance. The Marines don't fall under my command."

"Yes, sir," Davenport said. "But the RAB vessels—all combat vessels—fall under the authority of the wing commander. Once we're launched, there can only be one commander, and that's you." Then he gave a little smile and said, "Plus, the Marines have worked hard on this. They'd appreciate your nod of approval."

Bowman and Davenport entered the maintenance bay where the Marines had been working on the RAB vessels. To Bowman's surprise, the Marines stood in two rows, dressed from head to toe in the distinctive battle armor they were known for. The suits were all black, made mostly of a synthetic material that looked like leather, with a harder plating covering the knees, elbows, shoulders, chest, and back. The helmet was made of a tough dark gray alloy, with a flexible material extending to the shoulders. The faceplate was clear and covered the upper half of the face, while a breathing and speaker mechanism covered the mouth. Bowman had been told these suits were appropriate for fighting in vacuum. He wondered how long they could last without an oxygen supply and how much protection they offered from penetration. Standing at parade rest, they looked fearsome indeed. Bowman was reminded of images he had seen of the Spartans in full battle gear.

Behind the Marines stood the two renovated shuttles, now looking nothing like they had a few days earlier. Off to the side, looking weary and unshaven, was CPO Raymond. Bowman suspected Raymond hadn't slept much, if at all, in the days since the renovation commenced. He had what looked to Bowman like a wry smile on his face. Bowman thought how interesting it was that he could have known so little about someone he had worked with for years. Previously, he had seen him as only a steady and competent maintenance chief. In the past few days, he had learned a lot more about John Raymond.

Davenport called the Marines to attention. Even in the battle armor, they moved precisely, as one being, slamming to attention with a crash of metal. Then he said, "Marines, post!" Immediately, the Marines broke ranks and moved quickly to the RABs, some entering hatches, others taking up positions on the open deck behind what looked like heavy-caliber Gatling guns.

The vessels were dark and sleek. They were fifty feet long and thirty feet wide at the middle and aft, while the forward ends tapered to wicked points. The top was flat, with a waist-high railing with Gatling guns mounted at regular intervals. Bowman could see where the exterior had been reinforced with reactive armor. He noticed what looked like spikes extruding from the sides. All in all, he was amazed. He had never seen anything like them, nor even heard that such vessels were part of the Navy's inventory.

"Sir," Davenport said, "each of the RABs is manned by twelve Marine commandos and commanded by a Marine NCO. Gunnery Sergeant Wasp, front and center."

One of the Marines nimbly hopped down from the nearest RAB and came over at a jog to Bowman and Davenport. The Marine snapped to attention, saluted, and said easily, "Gunnery Sergeant Wasp, Commanding Officer First RAB, Achilles Expeditionary Wing, reports to the Marine Detachment Commander and the Achilles Wing Commander."

Bowman instinctively returned the salute. He was surprised to see how young the gunnery sergeant looked—no more than twenty-five. He reflected that the Marines had lost some of their complement during the attack by the Others and no doubt needed to promote the most competent marines from within the ranks. Although technically part of the Navy, the Marines were unique in some ways. For one thing, the skill set required to be a fully competent Marine commando could take years to achieve through constant training and qualification protocols. In addition to basic infantry skills, commandos needed to qualify in light and heavy weapons, communications, demolitions, and field medical. It was one of the reasons why the Marines always seemed to be training when they weren't on guard or sleeping. One result of this was that promotions tended to come more slowly, because Marines could not be promoted to a leadership role unless they had formally qualified at the level they currently held. Searching his memory, Bowman couldn't remember having seen a gunnery sergeant this young. Before his wartime promotion to captain,

Davenport himself had been a gunnery sergeant, but he was forty-five years old.

The Marines did have one tradition that applied to Davenport: Long-serving NCOs like him who were promoted to commissioned officer often skipped the rank of lieutenant and went straight to captain. It was a measure of respect, an acknowledgement of their experience. In Davenport's case, it was more than that. He was commanding what amounted to two companies of Marines as well as a platoon-sized element of naval security forces he had inherited after Admiral Chambers' post-ambush reorganization. His forces were stretched thin to undertake the missions that would normally have been allocated to a much larger force. His new rank was actually below that required for the post. Bowman knew that if Davenport could distinguish himself in this assignment, he faced significantly increased career opportunities.

All this besides, the Marines, when among themselves and off duty, did not consider rank as important as competence and achievement. On duty, however, obedience to the rank structure was nearly absolute. This type of organization was seen as necessary to accomplish any mission, and each leader had a sphere of authority. Within that sphere, the leader's word was law.

"Sir," Davenport said. "Gunnery Sergeant Wasp will escort you through his RAB for your inspection."

The next twenty minutes was quite an experience for Bowman. He was amazed at the progress they had made in such a short time. The interior of the shuttle had been converted to a mobile command center of sorts. Navigation had been modified for combat and upgraded for target acquisition. The command and control capabilities were upgraded to track multiple boarding parties and included the ability to track the life support of each Marine, as well as their ammunition status. It was far more sophisticated than Bowman had envisioned.

It was also very cramped. The space allocated for the pilot and navigator was only about four by six feet. The remaining open space was taken up by ten inward-facing seats. Aft of that was a bulkhead separating the seats from what Bowman expected was the rest of the interior of the craft. "What's behind this?" Bowman asked.

Wasp smiled for the first time and replied, "A Marine's best friends, sir. Ammunition, fuel, and propulsion."

The gunny was articulate in his briefing, pointing out the significant aspects of the RAB and answering the questions Bowman put to him in a forthright manner. "If you'll follow me, sir," Wasp said, "we'll go up on deck to inspect the firing platform."

Once on deck, Bowman could see six miniguns, each with four barrels and a ballistic shield to protect the gunner. There were two guns to port and starboard, and one each fore and aft.

"These are quad fifties, sir," Wasp said. "Officially Quadruple 13mm Self-Contained Vacuum-Rated machine guns, but that doesn't exactly roll off the tongue, so in this case, we use the old US Marine term. Each weapon is capable of firing six hundred armor-piercing, .50-caliber rounds per minute."

"No railguns?"

"Chemically driven projectiles are cheaper and work just as well at these distances, sir. Plus, they're less dependent on delicate tech, don't require ferrous-metal projectiles, and don't break down as often."

"I see. How many rounds does each weapon have?"

"Sir, the ammunition feed comes directly from below-decks and draws upon a central ammunition storage container. The amount needed for any one weapon is allocated by the RAB commanding officer. The total for the craft is five hundred thousand rounds when fully battle-loaded."

"So what are the spikes on the sides of the RABs for?" Bowman asked.

"Those are ramming grapples, sir. Once they penetrate the exterior of the enemy craft, the pointed tip expands and locks into the hull—actually fuses with it—thus making it difficult to disengage. This allows a stable platform for boarding."

"How many Marines actually board the enemy craft? I count six gunners, a pilot, and a navigator. That leaves four Marines to board. Is that enough?"

"Sir, the number of Marines to board is situationally dependent," Wasp replied. "The RAB commander or the detachment commander makes the call. The boarding party can be anywhere from four to the entire detachment."

"Do you mean you would leave the RAB entirely?" Bowman asked, astonished.

"Yes, sir," Wasp replied crisply. "If the situation required all hands to board, that would be what we'd do. The RAB is fused to the enemy vessel in any case, and mission success requires the complete submission of the enemy vessel."

He was beginning to understand the Marines' focus on training. A boarding operation was literally a do-or-die mission. Once committed, they had to succeed; there was no disengaging or retreating.

Bowman then inspected the second RAB and saw that it was exactly the same as the first, despite the fact that the second shuttle had been a different model of approximately the same size. Clearly, some effort had made to standardize these vessels.

When he asked Davenport about this after the inspection, he replied, "Standardization is key for Marines, sir. We need to be able to operate from any platform without having to relearn the entire setup. That allows us to be interchangeable, so to speak. When under pressure or during extreme fatigue, Marines need to function through training rather than conscious thought."

Bowman nodded, and Davenport said, "If you're ready, sir, we're ready for operational trials."

"Right now?" Bowman asked, surprised.

"Yes, sir," Davenport replied. "Gunnery Sergeant Wasp has your battle armor."

CHAPTER 12

TARGET PRACTICE

The shuttle slipped easily into space from a launch port in the aft section of the TS *Taipei,* where the Marines kept their headquarters, and where the majority of their troops were bedded down. It wobbled a bit but then steadied as the attitude jets fired.

Bowman sat in an elevated chair just behind the pilot and navigator in RAB One, which was commanded by Gunnery Sergeant Wasp; the gunny was just behind him and off to the right. The lack of room in the RAB had necessitated this awkward arrangement. Bowman could see that there had been no other way to get the key individuals into the space available. They were all in full battle armor, which also served as protection against the vacuum. Bowman was surprised to learn that the RABs were fully decompressed before launch. Wasp had explained that there was no need to pressurize the interior, since most of the Marines, maybe all of them, would need to disembark under fire in any case. Depressurizing from the start saved time. This convenience meant that the Marines had to suit up from the beginning.

The viewscreen to the front was wide and showed much more of the area in front of the craft than was visible from a fighter. Since there were no internal gravity controls, the occupants were technically in free fall, and that, combined with the wide viewscreen, made Bowman feel like he was constantly floating. Despite more than three thousand hours in space as a pilot, he felt an initial rush of adrenalin as the craft shot out into space. Taking off in the RAB felt more like driving a truck off a cliff, and he had to actively fight the sensation of falling. Looking around, he saw that none of his alarm was shared by the Marines. They all looked calm and professional.

He saw, and heard over his internal headset speakers, that the pilot and navigator, both corporals, worked well together, easily trading necessary information about relative speed, direction, clearance, and the status of the various systems on board. Bowman felt the propulsion kick in, and the gentle acceleration of the craft provided a sense of stability as the pilot maneuvered toward what the Marines called the firing range—a scatter of junk and salvaged spacecraft that had been set up to serve as targets and boarding vehicles.

The plan, as it had been explained by Davenport before departure, was to allow the Marines to engage various targets, moving at different relative velocities and distances, and then practice a boarding on an almost-intact salvaged spacecraft that had been modified to look something like one of the larger O-raiders—No, he was going to have to stop using that term.

"Stand by for exfiltration," came Wasp's voice over the intercom.

A moment later, the hatch blew open, and the Marines inside quickly exited the craft, each basically launching themselves out of the opening, one after the other. In seconds, the rear of the compartment was empty. Bowman was alarmed to see that they only had thin tethers attaching them to the craft. As their tethers pulled taut, each Marine fired a single small attitude jet on the back of his pack. This forced the trajectory into an arc above the craft, swinging each marine onto the deck overhead.

Clever, but terrifying, thought Bowman. Throwing oneself out of a perfectly good spacecraft and into space, tether or no, was completely against human nature. He knew they must have ironclad self-discipline to perform that kind of maneuver.

Bowman was in the process of thinking how lucky he was that he didn't have to do that when Wasp said, "Sir, it's your turn."

The gunny moved to the entrance and beckoned Bowman to move toward him. Unable to object, the captain did as he was bid. He realized that this was the Marine way: Leaders always did what their subordinates were required to do. In some part of his mind, he realized the Marines were paying him a high compliment by expecting him to jump out of the craft. *Strange sort of love*, he thought.

Wasp positioned Bowman in the hatch. Motioning with his hands, he indicated that Bowman was to place his hands on the outside of the hatch, thumbs down, palms inward. This was the position Bowman had seen the Marines adopt before propelling themselves outward. "Your static line is hooked in," Wasp said crisply over the tac-net. "I'll give you two commands: First, 'stand in the door,' then, 'go.' When you pull yourself out, tuck your chin to your chest; keep your arms close to your body, elbows in and your knees together and slightly bent. Don't worry about the jet. It will fire automatically when the line goes taut."

Bowman was about to ask how he should land on the deck when Wasp said, "Stand in the door!" He placed his hands as he had been shown and then heard, "Go!" and felt a sharp slap on his back. Without thinking, he pulled himself out of the hatch into a void filled with stars. It was an amazing thrill, like nothing he'd ever felt as a pilot. Almost immediately, he felt the snap of the static line going taut and the pop of the jet firing. His body rocketed upward in an arc toward the upper deck of the vessel. His stomach lurched, and the stars raced downward and past his field of vision. He saw the deck above him as it seemed to race to meet him. He desperately swung his legs toward the deck, not wanting to land on his head. He surprised himself at the agility he was able to muster to get this movement done and thanked his weeks of training with Mei-Ling Lee for that particular blessing.

He was pleasantly surprised that he landed on his feet and didn't stumble. One of the Marines came to him and wordlessly led him to a central position, where the marine strapped him in a sort of swivel chair. He found that he could use his legs to turn 360 degrees and see the entire target area. A second later, Wasp rocketed up to the deck, just as Bowman had a moment earlier. He looked like an acrobat as he unfolded from his curled position and stuck his landing.

Bowman saw that all the Marines were positioned behind their quad fifties, facing outward. Bowman couldn't see any targets, but he could see that each Marine had a targeting screen showing what he assumed was target data—position, trajectory, distance, and speed—of potential foes. He was gratified to see that friendly craft were clearly marked on their screens. This IFF (short for Identification Friend or Foe) system allowed all craft to distinguish between enemy and friendly spacecraft.

Unbidden, a small screen swung into place in front of Bowman. He was pleased to note that he understood most of what he was seeing, as it was similar to what he used on board his FA-300. He realized that each of the gunners had been assigned sectors of fire; individual Marines were responsible for any targets that came into their sector. The battle AI had color-coded targets by priority, using the standard scheme utilized by all pilots.

"Battery, stand by!" Wasp shouted. "Battery, fire!"

Immediately, the entire perimeter lit up, with six quad fifties belching fire into the sky. Bowman could feel the muzzle blasts and recoil through the deck and his chair. Tracers pierced the starry dark in a fantastic light show. In the distance, he could see flashes as the .50-caliber rounds found their targets. Occasionally, a larger blast showed where some of the junk had contained residual fuel, detonated by the heat generated by the tracer rounds and old-fashioned kinetic energy.

Bowman felt the craft alter course and heard Wasp command, "Cease-fire! Starboard team, prepare to board."

Instantly, all the gunners stopped firing; the Marines on the starboard side unhooked themselves from their firing mounts, drew what looked like rifles from slots next to them, and moved to the port side, where they huddled at the short waist-high railing. The port-side gunners remained alert, guns facing outward but silent.

Bowman realized they must be preparing to board one of the derelict vessels as part of the exercise, but he couldn't see anything.

But when he looked at the targeting screen in front of him, he saw with alarm that they were closing fast on a vessel at least five times the size of the RAB. *Holy crap*, he thought. They were going to crash into that thing—and he realized, for the first time at gut level, that this was the intent. Intellectually, he'd understood that, sure—but it hadn't really sunk in, until now, that the boarding was a controlled crash. Thus, the term *Ram and Board*.

Just before impact, the other vessel loomed before them, blocking out the stars. A moment later, they hit hard, and Bowman was thrown against his restraints. A split-second after that, he felt a shock run through the RAB and realized that the ramming spikes had detonated, fusing them to the OPFOR vessel.

"Demolition party, forward!" Wasp shouted.

The two forward-most Marines leaped forward, assisted by the jets at the rear of their backpacks, and came to rest on either side of a hatch. Moving quickly in what Bowman knew must be a well-practiced maneuver, the two Marines slapped explosive charges on the hatch. They both moved quickly to the side, faces averted from the hatch as one of them transmitted, "Fire in the hole!" A moment later, a flash blossomed from the craft, and Bowman saw the hatch blow down and away from the hull.

"Penetration team, forward!" Wasp ordered on the tac-net.

Two more Marines drove toward and through the now-open hatch, in one of the most coordinated displays of zero-gravity teamwork Bowman had ever seen.

"Entrance clear," one of the Marines reported almost instantly.

Wasp responded, "Boarding team away," and he himself leaped from the RAB and into the OPFOR vessel.

What followed was a series of clearance reports as the Marines boarded the vessel and reported their progress as they moved through the derelict ship. Bowman, who was watching a video feed from Wasp's viewpoint, noted with approval that they treated the training exercise as if it were real, taking nothing for granted, moving quickly but cautiously, clearing each passageway and securing the various areas of the ship: engine room, navigation, weapons control, communications, and finally the bridge.

He heard Wasp announce. "Det Six, this is RAB One Six, all clear. Enemy vessel is secure."

"Roger that," came Davenport's voice over the com channel. "RAB One Six, mission ENDEX. Disengage and return to base."

When he returned with Wasp to their base ship, he expected both Wasp and Davenport to be satisfied with (if not proud of) their newly proven capability. But instead, they both looked serious and grim.

Davenport noticed Bowman's surprise and, misunderstanding, said, "Sir, I want you to know the Marines will work this thing until it can be relied upon."

"Actually," Bowman said, "I thought it went very well."

Davenport's eyes widened in surprise for a moment, looking for sarcasm in Bowman. When he saw that he was sincere, he said, "Sir, the Marine standard for that type of operation is far higher than what you just saw. We will redouble our efforts."

Bowman, now serious, asked, "What went wrong? What needs to be done better?"

"Well, sir, first of all," Davenport replied, "that was done under no contact, no enemy fire, no resistance, with no casualties." He shook his head. "Next, the timing was off. A Marine boarding of a vessel under those conditions should be much faster."

Bowman was thinking just the opposite: that the boarding had been done rapidly indeed. *Oh, well,* he thought, *I guess that's just the Marine way.* He was already aware that they were never satisfied with their performance and were always their own harshest critics. The Marines were confident and proud, but in twelve years, he had never heard one brag, unlike many pilots he knew.

"I will have a training plan to get up to standards to you in twenty-four hours," Davenport said. "We're going to need some additional assets, sir, including some fighters to run OPFOR against us."

"Just don't shoot any of them out of the sky," Bowman said. "We don't have enough Marines as it is. Your men may be our most important resource." He turned to leave but then noticed that Davenport and Wasp were looking uncomfortable. "Was there something else?" he asked.

Davenport paused a moment and then seemed to nod to himself and said, "We do have a problem, sir."

"Yes?" Bowman said.

"We can't seem to work out some of the constraints, sir," Davenport said. "We have combat force ratios, redundancies, and firepower issues. We've been over it and have now seen it applied in exercise, and we just can't get it."

"What do you propose?'

"Speaking to the admiral, sir. He's the one with the most experience in RAB techniques. We'd like to consult him."

"Well, then go ahead," Bowman said, a bit baffled by this new timidity. "You don't need my permission."

"Actually, sir, we do," Davenport said. "You are the commanding officer for the combat aerospace force. We can't go over your head without your permission. No Marine would."

And there it was. *The Marine code is that strong*, thought Bowman. It sounded absurd under the circumstances, but he realized that the Marine code also kept them strong in the face of extreme adversity. It got them to jump out of a spacecraft under fire with only a thin tether to guide them, among other things.

"Captain Davenport," Bowman said formally, "you hereby have my permission to consult with Admiral Chambers on any issue concerning Marine tactics without prior consultation with me. Should the admiral issue you orders, you will inform me of those orders and then carry them out expeditiously. If time is of the essence or I cannot be located, inform me *after* you carry them out. This permission will remain in effect until revoked."

Davenport and Wasp came to attention and saluted. "Aye aye, sir," Davenport said.

Bowman returned the salute and walked away.

CHAPTER 13

COMING TOGETHER

Over the next several weeks, preparations to deal with their unidentified stalkers caused the crew of the Achilles Battle Fleet to work at an almost-frantic pace. Bowman was getting just four hours of sleep a day. At first glance, the bedlam resembled a disrupted anthill, but beneath the seeming chaos, Bowman could see both method and organization. He credited the admiral's leadership for this.

There were a number of projects running in parallel. First, the Marines were perfecting their RAB techniques. The admiral had come down to the training area and spent an entire day with Davenport and his people. Following that, the Marines worked tirelessly on their vessels, their weapons, and their training. Whatever insight Admiral Chambers had given them had motivated them to an even higher level of effort. The few times Bowman had seen Davenport, the Marine captain had the look of a man filled with holy zeal. Since he hadn't heard back from the captain, he was sure that whatever the admiral said had not been couched as an order. Otherwise, Davenport would have come to him with the news.

Second was the scheme for detecting the macro-wave collapse. Following the meeting during which CPO Raymond had been revealed as Dr. John Raymond, famous physicist, Chambers had appointed him chief science officer and had Lee allocate him a small office and lab. The admiral had also promoted him to warrant officer, the rarely used rank in between master chief petty officer and lieutenant junior grade. It was a promotion of sorts, in that he now outranked a master CPO of the Navy. It meant that the enlisted sailors would salute him, just as they would any other officer, but he wouldn't have to stand watch with the other junior officers. Nor would he be on the duty roster with the noncommissioned officers.

Raymond's lab was a modest affair: two rooms with a small living quarters, a shower, a bunk, a hotplate, and a coffeemaker. Technically, he was part of the headquarters staff and reported to Commander Lee. But the reality was that he reported directly to Admiral Chambers. In the meantime, he could access all the data he needed for his research.

Raymond's closest colleagues were those in the small intelligence section forming around Danner. Danner himself had received a promotion. At the beginning of the crisis, he had been a seaman apprentice, the second-lowest rank in the Navy. His training chief had admitted that Danner had in fact already qualified in every area only weeks after joining the fleet, but that he, the chief, had kept him in the training cycle, partly because he liked the young sailor, and partly because he worried that if it became known that Danner was a hotshot at taking tests, the other sailors and noncoms would hold it against him. In any case, he was declared a graduate of the apprentice program and promoted to seaman, a rank with which he was both happy and proud. Unfortunately, he had fallen into the leadership role of the new intelligence section, and several of the newly formed team were senior to him. There was no way he could hold that leadership role and keep the rank of seaman. As the intelligence section fell under Lee, it had been her responsibility to sort it out. She did some research and came up with a solution that surprised everyone and satisfied all but Danner himself.

"He'll be a midshipman," Lee said, as she was explaining it to Bowman over coffee during a rare break.

"Wait, how is that even possible?" Bowman asked. "Middies are cadets at the academy. He would need to be appointed, and we'd lose him for four years."

"True, in a peacetime Navy. But we're at war, a formally and legally declared war. And that means wartime rules."

"So in wartime, midshipmen need not attend the academy?"

"Correct," Lee said, smiling mischievously. "In fact, the Naval Academy is a relatively modern invention, going back only a few hundred years. It was an interim measure, never codified in law. It was established by the US Secretary of the Navy in 1842 after a mutiny led by three midshipmen aboard the Naval Brig *Somers.* The secretary apparently felt that a formal school was required to train aspiring officers. Before that time, all midshipmen were trained at sea. Their captain was responsible for their training, and they took their meals and bunked with the officers. After a period of training, any commanding admiral could convene a board of officers to examine midshipmen to decide if they were ready to receive a commission."

"Got it," Bowman said. "But that was seven hundred years ago. The Naval Academy has been there all that time. I thought that when the USA was brought into the Alliance, all of the laws then existing were to be respected."

"Correct again," Lee said. "But here's the catch: Believe it or not, the Naval Academy was never formally part of the US legal code, and no move was ever made to change that in all the centuries since. It was established by the US Navy but not originally funded by the legislature. Later, it was funded on a yearly basis but never formally charted. The original law for appointing midshipmen at sea is still on the books. And the decree of December 7 gives the admiral all the authority he needs."

"And so you prevailed upon Admiral Chambers to appoint Danner as a middie?" asked Bowman.

"When I approached him, he asked me why I hadn't already set up a program for midshipmen. He wants it done on a wider scale. We're already screening applicants."

"Wow. You move quickly." Bowman thought for a moment and then asked, "Aren't you worried that, once we get back to civilization, the commandant of the Naval Academy is going to make an objection to your interpretation of naval law? The last I heard, that was a four-star billet."

Lee looked sad and serious for a moment and then said quietly, "Yes, that might be the case, but Annapolis was destroyed during the attack on Earth, along with most of the East Coast."

Bowman was astonished. Though he hadn't been privy to the details, he knew, at some level, that the attack that had destroyed much of the Alliance government must have inflicted enormous damage and casualties elsewhere as well. He had no living relatives and had been so absorbed in his new duties and the effort to get the fleet up to fighting capability that he hadn't given much thought to what else might not be there.

"What contact do we have with Earth and the rest of the Navy?" he asked cautiously.

"Not much, really," Lee replied, heaving a deep sigh. "At the moment, their communications with interstellar vessels are almost nonexistent. We get a weekly, encrypted burst transmission that provides very limited information. That's how we found out the academy had been destroyed. We're not even sure our own reports are being received. In any case, all naval vessels have been directed to limit their transmissions as a security measure, so our efforts have been restricted."

"What do we know?" Bowman asked, feeling a bit stunned.

Lee replied grimly, "What little we know isn't reassuring. The messages we've received from other government agencies make it sound like there's some ... confusion back home."

"Confusion?"

Lee grimaced and tilted her head to the right as if struggling to find the right words. "Honestly, it sounds like there's confusion about who's in charge. We've received a number of seemingly conflicting decrees from government committees no one has ever heard of. I don't want to sound overly dramatic, but I fear the worst."

"What does the admiral say about all this?"

"He keeps his own counsel, but he's given orders that he is to see all communications we receive or intercept before they're published to the staff or the fleet in general."

Now that's interesting, Bowman thought. "Is the Navy chain of command clear?"

"No," Lee responded bluntly. "Again, the admiral has been very clear to Commodore Vance and me. We are to report to him any attempt to give the fleet orders, and he will decide how to respond. I think he understands that the Achilles Battle Fleet is a substantial combat force, and he's on guard against us being used inappropriately in case there's a squabble for power."

"Unbelievable," Bowman muttered. They were both quiet for a minute and then he asked, "So what do you think the admiral plans to do? Does he have a plan?"

"Oh, he has a plan, I'm sure," she replied. "I think he wants to make some progress on this thing Raymond is working on, and he wants the fleet up to fighting trim before we encounter any other Alliance ships or approach any of the colonies. If worse comes to worst, he wants the fleet to be able to defend itself and retain its freedom of movement. As you know, we can't jump yet because some of the ships aren't faster-than-light capable, and anyway, the admiral wants other repairs done first. He hasn't told me so, but I honestly think he wants the fleet to be completely combat-ready before it's able to jump."

Bowman stopped by Raymond's lab next. The man himself answered the door, and Bowman had a moment of surprise when he saw him. He had lost weight, was combed and groomed, and wore his new officer's uniform and insignia with a crisp pride. The change made him look ten years younger; Bowman thought he had never seen such a rapid transformation in a human being. Raymond looked good; he had a clear look of purpose in his eyes and stood straighter than he had in all the years Bowman had known him.

"Chief, ah …" Bowman trailed off. It was a bit awkward, because Bowman wanted to make sure he addressed the new warrant officer with the correct title, and for a moment, he had to search for it. Raymond had been a chief petty officer, and so "chief" was an acceptable, if somewhat informal, mode of address. Warrant officers were rare. In fact, Bowman hadn't known more than a handful in his twelve-plus years of naval service. In this case, Raymond had been promoted to warrant officer 2, meaning the second rank of four. This was technically a chief warrant officer, and thus, once again, the title "Chief Raymond" was correct. *Strange*, thought Bowman.

But Raymond didn't seem to notice Bowman's awkwardness. "Sir, I was hoping you would stop by," he said. "I wanted to bring you up to date and get your advice on something."

He led Bowman into his lab. It contained a number of workstations, with keyboards and screens of various sizes. Bowman saw with admiration that Raymond had data feeds from all the major systems on the vessel and throughout the fleet: navigation, propulsion, weapons, long-range surveillance, and target acquisition. Chambers must have pulled out all the stops to get this to happen in such a short time.

"Can I offer you some coffee?" the chief asked.

Bowman said, "That would be great, Chief," feeling more comfortable that he had the correct address down. "Congrats on your promotion, by the way."

To Bowman's surprise, Raymond positively beamed with pleasure. "Why, thank you, sir. I was very surprised and honored at the promotion. I felt sure I had sort of hit my plateau in the Navy. Never thought I'd be an officer."

Bowman didn't say what was on his mind: that as far as career status went, Raymond was already one of the most revered names in Alliance physics. His was a household name on dozens of planets, and every student of physics at the university level had to study his work. The Raymond Paradox Hypothesis had provided a key, of sorts, that allowed mathematicians and scientists to solve dozens of problems that had been considered unsolvable for centuries.

He remembered what Lee said when they had discussed Danner. He had asked her why a bright guy like Danner hadn't applied for OCS. She had replied, "I don't know. But I do know the fleet is filled with bright and motivated enlisted sailors. Let's not forget, military service is mandatory, and not everyone wants to be an officer."

Raymond joined the Navy to find anonymity and to escape persecution (and maybe even assassination). As a sailor working in the maintenance field, even rising to the rank of chief petty officer, he had been able to stay hidden from the forces that sought him. Perhaps he felt that rising to officer rank, something he was clearly suited for, would have drawn attention and blown his cover. But now that the war was on and his talents were needed, he no longer needed to hide.

"So how can I help?" Bowman asked.

Raymond looked at Bowman with a steady gaze and said, "We need to capture one of their vessels intact."

Bowman thought about that, nodded, and then said, "Tell me why."

"I've been going over it, starting from the big picture, the strategic level, and working it down to what we need, and then reversing it—working from the tactical to the strategic. We know that macro-wave function collapse can be accomplished; we've seen it. Our problem is that we don't have enough time to figure it out on our own. It would take years to recreate the process well enough to develop countermeasures, and that won't do, will it?"

Bowman nodded again. "You're right about that. We need a better grasp of what they're doing and how to defend against it, and soon, or we're going to have a big problem."

"And it's not just that," Raymond said. "I had a long talk with Danner. He's a bright boy, by the way. He pointed out that it won't be enough just to counter this new technology. He said no war has ever been won simply by countering a new weapon. If we are to be victorious, we'll need a more effective offensive capability."

"That explains why they never surrender," Bowman said. "They can't afford to. If they did, the technology would be in our hands."

"That's it, exactly. I suspect the craft we've been fighting have built-in self-destruct mechanisms. I seriously doubt every one of those pilots and crew would have chosen to die rather than be captured."

"I think we need to gather the team and talk to the admiral again," Bowman said.

CHAPTER 14

UNQUIET THOUGHTS

Midshipman Andy Danner was worried. As part of his duties overseeing the drone sensor net, he had been reviewing the telecommunications logs between the active and remote drones and the main command center. Something wasn't right, but he'd been reviewing diagnostics for days and couldn't find what it was that made him uncomfortable. He was having trouble sleeping and found that he was muttering to himself. Finally, he went to see Warrant Officer Raymond in his laboratory.

"What's up, Danner?" The Chief had a friendly expression on his face, but his tone said, "Let's get to it; I'm busy."

"Chief, I'm having some trouble with the telecom logs for the drone net."

"What's the problem?" Raymond asked, now totally focused on Danner. The drone net was the chief protective measure that allowed the fleet some measure of safety while it continued to repair and train. If something was wrong with the net, that was a serious problem.

"There's an anomaly with the logs, and I can't quite place it," Danner said with what amounted to a grimace. He was at heart an analyst. Identifying patterns in information was something he prided himself on. Having to turn to someone for help on an issue like this was outside his comfort zone.

Raymond returned to his terminal and began tapping the screen. "Okay, I've got the archive chapter headings. Where do you think the problem is?"

"Look at the log entries for 2 February," Danner said.

Raymond clicked away and then said, "Got it."

"Now look at the burst transmissions. The cycle is set to run an auto confirmation check every twenty minutes and then issue an update if any number of changes are entered into the system."

"What kind of changes?" asked Raymond.

"Well, of course, if the drones detect anything," said Danner. "Or if the fleet changes course, or if there's a malfunction in any of the com or data streams."

"What's this here at line Foxtrot Seventeen?" Raymond inquired, pointing at the relevant spot on the screen.

Danner hunched over to look at the monitor. "It's a maintenance query on drone Alpha Two-Four. The system monitors the drones and sends them a query, an interrogation, if any of the responses are off the mark."

"Off the mark?" Raymond turned to Danner with a frown. "This is a state-of-the-art drone, a Mark Nine. How could it be off the mark?"

Danner leaned in and tapped a few keys. "Let's see," he said. "Well, it seems the system detected a delayed response. The subsequent maintenance query showed no problem."

"How long was the delay?" Raymond asked.

Danner looked in and scrolled down. "Four microseconds," he said.

"That's an eternity for a Mark Nine." Raymond chewed his bottom lip. "That requires an explanation." They both sat in silence for a moment. Then Raymond asked, "Does this anomaly only occur in this same drone? Have any of the other drones been effected?"

"Let's see," said Danner. He pressed some keys. "No, the delay appears in other drones, but never the same one twice in the same cycle."

"Okay," said Raymond. "Let's run a quick program to analyze the sequence and timing of the delays." He brought up a new view and tapped in some commands. The computer showed a blue-colored bar that moved from left to right as the program made its calculations. In a moment, it popped up with some data.

"There it is," said Raymond.

"Shoot," Danner replied. "We have a traitor."

CHAPTER 15

WE HAVE A TRAITOR

Danner and Raymond discussed what to do with this new information. They both knew what the problem was: Whoever was messing with the drone net was connected to the project or had access to the system. Who could they trust?

"I hate to think it might be one of my guys," said Danner. "They're all good people. But all of us are new to the intelligence section, and none of us, myself included, have been vetted."

"We need to be careful, and we need to get it right," Raymond told him. "I've been on the receiving end of a conspiracy before. Maybe even the same conspiracy," he said with dawning realization. "If it's the same people, they can be vicious."

"We could go straight to the admiral," Danner suggested. "If he's the rat, we're screwed anyway."

"The problem is getting to see him without drawing attention. If the traitor finds out we're going straight in to see the CO, bypassing the chain of command, he might realize he's been found out."

"And do what about it? He can't very well flee, can he?"

"No," said Raymond. "He can't run, but he can do some damage before he's stopped. If that person is placed well enough to do what we've seen, they have access to all sorts of system commands that could cause a lot of problems, maybe fatal ones."

In the end, they decided to do it the military way and take it to the chain of command. Bowman and Lee were the commander and deputy of the intelligence cell and therefore responsible for this problem. Danner had the idea to ask for a meeting with the two of them to go over the progress of filling out the personnel roster for the intelligence section, since there were still a few vacancies, and Danner had been screening potential applicants. They agreed that wouldn't attract any attention. Raymond would come along in an advisory capacity as the senior science advisor.

They met in a ready room adjacent to the operations and intelligence work area. Danner and Raymond had gotten there before Bowman and Lee arrived and made a quick sweep of the room for listening devices. They didn't find any. When Bowman and Lee came in, Raymond shut and secured the hatch behind them. Lee shot Danner a quizzical look and waited for the briefing to start.

Danner spoke up. "Sir, ma'am, I'm afraid I've brought you here under false pretenses. We have a counterintelligence issue that needs your attention."

Lee asked, "And Warrant Officer Raymond is here because ...?"

"I sought him out to help me with a technical issue, and we discovered the problem together," said Danner.

"Okay, then, let's hear it," said Bowman.

Danner then reviewed the steps that had brought them to the conclusion that something was wrong with the data logs from the drone sensor net. "I don't understand. How do you know these anomalies are evidence of espionage?" Bowman asked.

"I think the chief can answer that best," replied Danner.

They all turned to Raymond, who said, "We knew there was a problem with the delays because the Mark Nine drone is state of the art; there's no way it would have a fault or a significant delay in transmission and then subsequently pass a maintenance query, unless there was something interfering with its operating system. We did check for that, though. Then I ran a program on the sequence and timing of the delays. The program shows a nonrandom coherence of nearly 100 percent. This is the same test we use on patterned radiation detected from distant sources to check for intelligent life. A near-perfect score for nonrandom coherence indicates an intentional sequence."

"Why would anyone interfere with the drone net in such a way?" asked Lee. "If there was a saboteur, why wouldn't he just damage the network or destroy it?"

"There are a number of possible explanations for that," Danner said, reasserting himself as the head of intelligence. "First, he might not be able to shut the network down. Second, shutting down the network would likely expose him as a traitor, and in any case, it would only cause a delay. The instant the network was down, the fleet would compensate with more traditional defenses, and we would have a new network up in a short period of time."

"So what is the traitor doing?" Lee asked. "What harm has been done?"

"Why, transmitting, of course," said Raymond. "I thought that was obvious, ma'am."

"Explain," said Bowman, tight-lipped and beginning to feel alarmed.

"The traitor has hijacked the network. The messages being sent are chopped up into pieces and transmitted from each drone in the first few milliseconds of each response to a query. That's why the drones are late in responding, each by a tiny bit. If Danner hadn't noticed the pattern, we might not have ever caught it."

"So the questions now are, who is transmitting the messages, what are the messages saying, and who are they being sent to?" said Lee.

Danner answered, "First, let me say that we haven't done anything about it yet. There's a good chance that whoever sent those messages has access to the networks and probably more of the fleet's systems. It's at least possible that he would be able to detect any activity on our part to uncover his or her identity."

"So you haven't done anything yet?" Lee demanded, with some tension in her voice.

Danner held his ground. "Ma'am, we haven't done anything that could be interpreted as looking into the transmissions. We *have* done some analysis completely offline, based on the information already in the logs. Chief?"

Raymond nodded and explained, "As I said before, the transmission is broken up into many small burst-transmissions at the front or end of the normal response-to-maintenance query. It's obviously encrypted, but it's not hidden. The digital maintenance logs have all the transmissions recorded. Because the unauthorized part of the transmission is short and otherwise meaningless to the network, the few bits are disregarded, because the system considers them garbage—background noise or simple errors."

"So what did you find?" Bowman asked.

"We've captured all the data transmitted by the drones and have been working on decrypting it. It's going to take time, and it's only coming in bits and pieces."

"So what *do* you have?' Lee asked.

"One phrase," said Danner. He paused and said, "'John Raymond is here.'"

CHAPTER 16

COUNTERINTELLIGENCE

They waited until the afternoon shift-change briefing to inform the admiral. First, because it was a regularly scheduled briefing, and second, because Lee, in her role as chief of staff, routinely published both the agenda and the list of those who needed to be in attendance. In this case, only Bowman, Lee, Danner, and Raymond were listed.

Admiral Chambers stood, rather than sat, during these briefings. It was his way of indicating he didn't want a long meeting. If everyone was standing, including him, it moved the presentations along quite nicely. After everyone was in position, Lee nodded to the admiral and he, surprisingly, started the meeting off himself, rather than waiting for Lee to do so.

"I suppose this is where you tell me we have a mole in the fleet?" Chambers said dryly.

Everyone was quiet for a moment, seemingly with nothing to say. As it was Lee's meeting to run as the chief of staff, she spoke first. "Yes, sir. Warrant Officer Raymond and Midshipman Danner have uncovered covert transmissions from the drone sensor net. They brought the information to Captain Bowman and me, and now we're bringing it to you. May I ask how you knew?"

Chambers drew a breath and thought for a moment before responding, "I knew there was someone in the fleet communicating to the outside. Let's face it: We've always known that something like that was happening. The ambush on December 7 required the attackers to have detailed information about our movements."

Danner burst out, "So you knew about this and didn't tell us?"

Lee glared at him, clearly furious with his breach of protocol.

But the admiral seemed to take no notice; he just nodded and said, "Hostile intelligence gathering is present in all conflicts. The question isn't whether it's there, but how best to take advantage of it. We could have done a witch hunt on the day after the ambush. What good would that have done? The traitor would have just hunkered down, and the search for him would have upset the crew and deflected our efforts. And in most cases, the information leaked isn't that valuable to the enemy, or if it is, they could have found it out from other sources. In any case, they've had us under surveillance for some time using their recon vessels."

They were all quiet for moment, and then the admiral said, "Danner, why would they use the drone sensor net? Why change anything when they obviously had an undisclosed source of communication before you set up the net?"

Danner thought a long moment before replying, "Well, sir, the drone net is larger; it's spread out over thousands of kilometers. It makes a better transmitter."

"And, of course, a better receiver," offered Raymond.

The admiral turned to Commander Lee and asked, "Why risk detection by using the drone net? Whoever is doing this must know that the net gets a lot of attention; people like Danner and Lee are looking at it daily. Surely the mole knew it would be discovered eventually."

Lee reddened a bit as everyone looked at her, awaiting an answer, but when she spoke, it was in a steady voice. "There are a couple of possibilities. First, whatever mechanism they had been using was no longer available. If they had a transmitter, it might have been destroyed in the attack, or it might no longer bc available with all the changes we've made since then. The second possibility is that something important has come up, and they need to get the additional boost the net gives them, so it's worth the risk."

The admiral asked, "Anything else?" He turned to his science advisor. "Mr. Raymond?"

Raymond spoke up right away. "It's also possible that protecting the identity of the source of the leak is no longer as critical as it was. Maybe something is about to happen that outweighs the secrecy."

"I fear you're right," said Chambers. "Have you decrypted the transmissions yet?"

"Only part of one sequence, sir. It read, 'John Raymond is here.'"

"That makes sense," said the admiral. "Up to now, the Achilles Battle Fleet has been one of many tactical units, a small element in a much bigger picture of Alliance capabilities. With the knowledge that the chief is aboard, we'll be seen as a strategic threat rather than a tactical one. Chief Raymond is one of the few people who has the background to interpret the macro-wave collapse technology. That makes him a threat to our adversaries, and the information that he's with the fleet now becomes worth the risk of exposure.

"Midshipman," the admiral said, turning to Danner, "am I correct in assuming you've taken no steps to indicate that you've discovered these transmissions?"

"That's correct, sir. Warrant Officer Raymond and I have done all our calculations offline, this room has been swept for surveillance, and only the people present know about the issue."

"Good," said the admiral. "You've all done exactly right." He paused and looked into the middle distance, a look they'd all seen before that meant he was thinking about something and shouldn't be interrupted.

Finally, he said, "Here's what I need you to do: First, protect Dr. Raymond, both his person and his work. If there's a traitor on board, they'll go for him if they can. If they can't get to him, they'll try to monitor his work. I want none of that to happen." He paused and looked directly at Raymond. "Dr. Raymond, I'm afraid your life is about to get a lot more difficult."

"Not a problem, sir," answered Raymond. "I'm tired of hiding. I'm up for whatever is required of me."

Chambers nodded curtly. "Second priority: Limit the number of people who know about this. I want Davenport brought in, because we can't go forward with a major threat on board without the head of security knowing about the problem. No one else—not Vance, not any of the techies, no one.

"Third: Mr. Danner, I need you to work up a confidential intelligence estimate. It should address the essential elements of friendly information. This will list the attributes and capabilities of the fleet that, if known, would be valuable to an adversary. Lay out our vulnerabilities, and offer recommendations on how to reduce them.

"Fourth, I need recommendations on how to identify the traitor without tipping him off that we're looking for him. Unfortunately, that will mean deceiving our own people. You'll need to come up with a believable cover story that makes your inquiry into the systems look like something other than a search for a saboteur.

"Fifth, we need recommendations on how best to take advantage of the mole, once he or she is discovered."

"Shouldn't that person be detained for court-martial?" Danner asked.

"It may come to that. But we also need to consider other options."

"Such as?" asked Lee.

"Captain Bowman, you're the history professor. Tell us how the British government handled German spies they caught during World War II."

Bowman nodded and said, "They detained them and gave them the option to serve British interests or face execution as spies."

"And what did they choose?" asked Danner.

"About nine in ten chose to serve the British as double agents throughout the war," said Bowman. "The rest were shot as spies."

Lee asked, "Didn't the Germans figure out something was wrong when they got bad intelligence from their spies?"

"No, they didn't," said Bowman. "The Brits actually gave them mostly correct information."

"What?" Danner exclaimed. "You're telling me they compromised their own operations?"

"Yes, they did," said Bowman. "They kept the spies credible in the eyes of their German masters until near the very end. Then, just before D-Day, they had every turned agent tell the Germans that the cross-channel invasion would come at Pas de Calais, not at Normandy. The Germans were completely fooled. It was, in fact, one of the most successful deception operations in history."

"Sounds pretty coldhearted," Danner said.

"It was," the admiral agreed. "And we will never betray our own people. But we still might make good use of a turned spy."

CHAPTER 17

THANKS FOR THE LESSON, HONEY

Despite her workload and its new tasks, Lieutenant Commander Mei-Ling Lee made time for training. It had been this way for her as long as she could remember. As the child of a martial arts legend, she often felt under pressure to perform. That was okay; she liked training, and to be honest, she liked the attention. But when things got stressed or complicated, she would sneak down to the training hall after everyone was in bed, light a few candles, and train on her own. She knew her parents were aware of it, but it remained an open secret. It was her time, and she needed it.

Lee was in one of the smaller training rooms, which was deserted at this hour. She started by warming up. A creature of habit, she went through the same series of exercises she always used. Then she went through a series of slow movements: blocks, stances, strikes, and kicks. With each controlled movement, she let her breath out slowly, tensing her muscles and then relaxing them. This let the body warm up slowly and reduced the risk of an injury when training at full speed. But more than that, it was a stress relief. She felt the tension pour out of her.

Her two jobs as chief of staff and deputy head of the intelligence section were very demanding. It was impossible to do all the things necessary for both jobs. That was fine; the academy had taught her how to prioritize and delegate. But even then, the number of things left undone at the end of the day often weighed on her. Thus, her training to help blow off the tension and refocus her mind.

And then there was Bowman. She knew he was attracted to her. One didn't grow up as a pretty girl and not know when men were into you. But he was different than many—well, maybe all—of the men who had looked her way since she was about thirteen. He was genuinely polite and modest, while being confident about his role as a naval officer. And oh my, he was way better than most pilots, who tended to be arrogant buffoons. Well, maybe that was too strong. Lee came from a culture where bragging and strutting around like a peacock was frowned upon. Her father was one of the best martial artists in the world, but he was a lovely, sweet, generous man, who was modest and reserved about his skills.

She started her forms. As always, she began with the basics. Many advanced martial artists eschewed the basic techniques, as if they were for children or beginners. Not Lee. She knew that the basic advantage of martial arts in combat, especially for someone smaller than her opponent, was the ability to generate power. The key, as taught in her art, was the correct coordination of limbs and joints in a relaxed, smooth movement, accelerating in speed until the point of impact. The forms, beginning with the basic ones, reinforced this technique.

After about twenty minutes, she moved over to the heavy bag. It weighed about seventy pounds and hung from the low ceiling of the training room (none of the ceilings on a war vessel were very high). As always, she started by throwing light punches and kicks, just barely tapping the surface of the bag. She did this for focus. Later, she would hit it harder, working on penetration and power.

"Hey, take it easy on that bag. Some of us would like to use it, and we can't if it's broke." The voice was male, sarcastic, and unfriendly.

She turned with her cold face on, the one her father had taught her to use in ambiguous situations. The speaker was a large man, about forty, with a barrel chest, beefy arms, and a bit of a gut. She recognized him as one of the Marines, a lance corporal. His name was Jenkins, from the security detail. Not one of Davenport's elite commandos—not with that gut, anyway. And he was old for a lance corporal, which meant he wasn't a top performer or had been in trouble in the past.

She stepped aside, wordlessly putting out her hand in a gesture to say, "It's all yours." He smirked and strode over, pulled some boxing gloves out of his gym bag, and put them on.

"Let me show you how this is done," he said.

He then began to hit the bag hard, but wildly, with no effort at focus or control. Lee watched his feet. He made no effort to balance himself, just leaned forward and hit the bag as hard as he could. After about twenty seconds, he stopped, breathing hard.

"Now you do it," he said, in a voice that presumed he was the superior. So it wasn't just the pilots who could be jerks.

"Thank you, no," she responded. "I'm finished with that." She turned back to the open areas to continue with forms training.

"You know, I saw you doing those kicks and stuff," Jenkins said. "That'll never work in a real fight, 'specially not in zero gravity. Not enough power. I suppose it's good exercise, though. You know, like ballet or aerobics."

"I'm glad to know it," she said, still with the cold face. The cold face showed nothing, neither interest nor anger. It was the face the Mongols, her ancestors, were reputed to have used when going into combat.

"No, really, I'm just saying. You know, in the Marines, we really have to fight, so we don't mess around with the fancy stuff."

Lee knew he was lying. The Marines had a system of combative training that drew upon a variety of martial arts, including the rare Hwa Rang, if she wasn't mistaken. She had watched Davenport and his commandos training. They weren't bad. Either this guy had somehow missed out on that training, or he was bluffing a bit, hiding some of his skills and training. "I could show you if you like, honey," he said with a creepy smile.

Though she would never show it, Lee was pissed now. When out of uniform in the training hall, rank need not be deferred to. But he clearly knew she was an officer and was intentionally baiting her by being overly familiar. She also knew that he'd never address a male officer in the tone he just used. But the word "honey"—that was far too familiar.

"I would enjoy that," she said, still with the cold face and the voice to go with it. She walked to her gym bag, drew out her protective gloves, and put them on. "North American freestyle rules okay with you?"

Jenkins looked taken aback for a second. He'd been teasing her, trying to intimidate her. Maybe that worked with women he had been around before. Probably not, she thought. But now he had to see it through or back down and seem the fool.

"Sure," he said, trying to muster his former bravado. "No biting or gouging, eh?"

North American freestyle was the least restrictive of the rules governing fighting used by competitors. It allowed strikes to all body targets, except penetrating strikes to the throat or eyes. It allowed kicks to the legs and groin, and grappling and sweeps, a technique in which one opponent kicks the supporting leg out from under the other, causing him or her to fall. It was the technique Lee had recently used on Bowman. In theory, the larger opponent should have an advantage, especially where grappling and throws were permitted. The fact Lee had suggested it meant she was confident.

Lee noted that other Marines were entering the training room, and she saw that Wasp, the young gunnery sergeant, was among them. She guessed that some of the Marines were coming down for a late-night training session, and Jenkins had arrived a bit early.

As Lee and Jenkins were squaring off, Jenkins turned to the other Marines and shrugged, saying, "What I can say? She asked for it." None of the Marines smiled at the double entendre, and Lee guessed that Jenkins wasn't popular with his mates.

Wasp walked over and said, "Hold up a moment. Did I hear North American freestyle rules?" As both Lee and Jenkins nodded, he added, "In that case, I'll referee, if you don't mind?"

Lee nodded. Jenkins shrugged as if to say it could hardly matter; this would be over soon.

Lee bowed to Jenkins, a courtesy he didn't return. Wasp stood in the referee's position, midway between them but off to the side a few feet. He put out his hand, chopped the air downward, and said, "Fight!"

Lee had been watching Jenkins. His face was flushed, his breathing rapid, and he was leaning forward as if he couldn't wait to jump her. In other words, he was making rookie mistakes, fully consistent with his performance on the bag minutes earlier. How had this moron been allowed to join the Marines, much less stay as long as he had?

Sure enough, he lunged forward, both hands outstretched as if to grab her. Not an elegant move, but clearly within the rules. Lee waited a fraction of a second to make sure he was fully committed. Then she deftly moved to the side, grabbed his right wrist, and drew his palm inward toward his forearm. As he moved forward, the pain of the joint lock, as it was termed, caused him to try to slow his forward momentum, but it was too late for that. He gave a little shriek as he fell, turning as he did to try to relieve the pain. Lee held on to his wrist just long enough that his body sprawled on the mat. At the last moment, she snapped a kick to his underarm as she released her hold. The result was that the kick added to his momentum, and his body continued to slide out of the sparring area. Had she wished to, she could have held the wrist and kicked hard enough to dislocate the shoulder.

"Break!" shouted Wasp.

Lee calmly moved to her position in the ring. Jenkins came up, furious and sputtering. "That was cheating," he shouted at Wasp.

"No, that was North American freestyle," Wasp responded with calm authority. "Point for takedown, penalty point for going out of the ring. Score, 2–0, Commander Lee's favor." He raised his open hand and ordered, "Fighting stances."

Lee and Jenkins squared off again, Lee still with her cold face, Jenkins now less cocky but clearly furious. "Fight!" Wasp said. This time, Jenkins came in with wild punches. Lee deftly sidestepped them. After the third, she moved in and hit him hard several times in the ribcage. She knew she had to hit him hard. He was fat, but there was muscle underneath, and he couldn't be a complete weakling, since he was somehow still in the Marines. She could hear the air *whoosh* out of his lungs. She could have backed off and let him catch his breath, as he was clearly outmatched. But she wouldn't do that. The fight needed to end decisively. Any sign of mercy would be taken by Jenkins as an intentional humiliation. And the other Marines were watching.

Yes, there was that. It mattered what they saw.

As Jenkins tried to straighten up, he instinctively placed his arms in a guarding position to protect his ribs. The moment he did, she struck his head with a roundhouse kick. It was a hard blow, and Jenkins went down in a heap.

Wasp broke in, placing himself between the two fighters, and yelled, "Break!"

Lee went immediately to her knees, facing away from Jenkins's crumpled form. She breathed deeply, focused on relaxing. Vaguely, she could hear the Marines, all of whom were trained as medics, begin first aid on their fallen comrade. She heard Jenkins sputter, groan, and then the unmistakable sound of him vomiting. Inwardly, she smiled. The fight was over in less than fifteen seconds of sparring time. Word would get out in the fleet, and that was not a bad thing. She was glad Wasp had been there, so Jenkins couldn't later say that she had cheated or pulled rank, or something like that.

"Competitors, back to the center," Wasp said. Lee stood turned and saw that Jenkins was standing unsteadily, his shirt stained with vomit, pure hatred in his eyes. "Winner," Wasp said, raising his open hand at an angle toward Lee, the universal gesture to show who was the victor.

Lee moved forward and offered her hand. Still the cold face. Jenkins waved it off, turned, and stomped off, muttering. She caught the word "bitch."

With calm authority, Wasp said, "Lance Corporal, return." With his back still turned, Jenkins straightened. For a moment, it looked like he would keep walking, but his training as a Marine got the better of him. Refusing an order from a gunnery sergeant, from any superior, would mean serious consequences: reduction in rank, for certain, and possibly expulsion. Jenkins then came back and reluctantly shook hands.

Lee grasped his hand and pulled him close. She whispered to him with a charming smile, "Thank you for the lesson, *honey.*"

She gathered her bag, put her sparring gloves back inside, and began to walk toward the hatch. As she passed the heavy bag, she shot a sidekick out, hitting the bag squarely in the center. It shot upward in a long arc, slamming against the ceiling. Every marine noted it.

CHAPTER 18

MIDSHIPMEN IN TRAINING

In addition to his heavy workload as head analyst for the intel section, Andy Danner had training and classes he needed to attend as part of his midshipman qualifications. This amounted to about twenty hours a week. Some of it could be done online from his workstation or quarters, but at least half needed to be done in a training environment with other middies. Lee had set up a training program, assigning various experts from the fleet to serve as ad hoc professors. Danner had never imagined there was so much to learn. A short list included weapons, navigation, propulsion, communications protocols, report writing, supervision, ethics, and administration.

And, of course, there was physical fitness. The Navy expected all officers to be fit. As an enlisted man, Danner had thought the physical demands of basic training were hard enough. Back during his pre-deployment training on Earth, he had had to run two miles and do forty push-ups, forty sit-ups, and six chin-ups. While on board, he had kept in pretty good shape using the treadmill in the training hall. He thought he was doing okay. Since he had never done sports in high school, and certainly not in college, he was secretly proud that he could meet the standards of the Navy.

That sense of accomplishment was challenged now. All midshipmen had to report for two hours of PT at the beginning of first watch, five days a week. Danner had heard that the training was to be led by one of the NCOs for the Marine commando unit but was surprised to see it was instead led by Captain Davenport himself. Davenport was an interesting guy. Danner knew he had been promoted from gunnery sergeant to officer following the attack on the fleet. As he had received a direct commission to captain, Davenport wasn't required to undergo any of the midshipman training. But he had voluntarily attended, as a student, almost all the offered training. Over coffee at the officers' mess, Davenport had explained to Danner and a few others his reasons.

"I joined the Marines at seventeen," he said. "I'm forty-five now. Yeah, I pretty much know how to work tactics and training at the platoon and company level. But keep in mind, Marine officers are still part of the Navy. There's a ton of stuff I've never been exposed to that I need to know. I've never even been a watch officer, never plotted a course for a starship, never done a single shift in engineering. I didn't ask for the promotion and would never have sought it out. But now that I have it, I'll be damned if I'll be any less than what's expected of an officer. And I'll be damned if I'll be any less than what the admiral expects of any of his officers."

The midshipmen—the oldest at least twenty years younger than Davenport—were impressed. Danner felt humbled and remembered that talk every time he wanted to feel sorry for himself.

And feel sorry for himself was what he wanted to do during the first few hours of PT. By tradition, Marine commandos were assigned to train fledgling midshipmen at the Naval Academy back on Earth. Here in the fleet, the admiral had decided the Marine detachment could handle that task, at least at first. Once they were at a basic level of fitness, Chambers wanted the midshipmen to rotate through leadership positions. As Davenport was to be present anyway, he took over the task of leading PT on most days.

It was horrible. It started out well enough with warmups, some stretching and jumping jacks, and other exercises. But then Davenport had taken the group to the Marine commandos' training facility. Once there, they were run through station training, which included ladders and climbing ropes, weight training, wrestling mats, heavy bags, even a swimming pool. One of the things Danner noticed was that the captain went first on every obstacle. It was the Marine way; leaders always went first.

One of the stations was a horizontal ladder suspended over a net some thirty feet below. The midshipmen had to go hand over hand for a distance of about twenty feet to reach safety at the far side. Although it was clear that if you slipped, you would just fall into the net waiting below, the immediate fear of falling was intense.

Danner realized he was terrified of this obstacle. He knew in his heart that without the peer pressure of the training environment, he would never have hung over that foreboding height. But when his turn came, he did it without hesitation and was surprised to discover that he made it to the other side in a reasonable time. He was definitely not the worst. One of the middies slipped and fell. At first, they all gasped; the poor guy who was falling let out a little yelp of fear. But the net did its job, and the midshipman bounced high with a nervous giggle. Davenport not only made the young man do it again, he made all of them do it second time because one of them had fallen. He wanted them thinking as a team, learning to feel responsible for each other.

After the obstacle course, Davenport put them in a running formation, and they ran two miles on the indoor track. They sang the same running songs they had learned at basic training and a few ribald ones they learned from Davenport, which had them smiling inwardly. By the time they finished, Danner could feel the energy coming from the group. Davenport was clearly an accomplished leader, and his magic was working on all of them. Danner began thinking about how he wanted to able to lead others with the same enthusiasm and confidence.

There was an interesting little technique that Davenport used when he wanted a volunteer. He would say, "Give me a volunteer." Then he would wait for what seemed like no more than a second and then order the midshipmen to do push-ups, do squats, or run laps. Then he would line them up again and repeat, "Give me a volunteer." Again, if no volunteer came forward quickly, the process was repeated. The message was clear: He wanted volunteers right away. By the end of the first day, if Davenport asked for a volunteer, midshipmen would be raising their hands, yelling, "Take me, take me." It was funny to watch, but it also made a point.

After the first few weeks, Danner found that he was in much better condition and felt more confident. He looked forward to the training and, when selected to volunteer, found he liked being the one to go first.

On one of the days that Danner got picked as a volunteer, Davenport introduced combative training. Davenport and a few of his NCOs, who were acting as assistant instructors, had shown them some basic kicks, punches, and blocks. The middies had been practicing in pairs, one holding a heavy pad while the other hit it. They had also done some grappling, practicing some holds and the counter that could be used to break each one. Danner found that he liked this part of the training and that he was reasonably quick at picking up on the maneuvers. Perhaps Davenport had noticed this, for Danner was selected among the volunteers to demonstrate with Davenport.

"One of the basic principles of combat is positioning," the captain explained. "If someone comes at you to attack, you need to pick a position that gives you a relative advantage. Mr. Danner here is going to attack me."

Davenport nodded to Danner, who realized with a start that he was supposed to do something. He shot out a roundhouse kick to Davenport's midsection. Davenport moved quickly forward, caught Danner's leg in the crook of his elbow, and gave him a slight push while holding the leg up. Danner went down but softened his fall by slapping the mat with his palm, as they had all been taught to do when falling. Danner immediately shot back up to his feet and squared off with Davenport. He wanted to show he was ready for more, and he was a bit miffed that he had gone down so easily and quickly.

Davenport held up his hand to show Danner the demonstration was over. "So tell me what happened," he asked the group. "Give me a volunteer." Several of the midshipmen raised their hands, and Davenport picked one to answer. "You."

"Midshipman Danner struck at you using a rear-leg roundhouse kick, and you caught the kick and knocked him down," he said.

"Correct, but more important was my movement," said Davenport. "I moved forward, taking away the full impact of the kick, and then pushed him backward while holding his leg off the ground. So let's try that technique with your partners."

As the training continued, Danner was amazed at how quickly he seemed to be learning. The thing with positioning really seemed to work. They rotated through various partners, and he found that it helped a lot and even gave him some leverage on heavier, stronger opponents. When they finished, despite their fatigue and some bruises, Danner could see smiles of the faces of the midshipmen, and inside he was a bit elated.

He could do this.

CHAPTER 19

AN INVITATION AND
AN EXPLANATION

The effort to capture an enemy vessel had moved forward on a number of fronts. Along with Danner and his team, Raymond had been working on interfering with the macro-wave collapse. When they thought they were ready, he arranged a briefing for the command group.

Lee was in the conference room early, as usual, making sure everything was set up for the briefing. A Marine sergeant and a private knocked on the hatch, entered, and stood at attention.

"Ma'am," said the sergeant, "with your permission, we'd like to check the room."

Lee nodded, and they entered. The private pulled out some sort of handheld electronic device, while the sergeant looked around at everything. They walked around the room and conferred with each other a few times. When they had walked the entire area, the sergeant came back to her and said, "The room is clear, ma'am; sorry for any inconvenience."

Lee responded, "Thank you, Sergeant."

He paused a moment, and Lee figured he had something else to say. "Is there anything else, Sergeant?"

The sergeant shrugged awkwardly and said with a sheepish smile, "Ma'am, I hope you don't mind, but I was in the gym when you sparred with Jenkins."

Lee looked at him closely now, interested in this unusual approach by the normally reserved Marines. "And?" she said.

"Well, I just wanted to say that we all thought that was a well-deserved smacking you gave him."

"Oh?" said Lee.

"Yes, ma'am," replied the sergeant. "Truth is, Jenkins isn't really one of us."

"No? And yet he wears the Marine uniform."

The sergeant nodded his head and grimaced. "Yes, ma'am. He does. Jenkins is really a contractor who was being evacuated from Achilles Nine when the war broke out. He was in the Marines about twenty-five years ago but washed out of basic training. Technically, he still has a reserve appointment. When the reserves were activated, his nearest unit was the Marine detachment with the fleet, so that's where he reported, and that's where he is. He's not meeting the standards, as I think you can imagine."

"If he's not meeting the Marine standards, why hasn't he been expelled?"

The sergeant shook his head and said, "There's a stop-loss order out for the entire fleet, Marines and Navy. No one can leave the service as long as it's in place."

"So what do you do with him if you can't get rid of him?"

"Well, ma'am, that *has* been a problem. He's on Gunny's bad list, though as you can imagine, the list isn't called that." He smiled and blushed, and Lee had to smile in return. "Gunny Wasp has been training him night and day, but nothing really takes." Then he smiled and said, "But that whupping you gave him helped some. He's not as loud-mouthed anymore, and he has tried a little harder."

Lee said, "I'm glad I was of help."

"Actually, you were. And you did him another favor."

"How is that?" Lee asked.

"Well, Gunny heard the way he spoke to you before the match. If not for the whupping he got from you, Gunny would have thrown him in the brig for speaking to an officer like that, off-duty or not. I guess Gunny thought you sorted it out nicely, and so Jenkins just had to pull some extra shifts of cleanup duty."

"Well, thanks for the information," Lee said, checking her watch and seeing that the meeting was about to start.

"Yes, ma'am," said the sergeant. "Just wanted to let you know the Marines think you're the best. And we'd really like for you to come train us some time."

"I will," she said, checking his nametag, "Sergeant Frasier; send me a request, and I'll find time to come down and train."

"Ma'am," Frasier said, came to attention and saluted, and walked out with his private following him.

Inwardly, Lee smiled. She'd been hoping for a chance to get in and train with the Marines. Also, she thought about the irony of the security detail checking the room for listening devices and other hazards. Everyone thought they were doing it to protect the admiral; that was the official story. But the reality was that they were doing it to protect Raymond. Wherever he went, a Marine was somewhere nearby.

CHAPTER 20

MACRO-WAVE COLLAPSE

Chambers, Bowman, Lee, Davenport, and Baker sat around a large table in the one of the conference rooms. Raymond stood at the podium with a large viewscreen behind him. Lee, in her role as chief of staff, started off the meeting. "Admiral, the purpose of this meeting is for Warrant Officer Raymond to present the status of research and development toward combatting the enemy's macro-wave collapse capabilities."

Chambers nodded. "Go ahead."

Lee nodded to Raymond, who began, "Sir, to review, we believe the Others are able to insert and withdraw their recon vessels by use of a macro-wave collapse technology, or MWC as we've termed it. Our research tasks have been twofold. First, we want to be able to detect when the MWC is about to be used, and secondly, we want to be able to interfere with that process."

Raymond took a breath and continued, "On the first issue, we believe that the wave itself must be using substantial power, and therefore we should be able to detect it. As you know, there are four major forces in physics, and we assumed when we started that the MWC must be drawing upon and impacting one or more of these forces. These forces are the electromagnetic force, the strong and weak nuclear forces, and gravity."

Lee showed signs of impatience at Raymond's lecturing the admiral on basic physics, but Chambers seemed attentive and unperturbed by his style.

"In the past weeks," Raymond continued, "we have equipped our drones with devices designed to detect each of these forces. The strong and weak nuclear forces are only effective over very short distances, down to the atomic level. Nothing in theory indicates that these forces could be harnessed for MWC purposes, but since we want to be able to rule out possibilities, we have set up detectors to account for them.

"There's no real problem monitoring in the electromagnetic spectrum. Here we're talking photons like visible light, x-rays, microwaves, and infrared, ultraviolet, and gamma rays. Of course, we already scan for these types of energy, but to increase our chances of detection, we've increased the sensitivity down to the individual photon level."

Raymond paused again, shuffled his notes. Lee thought he really did look like a professor. She wished he would get to the point, though.

"Finally, we configured for gravity. The fleet already uses mass detectors to check for obstacles in our path, so we've increased the sensitivity to detect even the slightest variations. This was difficult, because although gravity is a very weak force, all particles that have mass both influence and are influenced by gravity. Thus, we needed to account for and screen out the effects of the vessels, nearby stars, even the galaxy as a whole. This should have been just about impossible, but Danner and his team came up with some ingenious shortcuts that made it workable. Basically, we can detect individual gravitons if we so choose. If things ever get back to normal, these guys will be in for a Nobel of their own."

Raymond paused, and everyone looked over at Danner, who was blushing furiously. He said haltingly, "It was a group effort; can't take any credit myself."

Bowman nodded his approval at Danner's effort to share the praise with his team and thought what a good choice Danner had been to lead them. Shoot, Danner wasn't even formally trained as a scientist; he was a historian and an engineer, per his degrees.

"So what did you find?" the admiral asked, showing a bit of impatience at last.

"Absolutely nothing," Raymond responded with a satisfied look. "We detected no change in the monitored areas corresponding to the arrival or departure of the Others' vessels."

"How does *that* help?" Lee asked, with a touch of harshness in her tone.

Making no reaction to her impatience, Raymond answered, "The advantage of no observed changes is that we now know that either the methods we were using aren't sensitive enough, or the enemy's using techniques that don't fall within known physics."

"I thought you said you got down to the single photon and graviton level. What's more sensitive than that?" Bowman asked.

"That's precisely right," Raymond said, as if speaking to a bright student. "But there's simply no way these vessels could appear or disappear without having any effect on the gravitational field." Raymond paused. It was clear he was in full professorial mode and wasn't going to be hurried.

"Please continue," Chambers said, with a look of resignation.

"Next we looked at field theory," said Raymond. "We'd been monitoring particles. But we know that particles are a convenient fiction. The reality is that space is made up of fields; particles are the manifestation of excited fields. So we modified the detection devices to monitor the underlying field values."

"And what did you find?" asked Lee, now with her cold face on. She was irritated that Raymond was showing off and wasting the admiral's time with these theatrics.

"We found a substantial effect on the Higgs field. You'll recall that the Higgs field gives mass to particles. It's the only known field to have a positive value in empty space. Particles that pass through the Higgs field, which is everywhere, receive mass. Particles that aren't affected by the Higgs field, like photons and neutrinos, have no mass and travel at *c*, the speed of light. Everything else—electrons, quarks, protons, neutrons—gain mass and therefore travel at less than *c*."

"Higgs?" asked Bowman.

"The field and the particle are named after Peter Higgs, a scientist who predicted the existence of the field that gives matter its mass. In fact, the breakthrough on this was made by a number of different scientists working independently over a period of about sixty years."

Despite the length of the lecture, the group was now interested. "So what did you find?" asked Bowman.

"The Higgs field is definitely fluctuating during the MWC," said Raymond. "Somehow, they've found a way to lower the value of the Higgs field. This allows objects that should have mass to have little or no mass."

"And this process allows them to move through space as a wave?" asked Bowman.

"Yes and no," said Raymond. "It does allow objects to present themselves as waves. But to say that these objects *move* is technically incorrect. Without the Higgs field, space doesn't really exist. Once the Higgs field value drops to zero, all points in the universe are co-located. The Others, or whoever they are, simply move from one point to another, but without the need to *travel*, so to speak."

"So where does that leave us?" asked Chambers.

"First, we can absolutely detect when the MWC is about to occur. Midshipman Danner and his team have been correctly predicting the arrival and departure of the recon vessels with above a 99 percent rate of accuracy for the last few days."

"How much warning do we have?" asked Bowman.

"We're down to about two minutes so far," said Raymond. "We've been refining the techniques and believe there's a theoretical limit of about ten minutes of advance warning. We will, of course, keep working on it until we reach the limit."

"And can we interfere with the MWC?" asked Chambers.

"Sir, in theory, the answer is a definitive yes. Our problem is one of finding an engineering solution. The people who developed the MWC had decades of time and enormous resources at their disposal."

"Are you saying we can't do it?" the admiral asked.

"We can do it, sir," responded Raymond. "We just need a little help."

"What do you need?"

"I need one of the vessels intact," said Raymond. "And for that, Captain Bowman takes over."

"Sir," Bowman began, "Warrant Officer Raymond told me some time ago that he would need one of the recon vessels in order to further develop the technology we need to counter this MWC capability. Since that time, the command team has been working on various options to capture one or more vessels. We started by asking Midshipman Danner to work up some data to help us time our operations."

Danner stood and reported, "We plotted the locations and timings of their movements and believe we can predict within two minutes the appearance of the recon vessels within an area defined by a sphere twenty kilometers in diameter."

Lee was happy that Danner, who was her immediate subordinate, at least knew how to give a succinct presentation. She imagined if Raymond were giving this brief, he would have tried to explain what a kilometer was.

Bowman said, "The plan for the capture of the vessels was developed by Lieutenant Commander Baker."

Bowman looked to Baker, who stood and said, "Sir, the plan is to take advantage of the gap between the departure of one shift and the arrival of the next. We know from Danner's analysis that there's an operational window of between two and five minutes when there are no recon vessels on station. We're making a tactical assumption that they're blind during that time, and we have a good idea of where they'll show up next."

"How does this help? The recon vessels will be well out of flight range."

"Sir, we'll have our craft conducting normal reconnaissance and training, poised to make a rush. Danner can give us a one-minute warning that the recon vessels are about to rotate out. Once they're gone, he can feed us the coordinates of the estimated point of reemergence. We'll put on the afterburners and get into position," said Baker.

"How will you engage?" asked the admiral.

"In three phases, sir. First is the movement to the point of engagement. Second is the use of a tractor beam to disable to target craft. Third ..."

"Hold on. How do you know the tractor beam will disable the MWC vessel?"

"We can't know for sure, sir," responded Raymond. "But a tractor beam will freeze any known electronics system. In any case, it's our best option until we get our hands on one of them and see what technology they're using."

Raymond looked a little bit uncomfortable, and the admiral picked up on it. "What's concerning you, Chief. Raymond?"

The physicist responded, "The risk is that the MWC mechanism isn't located in the vessels themselves. If it's located elsewhere, the tractor beam probably won't work."

"Okay, got it so far. What happens next?"

"That's where the Marines come in," said Bowman. "Captain Davenport?"

Davenport stood, but before he could speak, the admiral interrupted. "You're going to take an RAB team with you as part of the capture element?"

"Yes, sir," said Davenport. "The RAB vessel can be fitted with the appropriate propulsion system and upgraded with gravity stabilizers to protect the crew during the acceleration. In fact, we've already made those changes." Davenport paused a moment in case the admiral had another question and then continued, "Sir, we'll take one modified RAB with a crew and boarding team of twelve Marines. Once the target vessel is immobilized, the Marines will ram and board."

"What if the vessel self-detonates?" asked the admiral. "All other combatant vessels did that to avoid capture."

"The tractor beam will disable any electronic detonation system. If the pilot has a manual backup switch, we won't be able to stop that."

Chambers nodded. He knew the risks they were taking; he'd taken the same risks himself. "What's the risk of the detonation taking out your team?" he asked.

"Sir, I am unable to make an estimate of the risk," said Davenport. "If we're outside our RAB and close to or inside the target vessel during a detonation, we'll suffer casualties. However, it's likely that the pilot will use his manual detonation switch, if he has one, as soon as he realizes he's trapped. Since it will take us a few minutes to position ourselves and board her, we might still be inside our own vessel when it explodes. We would survive that scenario."

"What about other recon vessels in the vicinity?" asked Chambers. "We've seen up to five at one time in the past."

"In addition to the RAB," Baker said, "we'll have a total of six fighters and a command and control vessel. We should have the element of surprise."

"Abort criteria?" the admiral asked.

"Based on the criteria given to us by the wing commander," Baker nodded toward Bowman, "we will only abort if the mission cannot be accomplished. That means we abort if the target is destroyed, if the RAB is disabled or destroyed, or if the fighter escort is degraded to the point that it can no longer protect the RAB. Otherwise, the mission continues until it's accomplished."

"Who will command?" Chambers asked.

Bowman said, "I'll command the overall operation. Lieutenant Commander Baker will command the fighter escort, and Captain Davenport will command the Marines."

"Rehearsals?" the admiral asked.

"In order to maintain operational security, we've had to rehearse it in parts," Bowman said. "The only time we've come together is for simulations, and that's been done offline from the network."

And there was the elephant in the room that no one wanted to acknowledge. They couldn't commit anything visible to the network because they didn't know who the spy was or what access he or she might have.

Chambers was quiet for a few moments and then nodded as if to himself. "Okay, I approve. Go forward with the mission planning.

Here's my guidance: First, security is paramount. There will be no discussion of this operation outside this group. Mr. Danner, if you need to bring any of your team in on this, clear it with Commander Lee first. Second, I accept that although the risk of mission failure is moderate, the risk to the fleet is high. All my key leaders and half my special operations capability are going into harm's way at one go. I want you to review the plans and brief me on ways to mitigate the risk. Third, I want contingency plans drawn up."

Lee looked quizzically at the admiral. "Sir, do you mean in case of failure?"

"No," he said. "I mean in case of success. Losing an intact MWC vessel is a game changer for both sides of this conflict. They already know we have Dr. Raymond. If we also have an MWC-capable vessel, this fleet will become their highest priority. We need to anticipate what they might do and be ready for any contingency."

"Questions for the staff?" Lee asked the group. No one responded. "Questions for the admiral?"

When no one raised a hand, Lee turned to Chambers, who said, "Dismissed."

CHAPTER 21

LEE LEARNS SOMETHING

Lieutenant Commander Lee did get the invitation she had been hoping to receive. It came not by message format, but in person. Gunnery Sergeant Wasp knocked on her bulkhead door and formally asked permission to speak with the chief of staff. The Marines were always so formal. She understood that because it was also the manner used in most martial arts; the external discipline reinforced the internal discipline. Her father had taught her when she was about twelve years old, "Once you have mastered yourself, the world opens up; you have true freedom."

"Enter," she called. Wasp came in, stood at attention, and said, "Gunnery Sergeant Wasp, Achilles Marine Commando Unit, ma'am."

"At ease. How can I help you, Gunny?"

"Ma'am, the Marine Commando Unit would like to invite you to train with us in our daily martial arts session tomorrow at 0500 hours."

"I accept your invitation; thank you, Gunny Wasp," she replied, deadpan.

Wasp snapped to attention, saluted, and departed. Lee smiled to herself. She had been hoping this invitation would come and was pleased that the Marines had thought enough of her to send someone senior to make the invitation in person.

Lee arrived at the Marine training room at 0454 the next morning. Unsurprisingly, a dozen or so Marines were already present, standing in formation. Wasp stood in front, and when he saw her enter, he brought the Marines to attention and faced away from them. Lee was puzzled. Wasp had just put the unit in position to receive a senior officer, and she couldn't see anyone else in the room. *Shoot,* she thought, *he's expecting me to take the formation. Oh, well, nothing else I can do.*

Lee strode out in front of the formation and stood in front of Wasp. He saluted her, held the salute, and said, "Ma'am, Marine Commando detachment instructor group is present for training."

So he had brought his own instructors together. *This should be interesting,* she reflected.

"Post," she said, returning the salute. It was a formal command when assuming leadership of a formation. She thought she saw Wasp smile just a bit. He was clearly satisfied and maybe a bit relieved that she would know the correct command used by the Marines in such a situation. He immediately moved to her left side, positioned himself a half-step to her rear, and faced the formation.

Although Lee had not expected to take over the training and was not quite sure what Wasp had expected, she knew from long experience that once in a leadership position, it was imperative to take command. The old saying was, "Lead, follow, or get out of the way." Now was the time to lead.

Using her best parade ground voice, she said crisply, "Extend to the left, march!" The Marines immediately spread out to their left, raising their arms and stopping when the fingertips were just touching. "Arms downward, move!" They snapped their arms down as one being. "Left face! Extend to the left, march!"

She continued with the commands until the unit was spread out in the correct formation for conducting exercises. She then continued with the traditional Marine warm-up exercises, giving the commands precisely and in accordance with Marine training regulations. The Navy had a slightly different set of exercises and commands for physical training. Not many naval officers would know the Marine version, but Lee had spent a summer at the academy going through the Marine Officer Candidate Program. This allowed middies who had completed it to select the Marine Corps upon graduation. Although Lee had decided to go with the Navy, she liked the Marine way of doing business. And though the Marines would never show emotion in formal training like this, she sensed they were responding well to having a squid who knew what she was doing. They had shown her the respect of inviting her to take the formation, and she was responding in kind by using commands they were familiar with.

When she had completed the set of training prescribed by the Marine training manual, she brought the formation back to attention and said, "Gunnery Sergeant, post!" This brought Wasp back to his initial position facing her. She said, "Please take the formation through the training. I will follow in the rear." They exchanged salutes, and she moved to stand behind the formation, the traditional position for an officer if a subordinate was leading.

Wasp then took them through a series of stances, punches, blocks, and kicks. Lee watched closely and adapted her own techniques to those being used by the Marines. She was intrigued. The slight variations the Marines were using were very similar to an ancient martial art form that, as far as she knew, was no longer being practiced on Earth. Her father had shown her similar techniques many years ago. He told her these techniques had been used by the Hwa Rang, a long-forgotten caste of warriors who had trained and studied together to protect their kingdom. She was impressed. She made a note to ask Wasp if he knew the lineage of this art form.

After about thirty minutes, Wasp had them pair up. Sergeant Frasier came over to her as her partner.

She smiled and said, "Good to see you again," but he was very earnest and serious.

Clearly, he was on the hook to make good in front of an important visitor. Lee understood. His somewhat informal invitation to her had probably not been fully in line with Marine protocol. She surmised that Wasp had not been pleased to learn of it, thus the much more formal invitation and reception she had been given.

Wasp took them through the basics of grappling, joint locks, throws, and holds. She could see the Marine penchant for power over movement and subtlety. In the type of combat they trained for, speed and overwhelming power were paramount.

Frasier turned out to be a competent and enthusiastic training partner. He didn't hold back because she was a woman or an officer. At the same time, he was clearly trying to both learn and assist her to learn the techniques used. Although he was average size and build, she could sense he was stronger than he looked. She suspected that this was because of the years of training with heavy protective armor, possibly under high-G. Lee guessed all the Marines had this trait.

Lee noticed a female marine, paired off with a male counterpart who was almost twice her size. She was a tough-looking woman with a shaved head, angular features, and rope-like, muscular arms. She was confident and moved quickly through the moves, easily throwing her sparring partner when the routine called for it. Lee made a mental note to introduce herself later.

After about thirty minutes of this, Wasp came over to Lee and politely asked if she would take over the training and demonstrate her own techniques to the Marines. Lee agreed and moved to the front of the formation. She had them form a semicircle around her and had Sergeant Frasier pair off with her as her demonstrator.

"Sergeant Frasier," Lee said. "Please attack using hand-foot combination number three." This was the standard move that the Marines had been practicing on the last few minutes of training. The Marines trained to meet the strikes squarely head on—block, parry, strike, and takedown.

As Frasier came at her, she met the attack exactly as the Marines had been taught to do. "That is a perfectly good way to meet that attack," she said to the group. "Now let's do it step-by-step."

Frasier came at her again, still at speed, but pausing between discrete attacks. On the second strike, she said, "Stop. Look where I am and where Sergeant Frasier is. What's wrong?"

The Marines watched closely, and she could see the realization come into their faces. One of them spoke up. "Ma'am, you are in a set position, both hands engaged in blocking. Your entire left side is open, and Sergeant Frasier has both his hands and one leg free to attack."

"Exactly right," she said. "Now let's do that again, this time full speed."

She nodded at Frasier, and he came again with the same attack, this time without pausing between movements. At the point of the second strike, instead of moving to meet the attack head on, as the Marines had been doing, she spun away just slightly, allowing his momentum to aid her movement as he continued forward, slightly off balance. She brought her elbow up to the back of his head, which accelerated his forward movement; he sprawled forward on the mat, deftly rolled, and was up on his feet in a guarding position. She nodded to him and faced the group.

"Sergeant Frasier is much stronger than me. If I face a stronger opponent, I need to find an advantage based on position or movement. In my martial art, this is called the Water Wheel. You spin away from the power of a river, but use that power to your advantage.

"Face your partners. Let's try it together."

The Marines jumped into the new techniques, though it didn't come easily to them. Some had been training for years on a different, more direct approach. Learning to slip away from an attack just wasn't in their mind-set for some of them. But Lee was persistent, even relentless. She had them do it again and again. Slowly, they all seemed to catch on, some better than others. At the end, she brought them up in pairs and had them demonstrate for the group. Nothing like a little individual attention in front of a group of peers to focus one's attention.

An hour later, Wasp politely asked to take back the training session, brought the group to formation, and asked Lee, as a courtesy, to formally dismiss the group.

After doing so, Lee walked over to the woman Marine, who came to attention, and Lee said, "As you were." The woman relaxed and looked at Lee, showing nothing in her face. Lee understood the woman's reserve. Women in the Marines were rare, and rarer still in the commando units, which were considered the elite of an already elite force. If she were believed to be speaking to a senior Naval officer, another woman no less, other Marines might consider it seeking favor, a kiss of death in such a unit.

Lee said, "Your name?"

"Private Jessie Johnson, ma'am."

"I saw you using a certain type of throw. Was that tomoe nage?"

"Yes, ma'am. I trained in jujitsu before joining the Corps."

"I've never seen it done the way you did it. Can you show me?"

Johnson simply bowed quickly to indicate she was ready, and Lee launched into a grappling move. Johnson was wicked fast. She grabbed Lee by her shirt and sleeve and then seemed to sit down, pulling Lee down with her and then used her foot to launch Lee over her head. As Lee was airborne, Johnson pivoted around in a seated position and pulled Lee closer, causing Lee to slam on her back on the mat.

Lee was pleased. It was a good move, and although she had studied the grappling arts, she had never seen anything like what Johnson had just done. Clearly, Johnson was an accomplished martial artist.

They both scrambled up to face each other. Lee bowed, and Johnson returned the courtesy.

Lee said, "Thank you." Better to keep it formal, she thought, as she noted the other Marines had stopped to watch.

Johnson saluted and moved toward the exit with the other marines.

Wasp came over to her and said, "Thank you, ma'am, for taking the time to train with us."

"Thank you for inviting me. The pleasure and honor were mine, Gunny."

Wasp started to speak, paused a millisecond, and looked a bit uncertain; very unlike a Marine, thought Lee. "Yes?" she asked.

"Um, I wondered, ma'am," he said slowly, "if you'd like to have coffee with me at the all-ranks' mess."

Lee had been taught, both as a woman and a martial artist, never to show the surprise she felt at such a moment. At the same time, she realized she was delighted and flattered. There was no longer any rule that forbade enlisted ranks and officers from social engagements, as long as there was no perception of favoritism, undue pressure, or public displays of affection. Fleet Admiral Robertson's wife had been a master chief petty officer when they were first married. She had retired after some thirty years of service, and no stigma had been attached to that relationship. Lee recalled with a twinge of sadness that they had both been killed in the initial attack. Maybe that was the best way for a warrior couple to go out.

Lee smiled brightly and said, "I'd like that. I should be free after third watch. See you then."

CHAPTER 22

COFFEE AND A KISS

Mei-Ling Lee entered the all-ranks' club a few minutes after third watch ended. Wasp was there at the bar, which was pretty much empty. A few couples were scattered around at the tables, and one fairly drunken sailor was talking a bit loudly to the bartender. Wasp saw her and waved. He picked up two cups and motioned her over to a table away from the other patrons.

When they sat down, he said, "Ma'am, I just wanted to thank you again for training with us today. You were a hit; the Marines really enjoyed it. The Navy has never stood so tall in their eyes." This last was said with a twinkling smile she had not seen on him before.

"If this is a date, you'd better stop calling me 'ma'am,'" she said with a smile. "My name is Mei-Ling, and yours is Theodorus. I know that because the chief of staff knows everything."

"Okay, then, Mei-Ling," he said. "I have a confession to make."

"That you've never been out with an officer before?" she said, still smiling.

He blushed. She thought it was the most charming thing she'd ever seen a man do. "Actually, I've been in the Corps for ten years, and I've never been on any date before."

The drunk sailor from the bar looked over their way and said loudly, "Well, looky here, an officer and a grunt. How charmin'. I wonder if I can get me some of that."

The bartender put his hand on the drunk's forearm and spoke quietly to him, but the drunk shook it off. He stood up, staggered a bit, and began to walk over to them.

"This should be fun," Lee said.

Wasp rolled his eyes and muttered, "It's always something."

The drunk came over, leaned in toward them, and slurred something about protocol and getting a room. Wasp stood up slowly. He was tall and fit, and Lee had the thought that no sober person would provoke such man without cause. Wasp raised his hand palms outward in a peaceful gesture and said, "Just a friendly chat over coffee. Can I buy you one too?"

"You think I need a cup of coffee, jarhead?" said the drunk loudly, and he swung a fist wildly.

Wasp easily slipped the punch, put the drunk in hug of sorts, and very smoothly applied a pressure point to his neck. The drunk slumped into Wasp's arms as if fast asleep. Then gunny lowered him to the floor gently and laid him on his back.

He looked up at the bartender and said, "Jack, I think this sailor has had one too many. Can you get the provost patrol to give him an escort back to his barracks?"

"Sure thing, Gunny," the man said. "And thanks for handling that."

Wasp sat back down.

Lee said with a smile, "That was smooth. Does that happen often?"

"Often enough. Someone's always looking to make a reputation with a Marine."

"And does it always end so peacefully?"

"Actually, yes. Most of the time," he admitted. "Our code doesn't encourage bar fights. Training is for combat, not for brawls with shipmates, no matter how obnoxious."

An hour later, he walked her to her quarters. She stopped, faced him, and looked up.

He said very softly, "Good night, Mei Ling," then bent down, softly kissed her forehead, and left her.

That night, she went to sleep in her quarters alone, but with a smile on her face. As she drifted off, she murmured, "And that was *my* first kiss, Gunny."

CHAPTER 23

THE SNATCH TEAM

Despite her years of training, both in the Navy and in the martial arts, Lee could feel the tension in her back. The Snatch Team, as they called themselves—only somewhat tongue-in-cheek—consisted of everyone in the know about the coming attempt to capture an MWC vessel intact. They had been rehearsing for weeks now, each sub-element training separately and offline from any central computer system to keep the mole from finding out about the operation.

Lee had been designated the battle captain in charge of the operations room. She had a central station that allowed her to sit in front of a low bank of computers and screens. Over the screens, she could see the other stations under her command: Communications, Navigation, Battle Tracking, and Weapons. At each of these stations sat two specialists, side by side. This arrangement was in part to divide up the tasks when the workload got heavy, but it was also to ensure redundancy in case one of the operators was injured.

They had briefed the plans to Admiral Chambers several times, and each time he had asked for options and details they hadn't thought of, so they had to go back and rework the plan. In the end, the plan for the snatch had remained pretty much as it had been briefed to Chambers earlier: Danner would predict the time of change-out of the enemy vessels and, within a twenty-kilometer sphere, the location of the reemergence of the next batch of recon craft. In the space of time between the disappearance of one shift and the reappearance of the next, the RAB and its fighter escort would rush to the estimated coordinates. Once the MWC craft were located, the fighter escort, under Baker, would lock one of the craft with a tractor beam while his fighters engaged the remaining vessels. The RAB, under command of Captain Davenport, would ram and board in an effort to capture the locked MWC vessel.

The contingency plan that Chambers had ordered drawn up was quite simple. The fleet needed to be fully combat ready, and it needed to be able to jump. As Lee had figured out a month ago, Chambers had been intentionally slowing the progress on achieving fleetwide jump capability. He wanted the fleet to be ready for combat *before* they jumped. As such, the fleet had been moving at sub-light speed for three months now. Once the plan for the snatch was approved, Chambers issued a revised work-priorities order that put propulsion at the top of the list.

Two days prior, all thirteen vessels had reached jump status. The fleet was now combat ready, and there was no small amount of speculation in the various messes about what the fleet would do now. Would they return to a major naval base? Go on offensive operations? Only the admiral knew, and he wasn't saying.

At the same time, the fleet had upped the pace of its training regimen. The Marines had continued to refine their RAB techniques, the aerospace squadrons were out almost constantly rehearsing tactics, while the various vessels in the fleet had practiced repelling boarders and firing their proximity artillery. Most of the sailors were working double shifts; they were exhausted, and yet the sense of combined purpose had a positive effect on morale. People came off their shifts and dropped into their bunks for whatever sleep they could grab before the next drill pulled them out again. Lee knew that part of this effort was to mask the preparations for the snatch. But she also knew that even without the upcoming covert mission, the pace of preparations would have happened anyway. Chambers was very serious about combat readiness.

The fleet personnel were, in general, comfortable with Chambers as the commanding admiral. He was far more visible and accessible than Admiral Robertson had ever been. He tended to show up at odd times and odd places. He clearly cared about the common sailor, checking in on mess halls, latrines, billets, and maintenance bays. Commanders and petty officers learned that they needed to check on their people regularly, to make sure they were taken care of and properly prepared.

Most of the time, he was friendly and supportive. But not always. He would not hesitate to show his displeasure, as he had on several occasions. To Lee, the admiral's priorities were taking care of sailors and readiness for combat. On this, he was relentless and uncompromising. No one was spared his wrath when he found out some sailor had not been properly fed or trained, or that a unit's equipment had not been maintained—or God forbid, a supervisor had turned in an inflated report. He had twice relieved section heads and once a ship's commanding officer. Upon the latter event, Chambers had called Commodore Vance in for what was clearly a dressing-down. Lee, in the outer office, had heard Chambers say, "Why was it my job to find out one of your ship's captains wasn't doing *his* job?"

She was brought out of her reverie by a familiar voice. "Estimated rotation in seven minutes," Midshipman Danner said from his station.

Now it begins, she thought. "Roger that." Turning to the command net, she broadcast, "Wing Six, do you copy?" Wing Six was Bowman's call sign as the Achilles' wing commander.

"Roger," responded Bowman. "Wing Five, Marine Six, did you copy?"

"Marine Six, copied," responded Davenport. He was leading the Marine Commandos on the snatch and was deployed on the RAB.

"Wing Five, copied," Baker responded in his calm Southern drawl. He was commanding the fighter component.

"Stand by for coordinates," said Lee. The plan now called for Danner to calculate the location for the reemergence of the next shift of MWC vessels, something he wouldn't be able to do until the current batch had rotated out.

The next few minutes were agony for Lee. She had nothing to do but wait. She watched on the forward viewscreen the activity in the vicinity of the fleet. There were lots of vessels out conducting training activities, just as there had been for the last several weeks. Any MWC vessels watching this would see nothing unusual.

"Vessels out!" snapped Danner. This was the notification that the MWC vessels had disappeared. Now it was a race. Danner needed to get those new coordinates; every second mattered. "Got it," he said after completing his calculations. "Coordinates transmitting now."

No one responded to the announcement on the net, but Lee saw the fighter escort, the RAB, and Bowman's command ship blast their afterburners en route to the intercept. "Shut the fleet down," she ordered.

Instantly, the fleet went dark. Except for Lee's operations center, the drone net, and the vessels already training, almost everything was shut down. Only life support, defensive weapons, and propulsion systems were operating. This was the plan to both protect the snatch operation and to hopefully to catch the mole. Danner and Raymond had come up with it after Chambers had repeatedly sent them back to the drawing board. He had said almost a month ago, "As soon as the snatch is underway, the whole fleet will see it on sensors."

Danner had replied, "Well, we could shut down everything, so they can't see what's happening."

"Yes," Raymond said. He thought for a bit but didn't say anything for a moment. Then: "But by itself, that doesn't solve the problem. The mole will know something is up and will send out some sort of warning."

"Is that such a bad thing?" asked Chambers.

"Sir?" responded Danner.

"If the mole is going to send a warning, let him do that. Let's be ready for it."

So that's what they did. Raymond, Danner, and the intelligence team had devised a master program to control all fleetwide systems. Lee had waited for the operation to start before ordering it activated.

Everyone in the fleet would see it start. Not everyone would know why certain vessels had broken off their training missions to rush toward some unknown spot, but the mole would know. The mole would know the MWC craft were compromised and would likely surmise that his or her presence was also known (or least suspected). By shutting down all normal means of communication, the mole would be forced to send out a warning message any way possible.

That was exactly what the admiral and his team were counting on.

"Counterintelligence sensors are on line," said one of Danner's team, the heavy kid with acne. "If any message is sent out now, we'll capture it and track it back to its source."

The drone net had been re-tasked to serve as a sensor net to track messages coming from the fleet.

Chambers wasn't in the command center. He was on the *Apache*, one of the hydroponic vessels, inspecting the farming operation in accordance with a schedule Lee had made up and published weeks ago. This was mostly for deception. If the mole was tracking Chambers' movements, he wouldn't suspect that anything substantial would happen while Chambers was away from the command ship.

"But sir," Bowman had protested. "You'll be out of position to command the operation."

"That's correct. I've already approved your command of the operation. My role in this is to make sure the mole is surprised. We want him to panic and use an emergency channel to warn his employers. Then we'll nab him."

CHAPTER 24

BOWMAN IN THE REAR

Captain Stephen Bowman, commanding officer of the Achilles Expeditionary Aerospace Wing, was currently undergoing maximum acceleration in an FA-300 modified to serve as a command and control vessel on the MWC snatch operation. It was his first time on an operation where he was commanding several elements, and he wasn't especially happy. The problem was that he wasn't up front, in the action.

In theory, the fact that the commander was removed from the immediate engagement with the enemy ought to have allowed him to better see the whole picture and make better, more informed decisions. But he didn't like it. Part of his discomfort came from the fact that he wasn't sharing the same risk as Baker and the escort team. But if he was honest, he was mostly uncomfortable because he liked being in the action. That was where he felt he could make his best decisions.

The command version of the FA-300 was a two-seater; in the seat next to Bowman sat Master Warrant Officer Matthias Nemeth.

Nemeth had almost forty years of flight experience, and Bowman knew he'd done a credible job as commander in chief for aerospace during the December attack on the flotilla. Not since flight school, almost thirteen years ago, had Bowman flown with a copilot. They had, of course, rehearsed and flown together many times in the past weeks, but Bowman still wasn't comfortable. As for Nemeth, he didn't show much of what he was feeling, and technically, Nemeth was the pilot, not Bowman. As the commander of the entire operation, Bowman was free to command.

"Sixty seconds to target," Nemeth reported.

"Roger, sixty seconds out." Bowman was busy tracking the combined fighter/RAB element well forward of his craft. He watched the fighters spread out to cover the entire area of the expected MWC appearance, while the RAB stayed on course for the center of the coordinates. As planned, the RAB had been modified for high acceleration.

"Wing Six, this is Ops base," Danner said over the command net. "We have detected an encrypted narrow-beam burst transmission from the fleet."

"Roger that. Go get 'em," Bowman replied.

"Marines are on their way now," Danner said. "Be aware the counterintel drones may not have been able to intercept and block the transmission. We're estimating a 50 percent chance you are compromised."

Okay, thought Bowman. *That wasn't supposed to happen.* The drones were supposed to detect and jam any unauthorized signal coming out of the fleet. "Wing Six, Wing Five," came Baker's calm voice over the net. "I copied last from Ops. Any further guidance on execution?"

And there it was. This was what Bowman was getting paid to do. Baker was asking if Bowman wanted to alter the mission or abort, considering the information that the mission—which depended mostly on surprise—might have been compromised. "Stand by," Bowman said. He looked over at Nemeth. Although Nemeth was here to be the expert pilot, not an operations officer, Bowman wanted his advice.

Without hurry or inflection, Nemeth said, "If the mission is compromised, what is the enemy's most likely course of action?"

Bowman thought for a moment and said, "They'll abort the next rotation. We just won't see them."

Nemeth prompted, "And if they know about the snatch and still come through, what does that tell you?"

"That they want a fight," Bowman said fiercely.

Nemeth smiled a wicked smile and said, "And what do *you* want, sir?"

"Wing Five, this is Wing Six," Bowman said over the tac-net. "Charley Mike." (Charley Mike was the universal shorthand for "continue the mission.")

"I copy. Charley Mike," responded Baker.

"Deceleration in five, four, three, two, one," Nemeth announced shortly afterward.

Bowman felt the afterburners shut off and the retro-rockets kick in. Despite the inertial dampers, he felt the craft slow, matching what his display told him. Must've been one hell of a decel to override the dampers even that much. He saw the fighter escort spread out exactly as planned. The RAB, on the other hand, had burned its jets a millisecond too long and was a kilometer forward of where it should have been. Bowman was about to mention it to Baker when he saw the fighter escort begin to adjust their formation to take the RAB's position into account. He nodded in appreciation of Baker's efficiency. The man knew his job.

"We have MWC rotation in thirty seconds, and they're coming in behind you, Captain Bowman; I'm sending revised coordinates to you now," Danner said from the Ops Center. His voice was strained, and Bowman could guess why. Danner was supposed to have given up to a minute's warning for the next MWC rotation. The fact that they were going to appear behind his current location in half that time meant the initial estimate was off by a wide margin.

"Repositioning," Baker said. Bowman watched as the fighter escort fired their afterburners to reposition for the new expected location. *Shoot*, thought Bowman. The RAB still sat where it had been. It had only been fueled for the one long burn to get it into position. It could maneuver locally under normal engine thrust, but that was pretty slow, considering the distance required and the time available.

"RAB Six, Wing Six," Bowman said. "Status?"

Davenport came back immediately: "Wing Six, RAB Six. We had an inertial damper malfunction during acceleration. I have two Marines down." There was a pause, then, "I have propulsion, navigation, and weapons. We are a go here."

"Roger," Bowman said. "Come about, make best speed toward revised coordinates."

"Wilco," responded Davenport.

Bowman tried to imagine what that had been like. The RAB would have lost some of its ability to dampen the effect of the acceleration and deceleration, meaning that the resulting G-forces had been very high, probably in the tens of Gs; strong enough to incapacitate, maybe kill, two of the twelve Marines aboard. Davenport had stuck with the burn despite what must have been agony. In the end, he had missed the burn shutoff and decel by only a fraction of second. The Marines were a sturdy lot.

"Chief," Bowman said to Nemeth, "let's hang back and cover the RAB."

"On it, sir." Nemeth brought the command ship around and headed for the RAB.

Just then, Danner broke in on the command net and reported, in an excited voice, "Multiple incoming MWC, your vicinity!" Bowman could hear shouting and what sounded like gunfire in the background. What the hell was going on?

CHAPTER 25

WHAT THE HELL
IS GOING ON?

From her command station on the HC *Centurion*, Mei-Ling Lee watched the snatch team approach the coordinates Danner had provided for the reemergence of the next rotation of MWC craft. The fighters spread out to cover as much of the twenty-kilometer sphere as possible. The RAB kept straight on a bit longer than it should have, and Bowman's command vessel stayed out of the immediate area of expected engagement.

She knew Bowman hated hanging back, but it was the right thing to do. One of the basic principles of combat was that the commander went wherever he or she could best perform the functions of command. That position might be forward, if for instance his example was needed to inspire those in a desperate fight. But in most situations, as with this one, he needed to be where he could see everything and remain free of the engagement himself to make the difficult decisions, should they be needed.

Danner said excitedly, "Ma'am, we have a tight-beam transmission from within the fleet."

That was expected. The planning team knew that the mole would try to get a warning out. "Send the Marine warrant team to its origin, and take everyone there into custody," Lee ordered. A warrant team was a military unit acting under the legal authority, or warrant, of the commanding admiral to detain or otherwise engage a criminal person or element. Gunnery Sergeant Wasp had been detailed with a squad of Marines to move on the mole the instant any unauthorized communication was detected on the *Centurion,* and similar teams were scattered throughout the fleet.

Just then, several things happened in quick succession.

"On it," Danner said. Then he reported crisply, "The communication originates from this vessel, Deck Nine, Compartment 22B. The Marines have been notified and are moving."

One of the technicians spoke up from his console. "Sir, we have a system failure on Drone 23. The message may have gotten through. I'm estimating a 50 percent chance."

Another spoke up, distress clear in his voice. "I'm reading multiple MWC vessels about to materialize near the snatch team, sir!"

Lee was about to have Danner warn Bowman of the new threat when they all felt an explosion outside the command center, followed immediately by gunfire. "Command, this is Provost Six," came an urgent voice over one of the internal nets. "We are under fire. I repeat, we are under fire. Four of my people are down. We are returning fire."

Provost Six was the petty officer commanding the guard force protecting the command center. His team had been placed outside the closed hatch because of the security precautions in place. Obviously, somebody was trying to breach the hatch and attack the command center.

She had no idea how anyone could have boarded the vessel without being detected. Or had they? How deep did this conspiracy go?

Lee heard Danner warn Bowman. The captain would have to handle his part of the operation without help from the command center, it seemed. She then heard Gunny Wasp's voice on the shipwide tac-net. Wasp, as the commander of the warrant team, should have located and detained or engaged the mole by now.

"Command, Warrant Six," Wasp said, his voice oddly calm. "We are under ambush on Deck Nine, Passageway Echo. One casualty; we should have this cleared in few moments."

"Warrant Six, Command Six," Lee said, struggling to keep her voice calm as well. "The command center is under attack. The provost element has suffered casualties."

"Roger," Wasp said without any indication of alarm or stress. "The warrant team is breaking off and will respond."

Though she hadn't ordered him to break off his engagement and come to her aid, she knew that was the correct decision. The command center needed to be protected at all costs. A tiny part of her mind wondered whether he was doing that because of her, or because his duty demanded it. Perhaps both. No time to think about that.

"I have reports of shots fired on the AS *Apache*," one of the technicians said from his station.

Lee realized that whoever was doing this was going after Admiral Chambers on the agronomy ship. Nothing she could do about that now, but ... "Open the weapons locker," she ordered. "Stand by to repel boarders."

In moments, the entire command team was armed. One sailor each remained at the consoles, while the others took up defensive positions facing the hatch. Lee told Danner to stay with the techs, to support the snatch team.

She could hear the fighting intensity increase outside the hatch and knew with certainty the provost guard was fighting to the last to protect the operations center. Tears stung her eyes as she thought of their valor. She swore to herself that they would not have died in vain. She knew the cold face had taken over her countenance, and she felt a rage steadily building toward the enemy she was about to face.

The fighting outside the hatch came to an abrupt halt, which Lee knew meant that the last of the provost team had fallen. "Brace yourselves," she ordered.

The defenders tensed and looked away from the hatch to protect their vision from the expected blast. When the hatch blew open, armed men in black battle gear and masks covering the lower halves of their faces burst into the ops room.

"Open fire!" Lee shouted.

Instantly, the dozen or so defenders fired into the mass of attackers. The first wave went down, and Lee was surprised to see more dark-clad attackers push through the narrow opening. She realized the provost guard had been heavily overmatched and revised upward her estimate of their valor, which was already quite high.

Again, this time without the need for her order, the defenders fired into the assaulting wave of attackers with their laser and low-velocity frangible-slug weapons. She aimed at one of the enemy and shot him through the throat, where she knew the armor offered the least protection. He went down immediately, grasping for his neck as he fell, but not before he dropped a grenade that rolled toward her defensive line.

"Grenade!" she yelled. She ducked down and immediately felt the blast wave.

She couldn't recall having heard the blast, but she could no longer hear the battle, just a constant ringing in her ears. As she rose to fire again, she saw the sailor who had been standing next to her, the kid with the acne, lying dead on the floor with a massive wound to his face and head.

She felt the battle rage overwhelm her. It was a cold, dark feeling, deeper than hatred, fear, or anger. "Advance!" she shouted.

She moved forward, firing for effect, her shots accurate and deadly. She could feel the remaining defenders advance on either side of her. Their volume of fire increased as they closed the distance to their enemies. She saw the black-clad adversaries falter, and a moment later, she was amongst them.

It was close combat now. They couldn't easily use their firearms because of the friendly-fire risk. Lee slammed the butt of her carbine hard under the chin of a man who was raising his weapon to shoot her in the chest. She felt the crunch of bone in his face as his head snapped back, and he fell away from her. Again and again, she struck out with punches, kicks, open-hand strikes, elbows, and knees.

For a moment, she thought they had won. None of the original attackers remained standing. But then another wave of them burst through the gaping hole that had been the hatch to the command bridge. All her team had been fighting with their hands and so were facing the new threat unarmed. *Okay*, she thought. *This was death, but at least it came with honor.*

She prepared to launch herself in one last, futile attack. But before she could move, a dozen Marines burst in behind the attackers, with Gunnery Sergeant Wasp in the lead—and dear God, they were fast, moving and shooting with an ease born of long practice. The black-clad assailants turned to face the new threat, but none of them even got a chance to fire a shot. The Marines were so confident, so accurate, and though her team of defenders were intermixed with the enemy and therefore in the line of fire of the Marines, none of them were shot. The Marines were hitting every target they aimed at, sometime inches from a shipmate.

It was over in seconds.

"Alpha team, on perimeter!" Wasp shouted. "Bravo team, secure the prisoners. Charlie team, tend to casualties." Instantly, the Marines moved to their various tasks. Lee was flooded with a relief she didn't know she could feel.

Wasp came to her and said, "Sorry for the delay, ma'am. We had to fight through." Then with a tiniest of smiles and a wink, he said, "What are your orders?"

Lee was astonished that Wasp could find humor in the middle of disaster. She realized this was the Marine way, or at least it was his way. Years of training and selection had bred him for combat. This was his place in the universe, and he knew it. And now, she knew it as well.

Lee steeled herself and said, "Once you're satisfied that the command center is secure, go get that mole."

"Already underway, ma'am," he said. "We held a reserve. After the ambush, I called them forward and sent them after the source of the transmission. There was no one there. The transmitter had been set up in one of the portal bays and triggered remotely. We have a forensic team down there now to see if we can trace the source."

"We have reports of fighting on the *Apache*. Anything we can do to help the admiral?"

"No, ma'am," Wasp said, "and no need, I expect. Anyone going after Admiral Chambers is about to have a very bad day."

Lee surveyed the operations room. Half the defenders were wounded or dead. The Marines were placing tourniquets and starting IVs on the wounded. She suddenly thought of something.

She turned to Wasp and said simply, "Find Raymond."

CHAPTER 26

NO PLAN SURVIVES CONTACT WITH THE ENEMY

On board the RAB, Davenport was struggling to deal with the situation. That long burn without the fully functioning inertial damper had been an eternity of agony. His copilot had lost consciousness, and he could hear the Marines to his rear struggling for breath, groaning, and vomiting. But he knew he couldn't cut the burn short. The RAB was the only element of the snatch team that couldn't be replaced. He took the controls manually, not trusting the onboard computer to time the burn. Something had gone wrong with the computer, or else they would have had warning of a malfunction.

Without a doubt, it was the hardest thing he had ever done. The pain was excruciating, and his vision narrowed to a tunnel view as the G-forces pushed the blood away from his brain. And then there were his Marines. His responsibility for their welfare was overmatched only by his duty to the mission. He knew he was doing the right thing by pushing ahead, but still, knowing they were suffering, maybe dying, was a torment. His copilot, Corporal Jennings, soon went into convulsions. Davenport cut Jennings' controls so his spasms wouldn't interfere with the flight.

He timed the burn cutoff and deceleration the best he could but saw immediately that he'd overshot the target point. He was a kilometer forward of the rest of the vessels in the snatch team. His first action was to check the status of his team and the RAB vessel. Not trusting the computer, he manually checked the individual system routines, even though that took a few seconds longer.

He spoke into the ship's intercom systems. "Marines, status check."

"Fire Team One, team leader is down, unresponsive. Weapons, ammo, and oxygen are all good."

"Fire Team Two, all good here."

Davenport checked the systems display and saw that the vessel itself was sound, or at least nothing was showing a malfunction. He knew not to trust that, but he had no option but to continue with the mission.

Bowman came on the net and asked for his status.

Davenport responded, "Wing Six, this is RAB Six. We had an inertial damper malfunction during acceleration. I have two Marines down." There was a pause as he rechecked his systems display, then, "I have propulsion, navigation, and weapons. We are a go here."

"Roger," Bowman said. "Come about, make best speed toward revised coordinates."

"Wilco," Davenport responded.

He manually brought the RAB around. Luckily, he had hundreds of hours of practice flying manually. It was the Marine way to plan for every contingency. Even so, it was difficult and frustratingly slow. He had to find a point in the starfield on which to orient and then manually control thrusters and stabilizers. He realized there was no way he was going to be able to do this and control the boarding team too.

"Sergeant Wilcox, I need a replacement copilot for Jennings."

"Roger," responded Wilcox. "Sending you Fredrick."

Corporal Fredrick came forward into the tight space of the RAB cockpit and, without ceremony, unsnapped and dragged Jennings' body out of his chair and took his place. This was their way. The Marines would fight the battle now and mourn their losses later.

Danner's voice came over the command net: "RAB One, multiple incoming MWC your vicinity."

Davenport spoke into his intercom. "Marines, clear for action."

Immediately, the Marines in the cabin unbuckled from their seats and began to check weapons and armor. The side hatch blew open, and the Marines jumped into the void one at a time, their tethers and jet packs propelling them toward the upper deck.

"Fredrick, you have the controls," said Davenport. "Keep us on course for the designated coordinates."

"Roger," responded his copilot.

Davenport concentrated on the tactical situation. He could see that Bowman in the command ship had dropped back to cover the RAB. He also saw on his tactical display that the rest of the squadron under Baker's command were now well forward of his position. He frowned at what he saw. At his best speed, he was still some ten minutes away from the new coordinates. There was very little chance the RAB would arrive in time to capture one of the MWC vessels.

"Weapons and boarding teams are ready and standing by," Wilcox said from the upper deck.

"Roger," said Davenport. "We are expecting bogies at any moment. You are weapons free to defend the RAB." This was Davenport's clearance to Wilcox to engage the enemy vessels, or any other hostile target, without further permission.

On the tactical display, Davenport spied the characteristic flickering that indicated an MWC vessel approaching. Then they appeared: three in his vicinity, and six more near Baker's contingent. The closest was about three thousand meters from the RAB.

For this mission, the RAB had been mounted with a 105mm howitzer in addition to its quad fifties. The weapon was of an ancient design, dating back to the twentieth century, but it worked just fine in vacuum. Sergeant Wilcox had found the weapon in storage. Apparently, it had been a museum piece on Achilles Nine and had been loaded onto one of the vessels during the evacuation. The Marines had been practicing on it for weeks and loved it.

He heard Wilcox give the command to engage with the main gun: "Gunner, target, port side, three thousand meters. Shell, armor-piercing, fire at will."

A second later, he heard and felt the howitzer fire. On the viewscreen, he watched the projectile streak toward its target. Davenport saw, with a bit of surprise, that the MWC vessel took no protective action, didn't even put up its shields. There had been some speculation among the intelligence section scientists that the pilot might need a few seconds to recover from disorientation following an MWC jump. He was glad to see that this was so.

The armor-piercing 105mm round plowed right through the enemy vessel, entering one side and exiting the other in a ball of fire and debris. Davenport heard the Marines cheer but saw that the other two vessels in the vicinity were raising their shields and beginning to maneuver. That's when Bowman's command vessel came screaming in to engage the two remaining bogies. Bowman had launched two missiles on a wide, arching path; the idea was to force the enemy vessels to face two threats approaching from different directions. The command craft came straight on towards the two enemy vessels, firing all its weapons.

Davenport was gratified to see that both enemy fighters chose to face Bowman's assault. They fired back at Bowman, their forward shields raised and enhanced. As Bowman broke off his assault, both craft remained focused on him, tracking and firing as he slid away. And then two great blossoms of fire filled Davenport's HUD as the missiles found their marks. The distraction had worked; in the haste of meeting Bowman's frontal assault, both enemy fighters had failed to take any precautions against the missiles, which had taken them from their rear.

Davenport turned his attention to the remainder of the snatch element, Baker's six fighters. What he saw surprised him, and he said out loud, "Well, that's different."

CHAPTER 27

WELL, THAT'S DIFFERENT

Baker and his five other fighters had turned and were undergoing maximum acceleration toward the new coordinates. In Baker's mind, the mission had clearly been compromised. He knew his best advantage now lay in getting in position as soon as possible. Thus, his decision to risk burning the extra fuel using the afterburners.

Sure enough, he saw the flickering of space that indicated six MWC craft entering the new coordinates. Something was different. What he saw was five fighters, not recon vessels, and a sixth larger craft. It was smaller than a frigate, maybe a fourth the size, but huge compared to the fighters.

"Wing Six, this is Wing Five," Baker said into the command net. "Are you seeing this?"

"Got it," Bowman said. "We've got three fighters here on the RAB."

On his viewscreen, Baker saw the RAB take out a fighter with a single round. *Good for them,* he thought. *That RAB's going to go down in Marine lore for that one.* No RAB had ever shot down a fighter, at least not with a five-hundred-year-old deck-mounted cannon.

"Snatch squadron, engage," Baker ordered his team. "Flight One, you're with me on the big one; let's call it a corvette. Flight Two, engage the fighters. Let's try and save one for the snatch."

Baker knew that the original plan, to surprise the enemy and capture one of their vessels, was unlikely to succeed now. Clearly, the mission had been compromised. Not only had the bad guys come in force, but someone was attacking the command center, though Baker couldn't see how that had been done.

"Flight One," he said. "Let's do a double tactical envelopment. I'll stay out of range and keep them looking at missiles. You two go left and right. Shields up; we don't know what that thing has for armament."

Instantly, the two fighters of Flight One split right and left, coming around on either side of the larger enemy craft. Baker came to a dead stop and fired two hypervelocity missiles straight on; then, a few seconds later, he fired two more. He was staggering them so the enemy craft would have to concentrate on the missiles while his two fighters moved in from either side. No vessel could keep its shields up in all directions for long; the pilot would need to project the shields in the direction of the greatest threat. Baker's plan was to present threats in as many directions as possible.

The first two missiles exploded with a flash about five hundred meters from the larger enemy craft. Just then, both fighters made their pass, firing all guns. Baker could see the direct hits on the enemy vessel as flashes of light with bits of debris flying away. He saw one of his fighters drop a mine as it passed. The mine floated toward the enemy corvette and attached itself to the hull.

Just as both fighters passed and were headed away from their target, the corvette fired what looked to Baker like a main gun. When the blast from the corvette caught one of the fighters from the rear, the fighter seemed to stretch out several times its normal length before disappearing in a flash of light. It was something he had never seen before.

"Flight One leader is down," the surviving pilot reported in a calm voice.

"Acknowledged," Baker said.

Less than a second later, the mine detonated. It wasn't a large explosion; it was designed to pierce the armor and force a breach in the hull. What Baker saw was a small flash followed immediately by a slight shudder of the corvette, probably caused by the venting of the ship's atmosphere through the breach hole.

And then the second pair of two missiles hit, and this time, no shield was up. The corvette exploded in an enormous fireball. All he could think was that it must have had nuclear munitions on board to have blown with that much force. He could actually see the blast wave moving outward at incredible speed. He'd never seen anything like it, not even when the command ship got taken out during the December ambush.

"Snatch squadron," Baker said. "We've got some blast pressure coming our way."

A moment later, he felt his craft rock a bit as the stabilizers adjusted to the blast wave. In an atmosphere, the overpressure would have sent him spinning end over end, but in vacuum, thank God, there was nothing to magnify the force.

He checked his viewscreen to see that his three other fighters were making quick work of their adversaries. Of the five they'd originally faced, only one remained. Baker's team was circling the enemy, staying out of gun range.

"Wing Five, Flight Two leader," said the senior of the pilots. "We've got this guy boxed in. Want us to try and freeze him up?"

"Freeze him up" meant to use their tractor beams and hold him for the RAB. The original plan had called for the snatch squadron to use the beams in the few seconds when the pilot of the recon vessel was still recovering from the MWC jump. This was different. The enemy was fully alert now and would probably expect something along those lines.

"Stand by," Baker said. "Wing Six, you copy?"

"I copy," came Bowman's reply. "Forget the tractor beam. Demand a surrender. Wait five seconds. If there's no response, light him up."

CHAPTER 28

FINDING WHAT'S LEFT

Bowman and Nemeth watched with satisfaction as the RAB took out one of the fighters. "Yes," Nemeth said with a slightly evil grin. It was a rare show of emotion for Nemeth, as far as Bowman could tell from their few weeks of training together.

"Let's go get the other two," Bowman said.

"With pleasure," replied Nemeth. Technically, Nemeth was the commander of the craft, while Bowman was the commander of the entire operation. Thus it was Nemeth, not Bowman, who made the pass. "Two missiles, wide approach. Fire when ready," ordered Nemeth.

"Missiles away," Bowman said almost instantly.

Bowman watched on the screen as both enemy fighters lit up the command craft. Their own forward shield held, but it was unnerving to see the projectiles coming directly for them, only to be deflected or detonated by the shields at what seemed like the very last moment. Nemeth pulled the craft away, intentionally presenting his undercarriage to the enemy fighters. He wanted them to focus on their target, not their own vulnerability. And they obliged, their attention on the command craft as both missiles found their mark in the rears of the enemy fighters.

Bowman turned to see the RAB was steadily making its way to the designated snatch spot. Not much chance of that happening.

"Rats," Nemeth said as they saw one of their own shot down by the larger enemy craft. But then they saw the mine explode, followed by two of Baker's missiles. They took out the enemy in a bright nuclear flash, accompanied by a hash of radio static as the electro-magnetic pulse passed through.

Bowman monitored the traffic between Baker and his team. They had the one last surviving enemy surrounded.

"Wing Six, you copy?" Baker said.

"I copy," came Bowman's reply. "Forget the tractor beam. Demand a surrender. Wait five seconds. If there's no response, then light him up."

Bowman looked over at Nemeth, who nodded. He knew that the chance of capturing one of these craft under the current situation was very slim. And yet, an enemy fighter could still be dangerous. They had all seen the enormous detonation of the corvette. If the cornered fighter had that kind of explosive force, it could do serious harm to anything nearby.

"Enemy craft, you are ordered to strike your colors," Baker said on the open frequency that all craft should monitor. "You have five seconds." Striking one's colors was the long-used naval term for surrender, going back to the days when vessels sailed the ocean. Lowering the ship's national flag, its colors, was a universal sign of capitulation. In modern warfare, the surrendering vessel would power down completely and lower its shields to show it was submitting.

No response … four, three, two …

What sounded like frantic gibberish came back over the net from the enemy craft. "Hold off," Baker said to his team. "If this guy is trying to surrender, let's give him a moment."

Just then, they saw a small explosion from the forward part of the enemy fighter. "What the hell?" Bowman said.

"Pilot's ejecting," Nemeth said.

And so he was: the pilot had used the explosive charges designed to eject his seat from an unstable craft about to crash or explode. The seat itself became a projectile, pilot and all. Bowman saw that it had a rocket propulsion device that pushed the pilot farther from the craft.

As soon as the ejection seat was clear of the craft, the fighter exploded—not the huge fireball they had seen when the corvette went up, but big enough.

"Wing Five, this is Wing Six," Bowman said to Baker. "Let's see if we can't pick him up, if there's anything left."

"RAB Six, Wing Six," Bowman said to Davenport. "Divert to the remains of the vessel you hulled, and let's see what might be left over."

CHAPTER 29

JOHN RAYMOND IS DOWN

"Find Raymond," Lee said.

Wasp understood immediately. Raymond was under Marine guard twenty-four hours a day. Normally, that was two Marines; today, that wasn't enough. Wasp keyed his internal net and said, "Papa Delta, this is Marine Six; report status and location." Papa Delta was the phonetic expression for "protection detail." Wasp was asking Raymond's protective detail to report in. There was no response. He checked his handheld display, which showed him the location of each Marine under his command, and did not like what he saw.

"Marine Reserve Six, this is Marine Six," Wasp said to the head of the reserve team. "Chief Raymond's protective detail is down and nonresponsive. Set up a four-deck perimeter and meet me with a Hotel Romeo team at his quarters." Hotel Romeo meant "hostage rescue."

In a few minutes, Wasp had arrived at the passageway leading to Raymond's quarters. Sergeant Phil Hoffer, the commander of the Marine reserve, and two privates were waiting for him. Wasp could see the unmoving forms of two Marines, one slumped in a sitting position and the other prone, in front of the hatch to Raymond's quarters.

"The detail is down, as you can see, Gunny. Both dead," Hoffer said heavily. "I've got two life signs from inside the quarters. One of them is in distress; I'm guessing that's Raymond."

"And the other?" Wasp asked.

"A traitor, Gunny," the sergeant said with a crack in his voice. "It's Jenkins."

Though he would never show it, Wasp was shocked. In his memory, no Marine had ever betrayed the oath. Even disobeying an order in wartime could be considered mutiny. Killing two fellow Marines and taking a hostage simply wasn't in the inventory of the possible. Wasp wanted to scream, "How could that happen?" But he knew he had to maintain control. Raymond was potentially the whole game. He might even be the reason for this larger attack on the fleet.

"And the HRT?" Wasp asked with forced calmness.

"We're it, Gunny," the sergeant replied.

Wasp nodded. He knew a fully prepared HRT wasn't likely under the circumstances; almost all the Marines had been deployed on the RAB or were involved in the fighting. All NCOs had training in hostage rescue techniques, in any case. They would have to settle this now with what they had available.

"I'll go in," Wasp said. "Give me a shooter just outside the door. I'll try to talk him down. If I can't, I'll take a shot if I can get it. You monitor and judge for yourself when to send in the shooter. Raymond's life is the primary concern."

The Marines glanced at each other. The term "primary concern" was a very rarely used criterion. It was literally a do-or-die command. It meant that Sergeant Hoffer and his team would do anything to save Raymond, including shoot Wasp if he were in the line of fire.

"We clear?" Wasp asked the Marines present. He wanted to make sure others had heard the order, in case there was a question later if he were killed.

"Clear, Gunnery Sergeant," they responded in unison.

"Who's the shooter?" Wasp asked.

Hoffer turned and nodded to one of the Marines standing near.

"I am, Gunny," said a tall, thin Marine with a clipped accent.

Wasp didn't bother asking about his marksmanship qualification score. He knew who he was: Lance Corporal Khalid Farmer. He was good shot, as all Marines were, and a solid Marine.

"It needs to be a head shot," Wasp said to Farmer. "We can't have him flailing about while he's armed."

"Aye aye, Gunny," Farmer said, without hesitation or emotion.

Wasp turned back to Hoffer and said, "Alert sick bay and have them send up a mobile trauma team."

Two Marines from the HRT began working quickly on Wasp, first fitting him with an armored vest, tailored to look like a normal uniform shirt, then microphones and mini-cameras so the team could monitor what was said in Raymond's quarters, and finally, weapons, all disguised and hidden.

"Sound check, Gunny," one of the Marines said, looking at a handheld receiver.

"Mary had a little lamb," Wasp said.

"Clear," the Marine said. "I have good visual forward direction only." This was said to remind Wasp that his team outside could only see in the direction his chest was facing.

Wasp nodded and said loudly, "Jenkins, this is Gunny Wasp. I'm coming in." He then stepped around the corner and through the hatch into Raymond's quarters.

Once inside, Wasp saw that Jenkins was holding a handgun pointed downward, directly at Raymond's prone form. He could see blood pooled beneath Raymond and realized the wound was probably severe.

"Stop right there," said Jenkins.

In his voice, Wasp heard fury, fear, and anguish. From his training, he knew this was the most volatile state of mind for a hostage-taker. Wasp understood the situation needed to be resolved quickly. He knew Hoffer was seeing this from his position just outside the door and would take the urgency of the situation into account.

"I've got to have Chief Raymond," Wasp said simply. "Tell me what you need."

"No ... I have, have to ... I n-n-need ..." Jenkins was stammering, blubbering, with saliva running down his chin. He was near, or maybe past, the breaking point. Then Jenkins shakily raised his weapon toward Wasp.

Farmer stepped around the corner and, in one smooth motion, aimed and fired.

Wasp felt a tingle in his left ear as the bullet passed on its path to the target. He saw a single black hole appear in Jenkins's forehead, a microsecond before his head snapped back. Blood and brain matter exploded rearward onto the bulkhead behind him. Jenkin's body went rigid, as if he had been electrified.

Wasp immediately snapped his wrist so the small-caliber gun in his sleeve came into his palm. He fired a single shot at Jenkins's wrist, which still held the firearm in his now-spasmodic hand. The bullet hit the wrist just above the palm; the explosive round severed the hand, which spun away still clutching the handgun. Then Jenkins collapsed.

"Jenkins is down," Wasp said. "Get me that medical team."

CHAPTER 30

POST-COMBAT ASSESSMENT

Twenty-four hours after the last shot in the engagement with the enemy was fired, the Achilles Battle Fleet was underway, outpacing the speed of light for the first time since before the December ambush.

Lee had coordinated the post-combat recovery efforts, and it turned out to be harder than she thought it would be. Her immediate assessment of the damage was substantial. The snatch team, minus one fighter, had limped back in, towing the remnants of the enemy vessel the Marines had hulled. Baker had been able to recover the pilot who had ejected. The snatch team had lost two marines who died from the extreme G-forces that leaked through when the inertial damper had failed on the RAB, as well as the pilot in the one fighter destroyed by the corvette. On the command vessel, all eight members of the provost guard had been killed. Raymond's two-Marine protection detail had been killed, along with one Marine lost when the warrant team had been ambushed.

Lee had lost four killed and two wounded in the attack on the command center.

Raymond was in sick bay in critical condition with a serious head wound; he had not yet regained consciousness. And one traitor had died. His name would be struck from the rolls. Per their tradition, the Marines would never acknowledge that he had ever been one of theirs.

One sailor was missing: a certain Admiral Jay Chambers. He had been attacked on the *Apache* and presumably kidnapped. From what she could gather from the bodies of the black-clad attackers, Chambers had put up one hell of a fight.

They weren't the only ones. The Marines had secured the eighteen wounded prisoners taken during the attack on the command center—and then they were gone, along with the pilot recovered from the snatch. Lee had watched it on the video recording from the detention center. One second, they were there; the next, a quick shimmer, and then nothing. The same with the bodies of the attackers. None remained.

For the last two hours, she had been getting the command team ready to brief the new commanding officer of the battle fleet, Commodore James Vance.

And that was a problem. Admiral Chambers had intentionally left Vance out of the planning for the operation. As such, Vance was not aware of the snatch, the reason for the fleet shutdown, or the subsequent combat operations. And now Lee was back in her role as the chief of staff responsible for bringing him up to date, and quickly. Needless to say, he was not happy.

The command team was assembled in the briefing room. In addition to Lee and Vance, Bowman, Baker, Davenport, Wasp, and Danner were present. Conspicuously absent was Chief Raymond.

"Commander Lee," Vance said. "You have convinced me to order this fleet to jump as a necessary precaution against further attacks. But now I have some questions: What do you mean, the admiral is missing?"

"Sir, Admiral Chambers was attacked while onboard the *Apache*," she said. "Our best reconstruction is that he was kidnapped by forces unknown. We're not sure what happened, but a search of all vessels and a check on his bio-telemetry shows that he is nowhere in the fleet."

There was short silence, and then Vance said, "Okay, got that. Now tell me about this snatch operation."

"Sir," she began. "Admiral Chambers ordered a covert attempt to try to capture one of the MWC vessels. An aerospace task force under the command of Captain Bowman, consisting of six fighters, a command ship, and an RAB, engaged eight MWC fighters and what is being called a corvette. The result of that effort has been that we have recovered one severely damaged enemy fighter. The aerospace task force lost one fighter and its pilot, and the Marines had two fatalities."

"And what about all this shooting?" Vance asked. "None of the ships reported any attempt at hostile boarding before the fighting broke out."

"Sir, it is unknown how the attackers got on board. Our best estimate is that they were somehow transported onboard and later departed, using MWC technology."

"And what happened?"

"There were four engagements," Lee reported. "The command center was attacked, during which the entire provost guard of eight sailors were all killed. The hatch was breached, and the command center staff, aided by a Marine squad, successfully defended the position." She paused as she remembered the emotions of that engagement and then continued, "The Marine warrant team was ambushed ..."

"Wait a moment," Vance snapped. "What warrant team?"

"The admiral issued a warrant, ordering a warrant team to detain a suspected spy," she said simply. It was too complicated to explain in detail; she was exhausted.

Vance raised his palms and said with sarcasm, "A spy. Of course."

Lee continued, "The warrant team was ambushed during its movement to intercept the spy on Deck Nine of the *Centurion*. However, Gunnery Sergeant Wasp broke off the engagement to assist the command cell when it was attacked.

"Warrant Officer Raymond was also attacked and held hostage in his quarters. A Marine HRT killed the hostage-taker. Chief Raymond is seriously injured and is in intensive care in sick bay. And finally,

Admiral Chambers was attacked, and we believed kidnapped on the *Apache*."

"And the total butcher's bill?" Vance demanded.

"Sixteen killed, three injured, one missing. In addition, the hostage-taker was a former Marine."

"What does that mean, 'former Marine'?"

"Sir, I believe Captain Davenport can best address that."

Vance turned to Davenport with a questioning look.

"Sir, former Lance Corporal Jenkins killed two Marines and took Chief Raymond hostage," said Davenport. "As his action is considered treason, his name will be stricken from the rolls of the Corps."

Vance was quiet for a long moment. He then said, in an uncharacteristically gentle voice, "Okay, I got the gist of it. First, I want to commend the snatch team and all who supported the operation. Clearly, there was valor here yesterday, as well as sacrifice." He paused again. "Now, let's hear what we got from the snatch."

All eyes turned to Danner, who looked exhausted.

"Sir, we recovered a damaged fighter. It had been hulled, through and through, with an armor-piercing projectile fired by the RAB. We have a forensic team going over it now. It's too early to report any findings."

"The RAB brought down a *fighter*?" Vance asked with astonishment.

"Yes, sir," Captain Davenport said. "The RAB gun section under the command of Sergeant Wilcox."

Lee thought how typical it was of the Marine leadership to publicly give credit to subordinates.

"And the enemy?" Vance asked.

Bowman spoke up. "Sir, the combined snatch team destroyed eight fighters and one larger craft we have been calling a corvette."

"And your losses?"

"One fighter, sir," Bowman said. "It was destroyed by the corvette using a type of weapon we haven't encountered before. There were no remains, unfortunately."

"What is the risk to the fleet from anything that came out of this most recent engagement?"

Bowman looked to Baker, who reported, "We defeated a larger force within minutes of engagement. Their pilots may have been recovering from the effects of their jump. And we did lose a fighter to the corvette. In a standard tactical engagement, the fleet aerospace division can handle what we've seen so far." He paused and thought for a moment. "That said, sir, we did get a surprise when the corvette blew. The explosion was out of proportion for a craft that size— any size, actually. We don't have an explanation for that yet. And of course, we don't know the numbers or capabilities of what they might have, beyond what we've seen."

Vance sat unspeaking for a moment and then said, "We're going to be under jump status for the next three days, and before the end of that period, we will need to sort out a few things. First, I will accept temporary command of the fleet only. I will not declare myself as primary. Admiral Chambers is missing, not dead. We will execute his intent as best as we can reconstruct it until he either returns or we receive another commanding admiral from higher authority. All his standing orders will remain in place until further notice. If there is any need to issue new orders, I want a formal decision brief presented to me by the command group.

"Second, I want a plan to recover the admiral ASAP. He would not leave a sailor behind, and we will not leave him behind. I will need options on how to recover him.

"Third, Danner, I'll need your team to work up a comprehensive threat assessment and update of your take on the recovered MWC technology.

"Fourth, we need to inform the fleet what has happened and, to the extent possible, what to expect next. I want to conduct a memorial service for those lost in the recent engagement.

"Fifth, I'll need an update on Raymond's status. If he regains consciousness, I want to be informed.

"Sixth, we need to review the fleet defenses in light of the recent attack, especially the insertion and exfiltration of forces on our vessels. Captain Davenport, I'd like you to have a look at that and then come brief me on options."

Vance rose to leave, and the staff came to attention.

After they left, Lee saw Danner standing where he was, apparently deep in thought. She said, "Mr. Danner, are you feeling okay?"

He came out of his reverie and said with a quizzical look, "He didn't ask about the mole."

CHAPTER 31

A CHANGE OF LIFE

Wasp heard the chime that indicated someone was at the door to his quarters. "Come," he said.

The hatch slid open, and Lee entered quickly, looking agitated. She came in and sat down on the only other chair in the small quarters, her hands tightly clasped. Wasp knew the signs. As a Marine, he had often seen it after a battle. He also knew that it was better to stay quiet and let her talk, so he waited.

"Do you have some tea?" she asked, her voice trembling just a bit.

"No," he said with a smile. "But I have something better. Instant coffee from Marine combat rations."

He got up, opened a small thermos, and poured the dark black liquid into the cap that served as a drinking cup. He handed it to her, and she held it in both hands, looking down at it, breathing in the smell. Then she took a long drink, set it down, and looked at him. She had tears in her eyes. Still, he said nothing. He knew what she was going through and was aware that nothing he could say right now would help.

She took another drink and said, "You smiled today, winked at me. After being in combat, after losing some of your Marines."

It was a statement, not a question. He looked back at her and said nothing. She started crying, gently at first, and then harder. Wasp put a hand on her shoulder and waited. After a minute, her crying subsided.

She said, "I lost half my team in minutes. You've done this before. Do you get used to it?"

"Yes," he said simply. "As a Marine NCO, my job is to train my people properly, lead them, and set the example. If I've done that, I can sleep at night."

"I'm so tired, but I feel like I'll never sleep again," she said.

"It's the close combat. It can change you."

"That's not what happened," she said forcefully. "I didn't change. I just became myself." She stared at him. "That's why you winked at me. You saw it in me, what you have in yourself. I've never felt anything like that; when we were fighting, everything slowed down. And that feeling, the battle rage. I felt only that, and I didn't want it to stop."

She started crying again and then suddenly reached up and kissed him, this time on the lips.

CHAPTER 32

RAYMOND WAKES

Lee was in her quarters, reviewing the staff planning calendars, when her com line chirped. "Go for Lee," she said.

"Commander, Danner here. I'm in the infirmary. Chief Raymond is awake."

"I'll be right down," she said, standing.

"Do you want me to inform the commodore?"

She paused and then said, "Let's confirm his status first. In any case, informing the commodore is my job."

Raymond looked bad. His head had been shaved for the surgery he'd needed, and the left side of his face was swollen and purple.

A female medical officer met Lee at the door and said, "He's awake and seems lucid. The risk now is stroke. We've got him on blood thinners, and he's still weak from the trauma and the operation. Please try not to get him excited. He'll need to stay here for a few more days and then face a longer recovery in his quarters."

Lee nodded and stepped through the hatch. Danner stood beside Raymond's bed, looking concerned.

"Chief," she said. "I won't ask how you're feeling; I can see that. I will say, I'm glad you're alive."

Raymond looked at her as if he was trying to understand and then nodded, saying nothing.

"I'm under doctor's orders not to get you worked up," she said. "But I need to ask you some questions. Are you up for that?"

Raymond continued to look at her and then looked at Danner and said in a hoarse voice, "Did you get me a ship?"

Danner laughed easily and said, "Most of one, Chief. The Marines shot a hole through it."

"I need to see it," he said, trying to rise, and was immediately constrained by the IV and a host of sensor wires attached to him. An alarm went off, which brought the medical officer back in with a frown.

She looked hard at Lee, who raised her hands and said with a smile, "It wasn't me."

After a moment of fussing with the wires and checking his bandages, the medical officer left again, but not before giving Lee a scolding look.

"Chief," Lee said. "You need to stay and heal up a few more days, then take it easy for a while. The Marines went to a lot of trouble to save you from Jenkins, and they don't want to lose their investment."

Raymond frowned and seemed to be searching his memory before he shook his head and said, "I don't think I know a Jenkins."

"He's the rogue Marine who took you hostage," she said. "The Marine hostage rescue team shot him dead."

Raymond shook his head and said, "I don't remember any of that."

"Chief, you were out cold the whole time," Danner said.

"What *do* you remember?" Lee asked.

"Well, my door chime rang, and I saw ..."

Just then, they heard a voice at the door. "Well, look who's awake." It was Vance. He was smiling and uncharacteristically boisterous.

Raymond stiffened when he saw him. Lee looked from Raymond to Vance and frowned.

"Commander, I thought I told you I wanted to be informed when the chief woke up," Vance said with a frozen smile.

157

"Yes, sir. I was just down here to confirm the situation." She paused and said carefully, while looking at Raymond, "The chief was just about to tell us what he remembers of his abduction."

All eyes turned to Raymond, who mumbled wearily, "I don't remember anything. My head hurts. I need some sleep."

"You heard him," the medic said from the hatch. "The chief needs a nap."

CHAPTER 33

AN AUTOPSY

Medical Officer Laura Zakany met the group as they entered the morgue. Zakany was young, maybe thirty tops, tall, and athletic-looking. Three months ago, she had been a nurse practitioner, actually a civilian refugee from Achilles Nine, onboard the *Centurion* as part of the evacuation. She had been helping out as a volunteer in the sick bay during the transit. On the night of the December ambush, she had been visiting a friend aboard one of the other ships when the central sick bay on the MS *Nickolay Pirogov* was destroyed.

In the aftermath of the attack, Zakany had thrown herself into the massive triage effort, and her work had drawn the attention of the two surviving physicians. Her education and skills had been just what were required. A nurse practitioner was a perfect bridge between physicians and all other medical specialties, and she knew how to train the technical personnel who were flooding into the medical unit to replace those who had been killed in the attack. She knew how to set up an emergency room, how to care for patients, and how to deal with grieving friends and relatives.

She very quickly became invaluable to the rebuilding effort. Based on the recommendation of the senior doctor, she had been offered a temporary appointment as a medical officer second class, which had the protocol equivalent of a naval lieutenant. She tried not to let it show, but she was hugely pleased with the new rank. She felt it was an honor. Admiral Chambers himself had held the promotion ceremony and had spoken quite sincerely about duty, sacrifice, and honor, all of which were important to her.

He had said, in a heartfelt manner, "While it may sometimes seem otherwise, no one is ever promoted as a reward for past service. They are instead promoted for their potential to serve in positions of greater responsibility. Medical Officer Zakany is joining the naval service at a time of great need for both her medical skills and her leadership. I have every confidence she will perform her duties in the highest traditions of the Navy."

Zakany had fought back tears at that. She hoped her father was still alive, and she wished he could see her now. *Every confidence*, he had said, and Zakany could tell he meant it. She would never forget it. She would never let him down.

She felt like her duties filled a void in her soul. She had been out on the far reaches of the galaxy on Achilles Nine, working at a clinic there, trying to ... do what, exactly? Find herself? Get away from herself? Nothing had clicked until now. She was good at her job; she was saving lives. For the first time, she felt like part of something larger, part of a team that mattered.

The most recent attack had been grim. So many dead, so many horrible wounds for the survivors. But this time, her team was ready. The emergency room was largely her design and her responsibility. Staffed almost entirely with newly trained medical personnel, they had handled the casualties with care and precision.

And then, of course, it had gotten weird. The enemy casualties, both injured and dead, had disappeared in a single moment of disorientation. It had since been explained to her that the enemy had used some sort of quantum-based transporter technology to remove them, just like something from one of those space operas everyone loved to watch so much. Luckily for the investigation that followed—and which was still ongoing—her medical techs had systematically in-processed all patients and remains before their departure.

For some reason, the commander of the aerospace fleet and the chief of staff were very interested in this particular autopsy, and so the job had fallen to her. She wasn't qualified as a pathologist, but neither were the other two doctors in the medical unit. She had assisted in a number of autopsies in the past, and of course she had the automated tech unit to do most of the exploration. She knew of Lee, had seen her a few times and spoken to her twice, once when Lee had come to see Raymond. She did not like Lee, who seemed haughty and dismissive, and wore her hair down like she was in a cocktail bar. Maybe it was just nature's way of trying to figure out the pecking order. Zakany had heard, everyone had heard, that Lee had fought this very man in the gym. Kicked his ass, is what they said. Okay, that counted in her favor, because he had a reputation as a pig. But still, did she need to attract so much attention to herself?

They all stood around the autopsy table.

Zakany said in her Hungarian-accented voice, "Recorder on. This is the autopsy of former Marine Lance Corporal Jeremiah Jenkins, age at death thirty-eight years, seven months." She paused, looked at those around the table, and said, "The time is now 0315 hours, 17 March 2542. For the record, those in attendance, please state your name and rank. I am Medical Officer Second Class Laura Zakany, assigned to HC *Centurion*."

"Lieutenant Commander Mei-Ling Lee, chief of staff, Achilles Battle Fleet."

"Captain Stephen Bowman, wing commander, Achilles Battle Fleet."

"Gunnery Sergeant Theodorus Wasp, Human Alliance Marine Corps."

Zakany nodded sharply and stated, "Autopsy begins. The subject has a single gunshot entry wound to the forehead, and a larger exit wound to the back of the head, consistent with a medium caliber intrusion. The right hand has been severed. The wound is jagged, as if from explosive impact." She paused and called up the body scan results onto the large screen, so all could see. "Based on initial scans, the subject shows signs of trauma to the back of the head and torso, and defensive wounds to both forearms."

"The injury to the back of the head is from the gunshot exit wound, and for the record, he was injured in a sparring match a few weeks ago," said Lee.

"No, Commander," Zakany said with a note of irritation. "The main injury to the back of the head was perimortem; it probably incurred minutes before the fatal gunshot. It was a severe blow, resulting in a substantial concussion. It would have caused serious disorientation, maybe even unconsciousness. The defensive wounds were also perimortem. I do see older injuries from a few weeks ago; three cracked ribs and a jaw injury. I treated him for those at the time, and they were healing nicely." She paused, looked hard at Lee, and asked, "That was you, was it not?"

Lee ignored the question.

"Are we saying Raymond fought with him?" Bowman asked, surprised.

Wasp shook his head and said, "Possible, but not likely. Jenkins wasn't the best Marine, but he could have made short work of Chief Raymond, no offense to the Navy. Look at the defensive wounds. Someone hit him hard and repeatedly. It was a fight."

"Doctor," Bowman said, "you treated Raymond. Did he have injuries to his hands and arms?"

"No, sir," Zakany responded.

"And Raymond says he doesn't remember even knowing Jenkins," Lee noted.

"Blast it," Wasp said, shaking his head regretfully. "Jenkins wasn't a hostage taker. He was attacked along with Raymond and was probably trying to protect him."

"Don't be too hasty. I've seen the tapes," said Lee. "He pointed his weapon at Raymond and then at you. Why would he have done that?"

"He was disoriented from the head injury," Zakany said, looking at Wasp. "He may not have been fully aware of the circumstances. It's possible in his confusion that he thought *you* were the aggressor."

Wasp's face froze, his jaw clenched. Everyone else remained silent for a long beat.

"Doctor," Bowman broke in finally, "what was used to strike him in the back of the head?"

"Let's have a look, sir," said Zakany. She was secretly pleased that Bowman had referred to her as "doctor," though in fact she wasn't one. She zoomed in on the wound that was displayed on the viewscreen. She tapped a few keys, and a stream of figures appeared in the margin. "There's no traces of foreign material. It was a severe blow, though. You can see the cracked atlas and axis vertebra and bruising to the internal artery. He was definitely in a bad way."

"Could this have been done with a hand or a fist?" Bowman asked.

Zakany paused. She wanted to answer instantly, to look knowledgeable and professional, but she really didn't know. She had done a rotation in pathology while qualifying as a nurse practitioner, but she had nowhere near the experience as a medical examiner to make such a judgment.

"I don't know," she said simply. "I can consult with my colleagues and get a better answer to you as soon as possible. I can say this: the injury was caused by a great deal of force. If it was a fist, and if the deceased was standing at the time of the blow, the assailant would have been striking downward, so they were probably taller than Mr. Jenkins and with greater-than-average strength."

Bowman asked, "Can you pull up the images on Raymond's head wound?"

"Yes, sir," Zakany said. She tapped a few keys, and a photo of a Raymond's wound, flanked by an accompanying x-ray, came up on the screen. "Actually, the wound is very similar. Raymond's scalp was torn, and that caused a great deal more bleeding than with Jenkins. But the location and general type of injures were the same. Let's see the surgery notes." She tapped again, and more text came up on screen. "Yes, the axis and atlas vertebra needed repair, as did the artery."

Lee said, "So we're looking for someone who attacked both Raymond and Jenkins, possibly someone strong enough to have inflicted serious head injuries to both of them." She looked around those present and said, "Are we agreed?"

All were silent but nodded, and then Wasp said, "And so Lance Corporal Jeremiah Jenkins died in the line of duty."

CHAPTER 34

A MYSTERY

Laura Zakany was nervous. Commander Lee had asked to meet her at the officers' lounge for a coffee. She wondered if she had overplayed her hand at the autopsy. Well, if Lee thought she was going to intimidate her, she had another thing coming. Zakany had risen from near-poverty to become a nurse practitioner in a time and place where many young women became housewives at best and prostitutes at second-best. Worse was dead. She had fought her way up and survived to become a respected medical officer on a war vessel in deep space. She wasn't about to let this tiny Asian woman push her around.

Lee was there before her, and to Zakany's surprise, she rose from the table with a smile and offered her hand in what seemed a genuinely friendly gesture.

"Thanks for coming," Lee said. She gestured for Zakany to sit and then sat herself.

The whole thing looked quite natural, and Zakany's mind was struggling to see a trap or subterfuge.

"It is my pleasure, ma'am," Zakany responded formally.

She was careful not to presume a familiarity that didn't exist between them, and as always, she was conscious of her heavy Hungarian accent. When she had time to think, she could mask it almost entirely. But when she was emotional or hurried, the accent was pronounced.

Lee smiled and said, "Please call me Mei-Ling, at least when we're out with the girls." Then she winked, and Laura felt herself laughing a girlish giggle.

Lee had selected a table near one of the viewports. The view was spectacular, as it always was when in jump status, with stars streaming by. Zakany knew this was a treat but also a show of power, because only high-ranking officers could easily reserve such a table. Lee was a lieutenant commander, only one rank ahead of Zakany. But she was also the fleet chief of staff, and that carried weight. Lee was one of a handful of officers close to the admiral. When she spoke, others assumed she spoke for the admiral. She punched above her weight class, as Zakany's dad would have said.

She thought of her father. Like everyone on board, she had no news of family, but she hoped they had survived the attack on Earth. Her family had originally lived on a farm in southern Hungary. When Laura was ten, the Zakany family sold the farm and moved to Budapest because of a crop failure and financial crisis. Those had been hard years. Her dad had worked odd jobs as a day laborer, a handyman, or delivery man. Laura had worked hard at school, getting good grades and winning honors. As a teenager, she had taken work as a waitress during evenings and holidays. All in all, it was not bad. But her mother had died suddenly of a stroke when Laura was twelve. That was hard, and yet, life had to go on. Her dad had cried like a baby for one whole day and then went back to work. Laura had done the same. There was really nothing else to do. They had to eat.

It was a great moment when Laura Zakany got her certification as a nurse practitioner. It meant she would rise above the very bottom rung of survival and social status. She had been able to make enough money to let her dad retire. She bought him a small cottage in the country near a lake, about an hour's drive from the city. Now she hoped that move had saved his life because it was rumored that the cities of Europe had taken a beating during the attack. She didn't know if Budapest had been hit or not.

Zakany realized Lee had been speaking: "... so I said, that's not really what I was looking for."

Lee broke into laughter, and Zakany realized she had missed the joke, but she covered by smiling and put her hand over her mouth as if she were politely covering a laugh.

The waiter came, and Lee ordered a cappuccino and said, "My treat; go wild."

There was that smile again, and Zakany had to admit to herself that Lee was charming, at least when she wanted to be. Perhaps she had misjudged her. *We shall see,* she thought. Zakany ordered a coffee, black, and a glass of sparkling water. When the drinks came, Lee was positively chatty. She asked Zakany about her experience and training, and she seemed genuinely interested in her story.

"And what about you?" Zakany asked.

Lee turned her head and smiled wryly in a "girls only" sort of way. "I grew up in Hong Kong. My dad was a martial arts instructor. Our family life sort of revolved around that. My mom died when I was six, so I don't remember much about her. I had an aunt, but she married a foreigner before I was born and left Hong Kong with her husband. Apparently, at the time it was considered taboo, so she was rarely mentioned. When I was sixteen, I went to the academy—a big deal in our circle, both because it was military service, which is highly respected, and because it was university, another plus for a Chinese family."

"How did you like it?" Zakany asked.

"It was hard being away from family at first. As you know, the academy is in North America. I liked the discipline, but the academy has its own pace and rules, and I don't think anyone comes to it naturally. But I came to like it. I was on the competition martial arts team, and we got to travel."

Zakany saw that Lee was smiling at the memory. "And after the academy?" she asked.

"I was commissioned an ensign and was shipped off to a year of naval warfare school. Would you believe I was the only woman in my class? Most female officers still go into the administrative fields or, if they're smart enough, into engineering."

"Let me guess," Zakany said. "You were the top graduate."

"Yes," she responded, laughing. "You got that right. My dad expected that. I could hardly come home as a runner-up." They both broke into laughter, and Zakany realized that Lee was much like herself.

The talk turned to men. "I hope I am not too bold," Zakany said, "but did I see with my girl's eyes that Captain Bowman looks at you with interest?"

Lee laughed and said, "Yes. He's not very good at hiding it, is he?"

"And what do you think?" Zakany asked.

Lee scratched her head and said, with a wry smile, "He's very nice, polite, and handsome."

"I sense a 'but' in there," Zakany said.

"The truth is, I've never had a boyfriend," said Lee. "There were a few dates at the academy, but those were formal affairs. No romances. Hmm. I don't want to be too picky, or I'll die an old maid. But to tell the truth, and may I speak in confidence?"

"Of course," Zakany said seriously, smiling and adding, "I pinky swear."

"Okay," Lee said with a smile. "As long as you pinky swear. Bowman isn't really focused. He was a college professor. Okay, that's a prestigious thing. But he didn't really like it, so he got into being a reserve pilot. He's good at that, and now that war has broken out, he's moving up."

"So what is the problem?" Zakany asked.

"I don't know," Lee said. "Things come easily to him. Where's the edge? Where's the substance? After he gets tired of playing captain, will he wander off to something else? *Someone* else?"

"And what is your ideal?" Zakany asked.

"I'll know it when I see it," Lee said. "Maybe someone who is *all in* to whatever he's doing. A man who doesn't do half-measures,"

Zakany was impressed. Here was a woman with standards who wasn't about to settle. How could she have thought Lee was putting on airs?

"Is there another, perhaps?" Zakany asked. "One more focused?"

Lee smiled wistfully and said, "It's too soon to tell. I better not jinx it."

"I understand," Zakany said.

"And what about you?" Lee asked. "I see you've spent some time with Mr. Nemeth. Is there something there?"

Zakany blushed and said, "We are countrymen, both from Hungary. Maybe. He is older, but in my world, that is not a problem. He is from old family, very prestigious."

"You mean like an aristocrat?"

"The monarchy no longer exists, for hundreds of years now. Most people don't know and don't care about the old families or titles."

"But you do?"

"His was a warrior family. His ancestors fought in the Black Legion for the king almost a thousand years ago. They won their titles by combat trial and loyalty," Zakany said. "He has it in his blood; he is a warrior. As you say, he is focused. And a good man, kind and thoughtful." She paused and then blurted, while blushing fiercely, "And he's never been married."

"Does that matter?"

"I hope you won't think me shallow," Zakany said. "But yes, it matters. It means that if we marry, my sons will inherit his title of Baron. It matters to me." And she blushed more deeply than before.

Lee was quiet for a moment and then said with sincerity, "I hope I can find a man like that. I wish you well."

Zakany was moved by this exchange, and she felt tears coming to her eyes, which she desperately wished to suppress. Lee saw this and was silent for a moment, pretending to check her handheld for messages until Zakany regained her composure.

Then Lee changed the subject. "Tell me, how is the forensic work coming on the hostiles who so inconveniently disappeared?"

Zakany paused for a moment to get her thoughts together. If this was a test, she wanted to pass. "Okay," she began. "The report is not done yet, and it will have to be signed off by the chief of medicine." She paused and saw that Lee understood. This was a back channel report on the autopsies. Zakany did not wish to be quoted as having gone out of channel and over the heads of her superiors. "We scanned the bodies before they were taken. We got tissue samples, blood, x-rays, and MRIs. High points: all humans, all males, all clones. Although they appear to be in their mid-twenties, the tissue and bone samples show that they are no more than three years old. Among those who were alive, none spoke. We thought that might be due to discipline, but it turns out they probably couldn't speak, at least not in the way a fully developed human adult might. In each case, including the captured pilot, the larynx wasn't fully developed, and some of the other structural arrangements of the throat argued against that. Each of them had a small artificial device in his frontal neocortex. Since we didn't retain any of those, there is no way to know its function."

"Can you speculate?" Lee asked.

"As a medical professional, no," she said. "There's just not enough information to make a judgment. Speaking for myself only, the neocortex is considered the most evolved and most recent part of the mammalian and primate brain. It controls memories, retention of facts, speech, and inhibition."

"Are we talking mind control?" Lee asked.

"Hmm," Zakany said. "That's not exactly what I'm thinking. There might be some control function, but 'mind control' is probably too strong a phrase. The human brain is far too complicated for anything close to full control to be feasible. The device was too large and complicated to be a simple tracking device, though. Given their young age and the fact that they probably couldn't speak, my best guess is that it had to do with communication and perhaps information. No three-year-old, no matter how physically mature, can learn to fly a fighter or conduct a coordinated raid. The device probably adds something that they wouldn't otherwise have."

Lee frowned and looked down.

"What is it?" Zakany asked.

Lee shook her head and said, "I killed some of them during the attack on the command center. I wasn't thinking of them as children being forced to do something they wouldn't do of their own free will."

"That wasn't your fault," Zakany said.

"No, it wasn't; of course, I know that." She paused and then said, "But I enjoyed the combat. When it was over, I wanted more of it." She paused again with a strange look in her eye and said, "I just need to think about that."

They were quiet for a long moment, and then Zakany asked, "So what are you working on?"

Lee came out of her reverie and said, "Well, I can't go into too much detail, given operational security, but of course there's finding the admiral and getting him back."

Zakany smiled and said, "Oh, that shouldn't be too hard."

Lee snapped, "Why do you say that?"

"Oh," Zakany said, a bit flustered at her suddenly hard tone. "I just meant that you already know where he is, so getting him back won't be hard."

"I'm sorry," Lee said, looking confused. "Please explain how I already know where he is."

Zakany looked confused and glanced around for a moment, seeming to realize that she had made some sort of mistake. "It's just that I assumed the kidnapping was some sort of cover story."

"What makes you say that?" Lee asked, now dead serious.

"Well, because *I* know where he is," Zakany blurted out.

"And how do you know that?" demanded Lee.

"Because I can track the telemetry from his artificial hand," Zakany said. "He's still aboard the *Apache*."

CHAPTER 35

A MYSTERY GETS COMPLICATED

Lee barked into her communicator, now in full chief-of-staff mode, "Danner, Wasp; meet me in the medical facility in five." She turned to Zakany with her war mask on. "Let's go to the lab so you can show us what you have."

Zakany nodded and got up. She felt stupid. She should have told someone about the trace on Chambers' hand, but she had assumed that they all knew. She was beginning to hope she hadn't screwed up her new commission as a medical officer or her new friendship with Lee.

When they got to the lab, Midshipman Danner and Gunnery Sergeant Wasp were already waiting. Zakany could tell from their faces that they knew something serious was up; Lee worked hard, long hours, but her organizational skills were such that she rarely called people in after duty unless there was an emergency.

Lee got right to the point. "Medical Officer Zakany has informed me that she can track the admiral's prosthetic hand, and that it shows he's still on the AS *Apache*." She turned to Zakany and said in a surprisingly gentle tone, "Laura, can you show us what you have?"

Zakany felt a flush of relief at the new tone. She quickly sat at one of the nearby terminals, typed in her password and opened the menu.

"Danner, please observe," Lee said.

Danner nodded and said, "Yes, ma'am," and sat next to Zakany.

In a moment, Zakany had a schematic of the *Apache* on screen. A blinking green light showed on one of the storage bays; next to the light was a series of data lines. "There he is," she said.

"Are you sure it's him and that he's still alive?" Wasp asked. "That it's not just his hand?"

"It's him," she said confidently. "The database has his unique biometrics on file. It's a match. And he's fine. Not injured, seriously ill, or under stress."

"Is he sedated? Is he moving?" Wasp asked.

Zakany tapped a few keys, looked for a moment, and said, "He's not showing signs of being sedated. Blood pressure and respiration are normal. He's not moving just now, but let's see ... he *has* been moving recently, at least within the confines of the bay he's in."

"Why do you ask, Gunny?" Lee said.

"Because the admiral is trained as a special ops warrior. He's trained to resist if taken captive and knows how to escape. If he's not drugged and not restrained, then he's not anybody's captive."

Danner was staring straight ahead at the screen.

"Danner, you're quiet," Lee said. "Do you have anything to add?"

He said nothing for a long moment, and then said, without looking up, "OPSEC. I'm under orders, ma'am."

Everyone was silent and still. Finally, Lee said, "I can respect operational security, Mr. Danner, but we have an urgent situation here. So I'm asking you, as adjunct head of the fleet Intelligence Division, what you know of this. What are your orders, and who gave them to you?"

Danner sat silent for moment, nodded as if he had decided something, and then began to speak. "The admiral is intentionally hiding. He said it was a counterintelligence operation designed to smoke out the mole. The idea was that if he were out of the picture, the mole would get bold enough to reveal himself."

"And your orders?" Lee asked.

"My orders were to modify the surveillance of his 'kidnapping' and to monitor key individuals for certain behavioral patterns."

"Who else is aware of the operation?" Lee asked.

"I wasn't told of anyone else," he said. "My instructions were to tell no one."

"And how do you communicate with him?" she asked.

"We have a secure channel. I check in once a day."

"Do you know who he is, who the mole is?" she asked.

"I do now, ma'am," he said. "But it's not a *he*. It's a *they*."

CHAPTER 36

CHAMBERS RETURNS

The command team was assembled in the briefing room again, with the admiral at the head of the table. His face was grim. Vance, Bowman, Lee, Davenport, Wasp, Danner, Baker and Raymond sat around the table. Surprisingly, Warrant Officer Nemeth also sat at the far end of the table with Medical Officer Zakany by his side, both directly across from Chambers. Two Marine commandos stood at the entrance, and Lee knew that two more stood outside the door on guard duty.

Lee had spoken briefly to the admiral only once since they had recovered him from his self-imposed exile. All he had told her was to assemble the people who were now present. He'd had a longer private meeting with Danner, Nemeth, and, for some reason, Zakany. Lee had no idea what was about to happen, so she just waited.

The admiral finally looked at her and said, "Commander Lee, please start the meeting."

Not knowing what to expect, she fell back upon Navy protocol and said simply, "The admiral has called this meeting to receive updates and to provide instruction." She looked at him and said, "Sir?"

"First, let me acknowledge the valor of those who fought in the last engagement. Many are dead, and others are grievously wounded." He paused. "Let me also apologize for the deception I engineered, encouraging most of you to believe I had been kidnapped. That was a violation of trust, which I regret, but which I undertook out of necessity."

Chambers looked around at each of the faces in the room as if to say, "I lied to you. This is your chance to look me in the eye."

When no one responded, he continued, "Midshipman Danner acted under my written orders when he withheld information from his superiors about my status. That fact has been entered into his record. There will be no further repercussions or mention of it," Chambers said. "Master Warrant Officer Nemeth was also under my instructions. His role in the investigation will become clear as we proceed."

Every head turned toward Nemeth, but as usual, he showed no emotion of any kind.

"Warrant Officer Raymond, I'm glad to see you on your feet again," Chambers said.

Everyone looked over at Raymond. He had lost weight, wore a neck brace and head bandage, and looked uncharacteristically blank. Only a slight nod showed that he had heard the admiral.

"We have a general overview of what happened during the snatch operation," Chambers said. "No plan survives contact with the enemy, and this operation was no exception. In this case, the entire team reacted well, with flexibility, forcefulness, and valor. But we do need to find out what happened and why some things *didn't* happen.

"We'll use the after-action review format," he continued. "What was the plan, what did each element do, what did the enemy do, and what was the result? Finally, what are the lessons learned? The key to our survival and our success is getting inside the enemy's decision cycle. We need to learn faster and apply what we've learned."

He turned to Bowman and said, "Captain Bowman, you were the commander of the operation. What was the mission, its objectives, and the constraints placed on you?"

Bowman stood, tapping a key that showed a schematic of the engagement area. "Sir. The mission was to engage the forces conducting reconnaissance of the fleet for the purpose of capturing an MWC vessel intact, with a secondary objective of flushing out and capturing the mole communicating with the enemy."

The display showed the originally envisioned engagement, with MWC vessels rotating out, the snatch team making its rush to get into position, and the following engagement, which resulted in one MWC recon vessel engaged with a tractor beam and the RAB boarding her intact.

"Commander Baker, your role in this?" the admiral asked.

"Sir, I commanded an aerospace detachment of six fighters. Our role was to accelerate to the coordinates provided by the Ops cell, get in position before the next rotation of MWC arrived, and engage the forces, while isolating one with a tractor beam so the RAB could board and secure her."

"Captain Davenport, your role?"

"Sir, I commanded the RAB," Davenport said. "Our mission was to board and secure the MWC vessel once it was immobilized and then return it to the fleet."

"Danner," the admiral said, "what was your role?"

"Sir, I was the intel chief," he said. "My job was to track the rotation of the MWC vessels, predict the location of the arrival of the next shift, and pass that information to the snatch team. My secondary mission was to identify any unauthorized transmission from the fleet, locate its source, and pass that information on to the warrant team."

"Gunnery Sergeant Wasp, what was your task?"

"Sir," Wasp said, "my role was to command the warrant team, move to the location provided by the command center, and secure the person or persons identified."

"And Commander Lee," the admiral asked, "what was your role?"

"Sir, I was the battle captain, in charge of the combined ops and intel sections."

"Chief Raymond," the admiral said, "your role?"

"I had no role in the operation, sir," Raymond said in a flat voice. "I was aware it was being planned because I had provided advice on the criteria for capture of an MWC. I did not know when it would take place or that it was underway."

"Master Warrant Officer Nemeth, your role?"

"Sir, I was the command pilot for the C&C vessel supporting Captain Bowman."

"And Commodore Vance, what did you do during the operation?"

"Admiral," Vance said somewhat stiffly, "I was not informed of the operation."

Chambers looked firmly at Vance and said softly, "That's not what I asked, but we can come back to that. Medical Officer Zakany, your role?"

"Admiral, I knew nothing of the operation," she said. "I supervised the triage function when the casualties started coming in. I also oversaw the mortuary process for the remains."

"You did something else, though. Tell us about that," Chambers said.

"Yes, sir. During emergency trauma, when the patient has multiple wounds, we inject a radioactive dye into the bloodstream. It allows the scanners to better identify damaged or malfunctioning tissues and organs."

"And were you able to apply this treatment to the wounded enemy?"

"Yes, sir. All of them."

Vance said somewhat abruptly, "And what's the point? They're gone now."

"Tell him," Chambers said to Zakany, not looking away from Vance.

"The dye binds to the patients' DNA and leaves a unique signature. We can track them," she said.

"I was on the *Apache* inspecting the hydroponic operations," Chambers said simply. "My role was to divert attention from any potential saboteur, so they wouldn't suspect an operation was pending."

Everyone was quiet for a very long moment.

Finally, Chambers said, "Captain Bowman, did the operation achieve its objectives?"

"No, sir," said Bowman. "We did not capture an intact MWC vessel, and we did not identify the mole."

"Why not?"

"As the commander of the operation, the results of the operation are my responsibility. My failure, sir."

"That goes without saying," Chambers said. "And I am your commanding officer. I approved the mission parameters. Did you execute the mission as directed?"

"Yes, sir," Bowman said. "But I made the call to continue with the mission even after it became clear the operation had been compromised."

"Baker, would you have made the same call had you been in command?"

"Absolutely, sir," Baker said in his distinctive drawl. "The abort criteria included the loss of the RAB or two-thirds of the fighter escort. We never met either criterion, so the mission went forward."

"Midshipman Danner," the admiral said, "please review for us the incidents that indicated outside interference in the snatch plan."

"Yes, sir." Danner punched some keys, and a list of events appeared on screen. "First was the tampering with the RAB's inertial damper. That caused the deaths of two Marines and the misplacement of the RAB for the operation."

"Do you think that was the intent of the saboteur?" asked the admiral. "To slow down their response, and put them out of position?"

"Probably not, sir," Danner replied. "Our forensic review showed the G forces rose to over ten times the normal level of a high-G mission. Whoever did this probably intended for it to disable the RAB personnel altogether. They misjudged the resilience of the Marines. Not only did Captain Davenport remain conscious throughout, he was able to manually cut the burn within a fraction of a second of the time the computer would have done it, had it been functioning, and the surviving Marines continued to fight."

"And brought down an enemy fighter, with a howitzer, no less. Continue."

"Next was the miscalculation of the position and timing of the shift change," Danner said. "There was no sabotage or interference. They just used a sequence designed to mislead us based on what we had seen before. It caused me to provide incorrect coordinates to the snatch team, along with a bad estimate on the timing."

"What does that tell you about the enemy's knowledge of your calculations?" Chambers asked.

"It tells me that they knew exactly how I was making my calculations and that it was likely we would rely upon them."

"Next?"

"A complement of fighters and a corvette appeared instead of the recon vessels we had been expecting," Danner said. "This indicated knowledge of the operation and an attempt to overwhelm or at least thwart the snatch."

Chambers shook his head and said, "I'm not sure it's that simple, but let's hold that for now. Please continue."

"The unauthorized signal from the fleet, and the tampering with the drones to allow that signal to go through," said Danner.

"That was set up in advance and remotely triggered, as I understand."

"Correct, sir."

"When did the signal begin? What was the trigger?"

"It came within seconds of the shutdown of fleet communications, sir."

"And what was happening during the operation?"

Danner checked his screen and said, "The snatch team was already en route to the coordinates, sir."

"Let me ask you to speculate," the admiral said. "What was the purpose of sending that signal, given the timing?"

Danner said, "To alert the enemy that the snatch operation was underway."

"How much time elapsed between the signal going out and the emergence of the enemy contingent of fighters and a corvette?" asked Chambers.

Danner checked his handheld and said, "Two minutes, eleven seconds, sir."

"Commander Baker," Chambers asked, "is 131 seconds enough time to reconfigure an aerospace task force from recon to a combat configuration?"

Baker responded, "Not likely, sir. Though Chief Raymond, when he was the maintenance chief for the 319th recon squadron during the December 7th attack, did something damn near that fast."

"Chief?" asked Chambers.

Raymond shook his head and said, "Not if there was no warning at all. The expected configuration was three to five recon vessels, and what we got was nine fighters and a corvette. On the seventh, we simply reconfigured from recon to fighter. The FA-300 is designed for that, and Commander Bowman, as the XO, had us a drill it a million times, so it came easily."

"Sir, can I ask why this is important?" Lee asked.

"In a moment. Danner, what was in the signal that went out from the fleet during the attack?"

"It was a simple numerical sequence, a burst transmission."

"So it was a signal flare, an alert that an operation was underway. It could not have contained enough information to describe the purpose or configuration of our snatch," Chambers stated rhetorically.

A bit confused, Lee said, "Sir, your point is that the enemy already knew about the operation, that they didn't find out about it from the signal, and that the purpose of that message was just to alert them it was underway? Is that correct?"

"Got it in one," the admiral said. "Let's stop there and discuss what the enemy did and how. Tell us, what's the common element in all these activities?"

Danner responded forcefully, "All of them were done by someone who had access to the com and data networks, and who had a reasonable understanding of how to plant viruses to manipulate our systems."

"You say 'a reasonable understanding.' Do you mean it wasn't sophisticated?"

"To be fair, it did get past us at first," Danner said. "But you will recall that Chief Raymond figured out that the drone net was being used to communicate unauthorized messages within a few minutes of me informing him of an anomaly. A real expert in computer network sabotage would have made that detection much more difficult."

Lee noticed that Medical Officer Zakany and Master Warrant Officer Nemeth were both looking at her handheld device; they spoke in low tones in what he assumed was Hungarian. Then Nemeth nodded, as if affirming what she intended to show him. Lee noted he shifted slightly in his chair and lowered his right hand below the level of the conference table. It was something that caused her to feel that tingling of impending combat. Something was up, and she didn't like not knowing what it was.

"So you've known for some time the drone net was being used to send out unauthorized messages?" Chambers said.

"Yes, sir," Danner responded. "At your orders, we monitored and recorded, but did not interrupt, the signaling."

"And were you able to decode the messages?"

"Yes, sir."

Lee was stunned at this response. She knew for a fact that only a fraction of the transmissions had been decoded. Why would Danner lie to the admiral?

"Commodore Vance," the admiral said, "do you have anything to add?"

At that moment, Vance rose from his chair, drew a palm-sized handgun from his sleeve, and raised the weapon toward Raymond. Davenport threw himself in front of the scientist. Before Vance could take his aim, Nemeth rose from his seat, drew a handgun, and fired in one blindingly fast motion. Two shots rang out, and Vance flew back against the wall, a spray of blood fountaining from his chest. The guards were still reaching for their holstered sidearms as Vance's body slammed against the wall. Nemeth lowered his weapon to the table and raised his hands behind his head in submission, a gesture to the guards, who were just then unholstering their weapons, that he was no longer a threat.

Chambers said calmly, "Commodore Vance, if he lives, is under arrest for treason. Captain Davenport, take charge of him and ensure he has an appropriate guard while in sick bay. Doctor Zakany, please do your magic and keep him alive, if possible. We have many questions. Master Warrant Officer Nemeth, once again, you've saved a life. Marines, do not shoot him; he was acting on my orders."

"Just like the old days, sir," Nemeth said. "I think I still owe you a few, though."

Things happened quickly after that.

CHAPTER 37

ONE THREAT DOWN

Zakany moved to Vance to take his vitals. "He's alive, but hemorrhaging," she said. She barked into her communicator, "Code Red in Conference Room One; trauma team respond."

Captain Davenport ordered the Marines to secure the prisoner and then used his communicator to order a guard detail to report to sick bay to take charge of Vance when he arrived. "Do we need to worry about our prisoner disappearing?" Chambers asked.

"No, sir," Zakany said. "The frequency of his chip is blocked."

"Good to know."

After the trauma team had taken Vance away under Marine guard, Chambers said, "Sorry for all the drama, but we needed to be sure Vance was the mole. I know I have a lot of explaining to do, but we have other pressing business right now." He turned to Wasp and asked, "Have you detained the other suspects?"

"Yes, sir," Wasp said. "All eight of them. They are in custody, and their chips have been jammed."

Lee asked, "Sir, how did you know it was Commodore Vance?"

"Danner, care to tell them?"

"When the admiral went into hiding," Danner said, "he had me monitor all the members of the fleet who would have had access to the networks that could have introduced the various viruses we saw. He felt his absence would encourage the mole to act aggressively. That led us to Vance. As I said before, whoever did the hacking wasn't a professional, and Vance only made a weak effort to cover his activities."

"So you've been tracking all of us?" Lee asked, a blush coming to her face as she thought of the time she'd spent in Wasp's quarters.

"Yes, ma'am. Sorry for the invasion of privacy. It's what I was ordered to do, it was necessary, and only unauthorized activities were flagged for review."

"And the other conspirators? How did you identify them?"

"I think Medical Officer Zakany can best answer that, Commander," Chambers said.

Zakany squared her shoulders, blushed a little at the attention, and said, "Once we realized that all the enemies who had disappeared had chips in their brain, we did a scan of everyone in the fleet to see who else might have one."

"And what did you find?" the admiral asked.

"Commodore Vance and eight others had the chip." She hesitated, as if she would say more.

"Continue," the admiral instructed.

"None of the nine are who they pretend to be," Zakany stated. "We have their DNA on file from when they entered the service, and all their genome profiles are different now. Somehow, their DNA is a combination of the originals and what we found in the clones before they were taken away."

"How is it possible we missed that?" Bowman asked. "Wouldn't we have picked up that our colleagues had been switched out?"

"Maybe we should have," the admiral admitted. "But remember, we don't know when the switch took place. It could have been years ago. Plus, the original flotilla was an ad hoc organization, put together quickly as part of an evacuation. After the attack, we moved people around to new jobs and new sections. This could have hidden any discontinuity of behavior, and any unusual behavior that might otherwise draw attention would be attributed to stress."

"And these imposters, who are they?" Bowman demanded.

Zakany said, "Well, the attackers who were captured and killed were all clones. Though physically they appeared to be in their mid-twenties, they were in fact no more than three years old. I believe they were grown and trained for their specific combat tasks. The others, the ones who impersonated our people, are older by a few years. We're assuming they had to be trained for a longer period of time in order to assume their more complex roles."

"But Vance was a commodore," Bowman said, "commanding thirteen vessels. How does anyone pull that off for months without someone noticing he's an imposter?"

"That's on me," the admiral said. "Truth is, the Vance imposter wasn't performing his job well, and I had counseled him about it several times. He let discipline issues slide that no naval officer in command would have missed. You may recall I had to relieve one of the ship's captains who reported to Vance. That's something that should never happen in a functioning chain of command. The real Vance would never have let it get that far. I was in the process of relieving Vance of his command; the paperwork was ready. My lack of confidence in him was why I left him out of the snatch planning."

Chambers turned to Raymond and said, "Chief, you've been through a lot. Was it Vance who attacked you?"

"Truthfully, I can't say for sure," Raymond said. "He did come to see me. It's possible he attacked me from behind. I don't remember."

"From what we can reconstruct from the Marine logs," Wasp said, "Lance Corporal Jenkins was the NCO of the watch. He must have entered Chief Raymond's quarters to check on him as part of his rounds. We think Vance took him by surprise and knocked him out long enough to leave."

"What about the two Marine guards killed outside Raymond's quarters?" Chambers asked.

"We think Vance shot them as he was leaving," Wasp said. "They would have come to attention for a commodore. He took them then, the coward."

"And Jenkins?"

"Shot on my orders, sir," Wasp said. "I believed him to be holding Chief Raymond hostage. I confronted him as he was pointing his sidearm at Raymond, and he raised his weapon in my direction. We learned later he was concussed and probably trying to protect Raymond from an unknown enemy. The HRT had orders to save Raymond as a primary concern. They did their duty, sir."

"As did you," the admiral said. "Lance Corporal Jenkins died an honorable death in battle and in the line of duty trying to save a fellow shipmate. The record will reflect that." He turned back toward Raymond and said, "You've had a look at the captured MWC vessel, Chief. What can you tell us?"

For the first time since the meeting began, Raymond smiled. "The results were better than I'd hoped. Whether they intended to or not, the Marines used a SABOT round."

"Captain Davenport, please explain for those of us not versed in ancient warfare," Chambers said.

"A SABOT projectile is designed specifically to penetrate armor," Davenport said. "It has an internal core of tungsten, shaped more like an arrow than anything else. The rest of the projectile is either a casing that protects the core as it's being fired, or an explosive charge that accelerates the arrow upon impact. Bottom line, the SABOT punched a relatively small hole, about two inches in diameter, though one side and out the other. It caused explosive decompression, killing the two-man crew and damaging some of the instruments. But the craft itself is basically intact."

"And what does SABOT stand for?" Lee asked.

"Actually, it's not an acronym. It's just the French word for 'wooden shoe.' I've no idea how it got that name. Keep in mind this howitzer design is five hundred years old, and the munitions were designed for a different threat."

"So, Chief," Chambers asked, turning back to Raymond, "what have we got?"

Raymond smiled broadly this time, looking like himself for the first time since the injuries suffered during his attack. "Sir, we have an intact MWC device, or at least, we have the half that is organic to the vessels."

"And what does that get us?"

"In the long run," Raymond said, "given the correct laboratory, we can reverse-engineer it and duplicate the function."

"And in the short run?" the admiral asked.

"In the short run," Raymond said, "it gives us enough to make sure these guys have a very bad day the next time we meet."

Lee spoke up. "I have a question for Midshipman Danner. You said you had decoded all the messages sent out. That's not true."

"You are correct, ma'am," replied Danner. "That was a lie ordered by the admiral, designed to get a response out of Commodore Vance."

"I don't understand," Lee said.

"If Vance believed all his transmissions were compromised," Chambers said, "he would believe his cover was blown. At that point, his most likely course of action would be to kill Raymond as a last act to impede our work toward MWC technology."

"And Mr. Nemeth?" Lee asked.

"Master Warrant Officer Nemeth is older than he looks," Chambers said with a smile. "He was my training instructor when I joined Special Operations a long time ago. Then, later, we served together for many years. He was my master chief when I was a squadron commander. I asked him to monitor Vance's biometrics along with Dr. Zakany during the meeting. I assumed that when Vance heard that his coded messages were compromised, his blood pressure, pulse, and respiration would spike. Am I correct that that did happen?" he asked, looking at Zakany.

"Yes, sir," she responded.

"And I wanted my old master chief to be alerted. I knew if Vance moved against any one of us, Master Warrant Officer Nemeth would do what was needed."

Chambers looked at Raymond and said, "Sorry, Chief Raymond, but you were bait. However, I can assure you that with Mr. Nemeth here, you were not at any risk."

"Not a problem, sir," Raymond said. "You got the guy who did this to me," pointing to his head.

Admiral Chambers turned to Lee and said, "Commander Lee, bring the fleet out of jump status. It's time for the Achilles Battle Fleet to go on the offensive."

CHAPTER 38

A FUNERAL ORATION

Chambers stood in front a row of seventeen coffins, a Marine honor guard with rifles at attention off to one side. Each of the coffins was draped with the national flag of its occupant's home country, except those of the four Marines, which were covered by the Human Alliance Marine Corps colors, as was their tradition. Chambers faced several hundred of the crew in the largest hangar bay of the command ship HC *Centurion*. The bay door was open to space, only the airlock force field keeping the vacuum at bay. The ceremony was being broadcast live to all vessels in the fleet.

He spoke steadily and calmly. "No man or woman is worthy to speak of these honored dead. They are all heroes, and their lives and their last moments were spent in honor of the greater good and in protection of their shipmates. But I am their commanding officer, and it falls to me to speak the words. They did not shirk their duty; and I will not shy away from mine. Not today, and not tomorrow.

"Marcus Aurelius, emperor of Rome, wrote in his meditations that all men die—but not all men die whining. These men and women died fighting against terrible odds, without complaint, and in some cases in the knowledge of the certainty of their deaths. Six months ago, we were a thrown-together, mismatched band of vessels, making a hasty withdrawal from a contested area. Today, we are a battle fleet, hardened by training, combat, and sorrow.

"Our president has ordered us to conserve our capabilities and to prepare for offensive operations. Thanks to the valor of those who have perished, and the good work of those who have survived, we are now in a position to take the fight to the enemy. That is what we will do in the following days, weeks, and months. And we will continue for as long as it takes to win this war, or until we ourselves fall.

"We now know the home base of those who carried out these attacks. We have the advantage of surprise, but far more importantly, we have the will and the skill and the duty to carry forward this attack. We will hit them hard, and we will be relentless. If they have a thought before they perish, it will be that they should never have attacked the Achilles Battle Fleet. We are going to hurt them; we are going to take away their ability to harm us or any other element of the Alliance. Every one of you is a combatant. These honored dead include great warriors who died in honorable combat. Here also lie technicians who refused to abandon their posts and fought hard, to the death, to see their duty through and to protect their shipmates.

"You are well-trained, well-led, and well-equipped. I have every confidence that you will perform well in the coming combat. But I also know there will come a time when this struggle will try the souls of the best of us. That is when we must remember these fallen, that is when we must force our adversaries to understand the consequences of attacking us, and that is when we will remember that we are the Achilles Battle Fleet."

The Marine bugler played the traditional melody for the fallen, and the honor guard snapped through the routine of firing three volleys of seven, for a total of twenty-one shots, out through the open bay door and into interstellar space.

CHAPTER 39

BECOMING WHO YOU ARE

The next few weeks were the hardest since the attack of December 7. Most noticeably, the grandfatherly, gentlemanly Admiral Chambers was gone. In his place was a leader fiercely determined to prepare for and win the next fight. Lee suspected his failure to have understood the treachery beneath his own nose had moved him deeply. Vance had been Chambers' direct subordinate. Chambers himself had promoted him to commodore, but somehow, for months, the admiral had failed to see the traitor in his own close-knit family.

Lee knew it wasn't just the failure that had changed him. Chambers had said several times that failure was a necessary part of moving forward, of achieving great success. No, it was that people had died because of it.

One day, she had come into his office when he didn't see her. He was watching on his screen the recorded security camera feed of the provost guard fighting to the last to protect the command post. She was behind him and could see what he saw, what she herself had seen many times, both on screen and in her dreams. The CPO in command was one of the first to fall, out front of his team, leading as he was bound to. The last to fall was an eighteen-year-old apprentice shore patrolman. He had expended all his ammunition, so he did exactly as he had been trained to do: he fixed his bayonet to his carbine and charged his enemy. At the very last, he took a volley of fire to his torso and legs. Mortally wounded, he fell forward and thrust his blade into the face of a black-masked assailant, shouting in defiance, "Come on, you bastards, take this!"

Lee could see in the reflection of the screen that tears streamed down Chambers' face, and his shoulders shook. She left quietly. Chambers had posthumously awarded the Navy Cross to the entire detachment and the Medal of Honor to the apprentice shore patrolman who had fought so bravely.

Nowadays, Chambers was like a man on fire. He was everywhere, overseeing training, preparations, planning. Lee thought she could see in him the man he was twenty years before, a SpecOps squadron commander. So strange that the war had brought forward the core personalities of all of them. Her dad called it the *agon*. It was the ancient Greek word for struggle, the basis for the modern English word *agony*. Sometimes, there was simply a time to fight, a time to grow into the warrior you were meant to be. Lee felt like her skin was on fire; she so longed for the combat, for the battle rage she had felt during the fight for the command post.

She trained hard in her martial arts during the few hours she had free, but she didn't trust herself to spar with anyone except Wasp— and even then, only with full protective gear. She knew her power now; it was deadly, and she wasn't entirely sure she could control it. Wasp understood. He was the only one who ever could, she decided. They would square off alone in the sparring area, when no one else was training. Something had changed in her style, in her power and speed. It was as if she understood her own martial art for the first time.

She went at him hard, blindingly fast. Her strikes accelerated throughout the movement and through her target. But for the heavy protection, her strikes would be breaking his bones. And he fought back, but despite his height and weight advantage, and the years of training as a Marine commando, he could not match her focused rage. Once, when they had been sparring for about twenty minutes, she lost track of everything but the fight. They were no longer in the sparring circle. She had driven him out, blow after blow. Even through the body armor she knew he was feeling it, but she couldn't stop herself. Finally, he was against the bulkhead, hands in a defensive posture as she hammered again and again. Each time he tried to strike at her, it seemed as if he moved in slow motion, and she easily slipped his strike, only to pound him again.

Then, as if in a dream, she heard a voice say, "Break!" Somehow, it penetrated through her rage-trance, and she stopped. She came out of her dream to see Admiral Chambers placing himself between them. Lee opened her mouth to speak, but nothing came out, so stunned was she. Chambers must have come around to check on the training, as he often did, and decided the time had come to stop what looked like something possibly out of control. To her surprise, he simply called them back to the center of the sparring area, gave the command for them to bow to each other, and formally ended the match. It was as if he understood what was happening to her. She knew Wasp understood, that he must have gone through something similar in his years of fighting. And then she knew, as surely as anything in life, that Chambers had been through this too—this becoming a warrior.

Lee started to speak, though she had no idea what words were about to emerge. But Chambers held up his finger to stop her and said simply, "Did you know that I knew your father?"

"My father?" she repeated dumbly.

"Yes, Grand Master Lee," Chambers said. "It was thirty-five years ago, when I did a tour in Hong Kong. I begged him to train me. At first, he said no. But I came back every day after my duty day. He completely ignored me. Finally, I picked up a broom and swept the dojo."

Lee was intrigued. "What did he do?"

"He brought out a mop and a bucket and went back into his office," the admiral said with a laugh.

"So did he let you train then?" she asked.

"Yes and no. He was training me already. The mop was my tool, my weapon, for learning patience. After about a week of doing that every night, he ordered me to line up with the other students. I spent the next twelve months learning from him; it was the best and hardest year of my life."

He paused for a moment and then said, "Beijing got hit on the seventh, not Hong Kong. I don't know if your father survived. I hope he did, but if he died, I know he lived as a warrior, a great teacher. And I know he would have been proud of you."

Then Chambers turned around and walked away without a word.

CHAPTER 40

THE RECONNAISSANCE

With Zakany's help, Midshipman Danner and his team of intelligence analysts tracked the enemy to a small moon of a gas giant, in a system well off any well-travelled area of the galaxy. The first part of the preparation had been reconnaissance. Chambers had made clear that, this time, surprise was key to success. Through long-range surveillance via drones, a picture of the scenario had come together.

In the work-up for the operation, Chambers had taken a more direct hand in running the staff. Lee, as the chief of staff, was supposed to run all the meetings and filter the information to the admiral so he could concentrate on making key decisions. Clearly, Chambers no longer wanted that. As a former SpecOps commander, he seemed most comfortable with a small staff that he directly supervised.

Lee might have been offended, but she wasn't. She had other duties as the deputy leader for the intelligence section. What she wanted, more than anything, was a chance to get into the coming fight. She worked closely with Danner and his team, sifting through the various bits of intelligence that came in, trying to get a clear picture of what they might be facing. They looked at everything they could find: old survey charts, accident reports, even the logs of merchant vessels that had traversed the area, going back a century. Most interesting to Lee was a record of a long-since-abandoned mining colony on the moon, so obscure that it was just called Alpha 51. Supposedly, it had been left untouched for about eighty years, abandoned after the mineral ores ran out.

Another interesting point was a fairly substantial asteroid belt in the system, which made it dangerous for starship navigation. These asteroids jostled one another gravitationally, and occasionally one or more would break loose from the belt and fall toward the system's star, often causing meteor showers on both the gas giant and its moon. This hazard was one reason the system had been considered unprofitable, as the occasional meteor strike caused damage and some casualties to the mining company crew.

She had Danner send out his drones mixed in with the various asteroids, to gather what intelligence they could. It turned out the moon was active; somebody was definitely using it. They saw a number of structures, and it was clear there was some subsurface activity occurring. They also detected curious energy readings, far larger than could be accounted for by normal generators or even a nuclear power plant.

She was meeting with the intelligence team when Raymond finally figured it out. "They're using the gas giant. Like Jupiter in our solar system, this gas giant is just shy of becoming a star itself. It generates its own heat. The gravity isn't so intense as to initiate a nuclear reaction, but there's definitely a lot of gravitational stress and pressure. Whoever is operating the moon base has figured out how to safely draw on that energy source."

Lee asked, intrigued, "Is it enough power to project the MWC vessels that we've been seeing?"

Raymond considered that a moment and then said, "Yes, it's more than enough to accomplish what we've seen attack the fleet. Whether it accounts for attacks and movements all over the galaxy, like those we saw in December, I can't say."

Lee said nothing. She sometimes found Raymond to be frustrating with his precise academic caution, but the point was taken. This was an enemy base; it was the base that had launched the attack on the fleet. The question now was how to get at it.

"What does the enemy use the power for?" Lee asked abruptly.

Raymond nodded and said, in his maddeningly academic way, "We know they use the power for the MWC movement. What else they might use it for, we can't say."

Lee closed her eyes and struggled for calm. "Would the power level fluctuate when the MWC process is in use?"

"Yes," he said. "As I said before, the power required to move vessels and people is enormous. It would be wasteful to keep power levels anywhere near peak requirements."

"So is it safe to say that when they use the peak requirements, the power output would be noticeable, even from a great distance?"

"Absolutely," he said. "Certainly, anywhere in this system, maybe even outside the system."

"That's why they're located so far outside the trafficked areas," Danner said. "If they were closer in, they would be detected anytime they used their MWC technology."

"And that's also why they haven't done more than they have, why the attacks have been limited so far," Raymond said. "They're either facing a limitation on their power supply or a restriction imposed for security reasons."

"Could they be conducting all of the MWC activity from this single location?" Lee asked.

"No," Raymond said. "In theory, if they have enough power, it *could* be done. But they have another problem that makes this so unlikely as to approach impossibility."

"What's that?" Lee asked.

"It has to do with timing," Raymond said. "At great distances— I'm talking here about light-years, maybe thousands of light-years— there's no single frame of reference in time that is privileged, in terms of the sequence of how things happen. That's because the universe itself is expanding, and so the objects within it, like star systems, are moving in reference to all other objects."

"Got you so far," Lee said with forced patience. "Now close the loop for me."

"Some of that motion is at relativistic speeds," Raymond said. "For example, this star system, which seems, and is, stable as long as we're in it, is actually moving away from our home star system at about 20 percent the speed of light. Not only that, both are moving laterally because of the rotation of the Milky Way, which is a spiral galaxy."

Lee said nothing, her frustration barely hidden.

Raymond seemed to notice her impatience and said, "So the bottom line is, there is no way, from a great distance, to know or even predict where and when things are or will be with precision, nor to even know in what sequence things take place. They have to be closer, in the same frame of reference, or at least not too far out."

"Could that be the reason for the corvette?" Danner asked.

Raymond froze, his eyes wide, and then said, "Yes, damn it. I should have thought of it. Well done, Danner. The corvette was needed because of the great distance from the home station. It wasn't there for combat power; it was there to control the MWC activity."

"And that might explain the very large release of energy when it was destroyed," Danner suggested.

"Precisely," Raymond agreed. "The energy release, that explosion, was too large to be accounted for by the vessel alone. Even if it had a nuclear weapon aboard, it wouldn't have been a fraction of that big. It must have been a conduit for energy required for the MWC activity."

"So what does that tell us?" Lee inquired.

"You remember when I said months ago that the enemy was like a child with a new toy with this technology? I meant it was lopsided. The enemy can do just this one thing, MWC, but the rest of their technology is no more advanced than ours."

"I remember."

"This proves it," Raymond said triumphantly. "Even the technology they're using has major limitations. They've known for months that the fleet was the biggest threat to their success. They had their spies near the top of our leadership, they've known our every move, and yet they haven't been able to stop us."

"You're right, Chief," Lee said. "It's not from lack of trying. They've done their best against us and failed." She looked around at the team and said, in a voice that sent a cold chill down Danner's spine, "And now they are going to feel *our* best."

CHAPTER 41

THE SHUFFLE

Chambers called a leaders' meeting in his ready room. Present were Bowman, Baker, Lee, Danner, Raymond, Davenport, Wasp, Zakany, and Nemeth. They sat around the table, with Chambers at the head. Since the admiral had called the meeting himself and hadn't told her the reason, Lee said nothing. Her only fear was that Chambers would somehow assign her duties that kept her out of the coming fight. She did wonder what Zakany was doing here, since she wasn't the head of the medical department. In fact, she was the lowest ranking of the three medical officers, though she had to admit to herself that she was one of the best medical officers she had ever worked with. She had heart, and it was clear she was desperately proud to be serving the Navy in wartime in a position of responsibility.

The new Chambers got right to the point: "I brought you here today to tell you about some changes I'm making in advance of the coming assault." Lee liked the sound of that. The Achilles Battle Fleet was going into battle. No more defense; no more hiding from the enemy. "The formal operations order brief is still two days away,"

Chambers said, "but we all know the outline of the plan. I'm making these changes now so you can have a chance to incorporate the new structure into your plans. The Marines are going to play a pivotal role, and I am assigning more naval personnel to their detachment to ensure a robust capability."

He looked over at Captain Davenport and said, "Captain Davenport is promoted to the rank of major of Marines. The entire naval security detachment is now under your authority, Major. Gunnery Sergeant Wasp, you are promoted to command sergeant major of Marines. If I'm not mistaken, that makes you the youngest CSM ever, or at least in my memory, which goes back quite a bit." Chambers' face wore a hint of a smile, the first Lee had seen in a long time. "Next: Sergeant Wilcox is promoted to gunnery sergeant." Lee knew Wilcox, a forty-something staff sergeant, had commanded the howitzer team that took down the MWC vessels. "Major, I know you have some internal vacancies, so I leave it to you to fill the ranks as you see fit."

"Aye aye, sir," Davenport said, with no discernible emotion. "I will inform him."

"Captain Bowman," Chambers said. "I know you aren't going to like this, but I need to do what's best for the fleet. You are therefore relieved of command of the Achilles Aerospace Wing." Gasps followed in the wake of this announcement. Chambers continued, "With the loss of Commodore Vance, I need a new deputy commanding officer. You are brevetted to commodore." (Brevet was a temporary promotion; Bowman would wear the rank and be addressed as commodore, but at some point, he would either revert to captain or be formally promoted.) "Sorry I can't make that permanent at the moment, but because of your reserve status and limited time in grade, it's beyond my authority." He moved on. "Lieutenant Commander Baker, you are promoted to captain. You will take command of the Achilles Aerospace Wing."

"Aye sir," Baker said in his unemotional Southern drawl.

"Midshipman Danner, you are promoted to ensign. I'm tired of seeing a middie running the intelligence section. You'll still need to complete your midshipman's training course in due time, but our operations will take priority for the present. You will serve as the battle captain in the command post for the coming battle." Lee knew assigning Danner to the battle captain position meant she was out of that job as well. "Medical Officer Zakany." Zakany straightened as if electrocuted. "You present a problem."

"Sir, I'm sorry, but ..."

"Please don't interrupt," Chambers said gently. "You present a problem because I need your skills on the upcoming operation. Normally, that wouldn't be a problem, but six months ago, you weren't even formally in the Navy. And although your medical qualifications as a nurse practitioner are beyond reproach, you are not a physician." He paused and looked hard at her. "As a medical officer, you have the protocol rank equal to naval lieutenant," he continued. "But an MO is a limited-duty position. You can't serve outside your medical duties, and your authority is restricted to medical personnel and to medical issues only. That will not do for what I have planned."

"Yes, sir," she said, tears starting to well up in her eyes.

"Therefore, I have transferred you to the Medical Service Corps. Your rank is now lieutenant. You will retain your authority to practice medicine, but you will be considered an unrestricted line officer. The reasons for that will become clear in the near future."

Zakany gasped with relief, tears now streaming down her cheeks. "Yes, sir," she said, her face gleaming with joy.

"Master Warrant Officer Nemeth," the admiral said next.

"Sir," Nemeth said, with the same deadpan look on his face that Lee had seen on him the first time she met him, the night of the attack on the fleet.

"Mr. Nemeth and I have a confession to make, don't we?" the admiral said, with a genuine smile this time.

"Sir, the first lesson I ever taught you when you were a recruit was not to confess to anything, ever," Nemeth responded with a rare smile of his own.

"And yet, the time has come," said the admiral. "The Master Chief Warrant was on the TS *Honolulu* on December 7 because he was being retired. He has extended beyond the mandatory age limit by special waiver twice that I know of."

"Three times, sir."

"Three times, then," the admiral said. "The final time, his request for a fourth extension was refused personally by the chief of Naval Operations. I know, because I argued with him myself. Apparently, my vote didn't carry much weight. The CNO claimed I sucker-punched him in a bar a million years ago when we were both petty officers, so he was not sympathetic to my request. I have no recollection of that."

Lee tried to imagine a young, brash Chambers punching someone in a drunken bar fight. Maybe that side of him, violent and undisciplined, was what her father saw in him and what made him reluctant to train Chambers in the martial arts.

"Of course, after the stop-loss order, all retirements were postponed. So we were able to use him. And to return the only compliment he ever gave me as a recruit, his service to the fleet has been adequate," Chambers said with a smile.

Nemeth nodded seriously, apparently taking it as high praise, and said, "Thank you, sir."

"Unfortunately, one of the few administrative instructions we received from naval command has stated clearly that sailors above a certain age must be released from active duty. So, in this matter, my hands are tied," the admiral said. "As of this moment, Master Chief Warrant Officer Matthias Nemeth, after forty-five years of service, you are honorably retired from the Navy."

The room fell silent. Nemeth showed no sign of emotion, as usual.

"Now that that's out of the way," continued the admiral, "one of the rights that I have as a CO in wartime is to recall to active duty any retired personnel, and on this, there is no age restriction. Master Chief Warrant Officer Matthias Nemeth, you are hereby recalled to active duty at your retirement rank, for duty as determined by the naval service, until the conflict is terminated, you voluntarily retire, or you die in service."

"Yes, sir," Nemeth said, this time with a distinct smile on his face.

The admiral turned to Lee. "Lieutenant Commander Lee."

"Sir," she said.

"You have served as my chief of staff and as the deputy of the intelligence section for six months," he said. "In the beginning, I needed a regular naval officer in that billet, an academy graduate who understood how staffs work. You did that well, and I am thankful for it." He paused and then continued, "But to be honest, I don't need a chief of staff any longer, and I think you will agree you've outgrown that position."

Lee nodded, knowing that what he said was true, but not wanting to say anything either presumptuous or offensive.

"And if I'm not mistaken," continued the admiral, "you would like to take on something a little more hands-on. Did I get that right?"

"Yes, sir," she said simply.

"I thought so," Chambers said. "As of now, you are assigned as naval liaison to the Achilles Special Operations Command. You will report to Major Davenport on operational command issues and to me in your role as liaison officer.

Chambers turned and addressed the whole group, asking, "Any questions?"

"No, sir," they answered in unison.

"Meeting dismissed."

CHAPTER 42

THE PRISONERS

Lieutenant Laura Zakany was nervous. Admiral Chambers and some of his officers were en route to see her.

For a week, she had been working with the prisoners who had been taken into custody along with Commodore Vance. The admiral had made it clear he wanted them treated humanely, as prisoners of war. But he also wanted to know more about them. Under her supervision, he had the provost investigators question them about their actions as spies. All but Vance. He was off-limits to interrogators until he recovered from his wounds, and even then only with the express permission of the admiral.

All the prisoners were more than happy to talk, and all of them claimed there was some big mistake. They stuck to their stories about their cover identities. Zakany had to admit, they seemed convincing. She had the biometrics equipment monitor their responses to see if there was any evidence of deceit. Nothing showed. As far as she could tell, they believed what they were saying and had no knowledge of ever having anything to do with the enemy. At one point, an investigator showed a twenty-five-year-old yeoman a video of herself tampering with a com device. She claimed the video must have been faked, and she started to cry and said she had done nothing wrong.

Since they were all willing to cooperate, Zakany had given them a battery of tests, starting with standard psych exams, the same ones the Navy used for recruitment to determine aptitude for skill sets, assess intelligence, and screen for undesirable disorders or personality traits. The normal testing routine asked both written and oral questions, checking the responses against a standardized key to develop a profile of the applicant. But Zakany had taken it a step further; she had the biometrics program check their bodily responses while they were answering. At the same time, she monitored the device each had in their head. From the beginning, these devices had been prevented from making any external communications, and the prisoners had been isolated from each other so there could be no possibility they could share information, act in unison, or contact the enemy. These precautions were also designed to prevent the enemy from trying to transport them away or perhaps even kill them.

The truth was, Zakany really didn't really know much about those devices. They were embedded in each prisoner's frontal lobe, and as far as she could tell, not by any type of surgery. There was none of the tissue scarring that should have been present, even if the procedure had been done by the best brain surgeon. In the meantime, there was nothing to do about it. Removing the device surgically might not be fatal, but it could certainly harm the prisoner, and harming the prisoners was forbidden, as Chambers had made clear.

Interestingly, it was the one area the prisoners would not or could not discuss. She had told the yeoman, "You have a foreign device in your brain. We don't really know what it does or how you got it. Do you know anything about it?"

"No, ma'am," said the woman.

"Will you give me permission to try to remove it surgically?"

"I would not like that, ma'am," she responded hesitantly. "I don't have that ... No."

And for a tiny fraction of a second, her facial expression went blank, and Zakany could see from her monitor that the device in the prisoner's brain had been activated, releasing just the slightest neural-electrical stimulation.

She asked the same questions to each of the prisoners and each time got a similar response. So she ran additional tests and asked more questions. What she found astonished her, and that was why she felt bold enough to notify the admiral. Of course, he had told her to call him if she found anything, though the idea that she would call the admiral directly seemed more than a bit presumptuous. But he had been very calm about it when she did call.

He just said, "I'll be down in twenty minutes, and I'm bringing some of the staff."

Chambers entered the detention area with Captain—no, *Commodore* Bowman, Major Davenport, Lieutenant Commander Lee, and Ensign Danner. The Marine guard called attention as they entered. "Lieutenant Zakany," the admiral said, "let's see what you have."

"Sir, I have been examining the prisoners, both mentally and physically, using biometric equipment and several oral and written tests."

Chambers nodded and said, "Please continue."

"First, they do not appear to be aware that they are clones or spies," she said. "At least, none of the biometric monitoring equipment can detect signs of deception."

"Hmm," Chambers said. "I have some experience with techniques to resist interrogation. We are trained to use them if captured. But to have several prisoners, eight of them, able to fool your equipment? Not even Oracle could do that. How do you think they're doing it?"

"Actually, sir, I don't think they *are* fooling the equipment. I think they believe they're who they purport to be. How this has been accomplished, I don't know, but I *have* found some anomalies."

"Tell me," he said.

"They don't show deception, but they do show stress, especially at some questions or even key words or formulations." She showed the group the video of her questioning the young yeoman, along with the data readout from the monitoring equipment. "As you can see, sir, at some point, their chip stimulates their brain and provokes a response.

And in each instance, the response is accompanied by an immobile facial expression and a slight pause, sometimes even a stutter."

"You said, 'In each case.' Am I correct in assuming you did this with the other prisoners?"

"Yes, sir. I repeated the same questions to all of them and got a similar response." Zakany paused and then continued, "I also conducted other psychological and psychometric tests, and I found a pattern. Some words and concepts cause a reaction. For example, if I mention a color, any color, there's a slight signal from the chip, a micro expression, and a hesitation. It is very slight. I would not have caught it most of the time, but the equipment catches it. Even the word 'color' will cause it. It's the same for shapes, spatial relationship, and names of things, especially if the name is unfamiliar to them."

"What do you think is the reason for this?"

"I can't be sure, sir," she said, now speaking quickly. "But I'm guessing the chip is designed for several functions. Clearly, it is used to keep them from answering or even seriously considering information that might conflict with who they are supposed to be. As far as the names go, that could be a learning routine, prompting the neocortex to store valuable information. As for the colors, shapes, and spatial relationships, I have a theory, but I wanted to show you it before I try to express it." When Zakany was nervous, her Hungarian accent became more pronounced.

"Let's see it, then," Chambers said.

"Please follow me, sir." Zakany led them into one of the detention cells. Inside was the young yeoman she had questioned earlier. The young woman looked up from her bunk and snapped to attention when she saw the admiral.

"As you were," Chambers said gently.

The young woman came to parade rest and looked directly at the admiral.

"Yeoman," Zakany said.

"Yes, ma'am?" responded the woman.

"I am going to ask you some questions, and I want you to relax and answer honestly. Can you do that?"

"Yes, ma'am."

209

Zakany held up a flip-book containing pages with different images on each. "Please tell me what you see as I show it to you. Describe the shape, color, or word you see."

As she said this, the yeoman blinked several times. "Okay," she said after a moment.

Zakany began by flipping up pages in rapid sequence, showing a new image as soon as she got a response.

The woman said, "Blue. Yellow. A pipe. John ... Jonathan, Johansson, Zachariah, Ezekiel. Black, buh, buh, Thomas, but without the 'H'; ha ha, what's that mean?" Then the woman froze, her face a mask, and said in a deeper voice, almost like that of a man, "Standing by." Then she collapsed. Zakany seemed ready for this and caught her as she fell, gently laying her down on the bunk. She then led the group back to her office.

Back in Zakany's office, Chambers asked, "So what did we just see?"

"My theory," Zakany said, looking at the group as if expecting to be contradicted, "is that the chip is programmed to put subjects into a state receptive for instructions if they hear a specific series of words, concepts, or names."

"So why did she collapse?" Lee asked.

"I am thinking that it is because we did not give her the right words or sequence. But the words we did use triggers the routine, if I can call it that. That chip uses it to begin looking for the code. Since it didn't find the code, it shuts down or resets."

"Lieutenant Zakany," the admiral said, "that's going to help a lot." She beamed at the praise. "But now I need you to do something more for me."

CHAPTER 43

THEY ARE US

Raymond's long-awaited briefing on the results of the examination of the MWC vessels was about to begin. For once, Lee wasn't in charge of the assembled group. Danner had sent out an invitation on behalf of the admiral, and that was it. No longer the chief of staff, she was just another participant in the meeting. She was surprised at her feelings about that. She was relieved not to have the responsibility any longer but also felt a bit of melancholy at the loss of her former role, where she felt she was in the center of things.

"Admiral, I think everyone is here," Danner said. Not very formal, thought Lee, but it wasn't her responsibility anymore. Danner was wearing his new insignia, and she had to admit, he looked the part. He'd matured a lot since that day just over six months ago when he had interviewed with Bowman to be part of the newly formed intel section.

She looked around and saw that in addition to the usual command group, the two commanding officers of the frigates *Alabama* and *Guangdong* were present. She didn't know them well. They were both commanders, regular officers; tough-looking, no-nonsense types, as most ship drivers were.

"Let's begin," the admiral said. "Chief Raymond, please present your findings."

Raymond stood behind a lectern with a holoimage pointer. "Sir, ladies, and gentlemen," he began. "Thanks to the sacrifice of many, we have had in our possession for the past few weeks an enemy macro-wave collapse, or MWC, vessel." He clicked the pointer, and a 3-D image of the spacecraft rotated in front of them. "It was damaged during the snatch, but the majority of the onboard equipment used for the MWC jumps was intact or at least salvageable." He paused and looked around, as if to see if his audience was following him. Lee felt her frustration rise at this bit of theatre, which the man was so prone to, but she reminded herself that Raymond's eccentricities were no longer her problem. Then Raymond surprised her, and probably everyone who had ever heard him speak before, by launching into a concise explanation of his findings.

"Here are the highlights of what we found." Raymond displayed a holo-slide with bullet points. "First, as we suspected, the MWC technology is a variant of the technology we were using years ago during the Jupiter orbital trials. What has been advanced since that time is the ability to modify the Higgs field to reduce the mass of any object and thus move it nearly instantaneously from one point to another.

"Second, the engineering is advanced to the point that large vessels with human pilots can be transported in relative safety. Third, the power requirement to do this is substantial, meaning that it presents a single point of vulnerability that, when in use, cannot be hidden easily, at least not locally within a star system.

"Fourth, we cannot reproduce the MWC effect at this time, but we *can* counter it, at least within a sphere with a radius of about a hundred kilometers. Within that sphere, we can alter the Higgs field such that their MWC technology will not function properly. Because we have not had the chance to experiment, there is a variance, or probability, of performance only."

"Let me just interrupt for a moment," the admiral said. "When you say we can interfere, but there is a variance, please give us examples of what we can expect."

"Sir, the MWC technology brings the Higgs field values to zero along the projected path of whatever they're transporting. That reduces the mass of the transported object to zero and allows the movement. When we alter the field locally, it prevents the MWC devices from dropping the Higgs field values to zero."

"What is the likely result?" Chambers asked.

"Without the chance to experiment, we don't know what effect that will have on the vessels transported into what we're calling our area of denial, or AOD. At one end of the spectrum of possible outcomes, the vessels will be catastrophically destroyed, as they regain mass unexpectedly while moving at relativistic speed. At the other end of the spectrum, the vessels will be unable to rematerialize and will continue through our area, either to reappear out of position or, possibly, to never reappear at all."

One of the frigate captains raised his hand: the thin man with a mustache.

Raymond said, "Yes, sir?"

"Commander Adam Montgomery, CO of the *Alabama*," the man said, with a faint British accent. "Chief, how will this defense apparatus be deployed, and will it interfere with our own ship's operations?"

"How it will be deployed is an operational decision for others to make," Raymond said. "For it to be effective, we'll need to place field amplifiers at several points throughout our formation. As far as any effect it might have on our own operations, we have no evidence that our field modification will impact the operations of our vessels at all. That said, the chance of a problem is not zero. This is entirely new technology."

Baker spoke up. "On the snatch operation, we lost a fighter to some sort of weapon fired from the corvette. What was that about, and can we expect to see that in the future?"

Raymond looked over at the admiral, who nodded. "That was the MWC technology being weaponized. The enemy basically emitted an MWC beam ... well, this isn't really what it does, but it's an approximation. As I've already mentioned, along the line of sight, the Higgs field is reduced to zero, and anything that has mass in its path instantly loses that mass. So I'm sorry to say that the fighter and the pilot basically came apart at the subatomic level. Those subatomic components then dispersed at the speed of light."

"What I don't understand," Bowman said, "is why they haven't used that weapon before? Why keep throwing fighters at us, when they could do real damage with this Higgs cannon thing?"

"I can answer that," Danner said. "Remember, they were pretending to be Others. They tried to hide the MWC technology altogether. That's why we think their base is so far off the well-travelled routes and why they haven't used these weapons."

"Yet," the admiral said. "They haven't used them *yet*, because they didn't want anyone to know who they really are."

"But they did use it during the snatch operations," Baker said.

"Yes, but only to try avoid capture, and only because you were pressing them harder than they expected," Danner said.

"Do we have any defense against this … ray gun?" Montgomery asked.

"Yes, we do," Raymond said. "It's twofold. The first line of defense is our own anti-Higgs field generator, which will weaken their ray gun, as you call it. The second is that we can, thankfully, modify our shields to protect against it. Used together, this is our best defense against the enemy's MWC technology."

Commander Montgomery raised his hand and stated, "Admiral, you said they were only pretending to be Others. May I ask if you know who they are?"

"Yes," said the admiral. "They are us."

CHAPTER 44

THE LIAISON ENDS

In the final days before the assault on the enemy's moon base, Lee felt she had no real duties in her new role as liaison to the newly formed Special Operations Command. Davenport was the commanding officer, and he reported directly to the admiral, who no longer needed a chief of staff, so she basically had no role to play, at least for the present. She reported this to Davenport, who suggested she fall in with their preparations for the "insertion," as he called it. He also asked her to help integrate the naval components to the SOC, which was fine with her.

In the days that followed, she got a good look at the internal workings of the Marine commando training and preparation. Of course, it wasn't *just* Marines; the upcoming operation was larger than could be accomplished by the Marines alone. The Marines were going to provide the heavy lifting, but they didn't have all the logistics, communications, fire support, transportation, or higher-level medical treatment capability that would be needed for this operation.

Davenport reviewed with her his concept of the operation, and she had to admit, she was fascinated. The objective of the task force was to capture the MWC generator on the moon. The problem was twofold: first, how to get in past the moon's defenses, and second, how to know the precise location of the generator to focus limited assets against that single point. There were other, secondary objectives: to secure prisoners, to preserve and gather intelligence, and, of course, to survive.

Chambers had made it clear that the Achilles Battle Fleet would sacrifice all, if necessary, to inflict damage on the enemy, but he didn't want to lose any more combat power than was necessary. He felt the fight against the enemy would be prolonged, and he wanted the fleet to be part of that struggle. Lee remembered the sight of him weeping while watching the recording of the death of the young provost guard. Clearly, he didn't want to waste lives.

Time for preparation was cut short. The admiral felt that the enemy would inevitably suspect that all the impostors imbedded in the fleet had been compromised. Although they seemed impervious to meaningful interrogation, their enemy could not be sure that something would lead the fleet to their secret base. Thus, the admiral wanted to hit them sooner rather than later.

In the meantime, Lee trained with the Marines daily. They seemed to accept her, perhaps because she'd led that class on combative techniques, but more probably because she knew their routine from having gone through the Marine OCS while in the academy. The Marines were relentless in their training: Fire, maneuver, communications, checking equipment, repeat. Over and over. They never got tired of it, and they were never satisfied. She loved it. She remembered how fast the Marines had been when they entered the command center during the attack—not a movement wasted, not a single round gone astray. She was beginning to understand why.

And for the first time in many years, she was struggling to keep up. They were training in specially modified battle armor for the upcoming operation. Although the gravity in the training area had been artificially reduced to match that of the moon, the armor was still heavy and bulky. But she struggled on, and some of what she could do surprised her. She found that she was a decent marksman; not as good as the Marines, but not bad, either. And she could move quickly, even in armor, her martial arts training having given her a sprinter's explosive speed. But what she liked the most was the EVMU practice. EVMU stood for extravehicular mobility unit, which was what they were calling the modified battle armor. These suits had been modified to do a lot more than just fight in the vacuum.

The Marines were just a little bit crazy, and some part of her wished she could go with them on this next insertion.

Two days before the operation was to start, Lee was summoned to the admiral's quarters. When she entered, she saw that Major Davenport was already present. She reported and waited for whatever was coming. The fact that Davenport was present caused her to think Chambers would ask for a report of the progress of the liaison.

"Commander Lee," Chambers said, "Major Davenport has told me he doesn't think he needs a naval liaison to the special operations command."

Since there was no question, Lee said only, "Yes, sir."

"How do you feel about that?" Chambers asked.

"I have to agree, sir," she said. "The communications channels are fully intact. The naval components have been integrated. There is no real role for a liaison, and it might even add an unnecessary step in communications back to headquarters." Although Lee knew what was happening was the right thing, she was disappointed that her short time with the Marines was coming to an end. She thought wryly, *Here's another job I'm getting the boot from.*

"The major has made another request," the admiral said. "He would like you detached to the SpecOps task force under his command."

Lee was surprised and delighted. "That would be an honor, sir," she said quickly.

"The problem is that you are senior to him by date of rank."

"That's not a problem for me, sir," said Lee. "I'll be glad to serve in any capacity the major wants me to."

"I'm glad to hear that," Chambers said with a smile. He turned to Davenport and said, "Major, say hello to your new deputy commander."

Davenport smiled and replied, "Thank you, sir." Clearly the two had discussed this before she arrived, and Chambers was feeling her out before making a decision.

Lee was stunned. There was no way she was qualified to be deputy commander of a SpecOps task force. She wanted to object, but her years of training, starting with the academy, kept her silent. No officer ever turned down a command position, much less one that involved personal danger.

In the end, all she said was, "Thank you, sir."

CHAPTER 45

INSERTION

Lee watched the gas giant they'd named Lilith rise above the horizon of the asteroid she and the thirteen other members of her detachment clung to. It was a beautiful sight, red with large swirling spots of blue and green. She knew it was deadly, mostly methane and nitrogen gas and other caustic chemicals, and far too hot to support life, even in the uppermost layers.

It was a killer in other ways too. It was a thousand times the mass of Earth, and its gravity was enormous. They had been inserted onto this asteroid twelve hours before. The asteroid had broken away from its cluster and had been falling inward toward the systems' star for a decade. Their projections showed that the asteroid would cut a path between Lilith and its moon within hours. It was the perfect cover for their insertion.

Because the asteroid was rotating, they saw Lilith rise and set every twenty-seven minutes. It was a sight Lee never tired of. They couldn't see the moon yet; it was too small and, in any case, would have been lost in the background clutter of stars this close to the galactic center. The moon would come later.

They had been inserted onto the asteroid early so as to avoid detection from the moon base. This asteroid was only one of many scattered through the system. They were a hazard to navigation, which was one of the reasons the mining facility had been abandoned so long ago. The intel section had surmised that the moon base's sensors would track the asteroid but otherwise pay it no attention since it wasn't on a collision course with the moon. The plan was to leave the asteroid, using only the propulsion jets in the EVMU suits, just as it was about to pass the moon and insert the team on the far side of a low ridge of hills that ran near the base.

They were in a rough circular perimeter formation, each in their EVMU suits—or as the Marines called them affectionately, "moo" suits. She was surprised at how comfortable the suits were and had been surprised further that she had been able to sleep for a few hours in hers. The Marines, who were accustomed to long hours and short breaks, were trained to sleep whenever the tactical situation warranted, and they did so now. A warning chimed in her ear, indicating an incoming call.

"Go for Lee," she said.

"You are approaching your kickoff point," the newly minted Ensign Danner said. "You should see the moon rise on your northwest quadrant right about ... now."

Just then the moon, a bright yellow, burst above the horizon. It was beautiful and terrifying.

"You should be feeling the tidal forces about now too," said Danner.

He was right. As the asteroid swung past the gas giant, its gravity pulled it inward and altered its course. The tidal forces kicked in hard.

It's a little like being on a roller coaster, she thought.

The asteroid was beginning to accelerate as Lilith's gravity whipped it past and away from itself. If not for their pitons hammered into the asteroid's rock surface, they would have been flung off their temporary home.

Here the plan got tricky. The team needed to push off from the asteroid at just the right moment, using the tidal forces of the gas giant to put them on the path toward their objective. "Marine Five," Lee said into her com channel. "Status check."

"Navy Six, this is Marine Five," responded Wasp. "We are a go, ma'am."

"Stand by for launch in sixty seconds," she said.

"Roger," Wasp said. "I have the count." Wasp was indicating that he would give the command to launch. They had worked out and rehearsed the sequence for the jump, as the Marines called it. Lee was in command of the detachment, but Wasp, as the sergeant major of the detachment, would translate her orders into actions for the Marines. "Detachment, stand up," Wasp ordered. The team stood up from their prone positions. They were attached to their pitons with a cable attached to their moo suits at the waist. "Status check," he ordered.

"Team One, ready."

"Team Two, ready."

"Navy Six, ready," Lee said.

"Marine Five, ready," Wasp said.

On her faceplate's HUD, Lee could see the relative position and movement of the asteroid and the moon. Her pulse quickened as she realized the speed at which the two were closing. Their path to the insertion point, or drop-zone, as the Marines termed it, was defined by a very narrow window of opportunity. They had modeled it and practiced it dozens of times in the simulator back with the fleet. Jump a second late, and they would miss the moon entirely and spiral out into space. Go a second early, and they would slam into the surface at over 100 kilometers per hour. The problem was that the asteroid wasn't entirely stable, so its rotation couldn't be modeled precisely, and therefore the moment to jump would have to be calculated in real time by the computers embedded in their moo suits and backed up by those in the operations center. Lee watched as the computer recalculated the trajectory as they approached the jump window. It was terrifying to see the rapid sequencing on the display showing the various trajectories, with their probability of success flashed up, only to be replaced by another scenario a second later.

"The gravity from the planet and moon have played havoc with your rock," she heard Danner say.

She looked up and saw that the moon and stars were beginning to career in a stomach-lurching way, which meant the asteroid had lost even its previous modest level of stability.

"Can we still get a good window?" Lee asked.

"Yes, but it's very tight," Danner said. "Your probability of success is dropping, and fluctuating wildly between 0 and 70 percent."

They had decided in advance to abort the jump if the probability dropped below 70 percent. If they missed the drop, they wouldn't get another chance for months, maybe never. It was only a matter of time before the enemy discovered the presence of the fleet in the area or changed up their security. This was their one chance, and they all knew it.

"I only need a three-second count," Wasp said in his eerily calm voice. He was indicating to both Lee and Danner that he only needed a three-second warning before giving the command to launch. If Danner's computer could give him that, the detachment could launch at a 70 percent probability of success.

"Stand by," Danner said. "Coming to you now." He paused and then said, "It's going to be a wild ride."

"Stand in the door," Wasp said. This was the traditional command for Marines to prepare to jump. Lee had been told that this command had originated with paratroopers jumping from aircraft in the wars of the mid-twentieth century. Now they used it to prepare to jump whether there was a door or not. Lee took up the ready position of knees bent, head forward so that her chin would rest on her chest. This was to allow the body to absorb the shock of acceleration.

Wasp said, "On my mark: Three, two, one, *mark*." As one being, the team launched themselves up and away from the asteroid. The connecting cables had small explosive charges that, when detonated, severed the connection to the piton and thrust the Marines in the direction of the jump. The tidal force was stronger than the weak gravity from the asteroid, and the team literally flew up into space.

Lee looked at her display and saw that Johnson, one of the Marines, had failed to launch.

"Team One lost one Marine on the jump," she heard that team's leader, Sergeant Frasier, report in. "Johnson, your status?"

"Team leader, I have a cable malfunction and am unable to jump."

"Roger; stay put. The fleet will send a recovery. Enjoy the show."

"Will comply," Johnson said. "Just send them in time to get me into the fight."

Lee knew that banter, though officially frowned upon, was ever-present during an operation. But she also knew that Johnson, the female private she had trained with during the martial arts session, would now be desperate to get back into the operation. This is what they lived for, and the thought of her mates going into harm's way without her would be torture for any Marine. Lee also knew that Johnson's risk was at least as high as that of the rest of them. There was no guarantee the fleet would be able to recover Johnson before her oxygen ran out; the asteroid could break up due to the conflicting tidal forces.

Lee privately wished Johnson the best.

CHAPTER 46

DESCENT INTO MADNESS

Lee felt the vertigo hit her like never before. Not even during parachute jumps on Earth had she ever felt anything like this. She was falling in space, the moon and Lilith flashing by in rapid sequence. She realized she must be spinning and adjusted her attitude controls to steady herself. Her heart was racing, and she knew her body was pumping adrenaline and other hormones into her system.

Danner's voice broke in on her thoughts: "Dr. Zakany is here with me, Commander, and she's indicating some concerns with your heart rate."

"Just enjoying my job," Lee said with a little laugh.

She could imagine Laura fretting over her bio-signs. They had grown close over the past two weeks. But she did try and steady her breathing. She also knew from her conversations with Zakany that the Marine commandos typically responded to stress by lowering their respiratory and cardiovascular rates. Zakany had explained that extreme danger actually had a calming effect on them. This was partly due to extensive training and partly due to the physiological and psychological profile that was part of their recruitment. Laura had explained that in centuries past, many Marines could have been classified as sociopaths. They were more than brave; they needed the challenge to survive.

She could hear the Marines on their internal com channel, making exclamations of excitement and joy, masked perhaps as macho statements of bravado.

"What a rush!"

"This is better than that time with your mother!"

"She says she doesn't even remember you. Are you sure you got it ..."

"Cut the chatter," she heard Sergeant Frasier order.

Lee looked at her display of the trajectory and saw a confusing mash of paths and probabilities. "Danner, what am I looking at?"

"Ma'am," Danner said. "What you have is the result of the launch criteria of 70 percent. The computer did what we asked, but the only option at 70 percent turns out to be pretty complicated."

"Simplify it for me," she said.

"You're going to have to orbit the moon twice in order to reach a spot near your initial insertion point."

"So what do we do to make that happen?" she asked.

"Nothing for now," Danner said. "Your current momentum and the moon's gravity will keep you in orbit. I'm here with Major Davenport looking at options."

"Navy Six, this is Marine Six," came Davenport's voice. "Your best option is to insert after the first full orbit. I'm sending the coordinates now. Tactically, it's not ideal, but it is the best option. Take a look and get back to me."

She looked around her and saw that the team was spread out in a rough line over about a kilometer. The asteroid was tumbling away from them and shrinking as it shot past the moon on its remaining two-year journey to the sun. The moon was close now, a huge ball of off-white. She could clearly see terrain features. Her heart gave a jump as her perception tried to tell her she was falling from a great height. She calmed her breathing and hoped that Zakany would stay quiet. Lee could imagine her clucking her concern as she looked at the biometric readouts. She could just see in her mind Danner raising his palm to her to cut off her exclamations.

She looked at the data that Davenport had sent. She knew Wasp was poring over it and could hear him speaking with the team leaders over his internal net. She had to hand it to them: Here they were, orbiting a moon in moo suits, calmly working out the details of an attack plan that had already gone a bit crazy. Lee could see the outline of what Davenport was proposing, but she knew that Wasp would be better able to work the various tactical options, so she stayed silent and waited for him to report to her.

"Navy Six, Marine Five," Wasp said.

"Go ahead," Lee replied.

"We can do this," he said. "It requires a change from the original COA." (COA was the Marine abbreviation for "course of action.") "We can split the teams. Team One serves as overwatch and provides supporting fire, while the other makes a direct assault."

Lee looked at the display he had been modifying and was surprised. "You mean an assault directly from orbit?"

"Yes, ma'am," he said. "The assault team can come in fast and hard, while the overwatch element can provide covering fire from the ridgeline."

Lee thought it was insane, but who was she to argue? If the Marines wanted to do something crazy, she had no better plan. "Sounds good to me," she said. "Tell me how it works."

"The teams will maneuver closer together now, so we have a tighter formation. Team One will slow their speed and drop out of orbit on the next pass to get in position to support the assault. I recommend you go with them."

Lee knew that if the teams were split, she and Wasp would need to split up to provide better command and control. It made it more likely that one of them would survive if one of the teams got hit hard. She also knew Wasp should lead the assault team. He was far more experienced, and his skills would be more valuable in that role.

"Got you so far," Lee said, burying her personal feelings for the man.

"I will take Team Two and make an additional orbit. That will give the overwatch team time to get into position."

"Then you come in, guns blazing?"

"That's it, in the main," he affirmed.

"Sounds good to me," she said. "Marine Six, do you copy?"

"Navy Six, this is Marine Six," Davenport said. "The plan is good here. Your call, ma'am."

"Roger," she said. "We will adopt the plan as modified by Marine Five. Can the fleet adjust to it?"

Danner cut in, "Fleet can adopt our plan to yours."

Wasp said, "Just get my Marine off that rock, sir."

"No worries," Davenport said. "Once the shooting starts, a search and rescue team will be ready to go get her." Marines always had one or more SAR teams on alert to recover Marines who might become separated by the flow of combat. Lee knew Davenport would need to wait until the operation was underway before attempting to recover the lone Marine; otherwise the enemy would detect the movement and the fleet would lose its element of surprise.

Lee noted that while this conversation was ongoing, the two teams had maneuvered into two distinct groups, separated by about fifty meters.

Danner said, "Team One, you are coming up on your deceleration burn."

"Roger that," Sergeant Frasier said. "Team One, prepare to burn."

Lee had to remind herself that although she was in overall command on the insertion, the team leaders were sovereign over their teams. As she was located with Team One, its chief—the same Sergeant Frasier she'd previously sparred with—would expect her to take his directions, at least as far as he was executing his orders.

Lee rotated her body so her feet were oriented in the direction of the moon, which was rapidly approaching. She had to admit, it was terrifying. It looked to her as if they were falling from a great height, which was in fact now the case.

"On my mark," Sergeant Frasier said. "Five, four, three, two, one, *mark.*"

The team ignited their jet packs. Lee could feel the abrupt deceleration, though her moo suit compensated for most of the G-forces she would otherwise have been feeling. Most notable, and a bit disorienting, was that in her view, Wasp and Team Two literally shot forward relative to her team. She watched on her display as her relative speed toward the moon dropped dramatically, from several hundred kilometers per hour to less than fifty. As they slowed, they fell toward the surface. Davenport had selected a short shelf, a sort of a mini plateau, near the peak of a low ridge of hills overlooking the base. The area was level and about thirty meters wide. The hope was that this distance would give the team enough room to both land and slow down before hitting the face of the hill.

"Stay with me, Team One," said the confident voice of Sergeant Frasier.

Lee could see from the projection that they were on track to make the landing, but it was tight. Go too fast, and they'd run smack into the rock face at the far end of the shelf. Go too slow, and they'd drop below the lower edge and slam into the near face of the hill. Lee felt herself being jostled, and an alarm sounded in her headset. *What was that?* she wondered.

"You guys are hitting the moon's atmosphere," Danner said, answering her thought. "It's very slight, and we missed it on survey."

"Not a problem," Frasier said. "Team One, I'm marking the aiming point for you. You can see it on your heads-up display. Just stay on that and take it in manually."

Lee could feel her blood racing again, and she realized what was happening. The original calculations done by the computer were useless now. She, and every member of the team, would have to manually guide themselves onto the shelf. This was the one area she had trained on only slightly when running the simulations back with the fleet. There just wasn't enough time to do everything, and so she had concentrated on practicing on the most likely maneuvers. That the moon might have an atmosphere, however thin, hadn't even come up.

"Navy Six, are you going to be okay, ma'am?" Frasier asked, as politely as if he were offering to help an old lady across the street. Lee noticed that the rest of the team were making maneuvers, and she was falling behind and below them.

"I'm good," she replied. "Just learning on the job."

She put the crosshairs of the reticle pattern from her faceplate display on the aiming point and fired her attitude jets in quick bursts until the aiming point centered in a small green circle that the computer considered a safe window for landing. At the same time, she had to keep two bar graphs aligned, which indicated her altitude and ground speed, with the computer's recommended approach settings. Every time the atmosphere buffeted her, she had to make a correction.

"Okay, team, we're coming in a little hot; there's no other way to make the shelf," said Frasier. "Just keep a good PLF position. Knees bent, feet together, elbows in, head tucked." This last little bit of advice was obviously meant for her, because no Marine commando needed to be reminded how to make a parachute landing fall. Again, so many terms borrowed from airborne warfare of centuries ago.

On her display, Lee understood what he meant. In order to compensate for the buffeting of the atmosphere, the jets had had to fire at greater strength to maintain altitude, and thus they were traveling too fast. There was nothing for it, though. Making the shelf was the safest—no, the *only*—way to land on this moon.

"Come to me, baby," said one of the Marines.

"Enjoy this one," said another. "It's the only one you'll ever get to take you."

"There was your mother ..." came the reply.

Lee stifled a crazy urge to giggle at the off-color joke. Then she saw the face of the hill race toward her. She got into her PLF position but couldn't keep her eyes off the approaching moon.

And then she hit. And then nothing.

CHAPTER 47

FIRE AND MANEUVER

Lee woke to the sound of communications traffic and the *thump, thump, thump* of automatic weapons fire. "Target, gun, four hundred meters."

"On it."

Thump, thump, thump.

She sat up and immediately felt her head spin, along with an almost overwhelming nausea. *Concussion*, she thought. Something was wrong with her lower lip, and she explored it with her tongue, only to realize her lip was a bloody mess and at least two of her bottom teeth were broken. Apparently, the suit had done something to stop the bleeding, or she would be choking on blood by now.

Her first sight was the gas giant, Lilith, enormous, filling the horizon and half the sky. She looked around and saw that two Marines had set up a firing position and were pouring fire at something she couldn't see from her position. She saw near her the unmoving body of another Marine. *Hard landing*, she thought.

"Navy Six is back up," she heard Sergeant Frasier say over her coms. He must be able to see her.

"Status, Frasier," she said.

"You and one other down on the drop," he said. "We set up a firing position. I saw the air defense guns on the base being set up, so I figured the assault had been compromised. I ordered our team to engage as suppressive fire. I'm moving up onto higher ground behind you with a sniper to get some additional coverage."

"How ish Team Two? The ashault team?" she said. God, she felt awful. She wondered if she was slurring her words.

"They're about thirty seconds out," he said. "The bad guys will know they're coming. Our best bet is to pour it on while they approach. Can you bring your weapon to bear? We could use it."

"Absholubley," she said. *Definitely slurring now,* she thought.

She reached to her shoulder, unsnapped her backpack, and drew out the case that held her automatic rifle. She quickly assembled the weapon. Wasp had trained her to put it together fast and under various conditions, including while blindfolded. Even while concussed, the steps came easily to her, and she thought she was feeling a little bit better—as if the process of assembling the weapon had steadied her. Now she understood why the Marines trained over and over and over again.

She quickly checked her weapon, fed in the magazine, and let the bolt slam forward. She crawled up to the low ridge and looked over, viewing a collection of small, one-story buildings surrounded by a fence line, punctuated by what looked like guardhouses and a single, reinforced gun position with a four-barreled antiaircraft machine gun. She saw the Marine's tracer rounds streaking across about four hundred meters of open ground, smashing into the revetment of the antiaircraft gun. She could see vague shapes of men in vacuum suits moving around.

"Ma'am," Frasier said, "the gun crew will keep its fire on the antiaircraft gun. If you could pick off anyone moving toward it on the left side, I'll handle the right."

"Gob it," she said. *I hope I can shoot better than I can talk,* she thought. She brought her weapon up into a firing position and took aim at the group of three men in EVMU suits running toward the gun. She focused on the lead one and, for no apparent reason, said, "Come to mama, moo man," and squeezed off a round. The rifle gave a satisfying recoil, and she saw a moment later that the man fell. *One moo down*, she said to herself. She quickly took out the second. The last one was beginning to run away. *Too late*, she said to herself and shot him in the back of the head. "Sorry, moo moo. Too bad for you."

"Nice shooting, ma'am," Frasier said. "Here comes the cavalry. Time to earn our pay, Marines. Watch your lane of fire. Let's not shoot any of our own."

Lee saw with dawning amazement that Team Two was coming straight over her head from behind their position in a V formation, and they were moving *fast*. They covered the last four hundred meters in seconds, and only at the last instant did they fire their jet packs in the direction of movement to slow down. Then Lee and the Marines from her position increased their volume of fire until it was fully automatic. Lee knew this was called suppressive fire. It was designed to keep the enemy from getting a chance to even aim at a target while the assaulting team closed on their position.

"Shift fire," Frasier said. This was the command to aim away from the point of attack so as not to hit your own. She immediately aimed to the left and fired at one of the outlying buildings. The idea was to keep up the volume of fire so an enemy shooter wouldn't be tempted to poke his head up and try and take a shot. Her team only stopped firing at the final moment before Team Two dropped the last few feet to the ground behind the first line of defenders; they immediately formed a circle, firing in all directions. In moments, all the enemy defending the exterior of the base were down.

"Team One, status?" Wasp barked over the coms channel.

"One Marine dead. Navy Six took a hard fall and had a short nap, but she's up and swinging."

"Navy Six, this is Marine Five," Wasp said. "I recommend you bring Team One forward. We'll need all hands for the breach."

"Robber," she said. "We're bone ah way."

Lee stood up and looked around for Sergeant Frasier; she tried to say something else but then fell over and, once again, saw only black.

CHAPTER 48

BOMBARDMENT

Rear Admiral Jay Chambers sat in the command chair aboard the *Centurion*, which was being used as the command vessel of the Achilles Battle Fleet. Altogether, he had thirteen vessels, most of which were not warships; they were designed for logistics, cargo, passenger transport, scientific research, or hydroponics. Today, they were armed with what amounted to heavy siege guns and a few torpedoes. The fleet was hiding for the moment, masked by the local asteroid belt. The two frigates were detached just now, with different instructions.

"The Special Ops team is about to make the breach, sir," Danner said. "They have engaged and have taken casualties. One Marine still on the rock, one dead on the jump. Commander Lee took a hard fall but is still in the fight."

"She is not well enough to be in such fight," Lieutenant Laura Zakany said in the heavily accented English she used when she was agitated. "She has concussion and broken jaw and ribs."

"Lieutenant," Danner said, irritated, "please do not interject yourself while the admiral is on the bridge."

Zakany looked exasperated; her face red, she turned away and mumbled something in Hungarian. Master Warrant Officer Nemeth spoke to her gently in the same language, and she nodded in apparent acceptance.

"No, it's all right," Chambers said calmly. "I have the doctor here for a reason. What's Commander Lee's status?"

"She is currently unconscious," Zakany said and then added, "though she bravely fought before with bad injuries."

"Are her injuries life-threatening?" the admiral asked.

"No, the autodoc in her suit will give her medicines to keep brain swelling down and control bleeding," Zakany said. "But more concussion, very bad."

"Thank you, Doctor," Chambers said. Zakany seemed mollified for the moment and seemed to settle down. "Major Davenport, picked up your stranded Marine yet?"

"SAR team is en route, sir," Davenport said. "They have a beacon from her moo suit, but no response from her as of yet."

Chambers nodded and said, "Please keep me informed. Danner, is there any indication that the fleet's been detected?"

"None, sir," said Danner.

"Okay, time for them to see us," Chambers said. "Take us in to our firing position above the moon base."

"Surely you will not fire when Mei-Ling and Marines are on surface," Zakany cried.

Danner turned toward her with an angry look on his face.

But before he could speak, Chambers said, "Yes, Doctor. We *will* fire, but we *will not* hit our own people. Stay ready; I will need you later. Stay focused."

In moments, they could see the gas giant and its tiny moon growing larger on the viewscreen as they approached.

"Signal the fleet to begin the firing pass," Chambers said.

CHAPTER 49

CONFRONTATION

Chambers ordered the fleet to pass the moon in a line formation. The plan was for each vessel in sequence to pass into range of the base, fire their siege weapons—heavy kinetic cannons hurling thousand-pound projectiles—and then continue into orbit around the moon. After the first pass, the fleet would basically have the moon surrounded and would be able to hit almost any target on the surface.

Danner had estimated that the moon would have shields to protect the main operating base. He had told the admiral that the bombardment would initially detonate on the force shields some kilometers above the surface, but that over time, the shields would weaken. The hope was that as the moon's defenses deteriorated, the defenders would call for help—which was what Chambers wanted. He wanted them to try to use the MWC generator so that it could be located and the Marines could capture it. But he also wanted something else: He wanted to see who would come to the aid of the base.

But as so often happened, the plan didn't work out that way. There were no shields. Instead, the base had a missile defense system. Before they could start the planned bombardment, the enemy responded first. "Firing ports opening on the moon's surface," said one of the technicians in the ops center. "Detecting multiple launches."

"Have the fleet hold course, shields up," Chambers said. "Target the firing positions and pass the coordinates to the gun batteries. Let's make sure they can't fire again."

"Sir," Danner said, "the Marines haven't breached the bunker yet. They're still in the open."

"They'll need to hurry," Chambers said.

Zakany let out a sort of hissing sound, that Danner assumed was some sort of Hungarian expression of frustration. But he was relieved she didn't blurt anything. Apparently, she knew that the best hope for her friend and the Marines on the surface was to let Chambers command the operation without interruption.

"Sir, the lead vessels are taking damage from the missiles," Danner said. "Their shields are providing only partial protection. We could call back the frigates."

"Negative," said Chambers. "Stay the course, and have our ships return fire as soon as they're within range."

"Aye aye, sir," Danner said, turning back to his console with a look of frustration.

Chief Warrant Officer John Raymond had been sitting silently on a swivel chair at a console with multiple displays. He normally wouldn't be in the operations center, but this wasn't a normal event. He had his reading glasses on, and Danner thought he looked quite professorial.

Raymond raised his hand to get Danner's attention and said, "I have an MWC generator start-up, subsurface. I'm sending you the coordinates."

"On screen," Chambers said.

What they saw was a three-dimensional display of the subsurface of the base. The generator was shown as a glowing red icon; the Marine team was shown one level above in blue.

"Direct the Marines to the target," ordered Chambers. "And let's get ready for company."

CHAPTER 50

THE BREACH

As she came to, Lee couldn't quite put all her sensations together. There was the jostling and an up-and-down movement that reminded her of when she was little and rode a horse for the first time. Then there was the image of someone's heels moving back and forth, running, and dust getting kicked up but settling back down in slow motion. And then there were voices.

"Team One, you need to close the gap now," said one voice. "The bombardment is about to begin, and we need to make the breach and get under cover before it starts."

"Roger," said another voice. "I've got Navy Six in tow. Moving with all haste."

Lee realized she was being carried, sack-like, across the shoulder of a Marine who was running at full speed. She tried to look around and saw that the three remaining members of the team were also running in the same direction.

"I'm awake," she said simply.

"Roger, ma'am," Frasier said. "I've got you. Stay still for now; it's the fastest way to get us to cover, and we're almost there. The fleet's about to begin the bombardment."

A few seconds later, they stopped, and the Marine easily hoisted her off his shoulder and gently set her down on her feet. He kept his hands on her shoulders to steady her and looked into her eyes to see if she looked fully awake.

"Can you stand on your own?" he asked.

"Yes. I think I'm good."

"Dr. Zakany said the autodoc in your moo suit has injected you with medication to control for pain, nausea, and hemorrhaging. She says to avoid getting hit on the head again," he said with a smile she could see through the faceplates. "When you hear 'Fire in the hole,' get behind this revetment until you hear the all-clear. Gotta run," he said, taking off toward the other Marines with that speed that the commandos always seemed to move with, which never seemed quite possible.

She saw that Marines from both teams were in the process of setting explosive charges in and around a door to what looked like a bunker. She knew from the intelligence estimate that this was the entrance to the underground complex that they hoped housed the MWC field generator. They needed to get inside quickly, because the bombardment from the fleet would begin soon.

Lee was starting to feel better. She didn't feel that awful nausea, and the autodoc had somehow corrected her slurred speech. But she knew she wasn't all right. Her insides felt jumbled, and she wasn't thinking clearly.

She wondered, *Why are they firing a bombardment when the SpecOps team has already been inserted? Why not just blow the thing from space and be done with it?*

Then it came back to her. The objective was to get to the MWC field generator. Intel believed it would be heavily shielded, even from an orbital bombardment. The other problem was that the underground complex included miles of old tunnels that had been dug out over centuries of commercial mining. And to make it more difficult, the intel section didn't know precisely where the generator was. Part of the reason for a bombardment was to prompt the enemy to use the field generator to try and defend the base. Once the generator was activated, its enormous power signature would allow Danner, Raymond, and the intel team to locate it precisely, and that's why the Marines were there. But right now, they needed to get under the surface. So the bombardment was a ruse of sorts, designed to get the enemy to show itself. And it had another purpose, one that was near and dear to Admiral Chambers' heart.

"Fire in the hole!" she heard over her coms channel.

She ducked down behind the revetment Frasier had indicated, just as several things seemed to happen at once. There was the blast from the entrance being breached; Lee saw from the corner of her eye a large part of the door go flying past her. Good thing she was down. And apparently, the moon had a substantial aerospace defense in place; dozens of missiles leaped simultaneously from multiple points on the surface and rose rapidly toward the fleet somewhere unseen and far above them. She hoped the admiral had anticipated this and assumed the fleet was taking defensive measures.

She looked toward the bunker and saw that the Marines were throwing grenades into the opening made by their explosives. She saw the flash from the explosions, but the atmosphere was too thin to carry the sound; immediately, two Marines moved through the opening, crouched over and firing.

"All clear," said a voice.

"Let's get everyone into the bunker," Wasp ordered crisply.

Just as she was moving, the explosions began on the surface. The fleet had commenced its bombardment. Huge fireballs erupted in every direction, the closest about two hundred meters away. These she could hear, if only barely; she could feel the ground shaking and knew that even in the near-vacuum, the overpressure would be substantial when it reached them. So she moved as fast as she could. Frasier ran back for her, grabbed her harness at the chest plate, and threw her like a doll toward the opening. A moment later, she landed in a heap on top of other Marines, with Sergeant Frasier on top of her a second later. The blasts from the bombardment washed over them through the open door, pushing them forward as if they were dust bunnies.

She estimated they flew about ten meters down a narrow passageway before slamming into a wall. Luckily, there were no sharp objects in their path, or they would have been impaled.

Lee moved to untangle herself from the arms and legs of her fellow Marines (she noted with interest that she thought of them that way). She looked down the corridor toward the way they had come, and outside the open hatch, she saw fires in the distance. Clearly, the fleet had been aiming at the missile launch sites, some of which were now burning. Burning required oxygen, indicating the base's structural integrity had been breached, causing it to vent atmosphere. How bad was the damage remained to be seen.

The Marines were moving quickly now; several had already untangled themselves and made progress toward the corridor that opened to their right. They needed to move quickly in that direction lest another blast enter the bunker from the opening. She heard the Marines performing their status checks, and it seemed they were all intact and accounted for. In seconds, they moved a few meters down the confined passageway and made a tight defensive formation. Wasp sent a two-man team forward to conduct a reconnaissance while the rest stayed put, alert for an attack. For all their bravery, the Marines were very careful when moving into unknown territory. They took risks when needed, but never without reason.

"Navy Six, this is Operations," said Danner's voice over the coms. "We have something for you."

CHAPTER 51

THE HEART OF THE BEAST

Lee responded, "Navy Six here. I'm passing command to Marine Five."

There was a pause, and Danner said, "Roger. Marine Five, do you copy?"

Wasp and Lee exchanged a long look, then he nodded and said, "Operations, this is Marine Five. I copy. I am primary for the SpecOps insertion team, over."

"We have a location for the generator," Danner said. "It's one level below you. Sending the schematics to you now."

After a moment, Wasp said, "Okay, got it. Do I have any bad guys to deal with before I get there?"

"Sorry, we can't see due to the energy distortion from the generator. Be aware: we expect visitors here shortly, so you may not get much support from us for a while."

"Understand. Marine Five, out."

On the internal net, Wasp said. "Team One, take the lead. Team Two, follow. Navy Six with me."

Lee felt a huge relief lifted from her. She knew passing command to Wasp was the right thing to do. She wasn't fit to make decisions in her current state, and the detachment needed a commander who was conscious most of the time. Now she was determined not to slow them down and to help when the fight started.

Wasp positioned the two of them between the teams as they moved down the narrow corridor. Lee was grateful that the pace of movement wasn't too fast. They could only move slowly because they had to clear the various side passages before the main group could move past. Her ribs were starting to hurt as the painkiller wore off, and she knew if she had to run, she would be in trouble. Luckily, her head seemed relatively clear, and her balance was okay as well. She watched in admiration at how efficiently the Marines cleared each passageway or obstacle. She thought, *I'm going to have to learn how they move so quickly, smoothly, and precisely.*

They found a stairwell, and after first clearing it, they descended two flights to the next level down. From the bottom of the stairs, they could see lights coming from around the corner and heard voices. Was it possible the enemy had no defenses for the generator? Surely they knew they were under attack. But then again, this was what Chambers had tried to accomplish. Push them from more than one point at the same time, and something would give, especially if this wasn't an eventuality they had anticipated. Lee recalled that the defense on the surface didn't look well organized. The defenders had been running around like startled chickens. It looked now as if they hadn't thought to keep a reserve, and the entire local security force had been taken out in one go. The people in the generator room might not even know what had happened on the surface.

The two Marines Wasp had sent forward came back and quietly gave their report. "The door's open, Sergeant Major," said one. "They're armed, but they look like technicians. They're not aware of us, and I don't see any security personnel or surveillance cameras."

"Is there another entrance?" Wasp asked.

The Marine showed a photo to Wasp on a handheld. "Couldn't see. There's a bank of computers, then a glass wall. Behind that, a room full of equipment. I don't know what's past that."

Wasp nodded and said over his coms channel, "Ops, we're sending you a photo of the generator room."

A minute later, Raymond's voice came on the line: "Marine Five, this is Raymond. What you're seeing there is the MWC generator. It has some pretty amazing components that we hadn't anticipated. We need to study it. The admiral is here and has approved my recommendation that you capture it intact, along with as many of the technical personnel as possible."

"Roger," Wasp said. "Ops, you copy?"

Lee knew that Wasp was following protocol. He didn't take his orders from Raymond, and he wanted to close out the session with clear guidance.

"This is Operations," Danner said. "I confirm the admiral has ordered that the generator and as many of the technical personnel as possible be taken intact."

"Generator and technical personnel captured intact, aye," Wasp said.

"Please be advised," Danner said, "our visitors have arrived as expected. The admiral doesn't want them to leave, so shut down the generator ASAP."

Wasp turned to the internal tac channel and said, "We go with flash-bang grenades and nonlethal force. I want them all alive if possible." The Marines immediately began to make adjustments to their weapons and equipment. In a moment, both team leaders reported ready.

"Let's do this. Team One, take the initial entry," Wasp said. "Team Two, secure this passage and hold back until I call you forward. Navy Six, you're with me."

CHAPTER 52

THE FACE OF THE ENEMY

"I have two vessels using MWC five kilometers to port. Two light cruisers," said one of the technicians in the Operations Center.

"Right on time," Chambers said mildly.

"Sir," the technician said with concern in his voice, "those are *Alliance* ships."

"Yes, I know." Chambers looked at Zakany and asked, "Doctor, are we ready?"

"Yes, sir," she said in a very serious voice.

"Hail from the command vessel, sir," said one of the technicians. "It's the commanding admiral of the Fifth Fleet."

"On screen," Chambers said.

He looked over at Zakany, who nodded and began to tap the keys at her keyboard. Behind Chambers' command chair was a large screen now displaying what looked like a stream of data readouts, video clips, and photos. It resembled an operations status board. Zakany was positioned so she could see both screens. She focused her attention on the screen Chambers was facing.

On the screen facing Chambers appeared a three-star admiral, sitting in a command chair almost identical to his own.

"Rear Admiral Chambers, I'm Vice Admiral Stuart," the man said, "commanding admiral of the Fifth Fleet. I'm ordering you to cease your assault on that moon."

Chambers' face was expressionless, as he sat for a long moment without answering. The silence dragged on, and Admiral Stuart's lower jaw twitched.

Finally, Chambers said quite conversationally. "Sir, it's good to see you again. You might recall we went through Officer Candidate School together."

The man's face reddened, and he said, "That's not relevant just now. Cease your bombardment."

"And we served together on the *Okinawa*," said Chambers.

"Admiral, I must insist that you ..."

"And in the Tenth Special Warfare Group, where we were both detachment commanders," Chambers said.

Admiral Stuart's lips began to quiver, and his head gave a slight but noticeable twitch to his left. He said nothing. At her terminal, Zakany watched Admiral Stuart intensely and typed feverishly on her keyboard. This was the task the admiral had given her, and she would not fail him.

"If you don't stop, I'll have to relieve you ..." The last word tapered off, as if Stuart was confused about something.

"And you will remember Master Chief Warrant Officer Nemeth," Chambers said. "He served as your weapons section head until he got promoted, and I stole him from you to serve as my squadron master chief."

Chambers looked to his right and motioned. Nemeth stepped up next to Chambers where he would be visible to Stuart.

"It's good to see you, Admiral," Nemeth said, without expression. "I haven't seen you since the christening of young Jay."

"I'm ... It's just that you have to stop," Stuart said with hesitation. "My cruisers will fire on you ... if necessary. Stop now."

Just then, Zakany said in a hushed voice, "I have it, sir; it's on your handheld."

Chambers looked down at a small screen in the palm of his hand and said to Stuart, "Blue dogs riding the square."

As soon as the words were out, Stuart's face went blank, and he said, in that same strange, deep voice Zakany had heard from the prisoner during interrogation, "Standing by."

"Be at peace," Chambers said.

Stuart immediately closed his eyes, lowered his chin to his chest, and stood unmoving, as if asleep. The screen went blank.

"Sir," Danner said, "the cruisers are powering up their shields and preparing to fire on us."

"Shields up, evasive action. Now is a good time for the frigates, please," said the admiral. He looked at Zakany. "Well done, Lieutenant."

She looked back with a proud smile.

"Patch me through to the fleet on broad channel," Chambers said.

"You're on, sir," said a technician.

"Achilles Battle Fleet," he said. "This is Admiral Chambers. Break off the bombardment. The two vessels in our vicinity, though they are flying Alliance colors, are enemy combatants. They are to be engaged until and unless they strike their colors."

"Admiral," Danner said, "the two frigates are back on station."

"Patch me through to Commodore Bowman aboard the *Alabama*."

Bowman came on screen and said, "Bowman here, sir."

"The vessels have been confirmed as enemy combatants," Chambers said. "Engage them with the *Alabama* and *Guangdong*. I am dispatching the Achilles Aerospace Wing to your command. If the cruisers will strike their colors, accept their surrender and board them. If not, destroy them. Be aware, until the generators are shut down on the moon, they may still have access to the MWC weapon."

"Aye aye, sir," Bowman said, and the screen went blank.

CHAPTER 53

THE MENTALIST'S TRICK, PART I

Lieutenant Laura Zakany had never been so excited. For weeks, she had worked to develop a system for identifying and neutralizing the clone-imposters. The admiral had taken her into his confidence, trusting her with a special task, and she had done it. Whatever happened now, nothing could take away that accomplishment. She prayed to God that her father was still living, so she could tell him of her success someday.

She had worked with the imposters in custody, showing them images, videos, words, and phrases until she detected the pattern that had been used to program them. At first, all she could do was get them to ask for the code. They would say, "Standing by," as had the young yeoman. But every time, when they didn't hear the correct authorization within a few seconds, they went into convulsions. The admiral wanted more than that. He wanted to be able to give them instructions. He wanted her to get the code for him. Finally, she had a breakthrough. With the help of some of Danner's computer people, they had discovered an algorithm that the people who had programmed the imposters used to select the code.

The next step had taken some research and some luck, actually. She had hit upon some old research done on brainwashing, as it was then called, from back from in the twentieth century. It was actually part of a mentalist stage show, where the performer could condition people from the audience to take certain commands. And sure enough, some of the commands this mentalist had used worked on her clones. The programmers must have used the same research.

The problem was that the code was different for each person. Through many trials, Zakany had narrowed down the phrases that could be used; she had worked out with Chambers that if they could show the images and phrases to one of the clones, she could monitor their facial expressions to unlock the correct code.

And it worked. Chambers had predicted that an Alliance force would appear to try to intervene with the bombardment. *He is so clever,* thought Zakany. He knew the enemy would try to infiltrate other formations, as they had done with the Achilles Battle Fleet. She had prepared a video presentation to look like an operational data stream. They had set it up so that it would be visible behind Chambers, and whoever was speaking to him on screen would see what was up there. If it was a clone, that person would begin to respond to the images, even if unconsciously. Zakany's task had been to watch the facial expressions and, applying the algorithm, determine the code needed to take control of the clone. And she had done it: "Blue dogs riding the square." She had given it to the admiral, he had said the words, and it worked.

The final touch had been the command, "Be at peace." It was from the mentalist's repertoire, and it had worked on every one of the clones to make them drop into a standing sleep.

And now the admiral had given her the biggest task of all, one that could make every difference in the battle to come. She turned to her computer and typed with an intensity she had not felt since she worked the emergency room in Budapest when she was a nineteen-year-old nurse. *Papa,* she said to herself, *your Laura is fighting on the front line and winning.*

CHAPTER 54

ACTIONS ON THE OBJECTIVE

It was over in seconds. Two Marines stood on either side of the open hatch, and both threw flash-bang grenades into the opening. No one on the other side called, "Grenade." They probably didn't even notice; these were not warriors, apparently. A moment later, the grenades detonated one after the other in rapid succession. Lee thought it was surprisingly loud, and she guessed it was the enclosed space. Immediately, four Marines poured through the entrance, shouting, "Get down, stay down, let me see your hands!'" Then there was a series of gunshots before the all-clear.

Wasp set two Marines to guard the entrance and motioned the remainder of the detachment into the room. It wasn't a big space, maybe fifteen feet square. It contained a bank of computers and few desks, a table with a coffeemaker, and a glass wall behind which was a larger room filled with machinery that she guessed was the MWC generator. Six of the seven occupants, all men, were sitting on the floor with their hands over their ears. One was on the ground, rolling around and moaning. The Marines were quickly disarming the occupants. There was no resistance.

Team One's leader said, "Sorry about that one, Sergeant Major," indicating the guy rolling on the floor. "He reached for his weapon. Took two dum-dum rounds, one in the stomach and one in the knee."

"It hurts," Wasp said with a wicked smile. "I've been there."

Lee made a note to ask him later about getting shot with a dum-dum round—a solid rubber projectile designed to inflict extreme pain without causing fatal wounds. She knew they were used for riot control or other situations where lethal force was not required.

"Gentlemen," Wasp said to the group of prisoners in a very loud, parade-ground voice, "I am Sergeant Major Theodorus Wasp, commanding officer of the Achilles Special Operations detachment. You are in my lawful custody. I will require your full and prompt compliance to my lawful orders. Because of the time constraints, and the fact that you were all armed, I have been authorized to apply coercive measures to gain your assistance. Who is in charge, please?"

While he spoke, the other Marines kept their weapons in a firing position, but not pointed directly at anyone in particular, and continued to move and watch the prisoners closely. Lee understood this was a well-rehearsed procedure, probably designed to make the captives anxious and more likely to comply.

No one spoke. Wasp nodded toward the oldest-looking prisoner, a bald man of about fifty in a white lab coat. Two Marines snatched him up and moved him roughly from the room out into the hall, where none of the other prisoners could see him. "Hey, hey, don't do that, please," the man said, in obvious terror.

Lee followed them out into the passageway.

"Did you get the recording?" Wasp said to one of his Marines.

"Got it, Sergeant Major," came the reply from a Marine looking at his handheld. "That should do nicely."

The Marines quickly put electrical tape over the bald man's mouth. The Marine made some adjustments to his screen and then nodded and said, "Ready."

The other Marine took the butt of his weapon and slammed it into the metal wall separating the passageway from the control room where the prisoners were being held. *Thump.* Still out of sight of the prisoners, the Marine with the handheld held it up toward the door, where it began to emit the sounds of a man in extreme agony. It was a perfect rendition of the voice of the man now standing with him mouth taped. "Oh, God, no, please, aghhh!" *Thump, thump.*

"Sir, you're going to need to tell us how to shut down the generator," Wasp said. "I assure you, if you do, this will stop."

Thump, thump. "I'm begging you," came the man's voice from the handheld.

"I'm sorry, we don't have time," Wasp said in his eerily calm voice. "Go ahead and take his genitals."

"But Sergeant Major, he'll bleed to death," one of the Marines said. "What if he's the only one who knows how to shut it down?"

"We'll just have to take that chance," Wasp said. "Plus, we've got a medical kit. All we need to do is keep him conscious."

Next came the most awful scream Lee had heard yet. It was long, pitiful, interspersed with crying and begging.

Lee could hear the other prisoners screaming from the room, "Stop that! We'll do it; we'll do it!"

Wasp smiled his mischievous smile at Lee and said, "Works like a charm every time."

"Not *every* time, Sergeant Major," said one of the Marines.

"True," Wasp said. "There was that one time in the Sagittarius system. Yup."

Wasp took a small packet from his pocket and bit off the top, spit it out of his mouth, and squeezed some red fluid onto his hands and forearms. He smiled at Lee and said, "Gotta stay in character."

Wasp left one of the Marines with the *tortured* prisoner and returned to the room. Every prisoner's eye was on his seemingly bloodied hands.

"Gentlemen," Wasp said. "Thank you for your cooperation. Sadly, your unfortunate friend did not survive his interview. Each of you will now be interviewed by one of my men. They will ask you a series of questions and video-record your answers. Please be as honest and complete as possible. Failure to answer promptly and accurately will be considered noncompliance. But first, we need you to watch a short video. Let's begin."

Immediately, a Marine paired up with each prisoner, and holding up a handheld device, they asked the prisoner to watch the screen. Lee knew this was a video designed to induce a seizure in a clone-imposter. Sure enough, after about twenty seconds, one of the prisoners, the one who had reached for his weapon and had subsequently been shot with the dum-dum bullets, said, "Standing by," and a few seconds later began to convulse.

The Marine caught him as he fell, gently lowered him to the floor, and then administered a shot, which Lee knew was a sedative designed to keep the clone down.

"Not to worry," Wasp said. "Your colleague has not been harmed. I will explain what happened in a short while." Then the interviews began.

"State your name, duty position, and organization, please."

Lee stifled a smile at how polite the Marines were being. She thought this must be part of the persuasion. Polite but deadly serious killers. *And that's not far from the truth,* she thought. The answers came fast.

"Robert Kiperman, scientist, Research Team Three ..."

"Fred Otte, technician on Team Three ..."

"Our task is to maintain the generator ..."

"I've been here four months ..."

"Kim Wong," said one man with a heavy accent. "Senior research engineer, Team Three ..."

This drew Lee's attention, and she looked up to see a man of Chinese features. She could tell from his accent that he was from Hong Kong. She looked over at Wasp with a questioning look, and he motioned as if to say, "Be my guest." She walked over to the man and addressed him in Cantonese, the language most commonly spoken in Hong Kong. He nodded quickly and responded. While a Marine recorded the conversation, Lee asked more questions, and each time, he seemed eager to get his answer out.

After a few minutes, Lee walked back to Wasp and said, "According to Mr. Wong, this is a small team of technicians and engineers. Their task is to maintain the generator, and some other equipment. He claims they're Alliance civilian contractors. They don't really know what the generator is used for. They're here on six-month rotations. A supervisor comes in with some other engineers about once a fortnight. They examine and adjust the equipment, but this team — Team Three—doesn't get to be present when they're here. It's always done when they're on their two-days' downtime, which they get every two weeks."

"Does he know how to turn it off?" Wasp asked.

"I'll ask," Lee said.

Lee spoke briefly with the man and came back and said, "They have an emergency shutdown procedure. He says they've never had to use it. Unfortunately, the only one who has the authorization code, Dr. McKenzie, he thinks has just been castrated and murdered."

"Well, time for a miracle, then."

He motioned to one of his men, who went out in the hall and returned with the unharmed prisoner. Every conversation stopped as the prisoners looked with astonishment at the unharmed Dr. McKenzie. Wasp carefully peeled the tape off the man's mouth and said, "Dr. McKenzie, all of you, please listen. Sorry to have had to put you through that subterfuge. I'm afraid you and your team have been working under a false flag operation. The people responsible for this base are *not* Alliance personnel. They have been using this generator to attack the Alliance.

"It is imperative that we shut down this generator right now and that it not be damaged. The man who went into convulsions is a clone-imposter, who has been specifically programmed for sabotage and espionage." Wasp turned to Dr. McKenzie and said, "Sir, I understand you have the code required to conduct an emergency shut down of this generator. Are you willing to help us do that?"

"Yes," the man instantly said.

"Good, I need you to speak with another scientist."

"And who is that?" McKenzie asked.

"Dr. John Raymond," Wasp said.

"Really?" McKenzie said. "I know Professor Raymond from way back. I took his class in quantum field theory when I was a graduate student. I thought he disappeared."

"He's back," Wasp said. "Let me patch you through."

CHAPTER 55

THE MUTINY

Bowman stood on the bridge of the *Alabama*. He had been designated as commander of Task Force Mars, which was made up of the two frigates and the Achilles Aerospace Wing, which was now under the command of newly promoted Captain Baker. Technically, the *Alabama* was to serve as the flagship for the task force. But Bowman had only brought a few of Danner's people to help him. For communications, he'd just use the C&C facilities of the frigate. Captain Montgomery, though very British and very polite to his commodore, made clear he was not relinquishing command of the *Alabama*. Bowman could give his orders to him, and they would be obeyed. But Bowman was not to presume to give orders to any of the frigate's personnel.

The task was daunting. The cruisers were larger and had greater firepower than the frigates. But they were slower to maneuver, and the task force had the aerospace wing. So far, they hadn't seen any enemy fighters. It might just be a fair matchup.

Chambers had ordered the remaining vessels, none of which were warships, into a defensive perimeter around the moon. He predicted that if the enemy was convinced they couldn't recapture the generator, they'd try to destroy it. Bowman thought about the SpecOps team on the moon; he thought about Lee. He'd monitored the transmissions and knew they'd made a spectacular and successful insertion. The generator was in their hands now, and they were working with Raymond on shutting it down.

Bowman turned to Montgomery and said, "Captain, your recommendation?"

"I say we get in close, stay in close, and let them have it," Montgomery said with his steady, aristocratic voice.

"Like Nelson at Trafalgar?" Bowman said.

"Quite so," Montgomery said. "The flagship should be in the thick of it. We can take the *Guangdong* with us in line formation, split the cruisers, and let the wing hit them from the sides. Our gunners are the Alliance's best. We can double their rate of fire."

Bowman didn't really like the idea of going straight up the middle against a superior force. His aviator instincts told him to maneuver for advantage. But the truth was, he really didn't know the tactics for major warships. Six months ago, he'd been a reserve lieutenant commander, XO for a recon squadron. Montgomery was regular Navy, a career ship driver, and at least ten years older—and fleet tactics were his business.

"Let's make that happen, Captain," he said.

"Right," said Montgomery. He turned to his bridge staff and ordered, "Line formation, *Alabama*, followed by *Guangdong*. Achilles Wing to strike outer defenses."

"Commodore," said one of technicians, "we're receiving a hail from one of the cruisers."

"I suppose we should give them a chance to surrender," said Bowman. "Put up the test video behind me, and put the hail on screen."

On the screen came the image of a Navy captain standing on the bridge of a cruiser. "Commodore, I'm Captain Namon McDonald commanding officer of the LC *Kauai* and now primary for Task Force Trump. I think you owe me an explanation."

"How so, Captain?" Bowman asked.

"Your vessels and fighters look like they're preparing to attack an Alliance task force," said the captain. "This is the flagship for the Fifth Fleet. Your actions are illegal."

"Captain, you're mistaken. I'm Commodore Stephen Bowman, deputy commander of the Achilles Battle Fleet and commander of Task Force Mars. I am under the lawful command of Rear Admiral Jay Chambers, who has authorized me to accept your surrender. Lower your shields immediately, or you will be fired upon."

The captain raised his hands in exasperation and said, "Sir, I don't think that's wise. Attacking us would be mutiny, not to mention suicide, as we have you outgunned."

Bowman could see from his personal display that the frigates were now moving in line formation, aimed directly between the two cruisers, and that Baker had split his wing so as to attack each cruiser from the left and right flanks.

"Your commanding officer is down, is he not?" Bowman said.

"Yes, he's had a seizure," said the captain. "What of it?"

"He's not your admiral. He's an imposter."

"*Please,*" the captain said with exasperation. "I'd know my own admiral."

"Check his DNA," said Bowman. "I assure you that you have been infiltrated. And he's not the only one. Ask yourself why you're out here in the first place, and how you got here so quickly. Did you even know there was moon with a base out here?"

Bowman could see from the captain's features that he'd made a point—or at least made him think.

"And how do you know I'm not one of them?" asked McDonald.

"We just tested you. If you were a clone, you'd be down now."

"I can't strike my colors on the orders of an admiral who's not even in my chain of command," said Frazier.

Bowman knew the man had doubts and probably had for some time. Captain McDonald opened his mouth to say something, but just then, a hole opened in his neck. He gasped and brought both hands to his throat, where blood poured through his fingers. He dropped out of their view as Bowman heard shots and shouts on the bridge of the *Kauai*, and then the screen went dark.

CHAPTER 56

THE LINE OF BATTLE

The *Alabama* and *Guangdong* were in line formation, aiming for a point that would take them between the two cruisers they were facing. The plan was to "run the gauntlet," as Montgomery termed it. They would cut between the cruisers and fire from the batteries on both port and starboard sides. The cruisers would, of course, return fire but would only be able to bring half of their big guns to bear; they'd also have to deal with the Achilles Aerospace Wing firing on them from the outside of their formation. Once through the formation, if they made it through, Bowman's frigates would double back and make the run again.

As they approached the narrow passage, Bowman was impressed by how much larger the cruisers were than the frigates: at least twice as long, and with a much larger bulk. Ominously, Bowman could see the gun ports opening on the cruiser on their right, the *Okinawa*.

"Sir, the *Kauai* has not opened its gun ports," said one of the technicians.

"Are their shields still up?" Bowman asked.

"Yes, sir," replied the technician.

"Treat them as hostile until they lower their shields."

Bowman knew there must be innocent men and women on both vessels, but he had no choice. Clearly, there was a mutiny underway on the *Kauai*. He hoped the right people would prevail. In the meantime, he had his duty, not to mention his orders. Chambers had told him to treat the vessels as enemy combatants until and unless they struck their colors.

His holoscreen split into three views, one showing the cruiser on the port side, the center view showing their direction of movement, and the right-hand portion showing the cruiser to starboard. What happened next was difficult to watch. As the *Alabama* slipped between the two vessels, the great guns on the port side fired a volley. On the viewscreen, Bowman could see the spherical muzzle blasts typical of vacuum artillery, consisting of ephemeral balls of flame threaded with smoke, and the projectiles streaking toward them. The first volley detonated on the shields, causing enormous explosions and shaking the ship like a rat in the jaws of an enormous terrier. The *Alabama*'s lights dimmed momentarily, and emergency lighting came up as an alarm sounded. The internal coms crackled with damage reports from various parts of the ship. Bowman noted how cool Montgomery was, as were his bridge crew, who took their cue from their captain. If he showed composure, they would also.

"All batteries, stand by," Montgomery said. "Batteries, fire!" Almost instantaneously, Bowman felt the frigate shiver as the batteries cut loose. Because railguns used magnetic acceleration, there were no telltale muzzle blasts. The frigates' five-inch railgun projectiles leapt toward their target at a significant fraction of light speed, too fast to follow with the eyes. Their effects were immediately apparent: the shells detonated on the shields of the *Kauai* and the *Okinawa*, as expected, but almost immediately another volley was fired, and then another. The point of this fire was to reduce the power of the cruisers' shields to the point that the projectiles could penetrate to the hull of the vessels.

"Sir, our fighters are engaging both vessels and are taking anti-spacecraft fire," said a technician. That made sense; the *Kauai*'s proximity defensive weaponry would fire to protect the vessels, no matter who was in charge. The commander of those weapons might not even be aware of the struggle for control of the vessel, so Baker was going to have a hard time of it.

"Patch me through to Captain Baker," Bowman said.

"Baker here, sir."

"Be aware, the *Kauai* went into mutiny about the time we asked them to lower their shields. It has yet to fire on the frigates, but is to be treated as hostile until it surrenders."

"Aye aye, sir," Baker said.

"Also, know that someone on that vessel is trying to do the right thing, and it's likely that many, perhaps most, of the hands are loyal to the Alliance and innocent of any wrongdoing. Make sure you break off the assault on the cruisers the moment they drop their shields."

"Acknowledged. Baker out."

"Sir, the *Kauai*'s shields are failing, down to 40 percent and dropping," said a technician.

Bowman saw that the *Alabama* was almost through its first run between the two cruisers, and the *Guangdong* was about to begin.

"Her shields won't hold long. The *Guangdong* will break through the remaining shields on her run," Montgomery said.

A technician broke in, saying, "Sir, we are monitoring an urgent message from Admiral Chambers. Apparently, the Special Operations detachment has discovered a bomb of stellar scale on their moon. They are evacuating civilian personnel and detainees, and command is warning the rest of fleet to pull out of the system."

CHAPTER 57

WE THOUGHT YOU WERE DEAD

Raymond's face appeared on the handheld's small viewscreen. "Chief Raymond," said Wasp, "I have the head of the team running the generator with me, a Dr. McKenzie. He is willing to help shut down the generator—says he has a code. Oh, and he knows you from his school days."

"Dr. Raymond, how are you?" McKenzie asked. "We all thought you were dead."

"Denis?" Raymond said. "Denis McKenzie? How did you ever get your doctorate?"

"Ha! Good one," said McKenzie. "Since you disappeared before giving me a passing grade on my dissertation, no advisor would take me. I had to switch to engineering."

"And how did you end up on this moon, working for the enemy?"

"I'm on this moon because I'm getting paid enough to pay off my mortgage and three kids' college loans. And until your sergeant informed me, we were all under the impression we were under contract with the Alliance. This has all been pretty straightforward. No cloak and dagger."

"Understood, but you should know, had Sergeant Major Wasp and his team not shown up, your employers would never have let you get back to your loved ones."

"I'm beginning to realize that," McKenzie said dryly.

"Okay, then, let's shut that generator down. I've got photos of it, and I've seen some of the interviews. Am I correct in saying you've got a working quantum flux generator?"

"Yes. It's the reason there's a team here at all. It needs to be monitored, or it will move outside safe parameters."

"And how do you handle the heat? That much energy must be a challenge."

"The moon is basically one giant superconductor; there are miles of superconducting coils beneath us," McKenzie said.

"What fluid are you using?" asked Raymond.

"Liquid hydrogen," said McKenzie.

"Seriously? You're sitting on a bomb."

"Thus, the reason the mortgage will be paid off."

Wasp, listening, realized this was the first time he'd ever heard Raymond sound alarmed.

"How is the temperature of the liquid hydrogen controlled?" Raymond asked.

"There's a regulator control room beneath us, but that's another team entirely."

"Have you been there? Can you lead the Marines to it?"

"Yes, of course," McKenzie said. "But I have to warn you, it's heavily guarded—or it was when I was there last, about a week ago."

Wasp interjected, "How heavily guarded?"

"Hard to say," McKenzie said. "I wasn't counting. The most I ever saw at any one time was about a dozen. We operate on three shifts around here. If they do the same, they'll easily have three times that number."

"Where are they billeted?" Wasp asked. "We didn't see that many coming in."

"They have a barracks about three kilometers east of here. I'd say about a hundred of them. Odd bunch, don't say much."

"And their armaments?"

"Sidearms, rifles. I never saw any more than that."

"Hand me back to the sergeant major," Raymond said urgently.

"Yes, Chief?" Wasp said.

Raymond spoke quickly and seriously. "The liquid hydrogen being used as a superconducting agent is volatile if it gets too hot. And unfortunately, *that* facility is not under your control."

"So whoever has control of it can decide to blow the place?"

"Not just the place, the whole moon, and Lilith too. With the quantum flux regulator at risk, it'll probably affect the sun at a deep quantum level as well. I'd say we're talking the equivalent of a supernova. The entire system is at risk. The fleet needs to jump out of this system ASAP."

"I need to talk to the admiral."

CHAPTER 58

THE BURDEN OF COMMAND

"Chambers here."

"Sir, I assume you've heard what Chief Raymond just told me?" Wasp said.

"Yes. I need you to conduct an abbreviated recon of the regulator. We have to know if it's possible to get to it before those guarding it try to destroy the facility."

"I can do that, sir, but if you'll permit, I'd like to make a recommendation."

"Please do."

"Let us just take the facility, sir. If they have only three dozen defenders, we can handle that many, twice that if needed. Pull the fleet out of system, sir; I'd recommend at least half a light-year. You can come back for us once it's secure, and if we don't make it ... well, you have six months to a year to get out of the way of the debris cloud."

Chambers was quiet for a moment. It was the first time Wasp had ever seen him hesitate. Then he said, "Yes, we'll do that. Shut down the generator. Secure evidence of its existence. Evacuate your wounded, the detainees you can spare, and the remains of any Marines killed. I'll send a shuttle."

"Will do, sir," Wasp said with obvious pleasure.

"Then go get that regulator," Chambers said.

"I'm staying," Lee said immediately.

"That's up to the commander of the SpecOps detachment," Chambers said. "I'll order the noncombat vessels out of the area. The frigates are still engaged, and Dr. Zakany is still working on some of her magic."

Chambers signed off, and McKenzie said to Wasp, "I'll stay and help."

"That's noble of you, sir," Lee said.

"No, it's actually our best chance of survival."

"Why do you say that? You could be safe with the fleet if this thing blows."

"No one is safe, and your admiral knows that. Or he soon will when Raymond tells him."

"Tells him what?" she asked.

"Tells him that if the liquid hydrogen goes, then the quantum flux regulator goes, the gas giant goes—and then the star goes, because the regulator will wildly unbalance the quantum flux in the star itself. That will produce not just a nova, but a supernova with as much energy as all the stars in the Milky Way normally emit in a day. Even if the fleet left now, it wouldn't outrun it. You can't jump this close to the gravity well of the gas giant. It'll take hours, maybe days, to get far enough out of the system to jump."

"Just the kind of motivation I like," Wasp said with his signature smile. "Although I don't think we've ever actually saved the universe before." He turned to McKenzie. "Can I ask you and your team to shut down the generator, and to take whatever records you'll need to establish the fact that this facility was here and what it did?"

"Got it. Team Three, on me," McKenzie said.

The civilians gathered around their boss in a tight huddle. Lee saw nods and heard a few exclamations as McKenzie explained the situation. To their credit, Lee thought, they broke their huddle quickly and went to their various stations to begin what she assumed was the shutdown procedure.

All but Mr. Wong, who came over to her and asked her in heavily accented English, "If your commander will permit, I would like to stay and fight along with the Marines. I was in the Territorial Forces as a reservist and am loyal to the Alliance."

Wasp heard and said, "Mr. Wong, if you can shoot, I can use you, though probably for security rather than breach. Every Marine I can take off rear guard is one I can use in the assault."

"It would be my honor," Wong said, bowing deeply.

Wasp called over one of his Marines and said, "Corporal Boyd, Mr. Wong here is a Territorial Reservist who has just volunteered to assist us. Give him a weapon, check him out on basic procedure, then the two of you gather up the scientists who are going back to the surface for pick-up. Use one of the docking bays to receive the shuttle so you won't need moo suits."

"Yes, Sergeant Major," Boyd said.

He turned and shook hands with Wong, and the two of them moved off to a corner of the room where Boyd ran Wong through the basic steps for using one of the carbines. Lee heard the words, "Safety ... chamber ... magazine ... front sights ... ejection port ... range to target ... reload." Wong was nodding, asking questions, and handling the weapon as if he understood. Lee was privately proud that someone from her hometown had stood up for the Alliance under dangerous circumstances.

As for herself, she was starting to feel better. She turned to Wasp and asked, "Well, do I get to stay, Mr. CO?"

"I was going to ask you to take charge of the civilians and the evidence and get that back to the fleet. But it looks like this is the Hail Mary play of all time, so I'll need all hands if you're cleared. How are you feeling?"

"Better," she said, realizing it was true. "But I'll check in with Laura to ask if she can give me a better readout from the autodoc."

Lee switched to her external link and said, "Ops, can you put me through to Dr. Zakany?"

A moment later, she heard Zakany's voice. "Mei-Ling, are you there? Are you okay?"

"Hi, Laura. I'm feeling better," she said. "We're getting ready to get physical here, and I wanted to know what you thought of my autodoc readout."

"A moment," Zakany said. A few seconds later, she replied, "You have three cracked ribs, a concussion, and a bruised left lung, and of course your lower jaw is broken and three teeth as well."

"So I'm fine," Lee said with a laugh.

There was a pause, and then Zakany said over what were clearly tears, "You are so brave, Mei-Ling. No, you are *not* fine, but I know the situation you face and accept that you cannot leave your team."

"I need to be able to tell Wasp I'm good to stay here, or I'm afraid he might send me back," Lee said.

"As a medical authority, I say you may stay. You tell him. But between us girls, as you say, you are hurt, and more trauma could be worse, maybe even bring death."

She stopped, and Laura could tell she was sobbing. Lee didn't know at what point her relationship with Zakany had become so close, but there it was. Maybe it was because they were two women far from home in a difficult, male-dominated world.

"Is there anything you can give me to make this go smoother?"

Zakany said slowly, "I can override the autodoc's safety threshold and authorize you to have a painkiller and a little boost. It is dangerous, so only if you say *yes* will I do it."

"Let me have it," Lee said, her voice strained. A second later, she felt a tiny pinch in her arm, which she guessed was the moo suit's autodoc giving her a shot.

"Do you feel it?" Zakany asked.

"Yes, thanks."

"Mei-Ling, you should know," Zakany said. "The battle here with the cruisers is fierce, desperate. Many have been lost, but the admiral and I have a plan to victory. You will be proud of me."

"I'm already proud of you, Laura. See you soon."

"Mount up," Wasp said loudly. The two teams assembled in the tight space of the control room. One was led by Wong, with a carbine slung over his shoulder, looking like a wannabe soldier of fortune, with a single Marine as escort; Wasp led the other, consisting of McKenzie and the rest of the Marines. Lee moved to join the Marines. "Did you get a clean bill of health from the doc?" asked Wasp.

"Better than new," Lee said with a smile.

"Good. Let's move out."

CHAPTER 59

THE MENTALIST TRICK, PART II

Laura Zakany stopped her work and sat back. *It is done,* she thought. "Ensign Danner," she said. "The program is complete. Now your part."

"Got it," he said, looking at his terminal. "Hmm."

"What hmm?" Zakany asked sharply. Although her rank as lieutenant was only weeks old, she was acutely conscious that she outranked young Danner, a point she frequently tried to make clear.

"Just checking," he said, still focused on his screen.

A long moment went by, and Zakany was about to ask again—no, to *demand* a better answer from this youngster, when he said into his communicator, "Admiral, I have Dr. Zakany's product, and it's suitable. Give us the word, and we'll try to insert it."

Suitable? His arrogance is amazing, Zakany thought.

But still, she was relieved. Everyone had been waiting for her to finish. According to the oh-so-clever ensign, it could only be so long, so many bytes. She had done what the admiral had asked. At least

Danner had correctly noted it was *her* product; he hadn't tried to take credit for himself.

The admiral said simply, "Put it through."

"Roger that, sir," Danner said.

He tapped a few keys. Although there was no obvious change, Danner could see on his system what was happening. Every communications channel began transmitting the data that Lieutenant Zakany had been working on so feverishly. It was two programs: the first, a data stream designed to disable the clones, the second a virus created by Danner and his team to infiltrate the enemy's communications and computer systems. Danner watched its progress as it made its way into the enemy's systems. If it worked, every clone who used a radio, operated a computer, or saw a viewscreen would get a dose of it. Most of it would be imperceptible to them, a subliminal message buried deep in the digital stream. But their subconscious minds would see it, and it would work its magic.

Zakany was brilliant, all right, thought Danner, but touchy—and a bit ridiculous with her insistence that her two-week-old rank made her something next to a god. But he had dealt with more difficult customers before. He had been an apprentice seaman leading an intel section that had much more senior people in it. And she *did* produce. *She may have just given us our best chance at winning,* he thought. *We should know soon if it's going to work.*

CHAPTER 60

A DESPERATE BATTLE

Captain Baker was feeling the burden of command as never before; maybe for the first time, really. The assault on the cruisers *Kauai* and *Okinawa* had been costly. They were fully capable Alliance vessels, and their defensive weapons were substantial. The cruisers had what was termed a layered defense. At long range, they fired missiles. These could be avoided and countered with chaff, electronic countermeasures, and shields. But they did a good job of breaking up attack formations. Closer in toward the vessels were anti-fighter point defense guns. The cruisers would emit an interlocking spread of Gatling, laser, and cannon fire that created a canopy of protection. Force shields helped protect the fighters, but they couldn't protect against fire from all directions at once, so if a fighter got caught in a crossfire, it often meant bad news. Baker lost almost a tenth of his fighters on the first pass, far more than he had expected. After that, he pulled back out of range and organized a volley-fire of missiles at their cruisers, timing and aiming them so the shields couldn't protect from every direction. That had worked, but the cruisers were tough.

They had armored hulls, and the interiors were compartmentalized, so a breach of the hull at any one point wouldn't necessarily be an incapacitating blow.

Baker saw the two frigates make their pass. The *Kauai* hadn't fired its main guns at the frigates, but the *Okinawa* let them have it broadside. *Oh, my goodness*, he thought. *That was some pounding.* He wondered what it must be like on board. They were was lucky the *Kauai* hadn't fired as well. But the frigates gave as good as they got. Both the *Alabama* and the *Guangdong* fired from both port and starboard batteries, and Baker could see the flames and debris that erupted from both cruisers as a result.

Then the *Kauai* went quiet; its shields were down, and it began to list and drift off course. He could hear repeated hails from the *Alabama* asking for its surrender, but there was no response. Baker figured the combination of attacks and the mutiny had probably disabled it. Clearly, nobody was exercising command of the vessel.

Bowman came on the net. "Baker, you seeing this with the *Kauai*?"

"Yes, sir."

"I'm sending in Davenport with a boarding party," Bowman said. "Be prepared to support him as needed. Keep an eye on the *Kauai*, but I want you to concentrate on the *Okinawa*."

"Aye, sir."

"Also be aware," Bowman said. "Zakany and Danner have worked up some cyber witchcraft to try to immobilize the clones. We may see some interesting results soon."

CHAPTER 61

AN UNWELCOME SURPRISE

Mr. Wong had organized the ragtag group of civilian scientists into a squad of sorts. Besides himself and, of course, the sole Marine with them, none of the technicians knew about firearms. He had gathered them together and given them the short course of weapons safety, how to aim and fire, and how to reload.

They made their way up to the surface and entered the docking bay where the shuttle was supposed to arrive. Wong placed his small team in a defensive perimeter and watched for the shuttle through the open bay doors. In minutes, they saw it coming in a few meters above the surface of the moon on a steady approach. Then Wong saw a single streak and a bright flash, and before he could register what it meant, the shuttle turned upside down and dived nose-first into the moon's surface.

"Rocket, probably shoulder-fired," the Marine, Corporal Smith, said in that calm voice that seemed so out of place. Wong could hear him reporting the attack to his commander on the comm channel. "Sergeant Major, the shuttle's down, looks like a shoulder-fired SAM."

Wong knew from his reserve training that SAM was an acronym for "surface-to air-missile."

"Understood," Wasp responded. "You and Mr. Wong and his team will need to hold the entrance. I think you're about to get a ground assault."

Wong felt a surge of pride as he heard the sergeant major refer to the force as "Mr. Wong and his team." He gave the Marine a thumbs-up signal.

"Mr. Wong, are you on the line?" Wasp said.

"Yes, Sergeant Major."

"What was your rank in the Territorial Reserves?"

"Color Sergeant," Wong said.

"Color Sergeant Wong, you are hereby conscripted into the Human Alliance Marine Corps, Achilles Special Operations Task Force," Wasp said seriously. "I want you to take your tactical guidance from Corporal Smith. Your objective is to hold the entrance to the facility. You will almost certainly receive a ground assault in the next few moments. I will be using all my forces to attack and seize the regulator, so don't expect any assistance from me."

"I understand and will comply," Wong said formally. As a color sergeant in the Territorial Reserve for Hong Kong, he had more experience than most reservists. He had trained, and trained others, in what was termed urban warfare. It was something he had taken seriously and did well at.

Wong reviewed the bay and the open area beyond. The shuttle was in flames; clearly there were no survivors, so there was no need to mount a rescue effort for the crew. There were a number of vehicles and larger containers in the bay that would unfortunately provide cover for the attackers he expected momentarily. He considered his own position and the personnel he had available. Only the Marine and he could make aimed fire hit a target at any distance. The other team members could be useful in laying down suppressive fire. That could slow down the attackers or perhaps force them to take less advantageous paths. He also realized that this was to be a tactical action of delay. If the attacking force was substantial, the best they could hope for was to slow them down long enough to allow the Marines to accomplish their task.

Quickly, he briefed his plan to Corporal Smith, who nodded and seemed satisfied that Wong understood tactics and was going to take responsibility for the deployment and control of the technicians. Wong knew them, their names, and temperaments. He would be better at controlling their fire and movement.

Corporal Smith moved out to get some higher ground. Since he was the best marksman in the group, he would set up a sniper position that gave him the best fields of observation and fire. Meanwhile, Wong called his crew of six together and briefed them on the plan.

He started by saying, "We are Team Tech. My call sign is Tech Six." This was to make sure that in any confusion that followed, that there was no mistake about who was to do what or who was speaking. Then he took them as a group and showed each of them three things: their firing positions, the area of coverage, and the route they were to take when the time came to fall back to the next position. He did something he had learned in the Territorial Reserves, which was to let everyone see where the others in the squad were and what they were doing. That did a few things. It let each man know that his flank was covered, and it also let everyone know where the friendlies were so they wouldn't accidentally shoot their own people. And finally, it also let them know that someone was planning this out and that no one was to be left behind or to fend for himself.

Then he did something that he hoped he would have time for: He paced off the distance into the area of engagement, stopped every fifty meters, and marked some object with yellow tape he had found in one of the equipment bins. As he did this, he made sure they could see him, and he called off the distance. This would allow them all to know how far away the enemy was when they aimed. He then got two of the men on his team to help him drag one of the mobile refueling pods out into the open. He opened the top valves and let some of the fuel spill out, and left it open so the fumes would escape into the bay. He was hoping this would allow him to leave a nasty surprise for the enemy.

As a final preparation, he searched the adjacent rooms until he found was he was looking for: ammunition. The guard force that been here, whom the Marines had apparently killed, had stored ammunition in one of the dressing rooms so they could arm-up quickly in an emergency. Wong called some of his men and had them deliver the ammunition to the rest of the team. He remembered that a defender was supposed to improve the position continuously until the attack came. He tried to think of what more he could do, but nothing came to mind. He felt he had done all that he could—and it was just in time.

CHAPTER 62

THE HARD THING

Wasp had sent two Marines to reconnoiter the heat regulator. The news wasn't good: There was a single corridor leading to a hatch that looked like it could be bolted from the inside. The enemy had placed armed guards in the corridor in front to the bolted door. Wasp reported the situation to Major Davenport and Danner.

"There's a vent that runs over the regulator," Danner said. "It's small, though. Very small. I doubt you can get a Marine through it, certainly not with any equipment."

"I can take the guards at the door," Wasp said, "but the door itself is going to take a minute to blow. There's no way they won't know we're coming."

"Raymond here. Is Dr. McKenzie on the net?"

"Yes, John, I'm here."

"How much of a lead time do they need to interrupt the regulator?"

"The sequence has to be done in order, but it doesn't take long to initiate," said McKenzie. "Maybe thirty seconds. That gets it started. Once it is commenced, it can still be reversed if you intervene in time."

"How much time?" Wasp asked.

"It's difficult to say," McKenzie said. "The regulator runs on a cycle, and the temperature of the hydrogen varies. If the hydrogen is at its coolest, you might have a minute, maybe ninety seconds. If it's at the other peak, if it's warmer, you're probably looking at thirty seconds tops."

Davenport said, "You've got a timing issue, then. I don't have any better idea than to take it as fast as you can. I'm on my way to a boarding operation on the *Kauai*, so I'll be out of touch until further notice."

Just then, Corporal Smith came on the line from his position in the docking bay. His voice was hushed. "I've got movement up here. I'll let you know when we drop back. Smith out." Before the line went dead, they heard the first few shots.

Lee started stripping off her moo suit. "I can get through the vent," she said.

Wasp nodded and said, "You feeling up to it? Honestly?"

"You bet. Dr. Zakany gave me some good juice through the moo suit. I'll be fine."

"Take a weapon."

"I will," she said, pulling a knife from a scabbard on her thigh. "The vent's too small for a firearm. If whoever's in the regulator room is armed, I'll use their weapons. If they're not, I won't need one." She looked at Wasp as if to say, "You know I can do this."

Wasp paused a moment, nodded, and then announced, "Marines, let's move. Standard breach, time sensitive. Be aware Commander Lee will be in the room when you make the breach." He turned to her and said, "Tell me when you're about to drop, and we'll go then." Then he turned to McKenzie and said, "Sir, I really need to keep you from getting killed, as we may need you to get the regulator back on line, so please stay back, out of the line of fire."

"I can do that," McKenzie said seriously.

Lee stripped down to the black, skintight leotard that amounted to underclothes worn under the moo suit. She re-sheathed the knife to her thigh and said, "Let's do the hard thing."

CHAPTER 63

TEAM TECH AND THE BATTLE FOR THE DOCKING BAY

Wong heard Corporal Smith report to Wasp that there was movement. He hadn't seen anything yet, and that frustrated him. He supposed the Marine had a better line of sight. Then he heard the sharp report of Smith's sniper rifle; and sure enough, a figure fell back from where he had been hiding. Wong guessed that the guy had tried to peek around from cover, and Smith shot him through the eye. This told Wong two things. First, the guy had snuck up *much* closer than Wong had thought possible without being detected. That meant the attackers were reasonably well trained, not the ragtag group of guards the Marines had so easily taken out during the initial assault. Second, it told him Smith was an excellent marksman. He'd shot out a man's eye at over one hundred meters.

"I'm changing position," Smith said. "In a moment, they'll return fire to where I took the shot. When they do that, you'll be able to see their position and can take action as appropriate."

"Got it," Wong said. To his team, he said, "Team Tech, stand by and return fire, but only at identified targets and only in your zone of fire. Do not expose yourself more than is necessary to fire at your target."

Just then, a fusillade of fire erupted from several points near the entrance to the bay, all of it aimed at the sniper's nest Smith had just vacated. Wong was astonished that they had gotten so close without him seeing them. But he was gratified to hear his team fire back. They were doing just what he had told them to do. Their fire wasn't very well-aimed, but it served its purpose. The enemy couldn't take aimed shots with so much lead flying over their heads. Instead, they did just what he hoped they would: they tried to change position. And when they did, Smith took his awesome vengeance. *Pop, pop, pop,* and three were down. Wong had never heard of anyone who could shoot that well. These Marines were *very* good.

One of the enemy moved toward him; clearly, he hadn't seen Wong's position. Wong took aim at the man's center of mass as he had been trained, and with a funny feeling in his gut, he squeezed off a single shot. The man went down. Wong could see that he was still moving, trying to raise his weapon. Wong aimed carefully and shot him in the head. The figure jerked as if electrified and then lay still. Wong felt the contrary desire to giggle and cry. He had never killed anyone before.

"That was the recon, now they'll do a frontal assault," Smith said on the tac net. "Is your nasty surprise ready, Color Sergeant Wong?"

Wong forced himself to concentrate. "Yes, I have the surprise ready." He saw that he had a good line of sight on the fueling pod he'd set up in the center of the floor.

"Good," Smith said. "Let them come forward until they're within blast range. Once you've detonated, then open up."

Just then, Wong heard vehicles approaching and saw two small trucks coming into sight from the right of the bay door. The vehicles turned into the bay, moving fast, directly toward Wong and his team.

"Hold your fire," Smith said calmly. "I'll handle them."

Wong heard the now-familiar sound of Smith's sniper rifle: *pop, pop.* The first vehicle's front tires burst, and it skidded to a stop. Two more pops, and bullet holes appeared in the windshield. Wong felt with certainty the two people in the front seat had just died. The vehicle behind swerved around the first and began accelerating directly toward Wong's position.

"Okay," Smith said calmly. "Now you can help."

Wong aimed at the windshield, switched his weapon to fully automatic, and fired a burst. He saw the glass of the windshield disintegrate and the two men in the front seat riddled with bullets. The vehicle came on, however, and Wong had to run to get clear of it. It rammed the cabinets he had been using for cover and came to an abrupt halt, its tires still spinning. Wong was glad he had selected in advance an alternate position to fire from, and he went directly to it and dove down on his stomach. It was just in time because a cascade of fire hit the wall over his head, right where he had just been running.

"Okay, there they come," Smith said. "Platoon strength."

Wong looked up and saw the enemy advancing on foot. They were in what was termed skirmish lines, five men side-by-side, followed a few meters back by five more, then two more lines behind that.

"Team Tech," Wong said. "Hold your fire until you see the detonation of the fuel tank."

He quickly switched out his magazine with one that held tracer rounds. Tracer rounds were designed to glow so that the shooter could track the rounds as they moved down range toward their target. The advantage here was that they were basically on fire as they moved, and that fire would serve his purposes.

The skirmish lines came forward steadily. The enemy wasn't taking any precaution or trying to use cover. They were just moving forward, almost like robots, and Wong wondered if they were under some compulsion.

"About now," Smith said in that calm voice.

Wong saw that the enemy were moving past the fuel pod. He took careful aim and fired his weapon on full auto. The tracer bullets raced toward the target, and then there was a flash so bright he automatically looked away, followed by an enormous explosion that bathed him momentarily in searing-hot air. He realized he should have known that would happen. He was blinded and deafened, at least momentarily; an amateur mistake he knew Corporal Smith wouldn't have made.

He couldn't see, but he knew the fuel pod trap had worked as intended. He said into his communicator, "Team Tech. Fire at will." While he waited for his eyes to adjust, he listened to the screams of the enemy as they burned and then heard the shots of his men. There was a small amount of return fire and then nothing.

"Nicely done, Team Tech," Corporal Smith said. "Tech Six, time to pull back. They're just getting warmed up. The sergeant major thinks there might be a hundred of them."

CHAPTER 64

A TIGHT SPOT

Mei-Ling Lee worked her way down the vent shaft. It was tight and completely dark. She lay on her stomach, unable to raise her knees more than a few inches at a time. It was slow going, and she could feel the pain in her ribs from the earlier injury tearing at her side. At least her head was clear. Soon, she heard voices and saw light a few meters ahead. Then she was over a grating, looking down into a small room.

She couldn't see the whole room, so she closed her eyes and tried to visualize the room based on what she could hear. How far apart were they, based on how loud they were speaking? How close were the walls, based on how the sounds rebounded? This was a technique her dad had trained her to use. When he tested her for her master's promotion, one of her tasks was to fight blindfolded against multiple attackers who were not impaired. Despite the time crunch, she closed her eyes, slowed her breathing, and listened. Four men, three standing, one sitting. One older, middle-aged, in charge, the others ... two were techs, and the third was not speaking, maybe a guard, maybe armed. She opened her eyes and looked into the room. Her line of sight was limited. A man in a chair, a computer screen. Like the generator room, a glass wall, something behind that, probably machinery. Okay, that was all she was likely to get.

She very carefully lifted the grate. It was heavy, and she needed to lift it soundlessly, straight up out of its bracket, without scraping metal on metal. Still on her stomach, she used both hands to lift it out. Her shoulders and back screamed with pain and fatigue, and her injured ribs seemed to take the full brunt of the additional weight. Keeping it elevated, she used her knees and feet to scoot forward until she could set it down soundlessly. By the time she'd finished, her stomach was over the opening to the room. She eased herself backward and looked into the room again. She pulled herself up in a ball, her hands on either side of the opening, her knees up to her chin in the small space. Then she spoke quietly into her communicator: "Lee, going in now."

She pulled her hands to her chest and dropped down into the room. It was a drop of about eight feet, and she landed easily. For a moment, no one reacted, and she thought they might not have noticed her. Then she heard the gunfire outside the door; the Marines had started their assault. She knew the guards outside the door would be down already, and she needed to act quickly.

She already knew the layout of the room and who was in it. Even as she was falling from the grate, her eyes had built upon what her hearing had told her. Five men, not four. One supervisor, two technicians, two guards, both armed. *Them first,* she thought. She drew the knife from its scabbard on her thigh and threw it at the guard on the left side of the door; she decided on him at the last moment because he was reaching for his sidearm. It hit him in the throat and sank in deep. Some part of her knew it was a fatal blow, the aorta severed; he would be dead in seconds. Before it had landed, she was already moving toward the other guard. He also reached for his weapon, but when the knife struck, his mortally wounded companion gave out a gurgled howl of pain and surprise. The other guard hesitated, and it was his last mistake.

Lee closed the distance quickly and slammed the heel of her palm into his nose, breaking it and slamming his head back against the wall.

At the same time, she pulled his sidearm from his holster, placed the muzzle against his stomach, and fired a shot. She could feel the jolt of the round as it tore into him. She spun around and faced the other three men, her weapon raised. "Step away from the computer." One of them reached toward the keyboard, so she shot him in the back of the head. Blood and brain matter sprayed forward onto the display, and he fell against the desk and then slid to the floor. By then, she had the other guard's sidearm; she pointed both pistols at the two remaining men. One was older, forty-something, overweight and balding. The other was younger, no more than twenty-five. They both wore white button-down shirts and looked like technicians.

Outside, she could hear the Marines using cutting tools and torches to get through the door. She said into her comm, "I'm in, three down. Two still standing."

"We're sixty seconds out. Door's tougher than it looks," Wasp said.

She pointed a pistol at the older of the two men and said, "Open the door."

"I can't do that," he said.

Lee swung the pistol toward the younger man and shot him in the left knee. He immediately dropped to the ground and began screaming. She said again to the older man, "Open the door." She kept her cold face on, the one that showed no emotion; but for once in her life, it wasn't an act. Her life and the lives of everyone she held dear were at stake. She would do what was necessary to live.

The older man ran to the door and started frantically pressing buttons on a keypad. Lee grabbed the younger man, who was still screaming, and pulled him away from the console, so he couldn't do anything to sabotage the thermal regulator.

She heard more gunfire outside the door, and then Wasp came on the line to say, "We've got company here. I'm going to have to break off the door for a bit. Keep trying to get it open from your side."

CHAPTER 65

SERGEANT WONG'S PENULTIMATE STAND

Wong had his men pull back two at a time so there would always be cover. He was the last to fall back. The motto of the NCO corps for the Hong Kong Territorial Guard was "First In, Last Out." He had always taken it seriously, as it meant that leaders set the example, and one way to do that was to be the first one to run into harm's way when things were difficult, and be the last to leave when things got desperate. Corporal Smith covered them from his mobile sniper nest, and Wong thought that was okay. He'd been ordered by the sergeant major to take his direction from Corporal Smith, so it was appropriate that Smith came last.

Their fallback position was through the hatch and into the corridor that was the only access to the regulator floor. It had some advantages. One was that the enemy would have to blow the hatch. That wouldn't take long, but every second counted. Another was that the enemy would have to come down the narrow hallway. That meant they'd be more vulnerable as they bunched up. But it wasn't ideal for the defenders, either. They too would have to bunch up. And the rule of thumb was, a corridor defense was a losing game if the attackers were both more numerous and determined to keep coming. That was why Wong had used the open bay as the first line of defense: to reduce the attackers' numbers and make them expend valuable time. He had accomplished that. He hoped the Marines would take the regulator and come to their aid. That would even up the score.

When they were safely in the corridor with the hatch bolted, Wong had his team start to drag furniture from the adjacent offices to use as obstacles and firing positions. As they did that, Smith used grenades to rig trip wires and other booby traps. Wong had seen this done before but had never mastered the skill. He was impressed that that the corporal had such knowledge. *The Marines must train constantly,* he thought.

Smith checked in with the sergeant major and came back to Wong. "Color Sergeant, the sergeant major would like us to delay, fall back, delay, fall back. Until we reach this section." He pulled up a schematic on his handheld and showed him.

"And then we stand and fight," Wong said. It wasn't a question. He expected to fight and die.

"Actually, the sergeant major has a better idea," the Marine said with a smile; he quickly briefed Wong on the plan.

Wong was delighted at the sheer audacity of it. It might just work. He called his men together, took a quick count of ammo, and redistributed it so it was about even. He briefed them on the plan, and they nodded their understanding. Then he quickly took them to their positions, set them in place, and went over the plan one more time. Then he returned to Smith, and together they walked through what they planned to do. Smith was careful to point out each trip wire and trap.

Then they came.

CHAPTER 66

A NON-FORCED ENTRY

Two Marine RAB vessels approached the Cruiser *Kauai*. Davenport had to chuckle to himself. The Marines didn't like to think anything was too big for them, but here was the *Kauai*. Fully manned, it would have a crew complement of over a thousand. His two RABs had a total of twenty-four Marines and a small contingent of Navy personnel to serve as a prize crew once the cruiser was taken. But there was nothing for it but to push on. None of his Marines had even raised an eyebrow when he briefed them. Twenty-four Marines against a thousand; what about it?

It was more than confidence in their ability. His Marines trusted him not to lead them into something they couldn't win. They were competent and ready for anything. But did he know what he was doing? Davenport had come up through the ranks. He had been a gunnery sergeant, a coveted rank for enlisted men, and had held that rank for over a decade before being appointed an officer. They had every reason to trust him. Now, somehow, he was a major of Marines, and for the first time in his life, he felt like he was faking it.

"Docking in five," the pilot said.

Davenport braced for the mild impact of docking. He had selected a docking port nearest the bridge and directed the other RAB to a parallel docking port on the other side of the cruiser. The plan was for each team to work inward and, if possible, to meet up in order to take the bridge and thereafter command of the cruiser. No one on the cruiser had responded to hails for over an hour, and it was currently drifting, so no one was navigating the vessel. He knew that a mutiny had been underway before the last hail was cut short. But something wasn't right. Why wouldn't anyone on the vessel respond? Even a mutiny should leave someone in charge. He had brought a naval prize crew with him to take control of the vessel once the bridge was secured, and that included a couple of top-notch petty officers. If it was something electronic or mechanical, they could sort it out quickly.

There was no need to ram and board. The boarding was unopposed, and so they just brought the RAB up to the docking bay, used an Alliance code, and were in. They simply set the RAB down and closed the airlock force field. He heard from the other RAB that they were also in.

"The cruiser has atmosphere," the copilot reported.

"Marines, dismount," Davenport ordered.

They exited tactically and took up a defensive perimeter, weapons ready. There was no movement and no activity. Nothing.

One of the Navy guys went to an interface panel, hooked in some of the portable equipment he had with him, and accessed the database. He keyed his com channel back to the technical crew back at the command ship. "You seeing this, guys?"

Davenport walked over to him and waited patiently for the man to finish his call. "What have you got, Chief?"

"Sir, you're not gonna believe this, but I've verified it with my team back on the *Guangdong*," said the PO. "The ship is practically empty. There are fewer than twenty crew still living. The ship's computer reports about an equal number dead."

"Will the vessel respond to us as Alliance authority?" Davenport asked.

"It already has, sir," said the PO, with a slightly astonished look on his face. "I've already stabilized the ship, and we can fly her once we get to the bridge."

Davenport checked in with the Marine team on the other side. They had the same situation status. No opposition, almost no one on board as far as they could see.

"Show me where the living are," he said.

The PO pulled it up on the display: A few in the mess hall and in the sick bay. No one in the gunnery batteries. No wonder they hadn't fired on the frigates. "Both teams, move out with tactical caution toward the bridge," Davenport commanded. He called Bowman on the command net. "Sir, this vessel is practically empty. We have no opposition facing either team. We're now advancing toward the bridge."

"The intelligence team on the *Centurion* thinks the *Kauai* was probably in dry dock, perhaps under maintenance," Bowman said. "They think the clone admiral basically stole the ship or ordered it out before its crew could respond. The other cruiser was probably at full strength and ordered out as well. They took a gamble that Admiral Chambers would yield to a senior officer. It was a bluff, and it failed."

CHAPTER 67

"CAPTAIN" DAVENPORT

In short order, the Marines made their way to the bridge, and the skeleton crew soon had the *Kauai* under control. They found about a dozen dead on the bridge; it looked like the crew had indeed been fighting amongst themselves. Had they all perished at each other's hands? He supposed it was possible. Why else hadn't the survivors stayed on the bridge and retained control of the ship?

He sent the other boarding team to collect the stray personnel, ordering those in the mess to be taken to sick bay and confined there, along with those who were truly sick or injured. "Take care," he said. "There may still be some saboteurs on board."

He turned to Gunnery Sergeant Wilcox and ordered him take his team and man the big guns. "Let's see if we can give the frigates a hand."

"Aye aye, sir," Wilcox said, with look of joy on his face.

Fifteen minutes later, Davenport reported to Bowman, "Commodore, we have the *Kauai* under our control. I've got a Marine crew on the big guns. We'd like to get into the fight."

"What was up with the point defense weapons?" Bowman said. "They gave Danner a hard time."'

"They were on automatic, sir. Our prize crew has that system shut down. Shields are at 50 percent. Just point us where you want some fire, sir."

There was a pause, and Davenport thought he heard Bowman speaking to someone. "Captain Montgomery is going to give the navigation details to the Navy prize crew," Bowman said. "We're going to bring you around to get you positioned to fire on the *Okinawa.*"

Montgomery came on the line and, very politely, addressing him as Captain, asked Davenport's permission to speak to the prize crew. Davenport was technically the commanding officer of the *Kauai,* and this was a distinction the Navy respected.

He said, "Of course, sir. Please proceed."

Montgomery spoke at some length to the Navy crew. Davenport saw them nodding and entering data into the navigation console as he did. In a moment, he felt the ship's thrusters, and they were underway.

Davenport realized with a start he was commanding an Alliance cruiser about to engage in combat and wondered if any other Marine major had ever done such a thing.

CHAPTER 68

IT NEVER HELPS TO BE RUDE

Lee turned her attention to the middle-aged bald man trying, or pretending to try, to open the door. "Sir," she said. "You need to get this door open in five seconds, or I will no longer consider you essential." Her voice was as cold as her expression. In another time and place, she would not have known herself. Was she really such a cold-blooded killer? No response. "Five, four, three, two, one." She raised the pistol, and the man screamed, "No!" She turned the weapon at the last moment and shot his earlobe off. He screamed and clutched his ear, which was streaming blood.

She grabbed him by his shirt collar, forced him up against the wall, and placed the muzzle of the gun at his crotch. "Last chance."

"The code is forty-seven nineteen," he gasped. "You have to wait five seconds after the first two digits."

"Do it," she said and forced him around to face the door, placing the weapon firmly at the base of his spine. In a moment, the door was open, and she said, "Was that so hard?"

"Chinese bitch," he snarled.

She punched him hard in the kidney, and he went down in a weeping heap. "You shouldn't be so rude," she said.

Outside the door was McKenzie, with a single Marine positioned to cover him from what was obviously a firefight farther down the hall.

"I'll take him from here," Lee said.

"Thanks, ma'am," said the Marine. "I'll get back to my mates." He took off down the hall toward the sound of fighting, with that supernatural speed the Marines seemed to use so effortlessly. Meanwhile, McKenzie looked around the room and saw the carnage. He glanced at Lee with a strange look and said, "You don't mess around."

She said with a serious expression, "They were very rude."

CHAPTER 69

THE GREAT HALLWAY DEFENSE

Wong and Smith were ready. Each had a good position behind desks and cabinets that they had carefully placed for cover and concealment. They had clear lines of fire toward the hatch, where the attackers now must come through.

Outside the hatch, they heard explosions, followed by screams.

"What happened?" asked Wong. "Did they misfire their breach?"

Smith called from his position, "No, I left them a surprise. I figured they'd be in a hurry and wouldn't clear for booby traps. It won't slow them for long, though."

It didn't. A minute later, the hatch blew, and black-clad attackers stormed through the door. Wong took aim and fired. One assailant went down. As usual, Smith's fire was more deadly: *pop, pop, pop*. With each shot, a man went down. Wong fired again and kept firing, and soon there was only a pile of bodies in the entrance.

"Fall back," said Smith.

As they had rehearsed, Wong moved quickly to his next position down the corridor, while Smith covered him. Then Smith moved while Wong kept guard. In a moment, another surge of attackers came through. This time, the defenders waited and kept low. The first attacker hit the trip wire at a run, and a grenade detonated. It was very loud in the tight space of the corridor.

For a moment, Wong was stunned. Then he realized Smith was firing. The attackers were in disarray, and many were down, but more kept pouring though the hatch. He raised his weapon and fired into the mass. No way to miss at this range.

"Fall back," Smith said.

Wong leaped up but immediately fell down. He looked around to see what he could have tripped on and saw he was bleeding from his thigh. *Must have been a ricochet or a fragment from the grenade*, he thought. He felt no pain, and the bleeding wasn't critical, but moving the leg took a lot of effort. He hobbled to the next position and yelled, "Set."

Smith got up to move, and Wong saw that he fired as he moved. Wong added his fire as well. The enemy would soon overwhelm them.

"Friendlies coming through. We'll be on your position in a moment," Wong heard Smith call to Wasp.

"Ready for you," Wasp responded.

Wong and Smith fell back to the final defensive position, a barrier completely blocking the hallway only a few meters before the hatch to the regulator room. Wasp and his Marines were already in place behind the barrier, weapons at the ready. Smith grabbed Wong, threw him over the barrier, and followed right after. They scrambled up and took their positions with the Marines just as the first wave of attackers came around the corner. Wong had to admire their bravery or pity the compulsion that forced them on. They filled the hallway, and the Marines sent their deadly fire, volley after volley. The attackers went down in waves, and yet more came on, relentlessly.

When it seemed they must be overwhelmed, Smith said to Wong, "It's time, Color Sergeant."

Immediately, Wong spoke into his communicator: "Team Tech, advance."

A moment later, the sound of weapons fire came again, but this time sounding different. The attackers hesitated; some of them turned back to face the new threat. Wong's team were firing and advancing from behind the attackers. They had been hidden in several of the rooms off to the side of the hallway and, as planned, had waited for the fight to pass them by and then come in at the last moment at Wong's order. And they were amazing, firing and advancing as if they were professionals. Wong felt the sting of tears in his eyes as he realized his ad hoc team of engineers was fighting with competence and incredible bravery.

In moments, the attackers were down, a giant heap of bloodied bodies. "Cease-fire," Wasp yelled. He turned to Wong and said, "A commendable performance, Color Sergeant. Please recover your team, take stock, and rearm. We may still have to fight our way out of here."

Wasp returned to the regulator room. As he entered, he could hear an alarm sounding and saw flashing lights. He smiled when he saw the chaos Lee had wrought on the occupants but then noted that McKenzie was frantically working the controls. Clearly, this wasn't over.

"How are we doing?" he asked.

"Apparently, one of the technicians set the self-destruct sequence before I could deter him," Lee said, pointing to the corpse of the man she had shot in the head.

"I'm working on it," McKenzie said. "It'll be close. It's too late for the coolant to stop its temperature climb, so I'm dumping the liquid hydrogen into the overflow vats. If I get the pressure down, I might just keep it from blowing."

As if in mockery of their hopes, an enormous explosion shook the entire structure. The lights dimmed, and dust sifted down from the ceiling. Danner's voice came over the coms channels. "SpecOps team, be aware the *Okinawa* is firing on your position. The fleet is engaging it, but I'm afraid you're in for a pounding."

CHAPTER 70

THE LAST FULL MEASURE

Davenport brought the *Kauai* around so that he could bring its guns to bear on the *Okinawa*. He only had enough Marines to operate one side of the cruiser's big guns, so he came at the cruiser with his starboard side facing his adversary.

Montgomery, aboard the *Alabama*, was managing the tactics and had directed the two frigates so the *Kauai* would have a clear path to close with the *Okinawa*. Both the frigates and the aerospace fleet were hammering the *Okinawa* now. Davenport was impressed that she hadn't struck her colors. Now that the *Kauai* had come over to the Achilles side, the remaining cruiser didn't have a chance in the long run, though to be fair, the *Okinawa* was still a force to be reckoned with. She let loose with her big guns and missiles, and her point defense kept Baker's fighters suffering a steady attrition.

"We'll be in range in five," said one of the prize crew.

"Batteries are loaded and ready," came the voice of Gunnery Sergeant Wilcox over the internal net.

"Batteries, stand by," Davenport said. "Batteries, fire!"

They instantly felt the recoil of the big guns launching their thousand-pound projectiles. On the forward viewscreen on the bridge, he saw the projectiles slam through the weakening shields and strike the *Okinawa* broadside. A cheer rose up on the bridge, and Davenport could hear the gun crews cheering as well, giving the "Ooh rah" the Marines were famous for. The *Okinawa* was hurt badly; he could see flames on several decks, clear signs that the hull had been breached in multiple compartments. This couldn't go on much longer. The captain of the Okinawa would need to surrender soon, or his vessel and its crew would be lost.

Davenport could hear the hail from Commodore Bowman demanding a surrender, but there was no response.

Then, without warning, the *Okinawa* broke off the engagements and began to accelerate away from the Achilles vessels. Davenport thought she might be trying to run for it, but he couldn't see any advantage there. The frigates were faster, and with the damage she had already sustained, there was no hope she could escape. But it soon became clear the *Okinawa* had another objective: the moon. Within moments, the big cruiser began firing what was surely all its remaining weapons at the base on the surface. It was a desperate and suicidal gesture, but Davenport understood. It was as Admiral Chambers had predicted. The moon base was everything; it was proof that a conspiracy had been taken place. By destroying it, the rebels embedded in the Alliance fleet, and probably the government as well, could always later claim that Chambers was the traitor, and they would scoff at claims of conspiracy.

Bowman's voice came on the line and said, "All vessels engage the *Okinawa*. She must not be allowed to destroy the moon base or the SpecOps task force."

Davenport had the prize crew adjust the *Kauai* so its big guns could continue to fire on the fleeing *Okinawa*. At the same time, the smaller, more agile frigates closed to within a few hundred meters and fired broadside after broadside at the cruiser. The *Okinawa's* shields were down now, and the punishment she was taking was extreme. All of a sudden, he realized what she was doing—and it took his breath away.

CHAPTER 71

WHAT LEADERS DO

Aboard the *Centurion*, Danner said, "The *Okinawa* is going to ram the moon, sir."

Chambers nodded as if he had been expecting this and said with calm assurance, "Set a course to intercept, and prepare to abandon ship."

Danner turned to look at the admiral as if he had misunderstood, and for a moment the entire bridge was completely silent.

Chambers said in that same calm voice, "Ensign Danner, please carry out my order."

Danner turned to his console and said, "Course for intercept is set, sir." Then he spoke on the shipwide channel: "All hands, prepare to abandon ship. I repeat, all hands prepare to abandon ship. This is not a drill. This is not a drill. All hands to escape pods."

"Transfer the conn to me. Evacuate the bridge, and well done, all of you."

Danner understood now: The admiral was going to ram the *Okinawa* in an attempt to force it off course in order to save the moon base. He wanted to save the crew, so he had ordered them all to leave the vessel prior to impact. Danner wanted to argue, and he wanted to stay with the admiral, but he knew that wasn't the right thing to do. They had only minutes to get everyone off. He had been given an order, and he would carry it out.

Danner said, "Aye aye, sir. You have the conn." To everyone else, he yelled, "Let's move, people!"

Zakany was nearly the last to leave. She was calm in emergencies; it was one of the reasons she was such a good nurse in the trauma wards, both in Budapest and in the fleet. As she was about to exit through the hatch, she turned and saw that Master Warrant Officer Nemeth had not moved. He was still at his post, so that only he and the admiral remained. She said to him in their native tongue, "Matthias, you must come now."

He turned, smiled at her, and said, also in Hungarian, "No, Laura, I cannot leave my *vazallus* in time of danger, just as he did not leave me many times."

Vazallus was an ancient term for "liege." She knew his roots went back to a time of honor long-forgotten among modern people. His ancestors had served under King Corvinus, as part of the Black Legion. For him, duty was all.

"Go on," he said. "We will be fine; we always are. We have our shuttle and will follow. Do you forget, I am the best pilot in the fleet?"

Tears filling her eyes, she said, "I want you to live; you must come back to me."

"I know, and I will," he said with such gentleness. "But first, I must do this thing."

She turned to the admiral and said, "The program might still work."

"It's worked already," Chambers said simply. "If not for your program, the *Kauai* would still be against us. It got to the clones. That's why the bridge was abandoned when the Marines took it. You have done all that you can; now go."

After she left, Nemeth said, "It was good of you to give her hope that her program might still work."

301

"I was being honest," Chambers said. "The program worked, and it *did* allow us to take the *Kauai* without a fight."

"And the *Okinawa*?" Nemeth asked. "Will it work there as well?"

"I'm sure it already has. But the *Okinawa* isn't commanded by a clone. It's commanded by a loyal Alliance naval officer who believes he's doing the right thing."

"And you know this how?" Nemeth asked his admiral.

"The CO of the *Okinawa* is Commander Jay Chambers Jr. My son."

CHAPTER 72

IT'S NOT GETTING
ANY EASIER

In the regulator room, the lights went out altogether. Backup lights came on a moment later. They were dimmer, and Lee thought the room looked a little surreal.

Danner's voice came though on the external net as if he were speaking through a long tunnel. "Marine Five, be advised the admiral has ordered us to abandoned ship. We will be unable to provide support until further notice." Then the line went dead.

"So they're having some trouble up there," Wasp said. "That doesn't change anything here. Dr. McKenzie, how are you coming on keeping us cool?"

"Okay, so I was about halfway through dumping enough hydrogen to keep it from cooking off," McKenzie said. "Now I've lost the connection. The battery backup doesn't extend to the control systems, only to basic life support."

"Options?"

"I'm blind here. There's nothing I can do. I can't even monitor the temperature, which is surely starting to rise again."

"Can it be done manually?"

"Yes ..." He paused, thinking. "All I was doing was electronically opening the valves, which are mechanical devices. The problem is that I don't know where they are."

"I do," said a voice from the door. It was Wong; he stood there covered in dust, with a Marine-provided bloody bandage on his thigh. "This was one of my areas of responsibility, the manual inspection of the coolant system. I have it in my head."

"Can you get to it?" Wasp asked.

"Yes," responded Wong. "But I will need help to get through the ducts and to swim to the manual valve controls."

"Did you say *swim*?" Lee asked.

"Yes, ma'am," Wong said. "Are you a good swimmer?"

CHAPTER 73

BLOOD TO ME

"Your son?" asked Nemeth. "You mean young Jay? I haven't seen him since he was a boy."

"I haven't seen much more of him. After his mother died …" Chambers shrugged. "These things happen. We drifted apart. He went to the Academy. After that, we were posted to different parts of the galaxy. I haven't seen him for years."

"And he's commanding a cruiser? He's young for that," Nemeth said.

"Yes," Chambers replied. "A fast riser and, by all accounts, a good officer."

"And you knew he was commanding the *Okinawa*? You said nothing. He is blood to you," Nemeth said, looking troubled.

"This battle fleet and my duty; they are blood to me as well," Chambers said. "That young provost guard who fixed his bayonet and went to his death to protect the control room; he was blood to me." Chambers squeezed his eyes shut at the memory.

"But why does young Jay continue? Surely he has seen the clones collapse. He must know there is a problem."

"You remember, he was always very focused, very literal. Even as a child, he wouldn't back down if he thought he was right or if there was a principle at stake. I expect he got his last orders from Admiral Stuart, his fleet commander. He may suspect something's wrong, and he's surely seen the clones go down due to the virus Danner and Zakany worked up. But he has no reason or authority to deviate from his last order. His admiral could have told him the moon was of primary concern. If he believes that and that his admiral has been killed in honorable combat, his sense of duty will be strong. He won't yield."

"Would *you* yield?" Nemeth asked. "To save your ship and its crew?"

"Not if I thought it was to a hostile adversary. Not if I thought the crew would be mistreated and the vessel used against the Alliance," Chambers said.

"Can you convince him you are *not* his enemy?" asked Nemeth.

"I must. I have no choice."

"I understand, vazallus. Shall we proceed as we planned?"

"Yes," Chambers said. "Slave the controls of the command ship to the shuttle, and let's get there. We don't have much time."

CHAPTER 74

TIME FOR A SWIM

"How much time do we have before the system blows?" Wasp asked.

"Minutes, no more," McKenzie said, sweating. "If the explosions damaged the containers, there's no way to tell what effect it could have on the temperature change."

"Can the moo suits be used while submerged?" Wong asked.

"They're not specifically designed for it, but in theory, they ought to hold up under just about anything," Wasp said. "They're designed to do EVA work under extreme temperatures and pressures, after all, and they have an oxygen supply that will last for days if needed. The problem is that they aren't designed to maneuver underwater. They'll be awkward."

"We have no choice," Lee said. "I have mine; can we get a suit for Mr. Wong?"

Wasp motioned to one of his men, who started stripping off his moo suit.

Wasp turned to the group. "Suit coming right up, but wouldn't it be better to send one of my Marines with Color Sergeant Wong?

They're all qualified in combat swimming. And Commander Lee, you are injured."

"Two reasons to send me. I'm smaller than all your Marines, and I was a competitive swimmer in high school. Not to mention, in a pinch, I can communicate with Color Sergeant Wong in his native language."

Two minutes later, Lee and Wong were suited up, standing over an open hatch that looked down upon a container of dark fluid. Even to Lee, this was a bit grim-looking.

Wong said, "There is a force field that contains the liquid hydrogen. It keeps the fluid in but will allow us to pass through. The fluid is cold, below minus 425 degrees Fahrenheit. Warmer than that, and it will begin to turn to a gaseous state, and that could explode easily, either with a spark or spontaneously."

"So what are we trying to do?" Lee asked.

"At this point, our only option is to open the vents leading to the surface. That will cause the fluid to expand and rush to the moon's surface and then into space."

"Won't that cause an explosion?" asked Lee.

"It will certainly cause the hydrogen to boil off to a gaseous state as it expands and escapes to the surface," Wong said. "It will be extremely volatile during that phase transition. When it hits the surface, it will cool again because it's nighttime up there, and the temperature on the surface is minus 300 degrees. Beyond that, the temperature drops to nearly absolute zero just a few meters above the surface."

Speaking in Cantonese, Lee asked, somewhat harshly, "Explosion or not?"

Wong responded stiffly, "I don't know, but I said it is the best option, and it is."

CHAPTER 75

THE ONLY OPTION IS ALWAYS THE BEST CHOICE

Lee took a quick hop, folded her arms to her chest, and plunged into another world. For a terrifying moment, she was in complete darkness, and then her suit lights came on, and she could see through the faceplate that she was submerged in swirling liquid. Her field of vision was only a few meters. Her suit was telling her in a smooth female voice that the external temperature had dropped and the suit would compensate. She could hear its internal mechanisms whirling in what she assumed was an effort to maintain her body temperature. She continued to descend, as expected. There had been no time to adjust the suits for buoyancy, so she had been told that they would drop to the bottom of the tank and would need to walk and climb to their destination.

She felt a disturbance near her and looked to see Wong dropping into the fluid beside her. She said, "Marine Five, we'll leave the channel open so you can monitor."

"Roger," Wasp replied. "Other than the coms, we can't monitor your progress, so you're basically on your own."

"Lead the way," she said to Wong over her suit-to-suit channel. Wong led her to their left until they came up to the wall of the tank. He moved parallel for a few meters until he came to a ladder. He turned to make sure she was with him and began to climb up. She was impressed, because she knew he'd been wounded in the leg during the fight in the hallway. She followed, and in a few minutes, they hit another level that opened up into a broad plateau.

"How much farther?" she asked.

He paused and looked around quickly, his head lamp cutting a path back and forth through the murky fluid. Finally, he said in a mildly panicked voice, "It should be right here."

Lee forced down the panic she felt trying to rise up inside her. "Should we split up and try to find it?"

He said nothing, and she wondered if Wong might have succumbed to panic himself. It would be understandable. After all, he was basically a civilian who had been through a lot in the past few hours.

Then: "No," he said with new confidence. "This is the right place. I was here a month ago, when the tanks were drained."

"So where is the valve?" she asked.

"They must have moved it during the last maintenance period, when I was on my two-day rest time," he said. "There is no other explanation."

"Not to rush you, Commander Lee," Wasp said over the tac net, "but we've just been informed the *Okinawa* is attempting to ram the base."

"Anything we can do about that?" she asked.

"Yes," McKenzie said. "The defensive missile system is still functional, though much degraded by your fleet. Apparently, its automatic systems still have power, and it's engaging the cruiser. We can hear the launches."

"How does that effect what we're doing here?" she asked.

McKenzie said, "If you can vent the hydrogen before the *Okinawa* strikes, we might just live out the day. The base is designed to survive meteor strikes. If the hydrogen is still underground when the cruiser hits, though, I think it will ignite."

"And if the missiles take out the cruiser?" Lee asked.

"We'll still get hit by debris. That's not as bad as an intact cruiser, but it's not good, either," McKenzie said.

"Wait," Wasp said. There was a pause, and then Wasp came back on the line to say, "We have the power back. Don't know how long it will last. Dr. McKenzie is searching the maintenance records for the new location of the release valve."

After a moment, McKenzie's voice came on the line. He sounded hurried as he blurted, "The temperature is too high; it's definitely going to blow. Your best bet is to open the valve—I'm sending the schematics to Wong now—and then get back to your entry point ASAP."

"How will that matter?" Lee asked. "If the hydrogen blows, the base goes with it."

"Maybe not," McKenzie said. "It looks like enough of the coolant drained out earlier. Yes, it'll detonate, but if you can get the valve open, it might just focus most of the detonation upwards and away from the rest of the base."

Wong was already moving at what amounted to an awkward run in the bulky moo suit. He must have received the new schematics from the last maintenance visit when the valve was moved. Lee moved to follow; she could hear him breathing hard over the net. He muttered, "The idiots may have saved us all."

"What do you mean?" she asked.

"They moved the valve into a stupid location, completely unwarranted. Had they told me, I would have objected," he said. "But the new location is better to redirect the blast. Now the fluid will go nearly straight up and out, with fewer turns at high pressure. It is better."

After another moment, he stopped in front of what looked like a large metal box attached to the wall of the tank. He flipped the panel door open. Sure enough, inside was a large wheel about two feet in diameter, comically large for the task. To Lee, it looked almost like what one might expect to see in an animated children's show on an old firetruck. Wong grabbed it with both hands and tried to turn it, but it didn't budge. Lee joined him at the wheel and took one side of it, and they both tried to turn it. Nothing; it was jammed. "Found the valve, but it won't turn," said Lee. "Any thoughts?"

McKenzie said quickly, "There's a safety override under glass on the left side. Smash it, flip the switch." Before he had finished speaking, Lee had smashed the glass panel with her fist and flipped the switch. A green light came on above them. Lee and Wong laid into the wheel and it began to turn, slowly at first and then more rapidly. They could feel the fluid begin to move past them. They hurried with the wheel until it wouldn't go any farther.

"Let's get back to the entry point," Lee said. But as soon as she said it, she knew that wasn't going to happen. The current was too strong, and it was pulling them in the wrong direction. "We have a problem here," she said with escalating panic.

"Yes, I can see it," McKenzie said. "My fault; I didn't think that through."

Lee and Wong were holding on to the wheel now, trying to stabilize themselves and keep from being dragged along with the current. "Any suggestions?" asked Lee.

"You can't stay there, because that tank is going to blow," McKenzie said. "Sounds crazy, but your only option is to go with the current and hope to be ejected with the hydrogen onto the surface. The moo suit will adjust to the lack of atmosphere, and it might protect you from the blast, at least the heat." He paused and then said, "I'm sorry; I can't think of anything else. If you stay where you are, you will die."

"Color Sergeant Wong," Lee asked, "are you ready for a ride?"

"With you, ma'am," Wong said, "I'd go anywhere."

They locked arms and let the current take them.

CHAPTER 76

THE LAST CLEAR CHANCE

Chambers and Nemeth sat side by side in the small shuttle anchored to the command ship. The navigation controls for the larger vessel were routed into the shuttle, so they were effectively steering the command ship. "Has everyone evacuated the *Centurion*?" asked Chambers.

"Yes, sir," Nemeth said. "Ensign Danner reports 100 percent of the crew are accounted for. He has the pods in formation, and they are moving away from the combat area, to the far side of Lilith. They're as safe as they can be."

"He did well, don't you think?" Chambers said.

"He has potential. He did very well under stress. His decision to be a person of substance lies in his future."

"You said the same about me after I finished the special warfare course," Chambers said lightly.

"And I was right."

"Time to impact?"

"Seven minutes."

"Hail the captain of the *Okinawa*, please."

On the screen appeared the image of a young naval commander with jet-black hair and a mixture of Asian and Caucasian features. "Commander Chambers, Alliance Cruiser *Okinawa*," the young man said tersely.

"This is Rear Admiral Jay Chambers, commanding officer of the Achilles Battle Fleet."

"I know who you are." The young man showed nothing, no emotion, a trait he got from his mother. Neither spoke for a long moment. Then: "You hailed me," said the younger man.

"Jay, I know you think you're doing the right thing," the admiral said. "But you've been misled. Your Admiral Stuart was an imposter, an enemy clone."

"And you have proof of this?" the younger man snapped.

"Of course we do," the admiral said. "We have him in custody. We have his DNA. He is *not* the admiral. He's an enemy agent. We had those here in the fleet as well. My own deputy, Commodore Vance, was one. Many died because I didn't see it in time."

"And this moon?" the commander asked.

"It houses something called a macro-wave collapse generator, a new technology that allows ships and personnel to teleport great distances," the admiral said. "It's why your clone admiral didn't want it captured, because it's proof of what they've been doing, that they're behind all these attacks."

"I have my orders," Captain Chambers said. "I was told the moon's base was a primary concern."

"I figured that," the admiral said. "But your orders are invalid and illegal."

Commander Chambers said nothing.

"Please don't sacrifice your crew," the admiral said. "They deserve to live. Their deaths will mean nothing."

"I haven't sacrificed them, Admiral. They've all left the vessel," replied the commander. "I ordered them to abandon ship. It's just me."

Admiral Chambers sighed. "I have a team on the moon. They have control of the generator; it's the proof we need. If you destroy it, they will have died for nothing."

"Admiral, you and I both know it's a SpecOps team. You have time to get them off. It's *your* job to protect your people, not mine."

"Jay," Nemeth interjected. "This is Uncle Matthias; you know me."

"Yes, Uncle," the younger Chambers said with a voice that had softened somewhat.

"Your father is speaking true," he said. "He does not lie. *I* do not lie."

"Duty is all, Uncle," the commander said. "You taught me that."

"Your duty lies elsewhere, Jay," Nemeth said.

The young commander stared back, the beginnings of indecision on his face.

"There is more, nephew. The moon has quantum flux generator. It's cooled by liquid hydrogen from the gas giant. If you hit, the moon will go, the generator will go, the gas giant will go, the star will go. None of us will survive."

No response.

"And on the moon, there is one who is blood to you. The daughter of your mother's sister, Mei-Ling Lee. Your cousin. She has fought with valor, many injuries. She cannot, will not, leave her duty. Even now she is in great peril. Do not kill her, Jay."

"I will not surrender an Alliance warship," the younger Chambers said.

"Agreed," the admiral said. "Divert from the moon, pick up your people. Under truce, together we will lead a joint delegation to the base and see what we will see."

Just then, a missile was launched from the moon's surface, headed straight for the *Okinawa*.

"Jay, that missile is for you. Your shields are down," the admiral said. "Eject!"

"Not today, Father," the younger Chambers said. "This is my command, and I won't leave it."

Just then, an enormous explosion could be seen on the moon. Flames erupted and rose hundreds of meters above the surface.

CHAPTER 77

A WILD RIDE

In moments, Lee had to release her grip on Wong, and they spun away from each other. She said with more confidence than she felt, "See you topside."

"You bet," Wong responded.

"Mei-Ling," Wasp said. His voice was strange, and she realized he was frightened for her, perhaps the first time he had ever felt that emotion. She remembered what he had said about casualties among his men: *"As a Marine NCO, my job is to train them properly, lead them, and set the example. If I've done that, I can sleep at night."*

"Yes, Theo," she said.

"We are evacuating to the surface, hoping to survive the blast."

"Last one to get there buys coffee."

He chuckled and said, "Dr. McKenzie has plotted your route."

"I'm listening."

"Your best chance is to make it to the central funnel before the ignition of the hydrogen."

"Not much we can do about that," she said. "We're just along for the ride now."

"Yes, we're tracking your progress," he said. "The most dangerous point is the turn into the main funnel. You're accelerating now. When the fluid makes the turn upward into the main funnel, the pressure will increase, as will your speed."

"Speed is good, yes?"

"Yes, good in that you get out quickly," Wasp said. "Bad in that you need to make that turn at high speed."

"You mean we may hit something," she said.

"You *will* hit something. The question is how hard."

"Any thoughts?" she asked.

"PLF is all I can think of," Wasp said.

"Got it," she said. "Mr. Wong, the sergeant major is recommending that we keep our elbows in, knees bent, and chin down."

"Thank you, ma'am," Wong said. "I am familiar with the PLF position. I attended the parachute training course in North America. I am in that position now."

"Me too," she said. "Wasp, how much time do we have?"

"Ten seconds. You should feel the acceleration now."

In the end, it wasn't as bad as she feared. She did slam into something, but it was a quick jolt, and then she was past it, racing upward toward the surface. She thought, *It hasn't ignited yet; maybe it won't, and we'll just get spat up onto the surface.*

And just as she thought it, the world caught fire. She felt like she had been kicked hard, really hard, right in the back; her field of vision was intensely bright for a fraction of a second until the automatic filter optics cut in and dimmed the view. The moo suit alarm went off to indicate extreme rise in temperature, and again she could hear the internal motors whining to compensate.

And then she was out and up, accelerating away from the moon. *I'm alive!* she thought. As her momentum started to slow and the gaseous flames dropped away, she stabilized her movement using the suit's thrusters and started to look around for a place to set down. Below her she could see a gaping hole that had been the external vent from which she had just erupted. The liquid hydrogen had changed to gas as it raced to the surface. When it ignited, the explosion had widened the funnel, leaving a smoking scar on the surface.

She picked a spot not far from where her team had first landed, on the low rise of hills above the now-smoking compound. As she descended, she saw what was left of a vessel that had been destroyed in low orbit drive nose-first into the surface, about ten kilometers away. It threw up a huge mushroom cloud of dust and smoke. She wondered if that was the remnants of the *Okinawa*, the *Centurion*, or some other vessel. She thanked her luck that she had not come out from the moon under that cascade of metal. "Color Sergeant Wong," she said over her suit-to-suit communicator. "Are you still with me?"

"Yes," came his excited voice. "I am alive, I think. But I am very high and unfamiliar with this suit. I do not wish to float away into space."

"Don't worry," she said. "Cycle though the commands until you get to automatic retrieval. The suit will set you down safely, and the beacon will allow us to find you."

"Yes, I see that. Thank you," he said. "That was something. Have the others survived? Do you have word of Team Tech?"

"Let's find out," Lee said. She switched to the external channel and said, "Any station this net, this is Navy Six. Please respond."

There was no response. Her pulse quickened at the thought that they might be trapped under surface. Did they have time to make it out?

CHAPTER 78

SEARCH AND RESCUE

Lee set down, got her bearings, and tried to think. She began to run toward the now-collapsed building that had been the moon base compound. As she ran, she switched to the broader operations net and said, "Any station this net, this is Navy Six, requesting SAR for military and civilians missing in action on Moon Base Alpha 51."

She immediately got a response: "Navy Six, this is Marine Rescue Six. What's your status and location?"

"I'm three hundred meters east of the compound, on the ridgeline," she broadcast. "I am not in need of assistance. I have been separated from the rest of the special operations detachment of eleven Marines. In addition, there are six civilians under arms who were assisting us. No response since before the explosion. Last known location, they were subsurface, making their way to the surface. One civilian friendly is on the surface with a beacon sounding."

"Stand by," Rescue Six said. Thirty seconds later, "Navy Six, we are inbound now, ETA five minutes with SAR teams. Sorry for the delay; we're spread thin with other recovery efforts."

"Who else is down?" she asked.

"The *Centurion*," Rescue Six replied. "You should be able to see it from where you are. Looks like the crew abandoned ship before it went in. We're bringing in the pods now. We've also got hundreds of enemy combatants in pods all over the place from the *Okinawa*."

"Did you get Private Johnson off that rock?"

"Yes, ma'am, we did," said the voice. "And she's pissing mad that she missed the fun. She's on the SAR team coming to you now."

She ran toward the destroyed bunker, but her heart sank when she saw the debris. Huge chunks of metal had been thrown hundreds of meters and more from the building. And then she saw it: a moo suit under the rubble. She ran over to it; it was face down, unmoving, covered in dust. She turned it over and saw that it was Dr. McKenzie. She checked the readout on his chest and saw that he was alive but unconscious.

"Dr. McKenzie," she said, "can you hear me? Where are the others?"

He groaned and opened his eyes; clearly, he was in serious pain. He finally focused on her and said, "Did you get them out?"

"You're the first. The SAR team is on its way. Where are the others?"

"Wasp put us civilians in front," McKenzie said. "He pushed us out through the bay door just as the explosion hit."

"Where are your people? The civilians?" she said.

"They got out," he said. "They were ahead of me. They must have been thrown forward by the blast. Help me up." Lee doubted McKenzie would be able to stand on his own, but he surprised her; once he was up, he stayed up. "I'll look for my guys now."

At that moment, the SAR shuttle landed. Lee remember how Wasp had rescued her on the bridge when the clones had attacked. This time, it was her turn to save others. The Marines exited tactically and cleared the area before the team leader, a sergeant, came over to her.

"Ma'am, I'm Sergeant Boyd," he said. Lee could tell his was the same voice that had spoken to her on the coms channel a few minutes ago.

She explained what she knew: that according to a survivor, the civilians had gotten out of the bunker before it blew, and that they had likely been thrown clear. And the Marines had not exited the bunker before it blew and were likely buried under the rubble.

"We got this, ma'am," he said. He sounded so confident, she wanted to believe it was true. She watched as his team of about a dozen began setting up lights, so the area could be quickly searched. They spread out and began the search. In moments, they were reporting, "I've got one in Sector Five," or "There are two in Sector Three."

From the back of the shuttle, they rolled out what looked like some sort of earthmover with a series of claws and levers extending upward from it. The sergeant stood near where Lee thought the entrance had been and waved the driver of the vehicle over to him. He gave instructions to the driver, and the large claws started reaching down and moving huge blocks rapidly, one after another.

The sergeant came over to her and said, "You've got one motivated crane operator there, ma'am. That's Private Johnson, the marine from your team who we just pulled off the rock. She had quite a ride before we could get to her—got slammed around, took some damage to her suit, and had to shut life support down to minimum to wait for her ride. She was near-frozen and suffocated when we got her. But after she came around, she wouldn't even see the medic. She wanted to get back to her team."

Just then, Private Johnson gave a shout, jumped down from the vehicle, and ran to the rubble to start digging frantically with her hands.

Lee ran over and joined her. "What have you got?" she asked.

Johnson ignored her and yelled, "Sergeant Major, I know you're hiding in there! Don't quit on us."

They uncovered a large section of metal siding; the three of them grabbed it and pulled it free. Underneath was what looked like a small, debris-filled room the size of a storage closet. Inside, she could see a tangle of moo suit arms, legs, and helmets. "Is it time to get up already?" said a familiar voice. "We were just having a nice nap."

"Wasp," Lee cried. "Why didn't you respond to the radio call? I thought you were all dead."

"It's good to see you too, ma'am," he said as he was pulled free of the rubble. "When we knew we couldn't make it out, we took shelter in the pump room, which had reinforced ceiling and walls. We had scoped it out earlier as we were coming through the first time. Then, after the explosions, when we knew we were trapped, we set our life support to minimum because we didn't know how long it would be until someone came for us. First thing that happens on minimum life support is, you fall asleep."

He turned to Private Johnson and said, "Johnson, I'm glad you made it. That must have been some ride, a story to tell your grandkids. And thanks for coming for us." He turned to the sergeant and said, "Boyd, what's the status on survivors?"

"Sergeant Major," Boyd said formally, "we have six civilians recovered, including one in a moo suit retrieved three kilometers east of here. All of them alive, all injured, two of them seriously, but no life-threatening injuries." He looked at the pit where the last of the Marines was being pulled out, all standing and stretching as if nothing unusual had happened. "And your team is intact, it seems."

"Not all," Wasp said. "We lost Private Simmons on the drop. He's still up on the ridgeline. Please bring him down."

Boyd turned to one of his corporals and issued instructions. The man set off at a run with two other Marines toward the ridgeline.

Wasp looked to the horizon at the flames from the starship crash. "What happened over there?" he asked.

"That's the impact point of the *Centurion*," said Boyd. "We have a team there, a recovery operation only. If anyone was aboard, they didn't survive the impact. We have vessels overhead collecting those who got out in pods."

"Did the admiral survive?" Wasp asked.

"As of now, he's missing," Boyd said. "He and Master Warrant Officer Nemeth stayed with the command ship after they ordered everyone off."

"Was the *Centurion* damaged in battle?" Lee asked.

"Apparently not, ma'am," Boyd said. "From what we can gather, the admiral intended to ram the *Okinawa* to prevent it from impacting the moon."

"So it worked. What happened to the *Okinawa*?"

"Apparently, the admiral came to an agreement with the captain of the *Okinawa*. They made a temporary truce until the moon base could be inspected."

"I'm confused. If they didn't ram each other, then how did the command ship get taken down?"

"The base fired a missile at the *Okinawa*. As her shields were down, the admiral used the command ship to intercept the missile and protect the *Okinawa*."

"What about the rest of the command team? Did they get off?"

"Yes, ma'am. Mr. Danner has them all together in orbit around Lilith. Since they're not in distress and are accounted for, we're giving priority to others for now."

"What about the *Kauai*?" Wasp asked.

"Now there's a story, Sergeant Major," Boyd said. "Major Davenport took it intact with two RAB teams and a naval prize crew."

Wasp smiled and said, "Ooh rah."

"There's more, Sergeant Major," Boyd said. "Gunny Wilcox took his Marines, manned the big guns, and the major got them into the fight with the *Okinawa*."

Wasp shook his head and said with a smile, "So you're telling me that a Marine unit captured a cruiser, turned it on an enemy cruiser, and fired on the *Okinawa* with a Marine gunnery crew?"

"Yes, Sergeant Major," Boyd said, also smiling.

"Gunny Wilcox will be unbearable in the NCO mess from now until forever," Wasp said with a laugh. "He took out a fighter and now a cruiser? The Marines will have to rename the artillery school after him."

Boyd held up a hand to indicate he had an incoming call on a line they couldn't hear. He nodded and said, "Yes, she's here. Patching you through now."

Boyd turned to Lee and said, "Commander, I have a Dr. Zakany for you. I've put her through on the suit-to-suit. The connection is poor, I'm afraid."

"Mei-Ling? Are you there?" came Zakany's voice. Though the signal was very weak and distorted, Lee could tell she was concerned.

"Yes, Laura," Lee said. "It's me. Are you okay? I heard you had to abandon ship."

"Yes, we are okay, though it is very tight here, and young Danner is apparently lord of all, despite his modest rank. How are you and the Marines?"

Lee smiled. She knew that for some reason, Danner irked Zakany. At least they were alive.

"We had the one fatality you knew about on the landing," said Lee. "Otherwise, everyone has some bruises, but they'll heal."

"You had more than bruises, Mei-Ling," Zakany said icily. "A concussion, broken ribs, and broken jaw and teeth. You must seek the aid station, as soon as duty permits."

"Well, thanks to your override of the moo suit autodoc, I got what I needed."

"Oh, my dear," Zakany said, sounding apologetic. "So sorry, but that was a little white lie. There is no override for the autodoc. I said that because I knew you would not be deterred, and maybe, I hoped maybe, the lie would help you through."

Lee was astonished and a bit pleased. She had no idea Zakany could, or would, so easily deceive her. *That's girlfriends,* she thought. She was also pleased because it meant she had done what was needed without exceptional help from painkillers or performance-boosting drugs. "Thank you, Laura," she said. "Whatever it was you did or said, it helped me through."

"I am worried, Mei-Ling," Zakany said. "They say Matthias and the admiral are not found yet. Do you know?"

Lee looked over at Sergeant Boyd, who shook his head as if to say, "Nothing yet."

"Laura," she said, "I'm here with the commander of the Marine Rescue Team. He's doing everything possible. When we know, I'll tell you."

"He promised to come back to me," Zakany said. "He would not lie. I will wait. I just found out he has something to return to. I will tell you in private."

Before Lee could think about that, she was distracted when she saw that the recovery party was bringing the body of Private Simmons down from the ridgeline. "I have to go now," Lee said. "Stay safe, and I'll see you soon."

The Marines stopped what they were doing and formed a line to honor the passing of the remains. Wasp looked at her and said, "You were his commanding officer when he died. It's for you to take the formation."

Lee took her position as commanding officer forward of the line, Wasp at her side. As the detail passed in front of the group on its way to the shuttle, Lee said, "Marines, present arms!" Every hand shot up in perfect unison as the body passed.

Lee said, "Marines, order arms!" Down came the salute.

Perhaps because of the exhaustion, she felt tears rolling down her cheeks. Wasp saw it and said, "Not the last time you'll lose those under your command." He paused and then said, "When I thought it might be you ..." His words came with difficulty, and she could see he was struggling with emotion. "It was different. Thank you for teaching me to grieve."

She looked up and saw he had a tear of his own, and she wondered if he had ever cried for a lost Marine before today.

CHAPTER 79

THE NEW NORMAL; NOTHING IS THE SAME

News of the battle and the discovery of the moon base had caused confusion and scandal throughout the Human Alliance. Commodore Bowman had briefed the Naval High Command by teleconference and had made a full written report as well. Investigators came out, surveyed the moon, and then questioned hundreds of crew members, including those of the *Kauai* and *Okinawa*, and the few survivors from the moon base. It was an awkward and unquiet time.

Lee's personal belongings had gone down with the command ship. Not much lost, really, besides a few mementos from her family life, and her uniforms, of course. Everyone who served on a starship knew not to bring along things that were too precious. So Lee stayed with the Marines on board one of the troop carriers after the battle. She felt more at home there, especially now that Admiral Chambers was gone. Technically, she had been assigned to the SpecOps task force as the deputy for the operation, and since no one had revoked that order, she was still part of the Marine detachment. Major Davenport had offered her one of the Spartan quarters reserved for Marine officers—a bed, a desk with a metal lamp, a sink, and a latrine down the hall—and she was glad to have it. It was more than enough for her. She went to the Marine supply room and drew two sets of battle fatigues, since they didn't have anything for a naval officer. She liked them and didn't care that they made her look like a Marine major instead of a Navy lieutenant commander.

With Zakany's help, she healed quickly from her injuries; and after a few days, she was back into a routine. She even got her teeth fixed; better than new, she thought. She spent her days training with the Marines—they never stopped, apparently—and her nights in the training hall working on her martial arts.

Like everyone else, she was interviewed by the investigation team members. It was an unpleasant experience. She didn't like those people, their tone, or their questions. They were a dour lot, pale-faced and flabby. But mostly she didn't like them because they hadn't been there, and yet they were apparently going to make judgments about the conduct of the people who had been. At the beginning of the interview, one of the unsmiling, doughy-faced, middle-aged men, a civilian apparently, put a form in front of her to sign that read "You have the right to have an attorney present while this interview is in progress." Lee, her cold face on, pushed it back to him unsigned.

The man asked, "Are you refusing to sign this?"

Lee looked at him and felt disgust for this person, not even a man, not a warrior, not someone who would ever face horrible death or great fear, not someone who would ever have to bury his own dead Marines who had died beside him on a godforsaken frozen moon.

Aloud, she said, "I'm a lieutenant commander in the Human Alliance Navy. I know my rights, and one of them is not to have to sign that form. I also do not have to talk to you."

"Are you refusing the interview?" he said.

"Am I a suspect in a criminal investigation?" she asked. "Am I in custody?"

He seemed flustered. She suspected he was used to intimidating people. This wasn't going the way he had seen it happen a hundred times. "Um, I suppose you are not a suspect … at this time," he admitted. "And, of course, you're not in custody."

"Fine. Put that in writing." She pushed the pad of paper he'd provided over to him.

'Um, well, I'm not, that's not how we do things," he said.

Lee got up and began walking to the door. She said, without turning her head, "You should really read up on the Uniform Code of Military Justice. It's a required course at the academy, and it's practiced in the fleet."

Lee went to the training hall, warmed up, and began her martial arts forms. She was angry that the investigator had tried such a shabby trick on her. The UCMJ was an ancient and well-crafted document. In addition to spelling out crimes and punishments, it also addressed the rights of suspects. Under normal circumstances, serving military didn't have the right to refuse to answer questions put to them by lawful authorities, and they certainly could be punished for withholding facts or making false statements. To protect them from being compelled to testify against themselves, the rule was that a service person had to be informed they were a suspect in a criminal investigation. That triggered their right to remain silent without fear of punishment. By getting her to sign the rights waiver, the creep could later say he'd informed her she was a suspect—"See, she even signed the rights waiver"—even though he clearly didn't want to say that.

To anyone in the military, that made a difference. Suspects had the right to remain silent, while witnesses in uniform did not. Clearly, these people were out for blood, and she knew the best course was to avoid giving a formal statement to any of them.

At the officers' mess, she found out all the Marines had refused to speak to the investigators. They had smelled a rat and acted accordingly. She felt better about the whole thing upon learning that. But she knew they were on safer ground than she was. Marines could only be tried by a Marine court. And although that happened often enough, they had confidence in their own leaders and their justice system. If they broke a rule, yes, they would get punished. But if they adhered to their code, their leaders would not arbitrarily punish them and certainly not just to find a convenient scapegoat for a mission that didn't fit clearly into some comfortable category.

This battle had been a confusing mix of conflicting loyalties. It was Alliance against Alliance. The admiral on one side was clearly some sort of imposter, which was bad enough. The admiral on the other side was missing, but whatever he had been doing, he had kept it secret, and the Navy didn't like secrets to be kept from it.

Worse yet, civilians on the moon had been killed, and Lee suspected that would be the real problem, especially for her. In the regulator room, she had killed three civilians, wounded a fourth, and tortured a fifth. Thanks to the Marines who dragged him to safety, the fat bald guy whose ear she had shot off had survived the explosion. She felt sure he'd made a complaint against her, and that was going to be a problem.

Was it a problem for *her*? Had she gone too far? No. The situation was extreme. If the regulator blew, the moon and the gas giant would have exploded, and the system's star would have gone supernova, killing every living thing in the system, including the entire battle fleet. She had had seconds to stop them from overheating the system. And though she did everything she could, they *still* overloaded the system, and it *did* explode, though thanks to some fast work by McKenzie and extreme scuba work by Mr. Wong and herself, the moon hadn't blown up, and the flux generator hadn't destabilized.

But it wasn't that simple, was it? She liked violence. Loved it. She felt zero remorse, then or now, about the men she had killed. After the fight in the command center, she had gone to Wasp and cried in his arms. But that was because she had felt herself changing, losing an innocent view of herself. It was not out of remorse for those she had killed.

Was she a bad person? Zakany had said the Marines were intentionally recruited and screened in part because they had a low sense of empathy. In past times, they would have been considered to be sociopaths. Was that her too? She didn't think of herself as a bad person. She didn't lie or steal or take advantage of people. She knew the difference between right and wrong, and she tried to do right if given a choice.

In the end, she decided she was who she was; there was some good and maybe some not-so-good. She needed to watch herself, to be aware of this newfound propensity for violence. She needed to make sure she was in control and responsible for her actions.

The day before the fleet was to make Earth orbit, Commodore Bowman, now the acting commander, called a meeting of the key staff. After everyone who had been invited was in the room and the door was closed, he cut through any preliminaries and said, "I've been in touch with the fleet staff judge advocate, who indicated some of us, or all of us, may be arrested upon return to Earth."

There was silence, and then Lee asked, "On what charges?"

"Treason, murder, conduct unbecoming an officer, destruction of Alliance property. There's more, but you get the idea," Bowman said.

"And their theory for this approach?" Lee asked.

"That Admiral Chambers was acting without authority," Bowman said, "and therefore any action he took against Alliance property, installations, vessels, or personnel was illegal."

Lee said, "Okay, that's crazy, but even if it were true, how does that implicate anyone under his command? Surely it's not a crime to obey an admiral in wartime."

"You would think that," Bowman said. "But they're saying commissioned officers should know not to obey illegal orders. They're likely to try to paint this as one big, out-of-control, renegade operation that resulted in the destruction of an Alliance war vessel and the deaths of dozens of naval personnel as well as civilians. The death of civilians, they are saying, is a war crime."

There was silence in the room. War crimes drew the death penalty.

CHAPTER 80

SAY GOODBYE

Two weeks after the last shot was fired in what became known as the Battle of Alpha 51, the Achilles Battle Fleet limped back into Earth orbit. The search and rescue teams had been unable to find any trace of either Admiral Chambers or Master Warrant Officer Nemeth. They were presumed dead, and so the search was called off. A final determination would have to await the results of a formal naval inquiry.

Lee said farewell to her Marines at a little celebration they had on their last night together. They were returning to their home base in the Rocky Mountains of North America. They would get some time off, a month or so, and then go back to their training cycle. The farewell was a modest affair, but Lee liked it all the more for that. They'd set up some tables and chairs in one of the unused hangar bays aboard the troop ship. It was just a dinner from the mess hall, good wholesome food. There was no alcohol, but she liked that even better. She didn't really like alcohol, and on her last night with her Marines, she wanted a clear head so she could remember everything perfectly.

After they had eaten, the lights were turned down, and a single candle was lit in the center of the table. Major Davenport stood at attention and everyone followed his example.

He said in a ceremonial tone, "Roll call."

"The company is present, sir," returned Sergeant Major Wasp.

Lee realized she was being allowed to witness a ceremony that outsiders rarely saw or even knew about.

"Lance Corporal Jeremiah Jenkins?" called Davenport.

"Lost in honorable combat, sir," Wasp replied.

"Private First Class James Simmons?"

"Lost in honorable combat, sir."

And the list went on, ten named in all. After each call and answer, a bell was rung. Lee remembered them all and wept without restraint, tears rolling down her cheeks as she stood steady at attention. And she wasn't the only one. Many of the toughest wept. This was their family. She knew Zakany had been wrong when she said they had low empathy. They had empathy, but theirs was an empathy that was earned in endless hours of training, sweat, and, yes, blood. Never had she felt so much a part of a family, even compared to her own, and never had she been so sad to leave it.

She could not imagine going back to the Navy. Her career there, which had once seemed so promising and exciting, now seemed something without joy or hope.

CHAPTER 81

SAY HELLO

The next day, Lee took the command shuttle down to the spaceport at Denver. The major ports on the American East Coast had been obliterated during the December attack, along with the cities that housed them. Denver was the new provisional capital of the Alliance on Earth.

She had waited until the last shuttle to go down to the spaceport. She wanted the Marines to go first, so they could get a head start on their hard-won R&R. The shuttle was nearly empty, containing just a few technical personnel who had stayed back to place the vessels in shutdown mode. The Achilles Battle Fleet was being disbanded. It was, after all, originally an ad hoc flotilla, whose only role was to transport passengers from Achilles Nine back to Earth. Chambers had made it into a fighting force. But that was no more.

Lee had been through the Denver terminal years ago during her travels with the academy's martial arts team on her way to a tournament. As she landed, she could see through the window that the base had been built up to expand its capability. There were many large metal containers and temporary quarters and offices seemingly arranged at random. At Passport Control, there was a young Asian woman in a border guard uniform directing travelers to various booths. When Lee approached, the woman directed her to a booth off to one side.

The immigration agent behind the desk said, "Passport, please."

Lee presented her passport. The Alliance wasn't a true world government; it was a quasi-federation with a strong central authority. It could and did tax its citizens, and it commanded a military. But each of the nations who were member states in theory kept their sovereignty and issued passports to their citizens. Lee, having been born in Hong Kong, was technically Chinese. Denver, although in the nation of North America, was considered part of the international zone, administered by the Alliance, where each member state would have an ambassador in residence.

The man behind the desk was also Asian; looking at her passport, he said to her in Mandarin, "Ms. Lee, welcome back to Earth."

"Thank you," she said politely. "It is good to be back."

"If you will pardon me," the agent said, "I will be back in a moment." He then left the booth and walked into a nearby room.

Lee thought that perhaps her name had been flagged and that he was going to get officers to arrest her. Surprisingly, this didn't seem to bother her. She was physically and mentally tired, and had been through a lot. And mostly, she was tired of waiting.

He came back in a moment, handed the passport back, and said cheerfully, still in Mandarin, "I hope all goes well with you."

At the baggage claim area, a tall Asian man in an impeccable business suit stood waiting for his bags. He smiled at her and nodded in a way that indicated he was Chinese and knew she was as well. Some gestures could not easily be learned by outsiders, and the Chinese nod and slight bow were among those, she thought.

Her duffle bag came; she grabbed it and started to walk toward the exit. The tall man said in accented English, "My bag has not arrived. I will go to the claims office."

He then very naturally fell in step beside her. This was a little odd, she thought; bags were still coming onto the roundabout, and so she wondered how he had known his bag would not arrive.

As Lee was exiting the baggage claim area into the spaceport proper, she was met by a delegation of military police, headed by a Navy commander. They blocked her way, and the commander said, "Lieutenant Commander Mei-Ling Lee, by order of the chief of Naval Operations, you are under arrest."

The tall man next to her stopped, smiled, and said, "Unfortunately, gentleman, Ms. Lee is a citizen of China and does not fall under your authority."

"And you are?" the commander asked.

"I am Xing Po, first consul of the Embassy of China. Also, kind sir, I am a registered attorney and member of the bar of both North America and the Alliance. I represent Ms. Lee."

Lee was astonished to hear that but said nothing. She decided to let this play out.

The Naval commander looked at Lee and said, "Commander Lee, is this correct?"

"Please, kind sir," Po said. "As she is represented by me, please address all questions to me."

The commander looked flustered and said with irritation, "I have a valid warrant for her arrest."

"Please to see," Po said and held out his hand, the smile dropping away.

The commander handed over a paper. Po took it and read it carefully, nodding as he did so. He took out a handheld and snapped a photo of it, then handed the paper back to the commander. He said, "Thank you for the courtesy, commander. This warrant is signed by the chief of Naval Operations, not by an Alliance or North American judge."

"And what bearing does that have?" the commander asked, now getting angry. "She is a member of the Alliance military and falls under the jurisdiction of the military. The warrant is valid."

Lee noted a group of about a dozen Marines in transit who had seen the confrontation and had gathered nearby. It was clear that they didn't like what they were seeing. Although they weren't the Marines from the Achilles Battle Fleet, she suspected that they knew who she was and what was potentially about to happen.

"You are an attorney as well, sir?" Po asked.

"No," the commander said, now starting to lose his composure. "I am an Alliance military officer executing a valid warrant, and I'm beginning to think you are interfering with a lawful arrest."

"Very understandable mistake," Po said. "I have just sent a copy of your warrant to my consulate, and they are contacting your authorities now. Soon you will get a call from a qualified Alliance attorney who will explain to you that the warrant is not valid. And while we wait, let me explain, with respect, sir, that it is you who are interfering with the free movement of a Chinese diplomat, which is itself an offense under Alliance law."

"I'm not interfering with your movement," the commander snapped, sounding exasperated. "You are free to leave at any time."

"You misunderstand," Po said. "It is Ms. Lee who has diplomatic protection."

"What?"

Po turned to Lee and said, "Please to pass your passport to the man."

Lee had no idea what was up. She had a normal tourist passport. She handed it over, and the commander took it and looked through the pages. He pressed his lips together and shook his head.

Just then, his phone rang, and he stepped away, listened for a moment, and then said, "Yes, sir. I understand."

He returned, handed the passport back, and said, with a red face, "Mr. Po, Commander Lee, I am sorry for the misunderstanding. You are, of course, free to go."

As Lee took the passport back, she noticed it looked different. She opened it, and sure enough, there was her picture, her signature, and the words "Diplomatic Passport, Delegation of China to North America" in both English and Mandarin. Then she understood. The passport agent had left with her passport and returned with a different passport, one that gave her diplomatic immunity.

As she walked forward with Po, he gestured to an Asian man, who was obviously waiting for him. The man stepped forward, bowed politely to Lee, and took her bag from her.

Po said in Mandarin, "Commander Lee, I'm sorry for the subterfuge. There was no time to do it any other way. We only found out about your arrival a few hours ago, and the arrangements had to be made quickly."

"What's going on?" she demanded.

"If you will agree," he said (now in perfect English; gone was the halting Chinese-accented pidgin he had used when confronting the arrest party), "I have transportation for you to the consulate, and my ambassador is in the car waiting to speak to you."

She thought, *The Chinese ambassador is waiting for me, here at the airport, in a car?* Nothing to do now but let it play it out.

When she walked outside, the first thing she noted was the cool autumn air. It was late afternoon, and she could see the pink sky in the west. She took a deep breath and realized she hadn't breathed Earth's air for over two years. It was good to be home and, at least for now, not in prison.

At the curb reserved for cars with diplomatic plates were two black cars: a limousine and a sedan in front of it. Po got into the sedan, and the man with her bag put it in the open trunk of the limousine. A chauffeur opened the door for her, and she got in the back seat of the limo. Immediately, the car pulled away from the curb and drove into the light airport traffic. Facing her was an older Chinese man who somehow looked familiar.

The man spoke to her in English and said, "Thank you, Commander Lee, for agreeing to see me. It is a great honor."

Lee said, "The honor is mine, Mr. Ambassador. And I am grateful for your intervention and the very professional work by Mr. Po. But I don't understand why you have gone to all this trouble on my behalf."

"I am Kim Wong, the elder," he said. "I believe you know my son."

CHAPTER 82

THE CALM BEFORE
THE STORM

The limousine left the city and proceeded northwest on the highway, heading toward Boulder. After a drive of about forty-five minutes, they pulled up to a compound manned by armed and uniformed guards who opened the gate and saluted as the two cars drove through. Shortly after, they passed what looked like a ranch house with several outlying cottages. There was even a barn in the back.

Wong said humbly, "Please forgive the rustic setting. When we had to relocate the embassy and consulate after the attack, this was the best we could arrange. I hope you will find it satisfactory."

The limousine pulled up to one of the cottages. Wong said, "This will be your residence during your stay, Commander Lee. I hope you will join me for dinner at 1900 hours at the main house. We have some things to discuss, and there are people I'd like you to meet. I hate to burden you after your ordeal, but you will have some decisions to make."

Outside the cottage was an elderly woman whom Lee assumed was a servant. She bowed when Lee and Wong got out. Lee noted that the ambassador returned the bow deeply, and that surprised her because he assumed that a man of such status would not show deference to a servant.

Wong said, "Commander Lee, please meet my mother, Mrs. Li Na Wong."

That explained it. Lee bowed deeply and said in Mandarin, "It is an honor to meet the grandparent of my brave brother-in-arms, ma'am."

Mrs. Wong came forward and said with tears in her eyes, "You have saved my grandson, the last of our beloved family. The honor is mine."

Mrs. Wong showed her the cottage. To Lee, who was used to the tight spaces aboard Navy vessels, it was luxurious; it had a separate bedroom with an en suite bathroom located in the loft, a small living area, and an adjacent kitchen with a stocked refrigerator. The back door off the kitchen opened to a small covered porch that looked out over the open grassland and the Rocky Mountains in the distance. The sun was just setting, and it was gorgeous. "It's beautiful, ma'am," Lee said.

"You must call me Mama," she said. "Everyone does."

"Yes, Mama," Lee said with a smile. She knew that it probably wasn't true that *everyone* called her Mama, but she liked this woman, and she liked the idea of calling her Mama. Her own mother had passed so long ago, she barely remembered her.

"In your room, I have left you a dress that you may wish to wear for dinner," the older woman said. "Please consider it a gift from me to you. It was to be for my granddaughter, but she was lost in the attack on Beijing." Lee opened her mouth to protest, but the woman raised her hand to cut her off and said, "It would my honor if you would accept it."

Lee nodded and said, "Thank you for your gracious gift. You are very kind."

Mrs. Wong shook her head, and said, "No, not just that. The people who attacked Beijing, they killed millions, including many of our family. You and your colleagues fought them when no one else would. You saved my grandson. That debt cannot be repaid in a lifetime. I have lived eighty years and had hoped never to feel such grief. But I pray I will live to see the bad ones brought to justice."

Lee nodded again. "Thank you for honoring me so, Mama. But I must tell you that your grandson, Kim Wong, himself took up arms against a superior force; he commanded a group of untrained civilians, and he insisted on taking up the most dangerous tasks, though he had been wounded. He saved all of us. *He* is the hero."

Mrs. Wong nodded and smiled. "I did not know this, though I suspected there was much untold to me. Young Kim is very modest; he always has been. He gave all the credit to you and your Marine warriors. Although he left out his own part in the battle, he did tell the truth about your part. Of that, I have no doubt. Nothing is changed. That he fought beside you makes the bond stronger. This house, any house of mine, will be your sanctuary as long any of my family lives."

CHAPTER 83

DINNER AND A SURPRISE

Lee wore the dress that night. She was surprised to find that it fit perfectly and was pleased because it looked good on her, though she would never have bought it for herself. It was black and strapless, and came to just past her knee. In the closet, there were many pairs of shoes of different sizes, and she found a pair that both fit and went with the dress.

At the dinner, there was a reception beforehand in the living room of the ranch house. It was a simple affair, and Lee saw about a dozen people, most of whom she didn't know. There was one distinctive, dark-skinned man who drew her attention. He was dressed in a business suit and was in his sixties, just short of average height but powerfully built. As her dad used to say about rough-looking men, his face looked like it had seen "bad weather and worse trouble." He looked familiar, and she assumed he was a military officer, but she couldn't place him.

There were two other men in civilian dress. Both looked military: short hair, fit, ramrod-straight postures; one in his mid-forties, the other twenty-something. She saw the ambassador, Po and Mrs. Wong. And to her delight, there was Color Sergeant Wong in full dress uniform.

She went over to him and hugged him. "Color Sergeant Wong, you look splendid."

"You are too kind," he said. "But you look recovered as well."

"Yes," she said. "The Navy gave me three new teeth and didn't even charge me." She smiled and pulled her lip down to show her lower teeth that, in fact, did look as good as new. They both laughed. "And your leg," she said, "has it healed already?"

"It was nothing. A scratch only, and caused by my own clumsiness."

Lee knew that wasn't true, but she also knew that Chinese decorum required that Wong, as a man, must never extol his own virtues or suffering. It would be considered impolite in a culture where courtesy was the sign of maturity. "I have met your father and grandmother," said Lee. "They are wonderful people and have been very kind to me. And thank you all for the help at the airport. Without Mr. Po's intervention, I think I would be in jail right now."

Wong looked serious and said, "Yes, that was a near thing. When Mama found out about your valor, she insisted that Father take some action to keep you safe."

Lee smiled and asked, "Does Mama have so much influence?"

Wong said seriously, "Yes, of course. She is a member of the Central Committee and has been for twenty years. She is very powerful. Even the foreign minister must defer to her."

"She has been very gracious to me," said Lee. "She gave me this dress."

"Yes, I know," Wong said with a melancholy look. "She told me. It was to be my sister's. She was lost in the attack on Beijing."

"I'm so sorry. I tried to refuse it," said Lee.

"Please do not be offended or think I am. I would rather you wear it than anyone on Earth." He smiled and said gently, "And if I may be so bold, you look lovely in it."

Just then, the ambassador held up his glass and tapped it lightly with a spoon to get everyone's attention. "Dear friends," he began. "Thank you for coming to our home tonight. We are honored to have with us here a number of honored guests. If I may introduce some you may or may not know: We have here General Mosi Motubu, commandant of the Human Alliance Marine Corps."

The elder man Lee had noted before smiled and raised a hand in greeting. So that's who he was. Of course; she had seen his photo in the Marine billets on board the troop carrier.

"We are also pleased to have Lieutenant Commander Mei-Ling Lee, recently returned from the Battle of Alpha 51." People looked at her and then, suddenly, broke into applause, and none more vigorously than General Motubu, who looked at her and nodded as if to say, "I know you, young lady."

Just then, the lights went out, and an instant later, Lee heard a sound she had heard before: the fuse of a flash-bang grenade. She closed her eyes and shouted, "Grenade, down!" But even before the words were out, the flash and pop went off. The effect was devastating on the room. Most of the people were down on the floor groaning, with their hands over their eyes or ears.

Because she had closed her eyes before the flash, Lee wasn't blinded. She looked around and saw the now-familiar sight of black-clad attackers swarming into the room through doors and windows. Lee looked around for a weapon and grabbed a knife from one of the serving trays on a table. She turned to look for a target and saw that General Motubu, old warrior that he was, had grabbed one of the assailants and snapped his neck as if it were a twig. As he fell, Motubu took the man's carbine and in one quick motion raised it and fired two rounds into the nearest invader, who went down in a heap. Lee for her part let fly her knife, and it found its mark in the throat of a third assailant.

Just then, the ambassador yelled, "Stop!"

Lee looked and saw what he had seen: Mama Wong being held by an attacker with a knife to her throat.

Mrs. Wong showed no fear and said to her son in Mandarin, "Kim, do not be childish. Kill these pigs. I have lived to eighty."

"I cannot, dear Mama," said the ambassador. He turned to the man holding his mother and asked, "What do you want?"

"Lee," the man said in a strange, raspy voice.

343

Lee knew this was another of the clones. She recalled that their voice boxes were not fully developed. She glanced at the general, who was still holding his weapon, though with the barrel slightly lowered. Clearly, he understood the situation. If he fired another shot, Mrs. Wong would die. He looked at Lee and met her eye. He nodded to her in a reassuring way.

She took it to mean she should go along with this kidnapping, so she said, "I will go with you now, as long as no harm comes to any of the others here."

Quickly, two of the attackers grabbed her arms and began to hustle her out the door. The man holding Mrs. Wong dragged her toward the door, waited for Lee to be taken outside, and then pushed Mrs. Wong to the floor and fled the room. Outside, Lee could see that the protective detail at the gate were down, probably dead. Another body lay a few feet in front of the door, probably a local security man on station outside the ranch house. The attackers had a van waiting with the motor running, and they ran with her between them toward the open back door.

Just before they reached it, there was a series of pops and thumps, and all the remaining black-clad men went down, obviously shot with silenced weapons. Lee dropped to the ground, snatched one of the weapons from the dead guard, and came up on one knee into a firing position, looking for targets.

"All clear," she heard a familiar voice ring out.

"Theo? What the hell?"

Six Marines stepped out of the shadows, Sergeant Major Wasp in the lead. "Check the house," he snapped, and two of his Marines moved off in their ever-so-quick fashion. They came out a moment later with General Motubu. Wasp turned to the general and said, "Sir, all the attackers are down."

"Well done, Sergeant Major," the old warrior said in a melodious East African accent. "Can I ask you to clear off these bodies? And then please stand fast for a moment so we can all have a chat."

"Got it, sir." Wasp motioned to his men, and they began to move the bodies into the van. Meanwhile, the three Wongs came out of the building. Along with Mr. Po, Lee, Wasp, and the general, they formed a rough circle in the moonlight.

The general said, "Ambassador, I'm sorry for this mess, and ma'am," addressing Mrs. Wong, "I'm sorry you were inconvenienced." Then, to Lee's amazement, he broke into clear, if accented, Mandarin and said, "Please know, Madam Minister, I would have killed the man before allowing him to harm you further."

Mrs. Wong responded in English, "I had no fear for myself but only for the honor of my house. If they had taken Commander Lee, who has sanctuary here, I could not have survived the shame. Thank you, General, and your men, for preventing that shame."

The general nodded and then said to the group, "I suppose an explanation is in order." He looked around, and when no one responded, he continued, "We knew there were elements of the Alliance government and the Navy that did not want the role they played in the attacks of last December 7 to come to light."

He turned toward Lee and Wasp and said, "What you did on Alpha 51 blew their plans up completely. Given enough time, all of it would have come to light. They desperately wanted to divert attention away from an investigation into the whole business. That's why they wanted you on trial, Commander Lee."

"Why would they attack here?" Lee asked incredulously. "This is a diplomatic compound; it's Chinese soil. Invading it is an act of war."

"You are correct," he said. "And it goes to show how desperate they are. But keep in mind that they have already done far worse."

"Did you know they were coming?"

"Commander," the ambassador said, "when I knew you would be our guest here, I reached out to my old friend, General Motubu. He commanded the Hong Kong garrison for many years, and I am honored to call him my brother."

"I asked the sergeant major to keep an eye on the place," the general said. "I figured he wouldn't mind giving up some of his R&R to help out an old shipmate."

Wasp said, "Ambassador, I'm sorry we couldn't save your protection detail. We were patrolling the perimeter and were not in a position to provide assistance when the attack commenced."

"You have saved us and the honor of my house, Sergeant Major," the ambassador said. "We are in your debt."

The general rubbed his hands and said, "Now we have some business to do." He turned to Wasp and said, "Sergeant Major, if your men can handle the remains, I'd like you to stay. I can drop you at the base afterward."

"Yes, sir," Wasp said. "Let me give them their orders, and I'll return." He walked over to the van where his Marines were now gathered, and Lee heard him speaking in low tones. She heard another voice say, "Wilco, Sergeant Major."

When Wasp returned, the general said, "May I suggest we go inside for a coffee? I'm not sure I'm up for dinner."

"Yes, please," the ambassador said. And they followed him back into the ranch house.

CHAPTER 84

A DEAL AND A COURT-MARTIAL

In the house, the ambassador led them to a room adjacent to the living room that had a number of chairs facing an old brick fireplace, complete with a roaring fire. They sat, and servants brought coffee and soft bread. Lee found that she was hungry and readily took the offered treat.

The general began the conversation: "Here is my estimate of the situation. The powers that be, including the leadership in the Navy, want you put on trial so they can paint the Battle of Alpha 51 as some sort of rebellion. The point is to muddy the waters and make *you* the problem." He turned to the ambassador and said, "Though I appreciate your ploy of granting the commander diplomatic immunity, that will not hold for long."

"Yes, of course we know this," Po said in perfect English. "The treaty requires us to register all diplomatic personnel with the Alliance thirty days before invoking diplomatic protection. This, of course, was not done in Commander Lee's case. She was registered only today. This rule is in fact designed to prevent such an abuse of diplomatic status. They will take it to court. We will fight it, but in time, they will win."

"So where does that leave us?" Ambassador Wong asked. "We still have options. I can fly her back to China, and I assure you she will never return for trial."

"That's one option," the general said. "But if I'm not mistaken, I don't think Commander Lee will take it."

They turned to her, and she said, "I don't want to go into hiding. I haven't done anything wrong, and this fight isn't over."

"I suspected you'd say that," the general said. "So I think I have another solution."

He looked at Lee and then at the ambassador, who said, "Please tell us, old friend."

"Mr. Po," the general said. "You are an attorney. What is the best way to ensure Ms. Lee is never convicted of any of the alleged crimes of which she is accused?"

"The only certain way is for her to be tried and found not guilty. In that case, the double jeopardy rule applies, and she cannot be retried."

The ambassador said, "But how does this help? You said if tried, she is likely to be convicted, despite her innocence. The men behind this do not care about justice."

"You're right, *they* do not think of justice," Motubu said. "But others do. The Marine Corps can try her."

"But she is a naval officer. The Marine Corps has no jurisdiction over her."

"Correct," the general said. "We do not. Not yet."

Lee's heart began to pound as she grasped what he was suggesting. She asked, "Are you suggesting I transfer to the Corps, and *then* stand trial on these charges?"

"Yes, I am."

"How long would that take?"

"Not long," he said, smiling. "Are you up for it?"

Lee looked at Wasp, who smiled and said, "Fine by me. You've already been through the Marine OCS, and you led a Marine SpecOps task force into combat. The Marines will follow you." Then he smiled and said, "I could get used to calling you *Major.*"

Lee took a deep breath and said, "I'm not qualified to be a Marine major. That wouldn't be right."

The general thought about that and said, "I understand your position, and I think we can accommodate your wishes, *Captain Lee.*" The general turned his head and called out to the other room, "Colonel, Captain, can you join us?"

Into the room came the other two men Lee had seen at the reception. One was older than the other; the colonel, she supposed. "Everyone, allow me to introduce Colonel James Russell, a Marine Corps superior judge; and Captain John Stack, a Marine Corps judge advocate prosecutor. Gentleman, are we ready to proceed?"

Servants brought up two chairs for the newcomers, and the general said, "First, Commander Lee wishes to branch transfer to the Marine Corps at the rank of captain."

The young lawyer brought up a briefcase onto his lap, opened the latches, and took out a sheaf of papers. He scribbled something on the top with a pen and then handed the papers to Lee. "Ma'am, if you'll sign where indicated, the application will be complete."

She looked at the papers and saw that she was applying for a branch transfer to the Human Alliance Marine Corps. The rank of major was crossed out, and "captain" had been written in pen above it. She signed.

"And now for the court-martial," Motubu said. "Mr. Po, in order to proceed, China will need to waive diplomatic protection for Mei-Ling Lee. Will you do so?"

Po looked at the ambassador, who looked at Mrs. Wong, who nodded. Po said to the general, "Yes, the government of China agrees to waive diplomatic protection for Commander ... I mean, Captain Lee."

The young lawyer handed Po a paper, which he read and signed.

The colonel said to Lee, "Captain Lee, you are charged with treason, in that you took up arms against the Human Alliance; with murder in that you killed Alliance personnel; torture, in that you inflicted grievous bodily harm on civilians while attempting to gather information from them; and with destruction of government property, in that your actions led to the destruction of an Alliance reserve facility on Alpha 51. Do you understand these charges against you?"

"Yes, sir."

"How do you plead?" asked the colonel.

"Not guilty, sir," she responded.

"Very well," the colonel said. "The prosecution may proceed."

The captain said, "I call to testify Marine Captain Mei-Ling Lee."

The colonel said, "Captain Lee, you are not obliged to testify in your own defense. Please consult with your attorney."

Lee turned with a questioning look to Po, who said, "I believe in this instance, it would be prudent for you to proceed."

"I will testify," she said.

"Captain Lee," the prosecutor said, "isn't it true that you in fact did kill many people, that you tortured and maimed a civilian, and that your actions led directly to the destruction of the facilities of Alpha 51?"

"Yes, those statements are true," she said.

"Thank you," the prosecutor said. He turned to the colonel and said, "The prosecution rests."

The colonel turned to Po and said, "Is the defense ready to proceed?"

"We are, your honor." He turned to Lee and said, "Captain Lee, please describe the circumstances of your actions on Alpha 51."

"I was assigned by Admiral Chambers, who was the commanding officer of the Achilles Battle Fleet, to be the deputy commanding officer of a Special Operations task force against an enemy facility. In that role, I was the commander of the team sent to infiltrate the moon base at Alpha 51 and to secure a device known as a quantum flux generator, which had the capacity to destroy the entire star system in which it was located."

"And during the operation, you were injured, were you not?"

"Yes, sir," she said.

"Please describe your injuries," Po said.

"Upon landing on the moon, I received a concussion, three broken ribs, a broken jaw, three broken teeth, and a lacerated lip."

"And did this injury incapacitate you in any way?"

"Yes, I was unconscious for a few minutes, I believe, and then later, I lost consciousness again for a few minutes," she said.

"And did you seek medical attention?" he asked.

"Not until after the operation was completed."

"May I ask why not?"

"Because the operation was ongoing."

"Based on your injuries, did you feel you were fit to continue as the commander of the operation?"

"No. I turned over command to the deputy commander, Sergeant Major Theodorus Wasp."

"So if I am correct, Sergeant Major Wasp was in fact the commanding officer for the remainder of the operations."

"Yes."

"And I see that Sergeant Major Wasp is present in court today. Your Honor, if you will permit, I would like to call Sergeant Major Theodorus Wasp to testify."

"Proceed," the judge said.

"Sergeant Major Wasp, can you corroborate Captain Lee's testimony up to now?"

"Yes, sir," Wasp said.

"As Captain Lee's commanding officer, were you aware of her actions, and did you authorize them?"

"Yes, sir."

"So if I can restate what we know, Captain Lee was severely injured, including an injury to her brain that caused two periods of unconsciousness, and furthermore, she carried out her duties after that point under your supervision."

"Yes, sir."

"And did you find that any of her actions were criminal?"

"No, sir."

"Sergeant Major Wasp, have your superiors reviewed this operation and evaluated your conduct as commanding officer?"

"Yes, sir."

"And was there any finding of misconduct on your part, or any failure by you to provide proper oversight of Captain Lee?"

"Sir, there was no finding of misconduct or failure to provide oversight."

"In fact, Sergeant Major Wasp, isn't true you received a commendation for your actions during the operation?"

"Yes, sir, along with the rest of my team."

"Thank you," Po said. "No further questions, Your Honor. The defense rests."

"Closing arguments, gentlemen?" the judge asked.

The prosecutor said, "Your honor, the accused admitted to the actions that led to the charges. As a commissioned officer, she cannot hide behind her injuries or the word of a person subordinate to her in rank. I move that she be found guilty on all charges."

Po said, "Your honor, this case should not have been brought. Commander Lee was in lawful combat at the time of the alleged offenses, she continued to engage the enemy despite being gravely wounded, and her lawful commanding officer has stated that her actions were justified. The Marine Corps has reviewed his conduct and found it to be praiseworthy. I move that the accused be found not guilty on all charges."

The judge considered a moment and said, "After having considered all the evidence and testimony before me, I find the defendant, Marine Captain Mei-Ling Lee, not guilty on all charges."

Mrs. Wong sprang to her feet and said, "Wonderful! Now you must all eat something, or I will be disgraced as a hostess."

EPILOGUE

SIX MONTHS LATER

Mei-Ling Lee entered the officers' club of the naval training base at Perth and paused for a moment, looking around. She spied Laura Zakany at a window booth. Laura smiled and waved and then stood up to greet her with some difficulty. Lee could see why: Laura was heavily pregnant, and her girth would make moving difficult.

They hugged, and Laura said through tears, "My dear Mei-Ling, my warrior princess. How I have missed you."

Lee hadn't seen Zakany since the fleet returned to Earth after the battle of Alpha 51. She had been busy with the aftermath of the battle, the public hearings, and the media coverage. And then there had been her training. Somehow, Lee had let slip the only friendship she had ever had, and now her best and only friend was pregnant, and she hadn't known! *Shoot,* Lee admonished herself. *I'm going to have to work on being a better friend. Time to try and make it right.*

"Laura, I am so sorry I haven't been in touch," Mei-Ling Lee said. "I have no excuse; please forgive me," and now she had tears in *her* eyes.

Laura waved away the apology. "My sister, my love, we are past any apologies." Zakany held out both hands and held Lee's, and they just let the moment rest with that. When they had regained their composure, Lee said, "So are you going to make me ask?"

"What is there to ask?" Zakany said. "Not 'who is the father?' Surely it is my husband, Matthias."

Lee was speechless. She looked at Zakany with a questioning look. She said, "Your ... husband?" Lee looked and saw that Laura was wearing a wedding ring on her right hand, as was the tradition in Eastern Europe.

"Ah, I see you do not know." Zakany nodded, as if she now understood the source of the misunderstanding. "Yes, Matthias and I were married before the battle, by the admiral. He had that power, as commanding officer. It was legally entered into the log." Zakany stared hard at Lee, as if challenging her to raise some objection.

"Laura, I am so happy for you. And of course, the child was conceived before ..." She trailed off, realizing she was treading on sensitive ground. Both Chambers and Nemeth had been declared dead after weeks of searching hadn't found their remains.

"Before he left with the admiral?" Zakany said. "Yes, of course, what else? He hasn't been back, has he?"

Lee was beginning to think this conversation had slipped into an alternate reality. "Hasn't been back ...?"

"He hasn't been back, no. I know he has his reasons. I miss him and trust him, but really, he needs to be back for the birth of his son."

Lee opened her mouth and then closed it. She said nothing.

"You think he is dead?" Zakany asked with astonishment. "No, not possible."

Lee said nothing, and Laura continued, "First, he *said* he would return to me, and this is not a promise to break, not from such a man. Second, he is not dead. Trust me, I am a doctor, or soon will be. There were no remains found: no bones, no hair, no DNA at all. Not for him and not for the admiral. And finally, the shuttle they were in was not among the wreckage. That has been well-established. No. He lives, he is my husband, and he will be the father of this child on the day of his birth, or he will have some explaining to do."

"I … don't know what to say."

"Say that you are happy for me, because I am happy for me," Zakany said, now bright red with emotion.

"Of course, sister of my heart," Lee cried out. "I am very happy for you." These terms of endearment came hard to Lee, who had always been very much a loner.

"The Navy came with a priest to tell me he was declared dead," Zakany said. "They want to give me insurance money and his things. I said, 'I will take his things, I am his wife, and you can keep the money. He is not dead.' Idiots."

"Where do you think they are?" Lee asked.

"Matthias and the admiral are out fighting the clones," she said. "You know this is not over."

Laura was right about that. The public outrage over the inquiry into the moon base was something to behold. When it became clear that some very high-ranking people were going to be arrested for treason, a civil war of sorts broke out. Part of the government and part of the Navy declared they were withdrawing from the Alliance. There had been some fighting, and the secessionists, as they were called, had occupied one of the colonial planetary systems and declared their independence. It was all very unsettling. Thankfully, all the Marine Corps had declared for the Alliance.

There was an awkward pause, and then Lee said, "And you are in medical school?"

Laura brightened and said, "Yes, here in Perth, there is a huge medical center. Isn't it wonderful? The admiral wrote me a letter before the battle, on the same day he married Matthias and me. Because I am nurse practitioner, they put me in fourth year. I got to keep my rank as lieutenant while in training. It is good. I outrank all the other students and some of the instructors, ha."

"And your family?" Lee asked. This was always a touchy subject these days, because so many people had lost family during the attack on Earth in December.

Zakany brightened and said, "My father is alive! Budapest was not hit. And now I have Matthias's family, very large, very wealthy. I am one of them. I bear the name and will bear the only male child of his generation, the heir of their line of nobility. They address me as 'Lady Laura,' as is proper. Matthias is baron; I am baroness. But our son will someday be duke, when Matthias's uncle—who has no children—passes."

Lee was trying to take in this new person who had been a shy nurse only a few months ago. Laura had found her path, and Lee was happy for her. She, too, had found a path of sorts.

A waitress came and took their order. Lee was hungry, having just come out of training, where food deprivation was part of the ordeal. She ordered a steak and a liter bottle of sparkling water. Laura ordered a salad and a glass of milk.

Laura said, "So you are no longer a commander in the Navy," looking at Lee's Marine uniform.

Here Lee felt a twinge of guilt for the lie she was about to tell. It was a story they had all agreed on after the court-martial. "Yes. It was something the admiral did for me before he ... left," Lee said. "He wrote a letter assigning me to the Marine Corps. I hadn't asked for it, but he must have known that this would be my chosen path."

"Can a Navy admiral assign a sailor to the Marine Corps?" Zakany asked.

"No, of course not. But it did add weight to my request for a service transfer. It helped that I had finished the Marine OCS while at the academy. Major Davenport was very gracious and supported it. Best of all, the Marines of the SpecOps detachment from the Alpha 51 raid all signed a letter basically demanding it. That meant a lot to me." This last was true.

"But you are captain of Marines, less rank than a lieutenant commander?" Zakany said as if she were about to be angry at a slight to her friend.

"Actually, I met with the commandant of the Marine Corps, General Motubu. He offered me a commission as a major, a lateral move."

"And you refused? Why would you do such a thing?"

Lee smiled and said, "Because it was the right thing to do. I need to command a Marine company, and that is done by a captain, not a major. Plus, I have a ton to learn."

"I see you have a medal; I know that one. It is the Silver Star."

"Yes, General Motubu awarded it to me." This part was true also.

"You deserve that and more. And I hear you have been in training?"

"Oh, my, yes. These courses are very challenging. I did the ranger course, the scuba course, pathfinder, and airborne qualification. There's so much more. Next the sniper course. In about a year, I'll be ready to command a Marine company."

"And your man, Wasp?"

"I'm not sure he's *my* man," Lee said. "But he's not going anywhere soon. He put in for Officer Candidate School and has just finished. He will earn the gold bars of a brand-new second lieutenant in a few days. I'll fly to Quantico to pin them on him. Then we'll take some time together, and we'll see if he *is* my man." She paused and then said with a wry smile, "I think he took the course for me, because he knew it would be easier for us if we were both officers. I didn't ask him to. It's not easy for him. In the Marine Corps, sergeant majors are next to God, and second lieutenants, though technically higher in rank, are not." They both laughed, and it seemed to Lee like they were settling into their friendship once again.

The food came, and Lee dug in with an appetite. Laura only picked at her food.

"And I hear you also have new family. Tell me?" Zakany said.

"Well, wasn't that a surprise?" Lee said with a smile. "Who knew I had a cousin?"

"And an uncle."

Lee shook her head as if to say she still couldn't quite grasp it.

"So Admiral Chambers is your uncle, and Jay Jr.—Commander Chambers—is your cousin? What did your father say? Did you confront him?"

"When I got back to Earth, I went to visit him. I said, 'Why didn't you tell me that Aunt Mei-Ling had a child?'"

"So you were named for your aunt?"

"Yes, but she died when I was young, and no one ever said anything about her husband or any children. She was sort of the black sheep of the family. I knew she had married one of Daddy's foreign students and sort of run off. Now I know that foreigner was a young petty officer, one Jay Chambers."

"What did your father say about it?"

"He tried to wave it off, but I got angry and started to leave. So he relented and told me that when my aunt left, it broke my mother's heart. He said that my mother died not long after. And although her death was from cancer, not from sorrow, he blamed my aunt for the sadness of her last years."

"And what did you say?"

"I said I didn't care about that," she answered. "It was in the past, and it was his burden, not mine. I said Jay was my cousin, and I wanted him to be part of my family."

"How did he take it?"

"He took it just fine. He acted as if he had expected me to take charge of the family and seemed relieved that I had put my foot down."

"So you have met with young Jay?

"Yes," Lee said. "I'll admit it was bit awkward. And at first, he was sort of stiff, maybe a little aloof."

"Yes, he can be like that," Zakany said. "But he is good inside."

"You've met him?" Lee said with surprise.

"Of course, my dear. Matthias is godfather to him. He knew young Jay when he was a child. Matthias was at his christening."

"Small world. I'll admit, I am a little angry that neither Matthias nor the admiral ever mentioned any of this to me."

"You have a right to be angry, Mei-Ling. Family is all, and that should never be hidden. When Matthias and the admiral return, you must speak strongly with them. I will do so also. It is not their right.

"And what of the others? Raymond, Danner, Baker, and Davenport?"

Lee smiled and said, "You will happy to learn that Danner is at the new Naval Academy. Since he already has a degree, they waived the first two years."

"And he is a midshipman? How the mighty have fallen," Zakany said with a mischievous smile. "I am so happy for him. The humbling will do him good."

"And I suppose you've seen Professor Raymond on all the news shows?"

"Yes, he is quite the celebrity."

"Let's see, Major Davenport has been put in charge of all Marine commando training."

"And Baker?"

Lee frowned and said, "He had to face an inquiry upon return. They were looking to find someone to blame for the Battle of Alpha 51, and his casualties in the aviation wing were so high; something like a third of all his pilots were lost."

"How did it go for him?"

"He was cleared, and he got to keep his rank of captain," Lee said. "But I think it was a difficult time for him. He was granted extensive leave, and it's not clear that he'll return to flight status when it's all over."

"And the commodore? How is Bowman?" Zakany asked.

"Well, of course he went back to academia. He's a big shot now that he commanded a task force in battle. I think they're going to make him the president of his university."

"He favored you. Do you have any regrets for not keeping that door open?"

"None," Lee said with certainty. "He's a good man, and I respect him, but he will always go from one thing to the next, and I will *not* let myself be one of those things."

On the large viewscreen over the bar, a flash news report was breaking into the programming. Lee asked the bartender to turn it up.

"We have reports of major fighting having broken out in the Stygian star system. We have unconfirmed reports of attacks on Alliance outposts, including civilian habitats. Initial casualty reports are in the thousands." A banner scrolled across the screen that notified all military personnel to report to their duty stations.

Lee stood and said, "Laura, my sister, I have to go. Take care of that baby. Take care of yourself. I'll need to find a way back to Quantico tonight. I think there's a Marine shuttle going out about midnight."

"I too must go back to the medical school," Zakany said. "It is my place of duty."

They hugged long and hard. Lee thought she could feel the child moving in Laura, and she was fascinated by it. A new life in the midst of so much death.

They cried and kissed each other on the cheeks, and then went their separate ways.

The End of Book One

ABOUT THE AUTHOR

Following twenty-five years of military service as a U.S. Army ranger and paratrooper, Brendan Wilson retired as a lieutenant colonel and then joined NATO where he served as a defense planner and diplomat for the next fifteen years. During the course of his forty years of work as a soldier and diplomat, he saw service in war-torn Libya, Ukraine, Kosovo, Bosnia, and Iraq. In addition, he commanded a fire base on the DMZ in the Republic of Korea.

A former coach and team captain for military martial arts competition teams in the 101st Airborne Division and the 18th Airborne Corps, he holds master ranking (8th Dan) in three different martial arts, and he won the silver medal in the 2009 U.S. Open for Taekwondo. He was one of the founding members of Aristos, a form of martial arts based on Classical Greek principles.

In retirement, Wilson turned his efforts to filmmaking. He wrote and produced two award-winning short films (*Doug's Christmas* and

A Child Lies Here) and served as executive producer for the award-winning web series, *Greetings! From Prison*. Moved by seeing human lives upended in war-torn areas, Wilson enrolled in law school and, as of this writing, he is in his final year. Once he qualifies as an attorney, he plans to volunteer to help refugees. Wilson, lives in Sycamore, Illinois. He spends his days writing, studying law, and practicing his martial arts.

Made in the USA
Columbia, SC
09 February 2025

53101544R00231